Available
from
Special

ROMANCING THE COWBOY

"Who are you?"

She crossed her arms. "I'm Sabrina Gonzalez."

"The bookkeeper who's taken up residence in my mother's house."

"And you're the rude, arrogant man who called earlier, the one with no manners."

Jared had been accused of worse, but he didn't take any guff from anyone. Never had, never would.

And he didn't trust Sabrina Gonzalez any further than he could throw her – something that wouldn't be too tough. She was just a slip of a thing, with a slinky veil of black hair that nearly reached her waist.

She was just over five feet tall. Her eyes, the colour of a field of bluebonnets in the spring, were big and expressive. She had high cheekbones. Lips that were kissable in spite of the pretty pout she wore.

He wondered what her hard luck story had been.

THE DIAPER DIARIES

"You wouldn't believe the number of people who want a piece of me."

Most of them female. Even before Miss Georgia, the newspapers had reported his dating exploits so comprehensively Bethany wondered how he found time to make it into the office. But evidently he did, because lately the press had been covering the foundation's charitable activities, and in that sphere at least it seemed Tyler was a saint. Albeit one untroubled by anything so pesky as a vow of celibacy.

"I want a piece of you, too," she said. Tyler raised his eyebrows, and she stuttered, "I – I want you to guarantee me that appointment to talk about my funding. Please."

"I like a woman who knows what she wants." Before she could decide if he was being provocative, he turned to his assistant. "Give Bethany some time next week. And when I tell you to fob her off, don't let me."

First published in Great Britain 2009
Harlequin Mills & Boon Limited,
Eton House, 18-24 Paradise Road, Richmond, Surrey TW9 1SR

Romancing the Cowboy © Judy Duarte 2008
The Diaper Diaries © Abby Gaines 2008

ISBN: 978 0 263 87635 2

23-0909

Harlequin Mills & Boon policy is to use papers that are natural, renewable and recyclable products and made from wood grown in sustainable forests. The logging and manufacturing processes conform to the legal environmental regulations of the country of origin.

Printed and bound in Spain
by Litografia Rosés S.A., Barcelona

ROMANCING THE COWBOY

BY
JUDY DUARTE

THE DIAPER DIARIES

BY
ABBY GAINES

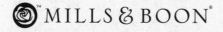
MILLS & BOON

ROMANCING THE COWBOY

BY
JUDY DUARTE

Judy Duarte always knew there was a book inside her, but since English was her least favourite subject in school, she never considered herself a writer. An avid reader who enjoys a happy ending, Judy couldn't shake the dream of creating a book of her own.

Her dream became a reality in March 2002 when the Special Edition line released her first book. Since then, she has sold nineteen more novels.

To Colleen Holth, who has been my friend for almost as long as I can remember. Thanks for letting me rope you into just about anything. I love you, Col.

Chapter One

"I need to talk to you about Edna." At the sound of Doc Graham's age-worn voice over the telephone line, Jared Clayton's gut clenched and his chest tightened. This, he suspected, was the moment he'd been dreading. The call he and his two brothers had known would someday come.

He'd been sitting in the worn, tufted-leather chair in his study, the ledger spread across the polished oak desktop, when the phone rang.

Edna Clayton, who was known as Granny to most folks in the small Texas community of Brighton Valley, had adopted Jared when he'd been a gangly adolescent. At the time, he'd had nowhere else to go except the county home for boys. And for the next twenty years, the elderly widow had been the only real mother he'd known.

Jared waited for the small-town physician to tell him

the reason he'd called. Instead, Doc asked, "How long has it been since you visited the ranch?"

"A year or so." Jared made of a point of spending the major holidays with her and whichever brother could make it, although he'd missed being home last Christmas, due to a crisis on his own ranch—a divorce that had caught him completely by surprise. "But I call regularly."

Oh, yeah? a small voice asked.

When was the last time he'd picked up the phone to chat with her, to ask how things were going?

A couple of weeks, he suspected. Or maybe a month.

Guilt rode him hard. He hadn't meant to let it go that long. And the fact that he'd been so damn focused lately—first on his divorce, then on his seriously injured brother—didn't help. At this point, neither Jolene nor Matthew seemed to be a good enough excuse.

"When did you talk to her last?" Doc had been Granny's best friend for as long as Jared could remember, but this was the first time Jared had felt as if he'd been called on the carpet by the man. Or maybe it was his own guilt doing a number on him.

"I meant to give her a call this evening," he lied, thinking he ought to actually schedule the time on his calendar so this wouldn't ever happen again. He'd make a point of checking in with her weekly, if not daily.

"It's just as well that you haven't yet done so."

"Why? What happened?"

"At this point? Nothing, but her memory is failing, and she's been having some health problems."

"Like what?" At seventy-nine, any number of things could wear out or go haywire. Maybe Jared ought to bring her to his ranch to live with him so he could keep an eye on her, but she'd always been so independent and set in her ways. And the old Granny, the one who'd raised him, would never agree. He'd have to hog-tie her and throw her over his shoulder in order to convince her to leave the Rocking C, the only home she'd had in nearly sixty years.

"I can't seem to control her blood pressure," Doc said, "even with medication. She has a heart murmur, and I'm afraid she may not have much time left."

A stab of grief shot through him, stirring up his memories—the *good* ones. Granny and his adopted brothers, Matt and Greg, were the only family he'd ever really had.

"Since I doubt Edna will let you boys know what's going on, I thought I'd better call."

Jared couldn't help thinking that Granny's heart had worn out over the years. The idea wasn't founded upon medical science by any means, but it seemed as though all the good deeds and charity work she'd done over the course of her life had finally taken their toll.

For as long as folks in Brighton Valley had known her, Granny had been taking in strays of all shapes and sizes— human ones, as well as the four-legged variety. And Jared thanked his lucky stars that he'd been one of them.

He had his own spread now, nearly a hundred miles away, but that didn't mean he didn't love her dearly. Granny was the only woman who had always come through for him and never let him down—one way or another.

"Give it to me straight, Doc."

"Well, I think she needs to go into Houston and see a cardiologist, but I've never seen a woman so dang stubborn in all my life." Since Doc had attended the local high school with Edna and was pushing eighty himself, that was saying a lot.

"Is she all right living out on that ranch alone?" Jared asked, thinking that they might need to hire a nurse to look after her if he couldn't talk her in to moving in with him.

"She's *not* alone," Doc said. "That's another issue completely. Right now, she's got a full house."

"What do you mean?" The last time Jared had gone by the ranch, the only ones living there had been Granny and Lester Bailey, the foreman, plus a couple of newly hired greenhorns who tried hard but didn't know much about cattle. Thank goodness the other hands knew what to do without being told. "Who's she taken in now?"

"A whole passel of women, one of whom looked pregnant to me. And there's at least one kid."

Oh, for Pete's sake. Jared, of all people, ought to be understanding of Granny's hospitality. But she was getting older now and was more vulnerable than she'd been in the past.

"Looks like I'd better make a trip south tomorrow." Of course, he'd have to find someone to look after Matthew. Jared had a bad feeling about leaving him alone, especially in his present frame of mind.

"You probably ought to consider staying at Edna's for a while," Doc added.

"Why is that?"

"I spoke to Grant Whitaker about her yesterday when we were eating breakfast down at Caroline's Diner."

Grant was Granny's CPA, at least he had been. He

had to be Granny and Doc's age. Or at least getting close. "Hasn't he retired yet?"

"Nope. He still works for Edna and a couple other longtime clients. And he was concerned about something. He decided to run it by me first, before bothering you boys with it."

Jared stiffened. "What was he worried about?"

"Grant seems to think there's a discrepancy in her accounts."

"What *kind* of discrepancy?" Jared asked.

"He says there have been a significant number of electronic withdrawals over the past few weeks."

"I don't know how in the hell that could have happened. Granny doesn't even have a computer."

"Apparently, she does now. Her new bookkeeper talked her into getting one."

She hired a new bookkeeper? One who had access to online banking, account numbers and passwords? Jared gripped the receiver until he thought he might choke the truth out of it. "I'm not going to wait until morning. I'll give her a call now and tell her… Hell, I'll think of something. Either way, I'm leaving this evening."

"Good. If she were my mother, I'd want to know."

"If someone *is* taking advantage of her, they'll wish they weren't."

"Now, don't go in there half-cocked, son. There could be a logical explanation for all of this."

Yeah. Right.

Granny needed him.

And now it was his turn to be there for her.

As he disconnected the line, a flash of lightning

briefly illuminated the oak-paneled study. He pushed himself away from the desk, then strode to the open window in slow steady steps as a rumble of thunder rolled across the evening sky.

The scent of rain mingled with smoke from the chimney. He could smell the storm coming. For a moment, he considered waiting it out and driving after it passed, but he didn't think on it too long.

He needed to get to Granny's ranch and find out what he was up against. He shut the window, then glanced at the clock on the bookshelf. 8:38 p.m. It would be late by the time he and Matt arrived.

Jared had a key to the back door, but he didn't want to let himself in without telling Granny he was coming. So he dialed her number.

"Hello?" a woman answered, her voice laced with a slight Latina accent, her tone soft and gentle.

All the frustration and worry that had been swirling inside caused Jared to snap in a manner that was more sharp and brusque than usual. "Who are you?"

She paused momentarily. "Why don't you introduce yourself first?"

Patience had never been one of his virtues, not when he wanted answers. "In case you didn't hear me the first time, who the hell are you?"

She cleared her throat, yet the softness remained. "I'm Sabrina. I work here."

"Let me talk to Mrs. Clayton."

"I'm not sure I want you to."

"Excuse me?" His voice, rock hard and determined, mocked her velvety tone.

"She's resting, and I'd rather not see her upset."

Jared didn't know who this woman was, but he didn't like her already. "Why in blazes would I call to stir her up?"

"You seem to be irritated about something, sir. And I can't see any point in raising her blood pressure."

"Listen here, Sabrina. *You're* raising *my* blood pressure. All I want to do is talk to Edna, to ask how she's feeling, to check on her."

She remained silent for the longest time, as if trying to determine whether she was talking to a friend or a foe.

"This is Jared," he said, although she didn't respond right away.

Hadn't Granny even told those women about him? About how she'd adopted not only Jared, but also two other boys, who loved her and would do anything to protect her?

Apparently not.

The memory lapses Doc had mentioned came to mind, and Jared was even more determined to set things right. Even if it meant backpedaling and reining in a conversation that he now realized had started off on a bad foot.

"Maybe we ought to slow down a bit and clear the air. I'm Edna's oldest son. And I'd like to talk to her. I get a little riled up when someone tries to put me off."

"She told me about you. I'm sorry. I'll get her."

When the woman set down the receiver, silence filled the line. A barrage of questions begged for answers. And not just questions about Granny's health, the women who'd infiltrated the ranch and the loss of money in Granny's account.

What had Granny said about Jared?

It could have been any number of things, he supposed. But sometimes Granny had a way of revealing secrets, things a guy would rather keep to himself. And her lack of discretion was one reason he hadn't gone into details about the divorce with her, just the irreconcilable differences part.

The *real* reason Jolene had left him remained deeply hidden within a ragged crevice in his heart.

"Jared?" that familiar, maternal voice asked. "Is that you?"

"Yes, Granny. How are you doing?"

"Fine as frog's hair," she responded. Then she made a fruitless attempt to cover the mouthpiece of the phone and speak to someone else, most likely Sabrina. "Thank you, dear. No, I'll lock up for the night. Go on to bed."

"Granny?" he asked, a bit put out that she'd be chatting with one of the moochers instead of him.

"I'm sorry. Where were we?" Granny asked.

"I asked how you were doing."

"Oh, yes. I'm doing just fine. How about you? Are you well?"

Jared had been doing okay until Matthew moved in. And until Doc had called this evening. "I'm all right. Keeping busy."

"What about Matt?" Granny said. "Is he doing okay, too?"

"Yes," Jared said, not wanting to worry his mother. But the truth was, although Matt seemed to be mending physically, he'd been depressed ever since the accident.

Of course, Jared really couldn't blame him. Matt had been the driver in the accident that killed his fiancée and her son. And he'd been the only one in the vehicle to survive.

"Does he still have to use a wheelchair?"

"Yes, but hopefully that's only temporary." Jared had built ramps to help him get in and out of the house, even though he seemed to prefer being inside. Or near the liquor cabinet.

"I'm sure it's tough on him," Granny said. "A man like Matt doesn't cotton to being laid up."

Jared wouldn't like it, either. And while he wasn't sure what Matt would say about the decision to go back to the Rocking C for a few days, he thought it might do him some good.

"You don't usually call so late," Granny said. "Is there something wrong?"

He suspected so, which was why he decided to lie about his reason for going back to the ranch and staying for a few days. "Matt and I have a couple of business meetings in Houston over the next week or so. We thought we'd come down, stay with you and drive back and forth."

"Why, of course. I'll ask Tori to make up beds in the den and in the guestroom."

"Who's Tori?"

"My new maid."

"Then who is Sabrina?" he asked.

"She's my new bookkeeper."

Aw. The suspected thief. "What's she doing at your house this late?"

"She and her nephew live here."

The hordes had begun to move in, ready to pounce and take advantage of one of the kindest little old ladies in Texas. And Jared wasn't going to let that happen.

"I guess I'll meet her when we get there."

"When are you coming?" she asked.

"Late tonight. But don't wait up. I've got a key."

And once Jared got to Granny's ranch, he was going to take control of a sorry situation, evict a few freeloaders and see to it the thief ended up in jail.

It was after midnight, but Sabrina Gonzalez had never been able to sleep very well in an unfamiliar house. So it was no wonder she was wide-awake on one of the twin-size beds in the small guestroom Mrs. Clayton had given her to share with Joey. Her new job, which had been a blessing in and of itself, came with room and board, too. That was a bit out of the ordinary for a bookkeeper, but Sabrina wasn't about to complain.

Besides, the room inside the Clayton ranch house was only temporary, since Mrs. Clayton planned to remodel an old cabin on the grounds. Sabrina and Joey, her six-year-old nephew, would move in as soon as it was ready for them. But God only knew how long that would be. The rustic structure hadn't been used in ages, so it would need a lot of work to be livable.

Sabrina stopped by Joey's bedside and gently caressed the top of his head.

Carlos, her twin brother and Joey's dad, had been convicted of a crime he hadn't committed and was currently serving time in prison, so Sabrina had stepped in as a guardian.

At first, when Mrs. Clayton's job offer came through, Sabrina had declined to take it, since the ranch was quite a drive from Houston and she hadn't found a competent and trustworthy sitter for her nephew yet. But the elderly woman had invited both Sabrina and Joey to live at the ranch, insisting that it was best for the motherless boy to be near a loved one at a time like this and not in day care.

How could Sabrina argue with that?

Joey stirred, and she shushed him until he grew still. Before leaving the room, she stopped by the closet for a robe, then hesitated. The door squeaked terribly when it slid open, and she hated to make any unnecessary noise.

Besides, what would it hurt to walk out into the kitchen wearing just her nightgown? There were only women in the house.

A night-light lit her way downstairs, the steps creaking under her weight. She walked into the living room, where she flipped on a lamp, illuminating the room. Then she went to the kitchen.

Connie, the new cook, was a sweetheart, but she hadn't been hired for her culinary skills. The oatmeal cookies she'd made, however, were the best Sabrina had ever tasted.

Rather than turn on every light in the house, Sabrina decided not to flip on the switch. She could make her way through the dimly lit kitchen easy enough.

She opened the fridge and poured herself a glass of milk, just as a car engine sounded outside. She glanced at the clock. 12:17 a.m. Surely, Edna wasn't expecting company. Maybe someone on the highway had made a wrong turn and was lost. The driver would figure it out soon enough, she supposed, and head back to the road.

She plucked two of the chewy cookies from the plastic container in which Connie had stored them and wrapped them in a paper towel to take into the living room, where she would eat them as she thumbed through a magazine.

But the vehicle didn't turn around or back out. Instead, the engine continued to idle, and the headlights remained on.

A door opened and shut.

When Sabrina heard a baritone whisper through a window that had been left partially open, she froze. Another voice responded, this one a bit louder.

One of the hired hands?

Maybe so.

She pinched off a bite of one cookie and popped it into her mouth, relishing the taste of raisins and spice, then took a sip of milk.

More voices—all male—sounded. Another door opened, then shut.

"Be quiet," a man said, as he neared the window. "I don't want to wake up anyone in the house."

"I hate this," another added.

"We don't like it, either. Just sit back and enjoy the ride, kid."

Footsteps sounded at the back porch. It might be the end of spring, but a winter frost crept up Sabrina's spine. Her heart pounded out an ominous dirge in her brain and perspiration beaded on her forehead.

As quiet as a cornered mouse, she tiptoed toward the kitchen counter, where the butcher block rested. She set down her milk and cookies, then grabbed the biggest weapon she could find—a meat cleaver—and held it with both hands, ready to defend herself.

Maybe it was Lester, the ranch foreman, and some of the hired hands. Maybe they had reason to be awake and milling about at this time of night.

That had to be it, yet her pulse escalated until she

could hear it throbbing in her ears. An avid mystery reader with a wild imagination, Sabrina often thought in terms of worst-possible scenarios. And she tried to keep that in mind, tried to remain calm.

She could scream, waking everyone in the house. And what if there was a perfectly good explanation for all of this?

Then the new ranch bookkeeper would look like a fool.

The lock clicked, as though someone had a key. Or perhaps someone was picking it.

Should she scream now?

The door to the mudroom swung open, revealing a group of men outside, their forms barely illuminated by the headlights of a vehicle. The one in front, a tall, thirty-something hulk of a man with wheat-colored hair, held a key in his hand and gaped at her. "Who the hell are you?"

If she'd witnessed a crime and stood behind a mir-rored window, looking at a lineup and listening to each voice, she'd recognize *that* one.

Jared Clayton.

She didn't know whether to cry in relief or anger. "Didn't anyone teach you to knock on doors?"

"Not at *this* house."

"Hey," a voice behind him said, "get a move on. This is heavy."

Jared stepped aside, and several of the ranch hands carried a dark-haired man and the wheelchair in which he was still seated through the service porch and into the kitchen, where they lowered him to the floor.

"I'm sorry," she said, more in response to the injured man's plight than anything.

From what she'd heard, the one-time rodeo cowboy

had been involved in a tragic car accident a while back, and he'd been recuperating at Jared's ranch. Yet her gaze and her focus turned to Jared. "You scared me."

"Oh, yeah?" Jared's features—quite handsome in the light—softened a tad. "And you don't think seeing a she-devil, wielding a meat cleaver in her hand and dressed like a ghost in flowing white didn't give me a start, too?"

Sabrina glanced down at her gown, realizing how threadbare the fabric had become, how sheer the material.

Her hair hung down her back, but she freed the side tresses, allowing them to cover the front of her gown the best they could.

As Matthew wheeled himself out of the kitchen and into the living room, the ranch hands backed out the door, closing it and leaving her with Mrs. Clayton's oldest son. He still hadn't formally introduced himself, although he really hadn't needed to.

He crossed his arms across a broad chest and shifted the bulk of his weight to one, denim-clad hip. "Who are *you?*"

She crossed her own arms, hoping that would help hide what her hair couldn't. "I'm Sabrina Gonzalez."

"The bookkeeper who's taken up residence in my mother's house."

It wasn't a question, yet his tone, his condescension, set her off, provoking a retort that was completely out of character. "And you're the rude, arrogant man who called earlier."

Jared had been accused of worse, but he didn't take any guff off anyone. Never had, never would.

Granny had done her best to teach him and his brothers to be cordial and polite, but it didn't come easy to Jared. Not when he had reason to believe someone was a liar or a cheat. And he didn't trust Sabrina Gonzalez any farther than he could throw her—something that wouldn't be too tough. She was just a slip of a thing, with a slinky veil of black hair that nearly reached her waist.

Jared, who'd always favored long-haired women, found it intriguing. Attractive.

But he didn't dare give this particular woman more than a passing glance. She was, after all, the one with the easiest access to Granny's accounts. And it didn't take much skill to put two and two together. He could do the math on that.

"Are you going to put down your weapon?" he asked.

She glanced at the cleaver, then replaced it into the butcher-block holder. Turning to face him again and re-crossing her arms, she gave a little shrug. "The ranch is off the beaten path, and I wasn't sure if this was a home invasion."

"My guess is that you watch too much television."

Her eyes, the color of a field of bluebonnets in the spring, were big and expressive. Her lashes, thick and dark, didn't need mascara.

She was a beautiful woman, even without makeup and dressed in an old gown. Of course, her bedtime attire and sleep-tousled hair had an appeal in and of itself.

To much of one, he decided.

He knew better than to allow himself to be swayed by lust and did his best to shake off any sexual interest in her.

"So what were you doing awake and prowling around in the house at this hour?" he asked

She paused, as if deciding whether to tell the truth or to lie. "Sometimes I have trouble falling asleep, so I came for a glass of milk."

"You might try whiskey. It works for me."

The hands that she'd tucked under her arms loosened, leaving him a glimpse of the gentle swell of her breasts.

Her white cotton gown had seen better days, but her body was damn near perfect. What he could see of it, anyway.

He pulled out a chair from the antique oak table, took a seat and studied her.

Early twenties. Just over five feet tall. High cheekbones, big eyes. Lips that were kissable in spite of the pretty pout she wore.

He wondered what her hard-luck story had been. "So how'd you meet Granny?"

She remained standing. "I was referred by Mr. Whitaker, and I came out to the ranch for an interview."

Grant referred her? If so, that was interesting. Grant had been the one to pick up on the discrepancies in the account.

"I'd originally applied for work at his office," she added, "but he's cutting back on his workload. He knew Mrs. Clayton needed a bookkeeper, so he gave her a call."

By the way she tried to cover herself, Jared suspected she was embarrassed to be standing before him in her nightgown, but apparently she was too proud to make excuses and flee.

And he was too ornery to give her a reason to leave.

Besides, he had some questions to ask her.

That is, until a young, sleepy voice sounded in the doorway of the kitchen. "Aunt Sabrina?"

The woman turned to where a small, dark-haired boy of about five or six stood, rubbing his eyes.

She crossed the distance between them, placing her

hand upon his shoulder. "It's okay, Joey. I'm sorry the men woke you. Why don't you go back to bed? I'll be there in a minute."

"I was worried 'bout you," he said. "Worried you left me here and wouldn't come back."

She stooped, her gown pooling onto the kitchen floor. She wrapped her arms around the boy. "I'd never leave you, Joey. Not on purpose."

"But my mommy…"

"I know, honey. But that wasn't on purpose."

Jared raked a hand through his hair. He wasn't sure what that was all about. But it sounded like the hint of a hard-luck story to him, and knowing Granny, she'd been more swayed by Sabrina's tale of woe than her qualifications, resume or references.

"Come on," Sabrina told the boy. "I'll walk you back to the bedroom."

As she ushered Joey through the doorway, her hair covered most of her back, swaying with her steps. But the thin material of her nightgown did little to hide her shapely hips.

Jared suspected she wasn't aware that the light was playing a trick on her, baring a slight outline of the panties she wore. Something decent and conservative. A pair worthy of any churchgoing matron.

Yet on Sabrina, with her ebony hair flirting with the elastic waistband, they fit her bottom in a way that would tempt a saint. And Jared was far from saintly.

Especially when he was determined to uncover a liar and a thief.

Chapter Two

On most nights, when those dreaded bouts of insomnia struck, Sabrina would finally fall asleep just before dawn, only to find it hard to wake up when it was time to begin the next day.

But that wasn't the case this morning.

After having had the liver scared out of her by Jared Clayton and his entourage last night, she hadn't been able to sleep at all. Of course, as much as she'd like to blame that on his unannounced arrival, it had been the tone of his voice and the implication in his words that had set her emotions on edge. He'd talked to her as though she were some kind of imposter or second-class citizen.

Standing in the kitchen, with his hand slapped onto his hips, golden-brown eyes narrowed with suspicion, square jaw lifted in challenge, he'd been a formidable opponent. And if he hadn't struck such an intimidating pose, she might have found the blond-haired rancher handsome.

Okay. So she'd found him handsome anyway. That didn't make him particularly appealing. Not to her. The kind of man she wanted for herself was caring and gentle, someone who pondered a situation before barking out commands or making rash judgments and snide comments.

Someone not at all like her employer's oldest son.

Sabrina's thoughts turned to the day she'd first arrived at the ranch. When Mrs. Clayton had given her a tour of the house, they'd stopped near the rustic stone fireplace in the spacious living room, where Sabrina had gravitated toward a hodgepodge of silver-framed photos gracing the mantel. When she had a family and a home of her own, she would display photographs, too.

One picture in particular piqued her curiosity, and she'd reached for the pewter frame of a young boy mounted on a black horse. His eyes fairly glistened with joy and a smile dimpled his cheeks.

"That's Jared the day he went out with the men for the very first time," the elderly woman had told Sabrina. "He was *so* proud. His early years had been spent in the city, so he had to learn to rope and ride first, but he was a natural. You would've thought he'd been born in a saddle."

Grant Whitaker, the elderly CPA who'd passed Sabrina's resume on to Mrs. Clayton, had mentioned something about the three boys the woman had adopted, all of whom had been down-and-out youngsters with nowhere else to go.

As Sabrina had studied the happy young boy in the photo, she'd been curious about his background. But since she'd always been one to keep her own…humble beginnings to herself, she didn't prod for any more information than her employer wanted to share.

"Jared's the oldest of my three sons," Mrs. Clayton had said. "He's grown up to be the kind of man a woman can depend upon. I suppose some would say he's loyal to a fault."

For a moment, Sabrina had wondered if the elderly woman had been trying her hand at matchmaking, but decided she was probably talking in a mother/son or family sense. Jared had certainly seemed to be looking out for his mother last night—if you could call a rabid dog protective.

Of course, he might have had good reason for being in a foul mood, like an abscessed tooth or a migraine headache. Still, try as she might, Sabrina couldn't imagine that scowling, brash man to be the same smiling boy she'd seen in the picture on the mantel.

As Sabrina had returned the frame to its rightful place, Mrs. Clayton had added, "Jared's a good boy. Of course, all my sons are."

That hadn't always been the case, though. From what Sabrina had heard in town, Edna "Granny" Clayton had opened her heart to people in need over the years, and no one had needed a home—or a firm hand—more than the three boys she'd adopted. Yet her generosity and kindness hadn't stopped there.

In the past few weeks, she'd not only taken in Sabrina and Joey, but she'd given Tori McKenzie and Connie Montoya jobs and a place to live, too. So now that Jared and his brother had arrived, the house was bursting at the seams. Of course, the living situation would improve once the cabin was renovated and one of the outbuildings was converted into two small apartments for the household staff.

Sabrina didn't know about the other two women, but she was really looking forward to the move.

As a child, she and her family had been forced to live with various relatives and she'd grown to hate feeling like a charity case. All she wanted was to have a home of her own, a place no one could ever take away from her, but she would be content with what she had now and do her best to create a stable environment for her nephew.

She plumped her pillow for the umpteenth time in the last hour or so, then rolled to the side of the bed and glanced across the room to where Joey slept. She was able to see his blanketed form without having to turn on the light, which meant morning had arrived, so she climbed from bed.

Before heading to the bathroom, she stopped at the window, drew open the white eyelet curtains and peered out at the grassy pasture where several horses grazed, then over to the big white barn. Near the double doors, some of the hired hands had begun to gather.

The Rocking C wasn't anything like the home she'd imagined having in the city, but Joey seemed to like it here, which was all that really mattered.

She let the curtains fall back into place and made her way to the shower. She was glad her room had a private bathroom she only had to share with Joey. She turned on the spigot, waiting until the water was the right temperature, then stepped inside. When she was done, she wrapped a towel around her and blow-dried her hair. Then she dressed in a pair of khaki slacks, a neatly pressed white cotton blouse and a black sweater.

Just months ago, she'd dreamed of living in the city and wearing business suits to work—a dream she would have to put on hold until Joey was older.

Still, she'd tried to dress the part of a professional on her first day at the Rocking C by wearing a skirt and blazer.

"Well, now, don't you look nice," Granny had said. "But dressing up all fancy isn't necessary around here."

Sabrina had glanced down at her outfit, then at the elderly woman who'd hired her. "I suppose this is a bit over the top for a bookkeeping position at a ranch, but I wanted to let you know I take this job seriously."

"I'm glad to hear it. But you'll be a lot more comfortable around here in denim and flannel."

Sabrina hadn't been able to go that far, so slacks and blouses had been a compromise. And even though Granny had purchased several pairs of jeans and some feminine-cut T-shirts as a surprise, Sabrina hadn't been able to wear them. Not for work.

Now ready to face the day, she took one last peek at her nephew, then quietly let herself out of the bedroom and started down the hall. The rich aroma of fresh-brewed coffee wafted through the sprawling, five-bedroom ranch house, letting her know she wasn't the first one up and moving about. A cupboard door opened and closed in the kitchen, suggesting that Connie had started to prepare breakfast. Sabrina wondered if the new cook had any idea there would be two more joining them for the morning meal—Jared and Matthew.

She supposed it didn't matter. Connie tried hard, and although her meals weren't anything to shout about, she usually prepared enough to feed an army.

Sabrina wasn't much of a breakfast eater herself, especially when she'd had a midnight snack. But last night she'd only had two cookies. If Jared hadn't shown up, she might have gone back for more, but she hadn't wanted to leave her room.

Before she could get three steps down the hall, she heard papers being shuffled in the dark-paneled, masculine office and stiffened. She'd become somewhat territorial about the room in which she worked. With Edna's permission, she'd spent the better part of two days arranging the furniture and setting up a filing system that suited her.

More paper shuffled and a drawer slid open.

Was Edna looking for something she'd misplaced again?

As Sabrina approached the open doorway, she spotted Jared seated at the desk, rifling through one of the drawers. Several open files lay across the scarred oak desktop.

"Looking for something?" she asked.

The rugged rancher glanced up. For one fleeting moment, he donned the expression of a boy who'd been caught with his hand in the church offering plate, but he quickly doused it.

Straightening, he leaned back in the seat, the leather and springs creaking from the shift in his weight. "Nope. Nothing in particular."

In that case, he'd been snooping, which she didn't appreciate one bit.

She crossed her arms and leaned against the door-jamb. "The office was a mess when I came to work, so I've organized it. I know exactly where everything is and can put my hands on it instantly. So if you ever decide what it is you need, just let me know. I'd be glad to get it for you."

His gaze traveled the length of her and back, as though he was trying to assess her—body and soul. A glimmer of masculine interest flashed in his eyes, and it was all she could do to remain ramrod straight. Calm. In control. She was determined to keep her pulse rate steady and her temper on an even keel.

"It's obvious that you've made a lot of changes," he said. "Granny used to file things in piles and stacks."

"I can't work like that."

"Ah, so you're a control freak."

She tensed. Over the years, she'd taken some ribbing because of her need to take charge of her life, but she couldn't help it. "I prefer to think of myself as organized."

He rocked back in the chair, causing it to strain and groan. "Where did you meet Grant Whitaker?"

Sabrina didn't like the idea of being interrogated and had the urge to tell Jared where he could get off. But she'd worked hard in college, choosing to bypass student loans and financial aid for reasons of her own, and didn't want him or anyone else to think of her as a charity case. Not anymore.

"I was majoring in accounting at the University of Houston and met Mr. Whitaker while applying for a job in his office. He wasn't hiring, but suggested I call Mrs.

Clayton, since she'd recently told him she was looking for a bookkeeper. I needed the job, and she needed me. It's as simple as that." She strode toward the desk. "While I don't usually waste my time speaking to rude, obnoxious people, you're my employer's son, so I'm trying to be polite. But I don't owe you anything, Mr. Clayton. Least of all an explanation."

A grin tugged at his lips, and a hint of—amusement? Admiration?—lit the gold flecks in his eyes. "I thought accountants were supposed to be mild-mannered. You've got a little spunk."

A part of her felt compelled to thank him, but she kept quiet.

"I suppose I've been…snappy," he admitted, "so I apologize. But there are a lot of people living here, all of them strangers, and I just want to make sure no one is taking advantage of Granny."

"Your mother strikes me as being a good judge of character."

"She always used to be."

Sabrina glanced at the files on the desk and eased closer so she could see what he'd been reading. "For someone who claims he isn't looking for anything, you sure have dug through quite a few files."

"Actually," he said, "I'm the executor of Granny's estate and I always go over the books when I'm in town."

"She didn't say anything to me about that."

"It probably slipped her mind."

That was certainly possible, Sabrina supposed. "Then maybe it's a good idea if we talk to her about it at breakfast. I'd feel much better if she gave me her okay."

Instead of responding to her comment, he studied

her. His hazel eyes, were compelling when they weren't narrowed or fired-up in anger. Mesmerizing, actually, so she broke eye contact.

About the time she assumed he wasn't going to respond at all, he said, "Your hair looks better down. Like you wore it last night."

The compliment, as well as the masculine appreciation in his tone, knocked her off balance, and she lifted her hand to feel along the side of her hair. Making sure the strands were in place, she supposed.

He cleared his throat. "Anyway, you don't need to worry. I'll put everything back where I found it."

"That's all right." Sabrina reached for a file, intending to gather them all together and make sure they ended up in the right place. "I'll do it."

Jared's hand clamped on to her wrist, and a jolt of heat shot straight through her chest, nearly taking her breath away. Time stood still, as sexual awareness hovered over her, unbalancing her.

She yanked free of his grip, a knee-jerk response that was more from the shocking zing of his touch than from being restrained.

Her parents had allowed themselves to be ruled by hormones instead of good sense. And look where that had gotten them.

Sabrina was determined not to make the same mistake, especially when she could clearly see that Jared Clayton wasn't the man for her.

"I'm not finished looking at those." As he withdrew his hand, his gaze softened ever so slightly.

"I have no problem allowing you to have the run of the office. But only if Mrs. Clayton gives her okay."

He leaned back in the chair, the leather and springs protesting again. Another grin eased across his lips, causing the warrior in him to relax some. "I value honesty, integrity and a good work ethic, Sabrina. So I hope that's what's going on here."

That's exactly what was going on. But the way he studied her made her wonder if he thought she had some kind of ulterior motive.

"Maybe we've started out on the wrong foot," he said, his eyes gentling even more.

He was right, but it wasn't Sabrina who'd set the ground rules. "I'm sure your mother would prefer that we be allies rather than adversaries."

"Is it too late to start over?"

She wanted to tell him it was. To insist the two of them might never see eye to eye.

Yet as her their gazes locked, as her heart rate slipped into overdrive, she wasn't so sure.

Jared hadn't been able to find anything suspicious in the office, so just before seven, he stopped by the kitchen to share a cup of coffee with the men who were downing the last bit of their breakfast—overcooked strips of bacon and misshapen, unevenly browned pancakes. Since Connie, the so-called cook, was nowhere to be seen, Jared suspected that she'd had been too embarrassed to stick around and witness the consumption of the meal.

But rather than hang out with the men any longer, Jared made small talk while he finished his coffee, then excused himself to check on his brother.

It was rare that Jared ever felt as though he was in

over his head, but in this case, with three women to question, as well as some of the ranch hands—if he could ever get them alone—he could use Matt's help.

His brother's bedroom door was closed, so he knocked lightly.

"Who is it?" Matt asked.

"It's me."

"Come on in."

Jared opened the door and entered the room. Matt was seated in his wheelchair. His dark brown hair was a tousled mess and he hadn't shaved in days. What most people might not know was that Matt's spirit had been more broken than his body.

"Want me to help you take a shower?" Jared asked.

"Maybe later." Matt nodded his head toward the office door. "Find out anything?"

"Not yet, but I haven't been able to go back too far. If worse comes to worst, I'll give Grant Whitaker a call."

"What are you going to do if you find out who's been tinkering with Granny's accounts?"

"Press charges for a start."

Last night, after Doc had called, Jared had given his brother the news. He'd hoped hearing about Granny's failing health and the missing funds might pull Matt out of the slump he'd been in ever since the accident.

"You have to come with me," he'd told his brother last night. "I'm going to need help convincing Granny to sell her place and move in with me."

But if truth be told, Jared had feared leaving Matt alone in his condition. No telling what he might do, even if he'd never made any outright threats to end it all.

Why else would he refuse to go to physical therapy?

If Jared had been the one laid low by shattered bones, he'd be champing at the bit to get better and back on his feet.

Now he was hoping that Matt's love for Granny would pull him out of the depression that threatened to keep him in that damn chair for the rest of his life.

"I need your help," he told Matt.

"What kind of help?"

In the past, Matt had always been just as protective and vigilant about the ranch and their mother's well-being as Jared was, but believing he'd caused the accident that killed his fiancée and her son had crippled him worse than the injuries he'd suffered that fateful night.

"I need you to keep your eyes and ears open. One of the strays Granny took in is a thief, and I'm not sure which one."

"What about the new bookkeeper?" Matt asked. "She has access to the bank accounts. Have you questioned her yet?"

"I wanted to do some poking around first." A small part of him hoped the lovely, dark-haired beauty with the skill and the opportunity to rob Granny blind was every bit as ethical and efficient as she claimed to be, although he couldn't say why. Someone was responsible for the missing funds, and heaven help whoever it was.

"Come on." Jared stepped behind Matt's wheelchair and began to push him out of the bedroom. "Let's go have breakfast, although I gotta tell you it smells much better than it looks. I just hope it tastes okay. When I was in there earlier, I didn't see any of the ranch hands go for seconds."

As Jared and Matt entered the hall, they blocked the

way of a tall, shapely redhead, who jerked back and gasped in surprise.

Jared opened his mouth to ask which of the freeloaders she was, but having already bumped heads with Sabrina, he decided to exercise a little more diplomacy this time. "We haven't met. I'm Jared Clayton, Granny's son, and this is Matthew, my brother."

"Tori McKenzie. The new housekeeper." Her gaze slid toward Matt, and curiosity played out on her face.

To her credit, she didn't ask any questions, which Matt probably appreciated. He didn't like talking about the car accident that had also ended his rodeo career.

"It's nice to meet you," Tori said.

"Same here." Jared forced a grin, yet doubted his brother made the same attempt. Matt didn't find much to smile about these days.

Tori stepped aside by entering the open doorway to the bathroom, allowing room for Matt's wheelchair to pass, and Jared continued on his way to the kitchen.

"Well, now," Granny said from her chair at the antique walnut table that had been in her family for years. "Isn't this a treat? All we're missing is Greg."

The youngest of the three boys, Greg, had always been in the limelight, first as a star football player in college and now as a country-and-western singer.

"Greg's on tour this month," Jared said.

After Doc's phone call last night, Jared had called his youngest brother, who was ready to cancel whatever shows necessary to come home, but Jared told him to hold off and that they'd keep him posted on the situation.

"Greg's getting pretty popular," Granny said.

"That's true, but the last time we talked, he mentioned wanting to come home for a visit as soon as he could swing it. I have a feeling he's going to surprise you one of these days soon." Jared didn't mention that the conversation had taken place last night.

The back door opened and shut, then a petite woman with short blond hair entered through the mudroom. She was attractive, Jared supposed, although he'd always been partial to brunettes.

Especially those with long dark hair—like Sabrina, he realized, although that was one attraction that wasn't going anywhere.

"Can I freshen anyone's coffee?" the blonde asked, as she headed to the sink and turned on the water to wash her hands.

Granny lifted her cup. "I'll have a tad more. And now that you're here, let me introduce you to my sons, Jared and Matt. Boys, this is Consuela Montoya. But she wants to be called Connie."

"It's nice to meet you." The woman smiled shyly, then reached for the coffeepot and replenished Granny's cup. "Anyone else?"

"Not yet," Matt said.

"I'll pass." Jared studied the woman, noting that her hair had been dyed. Had she been a brunette who'd come in to some cash lately?

Highlights like those were expensive. He knew because his ex had emphasized the blond streaks in her hair that way. And nothing about Jolene or her tastes had been cheap.

"By the way," Granny said, "someone made me an offer on the Nevada property."

Jared wasn't aware that she'd had any out-of-state land or holdings. "What property is that?"

"It's a large parcel that Everett purchased years ago." Everett was her late husband, a man who'd passed away just before Jared had been adopted, which meant Granny had owned the land for at least twenty years. "Didn't I tell you boys about it?"

Jared looked at Matt, who shook his head.

"Well, I plumb near forgot all about it. Everett bought it ages ago, although I can't remember exactly when."

"And someone wants to buy it?" Jared asked.

"Yep. And he's courtin' me, too."

Courting her? Jared furrowed his brow. "What do you mean?"

Granny laughed. "Not courting me like a moonstruck lover. He's just calling and sweet-talking me some, hoping I'll sell. And to tell you the truth, I think it's time. Everett said it would be a good investment for our old age."

"Where is it located?" Jared asked.

"Not too far from Las Vegas. Everett always thought the town would grow and that the property would be valuable someday."

"So do you want to sell?" he asked.

"If they make me a decent offer."

Jared feared, at her age, she might not be able to negotiate a real-estate deal—not without being taken advantage of. And who was to say what a "decent offer" was? "Why don't you let me talk to that guy the next time he calls?"

"All right." Granny took a sip of coffee, then watched as Connie took a platter of pancakes from the oven, where they'd been kept warm, and placed them on the table. Each one was an uneven shade of brown and shaped like the ink blots on a Rorschach test. Jared wondered if the hands had chosen the ones that looked more edible and left these behind.

"Hotcakes anyone?" Connie asked.

Matt merely stared at the stack, and Jared wondered if he'd make it until lunch if he didn't eat any of them.

"Thanks," Granny said, snagging one that was a little too dark around the edges for Jared's taste. "They're looking better each time you make them, Connie. I told you perfect flapjacks just take practice."

It seemed pretty apparent that Granny hadn't required her new cook to provide references.

Before long, they were joined at the table by Sabrina and her nephew, whose eyes widened when he spotted Jared. "We never get to eat with the cowboys." Then his gaze lit on Matt and his wheelchair.

Jared had to give the kid credit for biting his lip, rather than commenting.

After Granny made the introductions, Sabrina dug through the pile of hotcakes and found one shaped like an egg. It was a perfect shade of brown on one side, and nearly white on the other.

She placed it on the boy's plate, but he seemed more interested in Matt's chair. Curiosity grew in his eyes.

"My grandfather has a wheelchair," the boy finally said. "But it isn't as cool as yours."

"Mine's *pretty* cool," Matt said.

Was Jared the only one who sensed sarcasm in his brother's tone?

"What happened to you?" the boy asked. "My grandpa fell down and broke his hip."

"Matt broke his legs," Granny explained, probably assuming her middle son would shine the kid like he usually did when someone brought up the subject. Or maybe she was just trying to take the heat off him. "Thank God he won't have to stay in the chair forever."

Maybe not, although that was left to be seen. But either way, Matt would never compete in the rodeo again, which was his life. So Jared suspected his brother didn't get a whole lot of comfort from that. If he did, you'd think he'd be trying harder to get better.

"Have you started physical therapy again?" Granny asked.

Wrong question, Jared could have told her. But he didn't.

Matt tensed, then glanced at her, his expression blank. "No. Not yet."

Footsteps sounded, and the redhead—Tori—joined them at the table, taking a seat next to the boy.

"How'd you sleep last night?" Tori asked Granny.

"Only woke up once to use the bathroom," Granny said. "You were right about that medication."

"Good. I'm glad to hear it."

It was bad enough that three strangers had infiltrated Granny's life and home, but it was even worse to have them butting into her personal habits.

"Hey, cool," Joey said, as he pulled his fork out of the gooey middle of his hotcake. "They're cream-filled."

"Uh-oh. Sorry about that." The blond cook snatched away the boy's plate. "That's not cream filling, it's batter. I guess that one needs to be cooked a little more."

This was crazy. Jared wondered if Sabrina, the bookkeeper, knew how to run an adding machine or if Tori, the maid, knew which end of the broom was up.

He had to talk Granny into selling the ranch and moving in with him, where he could take care of her. Too bad she was every bit as stubborn as she was good-hearted.

A knock sounded at the door. Before waiting to be invited in, the ranch foreman entered the mudroom. "Sorry to interrupt breakfast, but Earl Clancy just split his head wide-open. He's refusing to go into town and see a doctor, but it looks pretty bad to me."

"He needs to go anyway," Sabrina said. "If he's worried about the cost, worker's compensation will take care of it."

Tori scooted her chair away from the table. "I'll go take a look at the wound. Maybe I can talk Earl into getting it checked."

"Thanks, ma'am." Lester turned toward the door and placed his hat back on his head. "I'd sure appreciate that."

The redhead reached into a cupboard near the refrigerator and pulled out a white metal box with a red cross on the front. Jared wondered if she had first-aid training, suspecting that she might have. Still, that didn't make her Florence Nightingale.

"You know," he said, getting to his feet, "I think I'll go check on the injured man myself. If he needs a doctor, I'll drive him into town."

And even if he didn't, Jared wanted to get the foreman off by himself. Lester Bailey had been working for the Rocking C for almost as long as Jared could remember, and if anyone had a handle on Granny's mental state, it was him.

"I'll keep the hotcakes warm for you," the cook said.

"Thanks, Connie. But don't bother." Jared would much rather pick up something to eat in town. As he reached the back door of the mudroom and grabbed his hat, footsteps sounded behind him.

"Wait a minute."

He turned to see Sabrina heading after him, a plastic container in her arms. "Why don't you take a couple of cookies with you? Think of them as a hearty bowl of oatmeal-on-the-run, only better."

Jared, who'd always had a sweet tooth, reached inside and pulled out one of the plumpest cookies he'd ever seen. "Who made these?"

"Connie did."

The cook?

"She's a whiz at making sweets and desserts. So I don't think one will be enough." She handed him a couple more.

He took the cookies she offered, then watched as she reached into the jar and pulled out one for herself. After taking a bite, she closed her eyes, relishing each chew.

Jared had never known that eating could be so damn sexy. His mind wandered to the vision Sabrina had made last night, wearing that flowing white nightgown and with that veil of hair sluicing over her shoulders and down her back.

Now, as she murmured a "Mmm" in delight, it set off a wave of hunger inside of him. And he wasn't talking about food.

But under the circumstances, the cookies would be a healthier choice.

Chapter Three

Jared's talk with the foreman would have to wait until after he'd driven Earl Clancy, the injured ranch hand, into the Brighton Valley Urgent Care Center for stitches.

Not only did Tori seem to have a good handle on first aid, she also had a way of dealing with a tough-as-rawhide ranch hand who didn't want "folks fussin'" over him.

When cajoling the crotchety wrangler into seeking medical help hadn't worked, she got tough and slapped her hands on her hips. "Earl, don't be stubborn. That wound is going to get infected if you don't get it treated."

Lester eased closer. "Ma'am, I'm afraid they don't come any more hardheaded than Earl. About five years back, he lost his big toe when he didn't take care of an ingrown nail."

"Is that right?" Tori shifted her weight from one foot to the other. "Well, listen here, Earl. There's not a whole lot above the shoulders you're going to want them to amputate. Now, get into Mr. Clayton's truck and let him drive you to town."

Earl grumbled some, but he did as the woman ordered.

"You'll be back and mending that fence before you know it," Lester told him.

But in reality, Jared and Earl hadn't returned until just after lunch. Tori had called it right, though. She'd guessed it would take close to fifteen stitches to close the wound, and Jared had counted sixteen.

As they approached the barn, the truck hit a pothole in the driveway, and Earl rattled off an "Ow," followed by a few choice swear words. "I told that damn nurse I didn't need a tetanus shot, but she was as pushy as that redheaded maid. And just to be ornery, I think she hit a nerve in my rump. And now my backside hurts worse than my head."

Jared parked the truck near the barn, where one of the hands had left Earl's horse waiting for him, saddled and ready to go.

"You need any help?" he asked the man.

"Heck, no. I've had about all the tender lovin' care I need for the rest of my life."

Jared watched as Earl climbed onto his mount, wincing as he settled his butt in the saddle. As he rode off, Jared headed for the barn, looking for the foreman. He found him in his office, placing an order for feed and grain.

When Lester hung up the phone, Jared asked, "Got a minute?"

"Sure." Lester pointed at a green vinyl chair that sat across the desk from him. "Have a seat."

Jared thought about shutting the door, but decided it was just the two of them. When he sat down, he tossed out the question that had been bothering him since the night before. "How do you think Granny is doing? I'm talking both physically and mentally."

"All right, I suppose. But she's getting older, and bodies naturally wear out. I guess you could say she's slipping a bit."

"In what way?"

Lester glanced at the open doorway, then back at Jared. "She's been a little forgetful."

"Give me an example."

Lester lifted his battered Stetson, raked a hand through his thick, curly gray hair, then adjusted the hat back on his head. "Can't say as I remember anything in particular."

Maybe Doc had been mistaken.

"Then how do you know she's 'slipping'?" Jared asked.

"I just do. And it wouldn't hurt none if you and your brothers started coming around to visit more often."

"It might be best if I took her home to live with me."

Lester's eyes grew wide, and he slowly shook his head. "Nope. That won't work."

"Why not?"

"It just won't. That's all."

A lot of help he was. If Lester hadn't always been a man of few words, Jared might have thought the aging ranch foreman was slipping, too. "Thanks. I'll let you get back to work."

A glimmer of relief seemed to cross Lester's face, and

Jared left him to it. Maybe it was time to go into the house and have a little chat with both the maid and the cook.

As Jared left the barn and headed toward the porch, he spotted Sabrina's nephew playing with Sassy, one of two Australian shepherds that lived on the ranch.

With his mind on Granny and her well-being, Jared had no intention of stopping to talk, but the boy stood when he approached.

"Hey, mister. Can I ask you something?"

Jared's steps slowed. "What's that?"

"Are you a *real* cowboy?"

Jared had half a notion to tell him no and go about his business. There was no need to befriend a kid who wouldn't be living on the ranch that much longer—especially if Granny sold out and moved in with Jared.

But he remembered his own first days on the Rocking C, his own wide-eyed interest in horses and cowboys and ranch life. In fact, the day Clem Bixby had taken him under wing had turned Jared's life around and set the course of his future.

"I suppose you could call me a cowboy," he admitted to the kid.

"And you used to live here, right?"

"Yep."

"But you don't anymore?"

"I own my own spread about a hundred miles north of here." Jared wondered where the little guy was going with all the questions.

"Then I guess I'm allowed to talk to you all I want."

"What do you mean?" Jared asked.

"Sabrina said I can't bother the cowboys who live here because they're working."

So Jared was free game, huh?

The boy eased closer, his small hand lifted to shield the sun's glare from his eyes. "Can I ask you something else?"

Again, Jared thought about making an excuse and leaving, but what would it hurt to stick around for a minute or so longer? "Sure. Go ahead."

"Did you have to go to school to be a cowboy?"

A grin tugged at Jared's lips. "Not the kind of school with desks and teachers and homework, if that's what you mean. But I had a whole lot to learn, and it wasn't easy."

"Sabrina says I gotta go to college, but I didn't even like first grade. And I don't think second grade will be all that much fun, either."

"Oh, yeah?" Jared hadn't liked school, either. Not when he'd lived in Houston. It was a lot better when he attended Brighton Valley Elementary, he supposed, but he'd dreaded every minute he'd had to spend away from the ranch.

The boy clucked his tongue. "I'd rather stay here and watch the cowboys work all day long. Maybe, if I did that, they'd let me help round up cows and ride horses."

"Cowboys don't need a college degree," Jared said, "although it might help some. But second grade is important. You sure don't want to miss out on any of the basic lessons all cowboys ought to know."

"Like what?"

"Well," Jared said, rubbing his chin and trying to recall some of the things Clem had told him. "Let's say there's an auction and you're in need of a few good horses. They advertise those in the newspaper. If you couldn't read, you'd miss out."

"Maybe one of my cowboy friends could call me on the phone and tell me about it," the boy countered.

Sharp kid. Jared tried not to grin. "Okay, let's say they did. How are you going to know how much money you can afford to bid? You need to be able to add and subtract pretty well to balance your bank account."

"I could hire someone like Sabrina. She's really good at math and could do that stuff for me."

"But then you'd have to trust someone else with your money. What if they ran off with everything you owned?"

"Sabrina wouldn't."

Jared hoped the kid was right.

But in Jared's case, he'd learned that some women, like Jolene, couldn't be trusted. And when they ran off, they took more than a man's money.

They took his heart and his pride.

Jared fixed himself a glass of iced tea, then took a seat at the kitchen table and watched Connie dry the last of the lunch dishes.

"Have you seen my mother?" he asked the so-called cook.

"She took her mare out for an afternoon ride." Connie turned away from a three-layer cake she was frosting—a chocolate masterpiece that rivaled any of those in a bakery display case and put this morning's hotcakes to shame.

So what was the deal? She could make moist, chewy cookies and cakes, but couldn't whip up a decent meal for breakfast?

Jared cleared his throat. "Well, then, I guess I'll have to wait to talk to her until she gets back."

Connie nodded, then returned to her work.

Jared carried his glass into the living room, where Tori the housekeeper was dusting the shelves in the handcrafted bookcase that Granny's husband had built many years ago. Matt had parked his wheelchair near the big bay window that looked over the driveway. He was holding a *Western Horseman* magazine in his lap and gazing through the glass into the yard, yet by his expression, Jared suspected his thoughts were anywhere but in the here and now.

He did look up as Jared entered the room, though.

"Did you get that guy stitched up?" he asked.

"Yep. He's back on the job." Jared slid his thumbs into the front pocket of his jeans. "Have you had a chance to talk to Granny this morning?"

"Not really." Matt glanced to the bookshelf, where Tori stood on a footstool, her back to them. "She was busy outside for a while. Then, just after lunch, she saddled Bluebonnet and took off."

If Granny hadn't given up her daily afternoon ride, then maybe she was doing okay after all.

"She should be back in an hour or so," the redhead said, obviously listening.

Jared would have to choose his words carefully, although now might be a good time to quiz the maid and get a feel for the kind of person she was. So he made his way to the bookshelf. "Tori, you mentioned something about Granny's medication earlier, and I'm curious. What was that all about?"

The attractive redhead, stopped her work and turned, a dust rag dangling from her hands. "Granny was complaining about having to wake up at all hours of the night to use the bathroom, so I asked her what meds she was taking. When she showed me the prescription bottles, I suggested she take the diuretic in the morning. She noticed a big difference."

"What's a diuretic?" he asked, wondering if Doc was the one who was slipping.

"Some people refer to it as a water pill. It helps rid the body of excess fluids and sodium, or rather, salt. She's taking it along with a beta-blocker for hypertension."

Tori seemed to have a better than average handle on Granny's medication. And after seeing how she'd dealt with Earl, Jared suspected she'd definitely taken some kind of first-aid course. But now he was beginning to think she might have had more training than that. And if that were the case, then what was she doing working as a maid and not at a hospital or clinic?

"You seem to know a lot about medicine," he said. "Where'd you pick up all that knowledge?"

She paused for a moment, then shrugged. "I read a lot."

As she returned to her work, providing him a view of her back, he pondered her response. She'd evaded his question, which made him wonder why she was holding back—and what other secrets she might have.

Tori was a pretty gal, with big blue eyes, a scatter of freckles across her nose and long, curly red hair pulled back with a clip.

Jared slid a glance Matt's way, only to find that his brother was watching Tori, as well. A hint of masculine interest in Matt's eyes suggested he found her attractive, and that he had noticed the way her snug denim jeans did justice to a pair of long legs and a sexy rear.

That was a good sign, Jared decided. Tori was the

first woman his brother had seemed to notice since the accident. Not that Jared would encourage anything. His brother wasn't ready for any kind of relationship, although it was a relief to know he might seek happiness with someone new in the future.

Of course, whether he found it or not was another question.

As for Jared, himself, Jolene had done a real number on him, so he doubted if he'd ever trust another woman again.

And although Jared suspected Tori hadn't been entirely honest with him about her medical background, when it came to stealing from Granny, that didn't make her any more of a suspect than Sabrina.

Any of the employees, particularly those with free rein in the household, could have taken Granny's money, yet the pretty, dark-haired bookkeeper was still the most logical.

Jared was open-minded, though. And if Sabrina hadn't stolen the money, she was also the most likely to help him find the real culprit.

Leaving his brother and Tori in the living room, he headed back down the hall to the office, where Sabrina worked at the computer.

The prim brunette was so intent on what she was doing that she apparently hadn't heard him walk up. So he watched her for a while, intrigued by the way she ran the tip of her tongue across her full bottom lip.

He decided not to interrupt her just yet, not while he was enjoying the view, but she glanced up and caught him looking at her.

"Got a minute?" he asked.

"Sure. Come on in."

He took a seat across from her and decided to lay the problem on the line and gauge her reaction. "I heard that Grant Whitaker found some discrepancies in Granny's account. There's some money missing."

"I'm aware of that." Sabrina straightened and leaned back in the desk chair. "Mr. Whitaker mentioned it to me a couple of days ago, but when I asked your mother about having an ATM card or utilizing the online banking service, she didn't have any idea what I was talking about."

"Then someone unauthorized must have ATM access to her account."

"You might be right, but your mother has been pretty forgetful lately. Just yesterday, I learned of an account she didn't even remember opening."

"How did you find out about it?"

"She received a letter from a savings and loan located in another town, telling her that the account would be frozen due to nonactivity."

Jared leaned against the doorjamb and crossed his arms. "I thought you went through her files. Wasn't there any record of statements being sent to her?"

"I might have missed it, but I don't think so." Sabrina pushed her chair from the desk and stood. In the course of her workday, a button on her blouse had become undone, and Jared couldn't help noticing a flash of skin and the white lace trim of her bra.

"I asked the bank to trace those withdrawals," she said. "I was told they were all made from an ATM card that your mother requested, a card someone activated through the main branch."

The question was, who had done that?

Sabrina was supposedly checking in to it, but Jared thought it might be a better idea if he stopped by the main branch himself. One of the girls he'd gone to school with used to be married to the vice president of the bank. Hopefully, she still was, although he knew the stats on break ups these days better than anyone.

The phone rang, and Sabrina reached across the desk to grab the receiver.

"Good afternoon. Rocking C Ranch." She paused, her body still bent, her blouse gaping open even more than before and revealing the gentle swell of a breast. A man would thank his lucky stars to cup his hand around the soft fullness of her flesh, to stroke, caress…

Damn. He tore his gaze away before she realized he'd been lusting over her.

"No," Sabrina told the caller, "she's not in right now. But if you leave your name and number, I'll pass along the message." She reached for a pink pad and pen. "Sure. I'll let Mrs. Clayton know you called."

As she hung up the phone and straightened, she turned toward him, the pink sheet of paper in her hand. As she did so, the pen she'd been using rolled off the desk.

"Oops." She stooped to pick it up from the floor, giving Jared a view of her from the rear.

His eyes fixed on the way the fabric of her slacks stretched across shapely hips.

Not bad, he thought. Not bad at all.

But Sabrina wasn't someone he ought to be looking at—from the front or the rear. At least not until she'd earned his trust, which could take years.

And he expected to have the problems solved at the Rocking C within a week, if not sooner.

* * *

After Sabrina had shut down the computer for the day and left the office, she went to look for Joey so they could spend some time together before dinner.

He tended to gravitate to the outdoors, so she usually knew right where to find him. Her rules were firm, though. He must always stay in the front yard and be able to see the porch.

It hadn't taken her long to spot him. He was sitting in the shade of an elm tree that grew in the middle of the lawn, one of the ranch dogs resting beside him.

"Are you up for an adventure?" she asked. "Mrs. Clayton mentioned that one of the broodmares is going to foal soon, and I thought it might be fun to take a look at her."

"Sure." Joey brightened. "Can Sassy go with us?"

"Sassy?"

"My dog."

Sabrina bent to scratch the Australian shepherd's ear. "Sassy belongs to Mrs. Clayton, Joey. And when we leave the ranch, she'll stay here."

"I know." Regret laced his voice. "But I can pretend, can't I?"

Just as long as he remembered they weren't permanent residents at the Rocking C. Sabrina might be trying her best to fit in and be accepted, to find a small piece of the ranch that they could call home, but eventually she wanted a place that belonged only to her. A place from which no one could ever make her leave.

"When we move into a house of our own, you can have a pet."

"Okay. I'd like a dog and a horse. Maybe a cat, too."

"A lot will depend upon where we move. Horses need a much bigger yard than most animals."

As they neared the white wooden fence that corralled the broodmares, a rider on horseback approached.

But not just any rider. It was Jared.

Seated atop a chestnut gelding, the sun at his back, he was a commanding sight. A woman, Sabrina realized, didn't have to be attracted to the rugged, outdoorsy type to perk up when she noticed him.

He tipped his hat in John Wayne fashion.

"Hi, Mr. Clayton." Joey started toward the man with a spring in his step. "Did you take your horse out for a run?"

A hint of a smile softened the rancher's face as he studied the wide-eyed child. "It wasn't a pleasure ride this time. I went to check on Earl, who's still out mending fences."

"How's he doing?" Sabrina asked. "He should be taking it easy after that accident."

"That crusty old wrangler is still hopping mad about wasting half a day at the clinic and about not being able to give one hundred percent because an uppity nurse insisted upon crippling him with a hypodermic needle in the…" He glanced at Joey, then cleared his throat. "Well, I guess you don't need a direct quote."

"I get the idea." Sabrina couldn't help but grin. "Thanks for taking him. If you wouldn't have done it, I might have had to drive him to see a doctor. And I have a feeling it wouldn't have been a fun trip."

"Earl's a tough old bird." Jared lifted his hat and raked a hand through his hair. "By the way, did you hear anything back from the bank?"

"No. Not yet. But I talked to Granny earlier and quizzed her about the accounts she has. She thinks there are about four or five, but isn't sure." The elderly woman had also given Sabrina permission to discuss any of her financial business with her son, which was the only reason why this conversation was taking place.

Jared's horse stepped to the right, no longer blocking the sun.

Sabrina lifted a hand to her eyes, trying to lessen the glare. "By the way, when I went back through last year's expenses, I saw property tax payments for that Las Vegas parcel. So if she forgot about owning it, her memory lapse was recent."

Jared replaced the hat on his head, then dismounted. "I was afraid of that. I asked her about having an ATM card, and she didn't seem to know what I was talking about."

"I'm inclined to believe her. But then again, if her memory is failing…" Sabrina looked at Jared. "Well… You know what I mean."

Unfortunately, Jared knew exactly what she meant. But he didn't want to believe it. Or accept it.

On the outside, it appeared that he and Sabrina had broached some kind of alliance, when in fact, he merely wanted to win her confidence.

He still wasn't convinced that she wasn't the one stealing from Granny. Hopefully, she wasn't. But he still didn't trust her. Not yet.

Maybe not ever.

As he prepared to cool down the gelding, he looked at the boy, who was gazing at him and the horse with stars in his eyes.

Joey was rail-thin, and a bit fairer than his pretty aunt, whose Latina roots were evident in a flawless, olive complexion. He also seemed a bit frail for ranch life, although he'd made no secret of his appreciation for horses and cowboys.

"If it's all right with your aunt," Jared told the child, "I'll give you a ride around the yard."

Joey's eyes widened, and he threw a pleading gaze at Sabrina. "Please, oh, please?"

"If Mr. Clayton doesn't mind…"

"I don't." Jared was going to suggest that Joey call him by his first name, but there was no need in them getting that familiar. Not when the length of Sabrina's employment was still in question.

He had no intention of going to the trouble of teaching the boy how to mount. Instead, he lifted him onto the saddle.

Joey gripped the saddle horn with both hands, his bright-eyed, ear-to-ear grin a dead giveaway that he was in hog heaven. "This is the very first time I ever rode a horse."

If anyone could understand his excitement, it was Jared.

As he began to lead the gelding around the yard, giving the kid a ride, he stole a glance at Sabrina. She smiled and mouthed a "Thank you."

He gave her a little shrug. It was no big deal.

"Do they give lessons on how to ride horses?" Joey asked.

"Yes, there are ranches and stables that teach people how to ride."

"Does it cost a lot of money?"

"It varies."

"Is it hard to learn?"

"Not for a cowboy." Jared glanced up at the kid. "And you seem to be a natural."

That wasn't quite true, but what would it hurt to make the kid's smile last a little longer?

"I'd like lessons, but Aunt Sabrina won't let me ask anyone here at the ranch to teach me. She doesn't want us to wear out our welcome. I mean, we're welcome to be here and all, but you know."

"You mean, she doesn't want you to take advantage of Mrs. Clayton's good nature?"

"Yeah. I guess. We're living here now, and Mrs. Clayton told me I could call her Granny and everything. So it's kind of like we're friends, you know? But Sabrina is big on manners and stuff."

"Oh, yeah?"

"Yeah. I think she even read a book on it and everything."

Jared couldn't prevent an almost-silent chuckle from erupting in his chest. Kids, he supposed, had an interesting view of life.

He led the horse around the side of the barn, then along the corral until he reached the outbuildings. When he figured they'd been walking for a good five minutes, he thought it wouldn't hurt to end the ride. But something wouldn't let him.

"You see that black mare in the corral?" he asked.

"Uh-huh. She's really pretty, but her stomach looks a little bit fat."

Jared chuckled. "That's because she's going to foal."

"You mean, she has a baby inside her?" The boy

turned his head to take a good look at the broodmare and shifted in the saddle.

Jared quickly grabbed a hold of Joey's foot to steady him. "Careful, sport."

"Oops."

"Hang on, will you? Your aunt would skin me alive if I let you fall off."

"She wouldn't be happy about it. But you could probably take her if she got *really* mad."

He could take her, all right. The thought of things getting physical between the two of them was an intriguing vision, though. And fighting wasn't what he had in mind. "You're right, Joey. I'm a lot bigger and stronger than she is, but real cowboys know how to treat a lady."

"You know what, Mr. Clayton?"

"What's that?"

"I never knew a real live cowboy before. And I'll bet you're the best in the whole wide world."

Jared hadn't been the subject of hero worship in some time—not since Greg was a boy—and it…well, it kind of touched him.

Maybe that's why he spent the next half hour wandering all over the ranch on foot, leading the kid around like an old man giving pony rides at the fair.

But what the hell.

When Jared finally wound up back at the barn, where Sabrina waited, she cast him a pretty smile that darn near turned him inside out. It was as if she saw him as some kind of hero, too.

And for some crazy reason, that touched him even more.

Chapter Four

Jared stretched out on the sofa in the den, the only room in the house that wasn't taken, and read a leather-bound volume of *Moby Dick*. He hadn't been able to sleep and didn't feel like watching television.

Outside, footsteps sounded on the front porch. He glanced at the clock on the lamp table, noting it was nearly midnight. So he set the novel aside and got up to peer out the window. Obviously, the dogs had decided that whoever was prowling around could be trusted to move about after dark.

When he drew back the curtains, he spotted Sabrina. She was facing the railing and looking out into the yard. Unlike last night, she wore a robe to cover her nightgown. But her ebony hair hung as long and loose as before.

The light of a full moon gave her a mystical aura, and a lovely one at that.

He watched from behind the glass for a while, then turned from the window and made his way down the hall and into the living room, where a lamp glowed softly. On the coffee table, an empty glass with traces of milk sat next to small plate bearing chocolate crumbs. Sabrina, he concluded, had been snacking.

The house was quiet save for the ticktock of the antique clock over the mantel. So, out of respect for those who were fast asleep, he carefully swung open the screen door. But the hinges screeched unexpectedly, causing Sabrina to gasp and nearly jump out of her shoes—if she'd been wearing them.

"Oh. Jared." The breathy, almost sensual, sound of his name as it slid from her lips stirred something deep inside of him. Something that had been dormant long before Jolene had walked out on him and moved back to Vegas.

Sabrina placed a hand over her heart. "You scared me half to death."

"Sorry. I didn't mean to." He eased toward her. "What are you doing out here?"

"Nothing." She gave a little shrug. "Sometimes I have trouble sleeping."

Like she had last night? "Why's that?"

"I don't know. Too much on my mind, I suppose. It's something I've had to deal with most of my life."

He closed the gap between them and joined her at the railing. Her scent, something shower-fresh and floral, laced the night air and set his senses reeling. He started to comment on her choice of lotion or soap, to tell her that he liked it, then clamped his mouth shut.

There was no need to make her think he was interested in her as a woman, even if his hormones insisted that, at this very moment, he was.

"I suppose Joey has already gone to bed," he said, trying to ditch any evidence of sexual attraction.

"Unlike me, that little boy can sleep anywhere."

"What's the matter? Isn't your mattress comfortable?" He figured that might be the case. He didn't like sleeping on the sofa in the den, but the only other option had been the barn, and that would be a whole lot worse.

"The bed isn't a problem. You'd think after all the different places I've lived in the past that I'd be able to sleep standing up." A little chuckle slipped out, but he guessed it was more from nervousness than actual humor.

"I take it you moved around a lot when you were younger."

"Yes, quite a bit. But it didn't seem to affect Carlos, my twin brother. He became a long-haul trucker."

"Is Carlos the boy's father?"

"Yes." She shifted her body, not exactly facing him, but no longer standing at his side. "Suzy, his mom, passed away nearly six months ago."

"From what?"

Sabrina cocked her head to the side and slid him an assessing glance, as though he was being a little too curious. But he couldn't help it. There was a lot he wanted to know.

"Suzy had a heart attack. It was sudden and completely unexpected. Joey never had a chance to say goodbye."

Jared blew out a little whistle. "Wow. How old was she?"

"Only twenty-two." Sabrina turned, resting her back against the railing. "The doctor said that she'd had a heart defect for years. And apparently, it had never been diagnosed."

"It must have been tough on Joey."

"It was."

"What about his father?"

"Carlos took some time off to attend the funeral, but it wasn't as long as he would have liked. He had to go back to work."

Leaving his son in the care of his twin sister. "If the boy needs him, maybe he ought to find another line of work. One that's closer to home."

Sabrina tensed. "It's tough supporting a family and providing health insurance when you don't have a high-school diploma."

Why was that? Sabrina obviously saw the value of an education. And her twin was a dropout?

"I'm sure it is. But it seems to me that a boy needs a dad, too."

"Believe me, Carlos would be here with Joey if he could."

Jared nearly asked why he couldn't, but let it go. Something told him that she wouldn't appreciate being prodded with more questions, no matter how many he had.

"Thanks for giving Joey that ride today," she said, changing the subject. "You have no idea how badly he wants a horse of his own."

Probably as badly as Jared had wanted one when he first came to the Rocking C. "No problem. He's a good kid."

She grew still for a moment, her gaze lifting to his and setting his senses on edge.

The night wind, as light as it was, blew a strand of hair across her cheek, and she brushed it aside. "Carlos loves his son more than anything. I want you to understand that."

Jared nodded, as though he did understand. But his childhood experience didn't allow him to be sympathetic for Joey's father, no matter how far Sabrina went to defend him.

When Jared's biological mother died, he'd been sent to Houston to live with his father, a man who'd gotten involved with drug dealers and had put his kid in foster care "for a little while."

"Just long enough for me to make a new start," he'd told Jared when he'd left him at a county office. But he'd never come back.

So rather than offer an opinion, Jared clamped his mouth shut. Families ought to stick together.

No matter what.

The wind kicked up a bit, sending another wisp of Sabrina's hair across her cheek, but rather than wait for her to sweep it away, he risked doing so himself. His fingers trailed across the softness of her skin.

Her breath caught, and their gazes locked. Her lips parted, as though she was going to say something, but no words came out.

His pulse began to pound out a ragged, primal beat, and his blood rushed through his veins, warming steadily.

The moment was too still, too tempting.

All he had to do was tilt her chin up, sweep his lips across hers. And he damn near had a mind to do it.

So why didn't she step back? Draw away?

It sure would have been easier if she would have told him where he could get off. Or if she would have made an excuse to head back into the house.

As it was, he had to do something himself. Something that didn't seem natural.

He let his hand drop to his side, empty. "Well, I guess I'd better turn in. I've got an early day tomorrow."

"Sleep tight," she said.

Yeah, right. He doubted he'd get any rest at all, because as much as he wanted to pat himself on the back for winning a daring battle with temptation, he had a feeling he'd be kicking himself all the way back to the den.

Sabrina remained on the porch for another few minutes before heading back into the house. All the while, she relived those last couple of moments with Jared on the porch.

He'd nearly kissed her; she'd been sure of it.

Not that she had all that much experience with men and romance. After the mistakes her parents had made, something for which she and Carlos were still paying a price, she knew better than to risk getting seriously involved with anyone until after she graduated and had a solid grip on her life and her future.

In the past, it hadn't been difficult to shy away from men and relationships. She'd just kept her nose in the books and her mind on her goal. But she'd never been faced with a rugged cowboy, whose musky, leathery scent set off something warm and fluttery in her chest, and she was afraid that keeping her focus might not be as easy on the ranch as it had been at the University of Houston.

Now, more than ever, a romance would be an unnecessary complication in her life. Especially when she found herself interested in a man who had a bossy, stubborn streak that brought out the worst in her. A man who threatened what little stability she'd found on the Rocking C.

Of course, he had a tender side, too.

"He's loyal to a fault," Mrs. Clayton had said about her oldest son, and Sabrina had reason to believe that might be true. His kindness had certainly been evident today as she'd watched him lead Joey and the horse around the ranch.

It was nice to see a grown man interact with a child like that, something Sabrina and her brother had missed out on while growing up.

But at this point in her life, she wasn't ready to open her heart to any obscure romantic possibilities. She wanted—and *needed*—to establish a home and a career first.

Still, in spite of her reluctance to allow herself to get involved with anyone, there'd been something almost magical about standing outside under the spell of a lover's moon. And Sabrina realized that if Jared had indeed tried to kiss her while they'd been on the porch, she just might have let him.

And then where would she be?

She looked over her shoulder to the far right, where a light burned beyond the curtain that draped the window in the den. Jared had said he was going to turn in for the night, but she suspected he hadn't done so yet.

Still, she didn't want to stay on the porch, where his presence seemed to remain long after he'd gone. She had a feeling that if she closed her eyes, she just might catch a lingering whiff of his scent. And that if she reached out, she might be able to touch him. To slide her hand around the back of his neck and draw his lips to hers.

So for that reason, she decided to return to the house and lock the door behind her. Stopping near the lamp table, she picked up the glass and plate she'd used earlier and carried them back to the kitchen, where she washed them and put them away.

As she tiptoed down the hall to her room, her steps slowed near the closed door of the den. As much as she'd like to write off Jared Clayton, to ignore the sexual curiosity he stirred in her, she couldn't.

She wondered when he and his brother would leave. It would certainly make her life easier when they did. But even then, she would still be living in someone else's house, eating someone else's food, following someone else's rules.

Shh! she remembered her mother telling her and Carlos as kids. *You're making too much noise, niños. Tio Jose will get tired of it and make us move.*

Stay out of Abuelito's flower garden, they'd been instructed time and again.

Don't touch those knickknacks. Your prima *Luisa is afraid you'll get them dirty or break them.*

Children adjust to rules, she supposed, but the instructions she and her brother had received changed from one house to another. So she and Carlos soon learned not to wear out their welcomes because, when they did, it was time to move all over again—to a new home, a new neighborhood, a new school.

As Sabrina quietly let herself into the bedroom she

and Joey had been assigned, she studied the gentle rise and fall of the little boy's chest as he slept, unaware of the past, oblivious to the cold ache of discomfort Sabrina felt in someone else's home.

She brushed a kiss across his brow, then turned away, removed her robe and climbed into the bed that had been provided for her.

Just last week, Mrs. Clayton had mentioned the empty cabin again.

"No one has lived there since Clem passed on, which has been a good ten years," she'd said. "so as soon as I get around to cleaning it, you and Joey can move in."

Sabrina hadn't wanted to rush her, but maybe it was time to do so now. She would offer to spend the weekend scrubbing the cabin herself. Hopefully, Mrs. Clayton would see the wisdom in the plan.

Besides the privacy she craved, there was another logical reason she should move out of the ranch house.

No good could come of her and Jared bumping into each other at all hours of the day and night. She lifted her fingers to her lips, tried to imagine the press of his mouth against hers.

She was afraid it was just a matter of time before they met again when the rest of the household was asleep, when defenses were down and vulnerabilities lay open.

And who knew what temptations might lurk under the silvery light of another lover's moon?

The next morning, Jared joined the ranch hands for breakfast, where the conversation was mostly small talk about the weather and the likelihood of rain on Sunday. No one made any comment about the meal laid before them, other than "Pass the salt" or "Hand over more ketchup, will ya?"

Connie had scrambled eggs and fried ham today. As usual, the moment she'd put the meal on the table, she'd skedaddled. And Jared could certainly understand why.

The ham, while unevenly sliced, wasn't half-bad, but the eggs were rubbery, and the toast both looked and tasted like buttered shingles. So Jared figured he'd let the working men have their fill before he dug in and chose to start with coffee.

Before he finished his second cup, Matt wheeled himself into the room, just as the foreman and the hands took off to start their day.

Jared made room for the wheelchair at the table. "Good morning."

Matt nodded in greeting. At least he hadn't barked, "What's so good about it?" That was a response Jared had gotten a time or two.

"Did you sleep okay last night?" Jared asked, making chitchat. He hoped Matt's mood was lifting now that he was back at the Rocking C, but something told him it hadn't and that Jared was expecting too much.

"I slept all right," Matt said. "How about you?"

"Like a rock," Jared lied. When he'd finally quit thinking about the kiss he'd nearly stolen... Well, he couldn't say that Sabrina would have been caught unawares or that she would have been unwilling. By the look in her eyes, he figured she'd wanted that kiss as badly as he had.

And that was the problem.

It's not as if Jared had sworn off women after Jolene took off, but he sure wasn't going to get involved with another one right away. And certainly not one he didn't know very well.

He'd met Jolene during one of the yearly trips to Las Vegas he took with some of the men who owned ranches near his. He'd never been what you'd call a gambler, although he did enjoy playing blackjack and poker once in a while and was more lucky than not.

But that was at cards. If he'd learned anything at all from a hasty marriage and subsequent divorce, it had been not to gamble on women.

Jolene had been a showgirl, with great legs, long blond hair, a sexy smile and, according to her, a fondness for cowboys.

They'd met in a bar at Caesar's Palace after one of her performances and had hit it off. He supposed you could say they had chemistry. They'd shared a few laughs, and one visit to Las Vegas to see her had led to another.

Looking back, he now realized their heated affair had been destined to crash and burn eventually. But one night on a whim—okay, so they'd both been drunk and decided to give forever a try—they'd stopped by the Golden Heart Wedding Chapel and made it legal.

But Jolene had loved the Las Vegas nightlife and the glamour of the stage. And whatever had burned hot through the end of their short honeymoon had fizzled shortly after she'd moved to Texas and got a real taste of ranch life.

Nearly kissing Sabrina last night had triggered a slew of bad memories that had kept Jared staring at the ceiling until almost dawn. But ironically, switching back to thoughts of Sabrina and the flicker of desire he'd seen in her eyes had finally taken him to a place where he was able to drift off to dreamland.

Still, Jared had slept like crap and woke up with a crick in both his back and his neck. But no need to complain about something that would ease once he walked it off. His brother, on the other hand, wasn't going to be that lucky—that is, if Matt ever decided to give his legs another workout.

The doctor had suggested physical therapy, but after the first session, Matt had refused to go back or talk about his reasons for doing so. Jared doubted it was because of the pain or hard work. Matt was one of the toughest men he'd ever known.

In a way, he still was.

Jared got up and poured his brother a cup of coffee, then brought it back to the table, along with a clean plate.

Matt peered at the platter in the center of the table and scrunched his face. "What the hell is that?"

"Scrambled eggs, I think." Jared grabbed a serving spoon and scooped out a helping for his brother.

Matt blocked his efforts with a high-five hand. "That's plenty. Something tells me I'm only going to want enough to keep my stomach from grinding on itself."

Jared chuckled. It was nice to have something humorous to share with his brother these days. It had been a long time since either of them had found a reason to laugh.

Footsteps sounded, and Jared looked to the doorway, where Joey entered the room.

When their gazes met, the boy's face lit up like a blasted Fourth-of-July fireworks show. "Hey, Mr. Clayton. Is it okay if I sit down with you guys? Or should I wait until after you're finished?"

"No, go ahead. You like eggs?"

Joey shook his head. "Are there any of those cookies left?"

"Good thinking," Matt said. "Better yet, I wonder if there's any more of that chocolate cake we had at dinner last night. I don't feel much like eggs this morning, either."

As Jared hunted for the leftover dessert, Joey said, "I wish I was at school."

"Oh, yeah?" Jared found what he'd been looking for next to the bread box. "Why is that?"

"So I could tell all my friends that me and a real live cowboy had chocolate cake for breakfast."

Jared carried his find back to the table and used a knife to cut three pieces. "Well, you'd have to tell them that you ate with two of us. You might not know this, but my brother Matt is a bronc rider."

"No way," Joey said, turning his focus to the man in the wheelchair. "Really?"

"Yep." Jared served the cake. "And he's got a glass case full of silver belt buckles to prove it."

The boy, his brown eyes wide and glimmering, was speechless.

"That was a long time ago," Matt said.

"Oh," the boy said. "You mean, 'cause you got hurt? Did a bronc buck you off and step on your legs?"

"No."

Joey gave the answer some thought. "Then what happened?"

Jared held his tongue. He hadn't start 1 this conversation for any reason other than to give ɔey a bit of a thrill. But things had taken an unexpected turn. Still, he figured he'd been bailing out Matt long enough, and maybe it was time his brother faced the facts. Cindy and Tommy were gone. And Matt was never going to compete in another rodeo.

"How'd you get your legs hurt?" the boy asked, prodding for an answer.

"I was in a car accident." Matt's gaze turned dark, cold and quiet, as though he wanted the memories to stay buried with his fiancée and her son.

Footsteps sounded again, giving them all a reprieve, it seemed. As Jared searched the door for an excuse to find something else to talk about, he spotted Sabrina.

He couldn't help but study her, noticing she'd put on a pair of jeans and a pale-blue cotton shirt. Her hair had been woven into a long braid that hung down her back. She'd dressed casually today, and it made her look as though she belonged here—even if the jury was still out on that.

"Good morning," she said, as she headed for the coffeepot.

"Can you please get me a glass of milk?" Joey asked.

"Sure." She offered him a smile, then froze in her tracks. "Joey? What are you doing?"

The boy's grin bore a smear of chocolate frosting on his lips. "Eating breakfast with two of the best cowboys in the whole wide world."

"Did you have any eggs yet?"

"Nope," Joey said. "Me and the guys decided we'd rather have cake."

"I can't let you eat sweets for breakfast," she told the little wannabe cowboy.

"Why not?" Jared wasn't exactly sure why he felt

compelled to jump to the kid's defense. Some kind of
Cowboy Code, he supposed. Or maybe because he'd
been the one to cut and serve the cake.

"It's important to have a healthy, balanced meal to
start the day," she said.

"But you ate cookies for breakfast yesterday," Jared
reminded her. "And you even passed a few to me."

"That's because they were made out of oatmeal,
which is clearly breakfast food." She crossed her arms,
and tossed him a pretty frown.

Jared ought to let it drop, but he couldn't help stirring
the pot. "I could be wrong, but chocolate cake has eggs
in it. And I do believe this is buttercream frosting. All
of which is clearly breakfast food, too."

She shifted her weight to one denim-clad hip. "Maybe I ought to let you chase him around if he gets hyper
from all that sugar."

"I'll just lasso the little buckaroo and wait 'til he
calms down." Jared couldn't help but grin. "Come on,
Sabrina, ease up on the kid." He nodded toward the
platter of eggs that were not only rubbery also but growing cold. "What do you think that grub is going to do
to him?"

Before Sabrina could offer an argument, Granny
entered the kitchen. "Well, now. Look at you, Sabrina.
Finally wearing those clothes I bought you. You ought
to be a whole lot more comfortable today."

"Actually," Sabrina said, "I was going to ask you if
it would be all right if I went out to the cabin this morning and spent some time cleaning it up."

"Oh, I hate to have you do that," Granny said. "It's
gonna be a real mess."

"I don't mind the work," Sabrina countered. "In fact, I'm looking forward to the exercise."

"Why are you volunteering?" Jared asked.

"Because Joey and I are going to move into it, but your mother doesn't want us to do that until it's clean. And I really don't mind." She brushed her hands along her hips.

"It's too much work for a woman," Granny said. "It's going to need some repairs, too."

"You might need some rattraps," Matt added. "No telling what moved in after Clem died."

Sabrina scrunched her face, obviously not nearly as eager to deal with a few critters than she was to scrub walls and mop floors.

"Jared," Granny said, "do you have any pressing plans this morning?"

Uh-oh. Granny was going to suggest that he help.

Of course, the sooner he got Sabrina out of the house the better. And if a few field mice—or whatever—made her reconsider living on the ranch and call it quits... Hey, that would solve half his problems right there.

Either way, if she moved out, freeing up the guest bedroom, he could get off the sofa in the den.

"Sure," he said, "I'd be glad to help."

"I hate to put you out," Sabrina replied.

"Actually, I wouldn't mind moving into your bedroom."

"I bet you wouldn't," Matt muttered.

"That's not what I meant."

But the idea, now that Matt brought it to mind, was far more appealing than Jared wanted it to be.

Chapter Five

Armed with cleaning supplies, mops, brooms, rags and buckets, Sabrina and Jared made their way to the small, clapboard building that everyone on the ranch referred to as "the cabin."

The structure sat on a knoll in a pasture about a hundred yards from the house. Neglect and weather had done a real number on the exterior, but Sabrina didn't care. She could envision it with a fresh coat of white paint, a pot of geraniums on the stoop and new curtains on the windows.

The yard wasn't too bad. A splatter of wildflowers at the side of the house added color. And thanks to the grazing cattle, the weeds had been kept to a minimum.

As they drew closer, Jared's steps slowed and he studied the cabin as though it were an aged photograph that had been misplaced and recently found.

"It's been about ten years since I've been inside this place," he said, carefully scanning the building from its block foundation to its roof. "But I have a feeling it's going to take a lot more than a weekend to make it livable again."

Sabrina didn't mind the time or the work. She'd been dying to have some privacy all of her life. And while this house wasn't officially hers, it was the closest thing she'd ever had.

As she began to step onto the porch, Jared grabbed her arm and held her back, the intensity of his touch sending a shiver of heat through her veins.

"Be careful," he said. "That wood is rotten."

She glanced at the flooring, which was cracked and bowed by age and neglect. Most of the planks appeared as though they would give way with the least bit of weight.

"Then how do you suggest we get inside?" she asked.

He stooped and reached for one of the boards, pulling at it with his bare hands until he'd ripped it away. Then he tore off several more strips of wood. "How's that?" He straightened and brushed his palms together several times. "I'll go into town later this afternoon and bring back enough lumber to rebuild the porch. But I have a feeling that's not even half of what will need to be done if we really want to get this place back into shape."

Nevertheless, Sabrina was still glad to have a place of her own. "As long as it's clean, I can move in and deal with the repairs as one fix-it project at a time."

"Maybe we better see what we're up against." He

stepped into the gap made by the missing planks of wood and opened the door, which, apparently, no one had seen a reason to lock.

As Sabrina began to follow his steps, he turned and reached out to her. She thought he was being a gentleman, intent on steadying her steps. Instead he slid his hands around her waist.

Her breath caught as he lifted her off the ground and swung her around. Her hands inadvertently went to his shoulders to brace herself, where she felt the bulk of well-honed muscles flexing beneath a soft cotton shirt.

As he set her down inside the house, she faced him, cheeks warm, heart pounding, senses reeling. Finding her tongue was going to be a struggle.

A glint of humor lit his eyes, and a smile tweaked one corner of his lips. "I figured we didn't need to risk another worker's-compensation claim."

She doubted liability issues had anything to do with his actions, but wasn't going to challenge his motivation. Not when her heart was still ricocheting throughout her chest.

Hoping to take some control of her response to his presence and touch, she cleared her throat and turned to scan the inside of her new home, where a layer of dust covered the floors and sparse furnishings.

"Damn." Jared lifted his hat and raked a hand through his hair. "I don't even know where to begin."

"Let's start by getting some air in here. It's musty and stale."

After they each wrestled with a couple of windows that were covered with a hazy film of grime and hadn't been opened in ages, Sabrina assessed her surroundings. The living room was small, with a bare minimum of furniture—a black Naugahyde sofa, a green recliner and a floor lamp in the corner. A television set rested on a shelf made out of boards stacked on cinder blocks.

She strode to the bedroom, which boasted a chest of drawers and a queen-size bed with a blue corduroy spread. The first thing she'd need to do was change the linen and turn the mattress.

Next, she went into the bathroom, which had an olive green sink and matching toilet, as well as a white tub with rust marks near the drain. With a little elbow grease, she'd have the room spic-and-span, but the faucets appeared to be fused by lime deposits. Hopefully, Jared knew something about plumbing.

In the hall, she found a small linen closet full of towels and sheets—no longer fresh and clean but still folded. Once they were laundered and hung out on the line to dry, she would feel comfortable using them.

Continuing her inspection, she moved to the kitchen, which would also take some work. The pea-green Formica countertops were chipped in spots, but they would clean up nicely.

A peek in the cupboards revealed dishes, dusty from lack of use. Pots and pans, too. She looked in the built-in pantry and found canned goods that had swollen to the point of leaking. "Oh, yuck."

"Where do you want me to start?" Jared called out.

"Wherever you like." Sabrina returned to the living room, where Jared stood by the mantel. He was gazing at a Polaroid photograph he'd found.

"What's that?" she asked.

"A picture of Clem." His voice was husky yet soft. "And of me."

"Can I see it?"

He nodded and handed it to her. It showed an older man—a full-fledged cowboy, judging by his apparel—and Jared as a boy. They stood beside two horses.

Young Jared balanced a fishing pole in one hand, and held his catch with the other. The smile he wore reminded her of the one he'd sported in the picture his mother kept over the fireplace in her living room.

"You were a cute kid." She gave it back to him, and he placed it on the mantel, propping it up against the wall.

She couldn't help thinking that he'd grown up to be an even better-looking man, but she kept that thought to herself.

"Well," he said, "standing around won't get us anywhere."

He grabbed the broom and began to sweep the floor, sending flecks of dust dancing along a ray of sunlight that shined through the open window.

Sabrina headed for the kitchen, where she'd decided to scour the sink and countertops first. The dishes and utensils would all need to be washed, but she wanted a clean place to put them.

As she went to work, wetting a cloth, then dumping cleanser into both sides of the sink, she began making a mental list of all that needed to be done. It didn't take long to realize that she ought to be using paper and a pencil.

Yet she easily imagined herself moving in by tomorrow evening. Maybe she'd even pick a few wildflowers, put them into a glass of water and place them on the kitchen table. In fact, she would look for more makeshift vases and adorn each little room with color.

As she began to put some honest-to-goodness elbow grease into her work, her heart lifted to a brand-new high, and she found herself humming a happy tune.

If she closed her eyes, she could almost pretend she'd finally found a place to call home.

Jared kept busy for several hours, washing the windows inside and out. It had taken him two go-arounds to get the bulk of the dirt and grime cleaned up, and he figured one more time ought to do the trick.

Still, his stomach was growling and he was ready for a snack. So he entered the kitchen, where he found Sabrina seated on the faded linoleum, taking pots and pans out from the cupboard nearest the stove.

"I thought I'd head back to the house for a minute. Need anything?" His words pierced the silence, causing her to gasp and jump. She sure was a touchy little thing, and quick to respond.

In spite of himself and what he'd meant to be an innocent assessment of her nerves, "touchy" and "quick to respond" sent an entirely different message to his hormones.

"Actually," Sabrina said, "I could sure use some shelf paper and a pair of scissors, although I'm not sure if your mother has any she can spare."

"I'll see what I can find."

As Sabrina returned to her work, Jared headed for the ranch house, intent on getting more paper towels, too. He also meant to get them something to eat. He probably should have asked Sabrina if there was something particular that she was hungry for, but decided to surprise her instead.

Twenty minutes later, he returned with a box in his arms that bore the items she'd requested, as well as lunch for two.

"I'm back," he said from the cabin door, thinking he ought to give her a heads-up. When he walked into the kitchen, he realized giving her fair warning had been a good idea.

She'd climbed on a chair and was washing out the inside of one of the kitchen cupboards. She turned to greet him with a smile, and he noticed that she had a smudge of dirt on her forehead and a strand of dark hair had loosened from her braid and now lay along her cheek.

He wondered if she knew. Probably not. And he wouldn't tell her. He actually liked to see her a bit mussed. It made her seem real, and he could almost imagine her completely trustworthy.

"I brought lunch, too." He placed the box on the table, which appeared to be clean. "I thought you might be hungry. Why don't you stop and take a break?"

When he glanced over his shoulder, he found her watching him from atop the chair. Then she cocked her head and touched her bottom lip. "What's that on your face? It looks like chocolate."

"It probably is." He shrugged, then swiped at his mouth with the back of his hand. "No one was in the kitchen, so I finished off the cake while I had a chance."

Sabrina climbed down from the chair, then washed her hands at the sink and dried them. "I hope Connie has something else to serve as dessert tonight."

"Me, too. Especially since more than one of us are

making meals out of her sweets." Jared pulled out the shelf paper and scissors from his box, then set them on the counter. Next he removed sandwiches, a Thermos and two glasses.

"Thanks for thinking about me." Sabrina joined Jared at the table.

"I brought iced tea to drink," he said as he set everything out, using sheets of paper towels as place mats. "It's sweetened. I hope that's okay."

"It's perfect." Sabrina glanced at her watch. "Oh. It's already after one. No wonder I'm hungry."

"Everyone else at the house had meat loaf, so count yourself lucky to get a ham sandwich."

"I take it that meat loaf isn't one of your favorites."

"It's okay. I don't normally mind it, but Connie could really use some cooking lessons. Or maybe she just needs to pay more attention to the stove timer. That meat loaf looked pretty dry." He handed Sabrina a paper cup filled with iced tea, trying to get some of the ice cubes into her glass. "So what's her story? Obviously Connie isn't a chef by trade. But I figure it was the only job Granny had left to offer."

"You might be right. I don't know Connie very well. She's pretty quiet and keeps to herself. I think she's probably very shy."

"Where did she meet Granny?"

"At the doctor's office in town. Connie had fainted while sitting in the waiting room, and when Granny overheard her say that she needed a job and a place to stay, she offered her both. Connie hasn't been living here very long."

Jared unwrapped his sandwich, hoping whatever illness Connie had contracted was no longer contagious. All they needed was an epidemic on the ranch. "What was wrong with her?"

"Nothing really." Sabrina peeked under the top slice of bread, then covered it back up. "She's pregnant and had morning sickness when she first arrived, but that seems to have passed now."

Jared fought off a curse. Doc had mentioned one of the women might be pregnant.

What was Granny going to do with a baby underfoot?

Besides that, the house was packed as it was. So even if Sabrina moved out to the cabin, it wouldn't help the overcrowding for very long.

If anything, Jared was further convinced that he needed to run off the freeloaders, pack up his mother and take her back to his ranch so he could take care of her. She was only going to get older and more vulnerable.

He took a bite of his sandwich. While he chewed, he scanned the kitchen, noting the progress Sabrina had made. There'd been some, he suspected. But not enough. "Have you had a chance to see if everything is in good working order in here?"

"The oven doesn't heat, but I can get by without it for a while."

"I'll take a look at it. Maybe I can fix it. I'm going to need some new faucets for the bathroom, as well as some valves and a P-trap. I plan to go to the hardware store in town and pick up parts and supplies later today. So if I need anything for the stove or oven, I can get them while I'm out." Jared slowly shook his head. "See?

I told you it would take a lot to whip this place into shape."

Sabrina slid him an easy smile. "You're probably right, but I don't mind the work. It's actually…kind of fun."

He couldn't help but take another note of the smudge on her forehead and the loose strand of hair that fell near her ear. Yet a gleam in her eyes suggested that she meant every word she said.

"And you're actually happy to move in here?" Not that he was trying to talk her out of it.

"Absolutely."

"That surprises me."

"Why?"

"Because something tells me you're used to so much more."

"Then that *something* is lying to you."

Was she pulling his leg?

"You seem so prim and proper, Sabrina. So tidy. It's hard to believe you weren't brought up in the lap of luxury."

She lifted a delicate brow, which placed a furrow right through the dirty spot on her face. "I'm not sure if I should thank you or not. Either way, things were never easy for me or my brother. My parents were little more than kids themselves when my mom got pregnant—and not with just one baby but two. So we spent our early years moving from one place to another."

"You mean, you were raised in foster care?" Like me? he wondered.

"No. Our parents moved with us. At first, we bounced back and forth between our grandparents' houses. But our mom and dad both came from big families, so there was never a lot of room. And then things would always get…weird. Or awkward. And we'd have to leave."

"How long did that go on?"

"Let's just say that whenever we wore out our welcome at one place, we'd move to another. Living out of boxes didn't seem to faze my parents or even my twin brother. But I guess, by nature, I crave stability."

And her brother, the trucker, didn't? Talk about not having a place to lay his head at night.

Jared wanted to quiz her about Carlos, Joey's dad, but he didn't. There was still so much about *her* he had to learn. Yet, sometimes, her answers just left him with more questions.

She set her half-eaten sandwich aside. "When I was a little girl, I tried my best to control my life and organize my environment, but it was almost impossible to do."

"So you're trying to make up for that now at work by filing everything carefully and keeping the office in order?"

She smiled wistfully. "Actually, it's been an ongoing thing for me. I remember one of my teachers telling my mom that she'd never seen a child with such a neat and organized desk. She went on to say that she wished all of her students were that responsible."

Jared took a swig of iced tea, letting it wash down the last of his sandwich. If Connie hadn't overcooked the ham a bit too much, it might have tasted better. But it had to beat the heck out of that meat loaf.

He turned his attention back to Sabrina and the story

she'd been telling him. "Did your folks ever find a permanent place of their own?"

"They divorced when Carlos and I were eight, and the moves merely continued. First we lived with my mom and her boyfriend. Then with my dad and his new wife."

"I did a lot of moving around when I was a kid," Jared admitted. "And it sucked. It was hard to make friends. Or to give a damn about going to school."

"You're right. But in spite of the constant upheavals, I survived. I also studied hard."

"Don't tell me. Let me guess. You found an aptitude for math, a subject with rules and properties that remained constant. And so you decided to become a number cruncher and put that skill to use."

She lifted her glass and took a sip. "That's about the size of it. I was determined not to make the same mistakes my parents made—like getting pregnant too soon or married too young."

She was still young now. Early twenties, he suspected.

"Does that mean you don't date very much?" He wasn't sure why he asked, why he cared.

She paused and bit down on her bottom lip, as though trying to decide how much she wanted to confess. "I guess you could say that. I've had boyfriends, but when they realized I wasn't going to risk getting physically involved, things sort of fizzled out."

Did that mean she was a virgin?

He found the possibility…intriguing. And somewhat challenging. That is, if he wanted to risk getting physically involved with a woman he wasn't yet sure he could trust.

"When my brother was sixteen," Sabrina said, "he and his girlfriend weren't as careful as they should have been, and she got pregnant. When I saw what he and Suzy went through, I was even more determined to focus on the future, rather than the here and now."

"So Carlos got married young?"

"No. He claimed he wasn't in love with Suzy, although I don't believe that. Instead I think he was afraid of repeating family history."

Jared tensed, not liking the thought of a man who refused to take responsibility for his mistakes. After all, Carlos was off driving big rigs across the country, and his sister was stuck raising the kid he'd fathered.

Not that Joey was a problem child. He was polite, appreciative and nice to be around. It was obvious that he craved a father's attention, though. And that made Jared feel sorry for him.

Sabrina must have sensed Jared's disapproval because she added, "My brother dropped out of school and went to work so that he could pay child support. But he didn't think he was old enough to know what love really was and didn't want to make a commitment he couldn't keep."

As far as Jared was concerned, her brother had an unspoken commitment to his son the moment he'd been conceived. Fathers weren't supposed to walk away from their kids, leaving them for someone else to raise.

A piece of lettuce dropped out of Sabrina's sandwich and onto the paper towel. She picked it up and popped it into her mouth.

"But what about now?" Jared said. "Joey needs him."

"Yes, I know, but..."

"Your brother ought to find another job and stay home."

"You don't understand. Carlos has...reasons why he can't do that."

"What are they?"

She didn't answer right away, and for a moment he wondered if she would. Finally, she said, "I don't feel right discussing them with you. You'll just have to believe me when I say that for the past seven years I've felt sorry for all of them—Carlos, Suzy and Joey."

"Okay," he said. "We'll leave it at that. But surely there was someone other than you who could have stepped up to the plate."

"Suzy's family...well, they weren't much help. And to be honest, none of the relatives on either side were willing or able to take him, so it was up to me. I put my schooling on hold to take care of Joey."

"You gave up college?"

"I'll go back someday."

Her tone lacked all but a spark of determination, and he suspected that she might not be so sure about that.

"Besides," she added, "Joey was closer to me than to anyone else. And I love him like my own. There really wasn't any question about who would be the best one to take him."

"And now you're here," he said.

"Yes. And since your mother offered me a place to stay and let me bring Joey, it seemed to solve most of my immediate problems."

Her gaze snagged his, and something twisted in his chest. Something that had been ramrod straight and as tough as cowhide.

All right. So the story she'd shared had touched him, just as it must have done to his mom.

But did it also give Sabrina a motive to steal?

The next morning, as Jared stood on the porch scanning the dark clouds that were gathering overhead, Hilda Detweiler, an old friend of Granny's, drove into the yard in a red '86 Cadillac Seville, parking only steps away from the front porch.

Hilda used to own and operate the Pampered Lady Beauty Parlor in Brighton Valley, but sold it about fifteen years ago and retired. To this day, she continued to work part-time out of her home, though, fixing the hair of some of her oldest and best customers.

Granny was one of them.

For as long as Jared could remember, and probably decades longer than that, Hilda and Granny had been good friends. Each Sunday morning, they spent the day in town, where they attended church, had lunch at Darla's Diner and then either went shopping or to a movie.

The perfectly coiffed silver-haired lady rolled down the window of her car. "Why, Jared Clayton. Aren't you a sight for poor eyes."

"Good morning, Hilda," Jared said. "I see you and Granny are off to church."

"At our age, your mother and I figure we ought to watch our spiritual p's and q's. You never know when we'll find ourselves standing at the Pearly Gates, hoping someone will recognize us and invite us inside."

Before Jared could do much more than chuckle, Granny walked out the front door, dressed in a pair of pink slacks, a white blouse and a sweater. A white leather handbag and a black raincoat dangled from the crook of her arm. "Are you sure you don't want to go with us, son? That new preacher isn't half-bad. And better yet, he's not as long-winded as the old one."

"Not this time," Jared said, providing the same response he always gave her whenever she invited him to church. "You two go on. I've got some work to do out at the cabin."

"That's good to hear." Granny grinned, eyes twinkling. "I sure appreciate you helping Sabrina. That little gal has taken on a huge chore. The cabin was nearly falling apart when Clem died."

She had *that* right.

Late yesterday afternoon, Jared had driven to town and picked up the lumber, parts and supplies he needed at Riley's Hardware Store. All the while, Sabrina had stayed behind and continued to work.

By the time he'd unpacked everything at the cabin, it was already dusk, and he'd had to convince her to quit for the day. Since the lighting wasn't that good, she'd been forced to agree. But then she'd spent the evening washing towels and sheets she'd found in the cupboards.

He wondered if the physical labor had helped her sleep better last night, suspecting so. He hadn't heard a peep out of her after the washing machine finally finished its last spin cycle and shut down.

As Granny climbed into the car, Jared told Hilda to drive carefully. "The weather report says there's a storm heading our way."

"It's not supposed to hit until this afternoon," Hilda said. "We'll be back by then."

Jared nodded, then strode toward the cabin, intent on

repairing the porch before the rain came. As he approached, he found the front door open wide.

"Sabrina?" he called.

"I'm in the bathroom," she answered.

He made his way inside, where he found her bent over the tub, scouring out a rust spot that wasn't likely to recede. The denim stretched and molded around her hips, offering him a view that sent his testosterone levels surging and damn near pumped him full of ideas he had no business having.

She turned and cast him a smile. "Good morning."

"You're up early," he said. Bright-eyed and bushy-tailed came to mind, but he wouldn't go there.

"I wanted to get as much done today as I could. There's a chance we could move in this evening."

"There's an even bigger chance of rain," Jared said. "So moving may have to wait until tomorrow."

She shrugged. "Well, I can hope, can't I?"

"You're really eager to get out of the house."

Her expression sobered. "It's not as though I'm not grateful for the room we were given—"

"I know." At least, he thought he did—if the story she'd told him had been true. Still, he was certain she'd been holding something back about her brother, and that didn't sit well with him. But he tossed her a crooked grin anyway.

He supposed she'd read sincerity and compassion in his response, because the pretty smile she threw back at him shot straight through his chest, knocking him off balance.

"I…uh…" He nodded toward the tub, wanting—no, needing—to put some distance between the two of them. "I'd better mend that porch and let you get busy, or this place will never be ready."

"You know," she said, cheeks flushing a pretty shade of pink, "I didn't think much of you when I first met you. But I was wrong."

He hadn't thought much of her, either. And he still had a hard time believing she was everything she appeared to be—a loyal sister, a loving aunt, a dedicated and honest employee.

For cripe's sake, she even implied that she was a virgin. But Jared didn't take anyone at face value anymore.

He'd been burned by one pretty face already.

Chapter Six

A couple of hours later, Jared had repaired the porch, changed a few light switches and replaced the bathroom plumbing. Sabrina had kept busy, too, which made it easy for him to stay out of her way.

At least, until she called out his name.

"Jared? Will you please come here? I need your help."

He followed her voice into the bedroom, where she stood beside the bare mattress and box springs of a queen-size bed, hands on her hips.

"I stripped this down yesterday and washed all the linen, so I'd like to make it back up again. But first, can you help me turn the mattress and move the bed against the other wall?"

"Sure."

Two pairs of hands made it an easy task.

"Thank you," Sabrina said. "Not just for this, but for all your help with the cabin. You've been a godsend."

He didn't know about that. "You're welcome, but I think it's only fair to tell you that my motives are purely selfish. The sooner you can move in here, the sooner I can get off the sofa in the den."

A smile dimpled her cheeks and added a sparkle to her eyes. "Well, I can't fault you for being honest."

"Hey," a small voice called from the open front door. "Sabrina? Are you in there?"

"Come on in, Joey." Sabrina left the bedroom, with Jared bringing up the rear like a little lapdog.

Of course, he had to admit that following behind Sabrina had its perks, like being able to watch the way her shapely hips swayed with each step she took.

As they neared the living room, he tore his gaze from the sexy view of Sabrina's backside, focusing on her nephew instead. Joey held a brown sack in his hand as he carefully scanned the interior of the cabin.

"What do you think?" Sabrina asked the boy.

"You were right. It's *really* cool." He beamed as though he'd entered a mansion. "Wow. We get a fire-place and a TV, *too*."

Jared hoped the television worked. And that the antenna was still receiving. Every once in a while, after a strong wind, Clem would have to climb on the roof and readjust it so it would pick up a strong signal.

"What have you got there?" Sabrina asked the child.

Joey glanced at the bag. "Oh, you mean, this? Connie wanted me to bring it to you."

Lunch? Jared wondered. If it was, that was too bad. He'd planned to go back to the house and rustle up something for him and Sabrina to eat—something Connie hadn't made. But apparently, he should have done that sooner.

Sabrina took the brown sack from him. "What's in here?"

"Apple stu... Apple stru..."

"Strudel?"

He nodded. "Yeah, that's it. Connie made a whole bunch this morning because everyone loves her dessert so much that they've been sneaking the leftovers."

Sabrina pulled out a foil-wrapped container and three plastic baggies. One was filled with coffee grounds, another with sugar and the last one held what appeared to be instant creamer. "How thoughtful of her."

If the strudel tasted as good as her cakes and cookies, the gesture would be appreciated by everyone who had to depend upon Connie for sustenance, especially Jared.

"Joey," Sabrina said, "why don't you come with me into the kitchen? I'm going to cut this into three pieces so we can share it."

"Oh, that's okay." The boy rubbed his stomach. "I ate two helpings already. Connie just told me to bring that to you. But I gotta hurry back. Me and Tori and Connie are playing Go Fish. It's a really cool game."

Jared could see that it didn't take much to make the boy happy: a ride on the horse; a fifteen-year-old television in a run-down cabin; a card game.

"Okay," his aunt said. "I don't want to keep you from having fun."

Joey turned and dashed out the door, obviously in a hurry to get back to the house. He sure seemed to like it on the Rocking C.

How could he not?

Jared had been a city kid, too, and he'd thrived in a ranch environment. Of course, it had been more than just the wide-open spaces, the cows and the horses. There'd also been a masculine camaraderie, too. Clem and the other cowboys had taken Jared under wing, making him one of them and filling the empty gap in his life that his old man had left. They'd taught him everything he knew about roping and riding and being a man. And lessons like that couldn't be bought.

Jared's thoughts drifted to Joey, who'd mentioned how much he'd like to learn how to ride a horse all by himself. The conversation they'd shared replayed in his mind.

But Aunt Sabrina won't let me ask anyone here at the ranch to teach me, he'd said. *She doesn't want us to wear out our welcome.*

If that were the case, then maybe, one day soon, Jared would surprise the boy by saddling up one of the old mares and giving him a couple of tips about horses and riding. That ought to really slap a smile on his face.

And maybe, after a couple of weeks on the ranch, Joey would bulk up and get some color in his cheeks.

"Mmm," Sabrina said, drawing Jared's attention. She held the foil-wrapped package under her nose and closed her eyes. "This strudel smells so good. And it's still warm. I'm going to put on a pot of coffee to go with it. Are you ready to take a break?"

"Sounds good to me."

"Good. If you don't mind, I'll finish making up the bed first."

He watched as she left the room, hips swaying in a mesmerizing fashion.

Damn. He was going to have to watch his growing fascination with her backside.

A light lit the cabin like a camera flash, and moments later, thunder rumbled in the distance. There was a chill in the air, he realized. One he hadn't noticed earlier.

He made his way to the window and peered outside. The sky had grown dark and threatening, especially in the east. The weatherman had been right when he'd predicted rain, but it looked as though it was moving in sooner than expected.

If Sabrina actually planned to move in later this afternoon, it might be a good idea to make a trek to the woodpile and start a fire in the hearth. So he strode to the side of the barn, where the wood was stacked, and loaded up an armload. It took him several trips to get enough to last her through the night.

He had no more than stacked the last piece on the porch, when Sabrina let out a scream that nearly blew off the roof.

Damn. What in the hell happened?

A shot of adrenaline raced through him, and he ran to the kitchen.

Had she sliced her hand open while trying to cut into the strudel?

He found her crawling on the table, her eyes open wide, her complexion pale.

"What's the matter?"

She pointed into the corner near the fridge. "A mouse. A big one. It ran across my foot and scared me half to death."

His heart was pounding so hard it damn near jumped out of his chest. "Is that all?"

"What do you mean, *is that all?*" She shuddered. "They're...ooh." She pushed up from the tabletop with her hands, straightening until she was kneeling and her bottom was resting on her heels. Then she shimmied in fright. "I hate mice."

"I can't understand why. Those little things won't hurt you."

"I don't care. I can't even stand the sight of them."

"You've convinced me of that. But you'd better get down from that table. It's not very sturdy, and if it collapses with you on it, you'll be at a real disadvantage. With a broken neck or leg, you won't be able to escape the little critter."

"We'll need to set traps. Lots of them. No matter how badly I want to move in, I can't stay in here with a mouse."

Jared had a feeling that there was more than one small, furry varmint taking up residence in the cabin. But what did she expect? This building was old, and the field mice had probably been nesting in it for years.

"I wouldn't worry about it," he said. "I have a feeling that little critter is on its last legs."

"You think it's dying?" She scrunched her face. "No way. That thing looked as healthy as a horse."

"Maybe, but that banshee scream you let out was loud enough to chase every animal within a hundred-mile radius to go charging into the Gulf of Mexico." He slowly shook his head, then reached for her. "Come on. Get down. You probably don't weigh much more than a hundred pounds, but that table has always been wobbly."

She scanned the floor, no doubt looking to make sure the mouse was long gone, then let him help her.

He placed his hands around her waist, then swung her around. As he did so, she slid down the front of him. The buttons of their shirts clicked against each other, but all he could think of was the way her breasts splayed against his chest, how their hearts beat warm and vibrant.

How he wished their clothing hadn't stood in the way.

He could have let her go and stepped aside. In fact, he *should* have.

But as their gazes locked, so did their arms—his around her waist, hers on his shoulders.

Something powerful snaked around them, something far more threatening—and imminent—than the storm on the horizon.

Sabrina's lips parted as though she was just as aware of what was going to happen as he was. And just as powerless to stop it.

Every lick of sense Jared had ever possessed, every ounce of self-control, deserted him as he drew her close and lowered his mouth to hers.

He took it slow and easy at first, his lips brushing hers gently, but when she slid her arms around his neck and lifted up on tiptoe for a better reach, he was lost in a surge of heat and desire.

A sense of urgency swept over him, and he drew her close. He felt a growing compulsion to run his fingers through her long, silky hair, something he'd been dying to do ever since he'd seen it loose that first night. But she'd woven it into a braid again today, so he had to be content with what he did have access to—her sweet, willing mouth.

She'd implied that she had very little experience with

this sort of thing, but that sure as hell didn't seem to be the case right now. And as much as he'd wanted to keep his distance from her, he lost that fight and savored one of the most arousing kisses he'd ever had.

She tasted of apples and cinnamon, no doubt from a bite of strudel she'd snagged for herself moments earlier, and he couldn't seem to get his fill of her sweetness.

But he might have, if a flash of lighting and a subsequent boom of thunder hadn't rolled across the Texas sky.

He drew back, mourning what they'd shared instantly, yet knowing how crazy it had been to lose his head like that. He wanted to apologize. Or to laugh it off. To make an excuse that would turn back the clock and put them both on an even keel. But he couldn't think of a damn thing to say.

Her lips, still plump and rosy from the assault of his mouth, parted. Apparently, when it came to conjuring some kind of verbal response, she was in the same quandary as he was. So he decided to make it easy on her—and on himself—by pretending the kiss had never happened.

"Why don't you start the coffee while I get a fire going," he said.

Trouble was, it was hotter than hell in the cabin already, and he hadn't even struck a match.

Sabrina, her mind still numb from the intoxicating kiss she and Jared had shared, struggled through the steps of making coffee in an old, electric percolator she'd found while cleaning the cupboards yesterday.

As she inserted the plug into an outlet near the counter, she trailed her fingers over her lips, amazed that a man's mouth and tongue could make her feel so weak-kneed and dreamy.

Never had she been held so close, kissed so thoroughly, and something told her she would never experience the like again. Not that she was any kind of expert on kissing or sex. But she *was* human.

And her hormones had certainly been in good working order today.

She tried to keep her mind occupied with thoughts of anything other than Jared, but she couldn't seem to focus, not even on the brewing coffee, something she'd been craving earlier.

Unfortunately, she was craving something entirely different now.

But kissing her employer's son had certainly been a complication she hadn't planned on. Of course, he lived nearly a hundred miles away and was only here temporarily, so nothing would become of it anyway. Still, it hadn't been a wise or professional thing to do.

Yet as much as she knew better than to ever let herself get in that position, she feared that when faced with another opportunity to kiss Jared, she might be tempted to do it again.

She shot a glance at the refrigerator, where the pesky mouse had run.

Had Jared been right? Had her scream frightened the little creature to death?

Surely not. But maybe it had scurried outside, trying to find a safe place to hide. She hoped so. She couldn't handle seeing it again.

Either way, the sooner she could get out of the kitchen, the better.

As Clem's old percolator whished out one long, last burble, indicating the coffee was finally done, Sabrina glanced at the kitchen window and saw that the rain had begun to pelt the glass.

From in the living room, she could smell the fire in the hearth.

She both dreaded and looked forward to facing Jared again. But there was no way around it, she supposed. After removing the built-in cutting board from the counter, she covered it with a paper towel and used it as a tray to carry the plates of strudel, cups of coffee, sugar and cream into the living room.

Jared, who'd been kneeling by the hearth, staring as the flames licked the logs, turned and stood as she entered the room.

"Need some help?" he asked.

"Thanks, but I've got it under control." She set the cutting board on the lamp table. "How do you like your coffee?"

"Black."

She nodded, then handed him a cup and took a seat on the sofa. He joined her, leaving a physical gap between them, but not nearly as pronounced as the invisible one that the kiss had created.

The warm, flickering fire, the aroma of fresh-brewed coffee and the taste of apples and cinnamon made the little cabin feel much cozier and warmer than Sabrina had ever imagined it could be, yet she was still on edge and not sure what to say.

Bringing up that kiss certainly wasn't something she

was willing to do, so she chose a subject that was easier to discuss. "Do you know if Mrs. Clayton—or rather your mother—returned Wayne Templeton's call yet?"

"Who's he?"

"I'm not sure exactly." Sabrina added creamer and sugar to her coffee. "He said that he's with Dazzling Desert Ventures."

Jared took a sip from his mug before setting it aside and reaching for a plate of strudel. "When did he call?"

"On Friday. I passed the message on to her, and she said she wanted to run something by you and Matt about it first. So I was just curious, that's all."

"She never said a word to me." Jared used his fork to break off a bite-size portion of the dessert. "But if it's the guy who wants to buy that property, I'm a little worried about her negotiating a land deal, especially with a company called Dazzling Desert Ventures."

"I suppose it could have been a telemarketer trying to sell her a time-share or something."

"It's possible. But maybe I ought to call the guy back. Did you keep a record of his number?"

"Yes. In the office."

They ate in silence, each deep in thought. But Sabrina suspected it was more than real estate that had Jared so quiet.

Just as it was for her.

The coffee break didn't last long, and after another hour of work in the cabin, the rain slowed to a sprinkle.

"There seems to be a lull in the storm," Jared said, "although I don't expect it to last long. Maybe we ought to head back to the house while we have a chance to stay dry."

Sabrina agreed, so they sloshed through the water-soaked yard and entered through the mudroom, where Jared kicked off his boots and Sabrina left her shoes.

In the kitchen, Connie stood over the stove, frying up chicken, while Tori sat at the table with a coffee mug in front of her. They'd been chatting, but their conversation suddenly stilled, which made Jared wonder whether they were conspiring about something.

He glanced at a platter filled with golden-brown chicken—legs, thighs, breasts. Had Tori been giving Connie cooking lessons? If so, he didn't mind them being in cahoots about that.

"Thanks for sending Joey with the coffee and strudel," Sabrina told Connie. "It was delicious. And a real treat."

"You're welcome. I thought you might need a break."

"We did, so your timing was perfect." Sabrina looked toward the doorway that led to the rest of the house. "Where's Joey?"

"He's watching a cartoon on television in the family room," Tori said. "I know you're careful about what he can see, so I made sure it was appropriate."

It was a good thing Jared didn't have to make decisions about what was appropriate for kids to do or see. He wasn't up on current child-rearing practices, and since Jolene hadn't wanted to have a baby, he hadn't given it any thought.

"Your brother's in the living room," Tori told Jared.

"I hope he's behaving himself, too." Jared had meant his response to be tongue in cheek, as if Tori would have made sure Matt, like Joey, was involved in some kind of age-appropriate activity.

"Has your brother always been grumpy?" the red-headed maid asked. "Or did his attitude change after the accident?"

Jared didn't normally like discussing his brother's depression with anyone other than one of the doctors, but he figured a truthful answer wasn't going to hurt. Yet it didn't take a board of surgeons to see that Matt could be an ass, whether he had reason to be or not. "He lost someone he cared about in that accident. And he's had to give up a career in the rodeo. I can't really blame him for being miserable."

"The poor man," Tori said. "Maybe I ought to talk to him."

Jared wasn't sure what she could say that would help. But he figured it wouldn't hurt if she tried. Matt might look vulnerable, but he'd always been scrappy and strong-willed. In fact, in some ways, he was probably even more so now.

"Well," Tori said, getting to her feet and carrying her cup to the sink. "I'd better get back to work. My coffee break is over."

As she left the kitchen, Connie, who'd been listening intently to the conversation, turned back to the stove and sucked in a breath. "Oh, darn it. Now, these are going to be extra-crispy and a bit on the dark side."

Apparently, the new cook was easily distracted and did a better job when she was able to throw a dessert into a preset oven and not pay it any mind until the timer went off.

Jared turned his attention to Sabrina. "When you get a chance, will you please get me Wayne's number?"

"I'll get it now," she said. "For what it's worth it had a 702 area code."

Jared had called Jolene enough times to know the guy was calling from Nevada. "It must be the man who wants to buy her property."

"That's what I was thinking," Sabrina said. "If you'll excuse me, I'll be right back."

Jared followed her as far as the living room, where the front door suddenly swung open and Granny stepped inside. Once she'd shut out the dreary weather, she whistled out a "Whew."

"You're home earlier than usual," Jared said.

Granny wiped her feet on the rug in the entry, then shucked off her black coat. "That's because Hilda doesn't like driving in the rain anymore. And I can't say as I blame her. When you're our age, the damp weather is tough on the bones and joints."

"Mrs. Clayton," Sabrina said, "did you ever get a chance to call Mr. Templeton or talk to your sons about him?"

Matt glanced up, his brow furrowed. "Who's he?"

"Wayne Templeton is one of the fellows who are interested in the property in Nevada. He wanted to know if I received the offer he mailed me the other day." Granny hung her coat on the hook by the door, then shuffled into the living area and took a seat on the sofa.

"You got an offer?" Jared asked.

"Yes. Hilda and I picked it up from my post-office box while we were in Brighton Valley. And to tell you the truth, I'd just as soon sell it. What do I need a bunch of cacti and scrub brush for?"

"Before selling it, I think someone ought to fly out to Las Vegas and see just where it's located." Jared leaned his side against the backrest of the recliner and crossed his arms.

"Good idea." Granny smiled at Sabrina. "I'll give you power of attorney and let you handle the deal with those casino bigwigs."

"Now, wait a minute," Jared said, straightening. "You can't just send her out there alone."

"Why not?" Granny asked.

Because that "desert property" could be worth a hell of a lot more than either Granny or Sabrina imagined. And if a casino was interested in it… Hell, if that were the case, neither one of those women were prepared to negotiate a deal of that type.

Jared would insist upon going to Las Vegas for Granny and leaving Sabrina behind, but with both women eyeing him as though he'd just walked into the room buck naked, he figured he'd better be careful how he worded it.

"I have a friend who's a real-estate attorney in Vegas," Jared explained. "I'll call in a favor and ask his opinion on the deal."

"Fine," Granny said. "Then you and Sabrina can both go on my behalf."

Together?

That hadn't been what Jared had in mind.

"Actually," Sabrina said, "I really don't want to drag Joey to Las Vegas."

Jared felt the tension slip off his shoulders. Good. He'd much rather handle this on his own.

"Don't you worry one little bit about Joey." Granny grinned and eased back into the comfort of the sofa cushions. "I'll watch him. And Tori and Connie will help me."

Jared stole a glance at Sabrina, who appeared to be just as surprised by the travel arrangements as he was. But he figured there wasn't anything either of them could do or say to change Granny's mind when she got something wedged in it.

And apparently, she was dead set on being represented by both of them.

"Well," he said, wondering how Sabrina felt about all of this and taking a good, hard look at his mother, "I guess you've made up your mind."

Granny beamed, as if she had it all aced—the deal and the sale.

Jared's gaze drifted to Sabrina. As their eyes met and locked, something rushed between them. Something breathless and hot.

It was just the memory of the kiss, he supposed. And the thought of a repeat.

But, hey. What happened in Vegas, stayed in Vegas.

Chapter Seven

On Monday morning, Jared entered the kitchen after the men had gone to start their chores. He drank a cup of coffee and munched on a couple of pieces of toast, then grabbed an apple from the fruit bowl on the table and went outside.

The sky was smudged and spotted with gray clouds, remnants of yesterday's storm, but the rain had passed. That was a good thing, he supposed, since he and Sabrina would be leaving today.

The first afternoon flight out of Houston that still had seats available didn't depart for Las Vegas until one o'clock, so there was no need to leave the ranch until nine.

For that reason, Jared stepped off the porch and headed for the barn, where he found Lester just outside his office, lighting up a cigarette.

"Got a minute?" he asked the lanky, weathered ranch foreman.

"Sure." Lester pulled a long drag, no doubt savoring the taste of tobacco, then blew it out. "What can I do for ya?"

"I'm looking for a dependable horse for Joey to ride while he's here. You got any suggestions?"

Lester stroked his chin, fingers brushing two-day-old whiskers, and gave it some thought.

Jared, who still held the apple he'd picked up in the house, rubbed it on his flannel shirt, giving it a shine, rather than a bite.

"You know," Lester said, "I've got a couple that might work out. Let me show 'em to you."

Five minutes and three horses later, they settled on Smokey, a sure-footed black gelding that had done his share of ranch work over the years, but was ready for an easier life. Smokey didn't know it, but he'd won a short reprieve from the auction block.

Jared thanked Lester, letting the foreman get back to work. Then he strode across the yard, making his way to the house. He spotted the boy seated on the steps leading to the mudroom.

Joey lifted his hand and wiggled his fingers in a fluttery wave. "Hi, Mr. Clayton."

"Well, now." A slow smile stretched across Jared's face. "You're just the guy I was looking for. I have something I need you to do for me."

The boy jumped to his feet. "Sure, Mr. Clayton. What is it?"

"We've got an old horse that needs someone to take care of him, and most of the cowboys are too busy to give him the kind of attention he needs."

"A *horse?*" The boy's voice was laced with awe. "A *real* one? And you need *me* to take care of him?"

"Absolutely. His name is Smokey. He's getting on in years and has pretty much been retired. But he was one of the best cutting horses we ever had. And it just doesn't seem fair for him to be stuck in a corral most of the day." Okay, so he'd stretched the truth, lending a bit more importance to the old black gelding's job on the ranch than was the case.

"What do you want me to do?" Joey asked.

"Well, it's probably a good idea for you to get to know him first, I suppose. You might start by talking to him and giving him some oats or chunks of carrots." Jared glanced at the apple in his hand, deciding on a better use for it than a snack before leaving for the airport. "Smokey was one heck of a good horse, so he deserves to be treated well. And something tells me you'd do right by him."

"Oh, I *will.* I'll take super good care of him."

"Come with me." Jared put the apple into his left hand and slid the right one into the front pocket of his jeans, withdrawing his Swiss Army knife. "Let's go meet him."

They walked toward the corral where the black gelding had been penned with a piebald mare.

"Which one is Smokey?" Joey asked.

"The biggest one." Jared whistled, and Smokey perked up his ears, but remained where he was standing.

"It looks like he's not too sure about us." Jared opened up his knife, then pared off a small chunk. "We're going to have to bribe him a little."

Slowly but surely, Smokey plodded toward the fence, where the man and boy waited.

"Here, Joey." Jared gave the child a piece of apple. "Hold your hand open flat. Like this. Keep your fingers out of the way and make Smokey do the work."

As the gelding sniffed, snorted then gobbled up the apple, the look of wonder that crossed Joey's face was priceless, and it released a flood of warmth in Jared's chest.

Was this how Clem had felt when he'd taken Jared under his wing years ago?

As the boy fed the horse another small piece of apple, the piebald figured out what was going on and tried to nose her way into the party.

Just like a female, Jared thought, as the memory of the night he'd first met Jolene settled over him.

He and his buddies, all Texas ranchers wearing Stetsons and boots, were kicking back and having a drink in one of the lounges in a prominent Las Vegas casino when she'd sidled up to the table.

"Is this seat taken?" she'd asked before claiming the one next to Jared. "I love cowboys."

If he'd realized the truth of her statement then and had known what the future would bring, he would have told her the seat wasn't available. It would have saved them both a hell of a lot of grief.

As Joey continued to feed the horses one small piece of apple after another, he giggled each time they nibbled against the palm of his hand.

The boy's delight made Jared chuckle, too, and he realized he was playing the same role in Joey's life— albeit temporarily—that Clem had once played in his. But, hey. That was okay. It seemed only right to pay it forward.

"You know," Jared said, "part of taking care of ol' Smokey will be to exercise him."

"How do I do that?"

"Well, you'll need to ride him, of course."

"*Ride* him?" The boy's eyes couldn't have grown any wider, his smile any broader. "Oh, wow. That would be *way* cool."

"I suppose I'll have to give you a few lessons, though. Can you wait until after my trip to Las Vegas?"

"If I have to." Joey bit on his bottom lip. "I mean, sure. I can wait."

"It would probably be a good idea if you came out and visited Smokey several times a day until I get back, though."

"Joey?" Sabrina called from the house.

"I'm over here," he yelled, before taking off at a run. He met his aunt before she could step a foot into the yard.

Jared followed behind at a normal pace, arriving in time to hear the boy try to catch his breath while blurting out, "Guess what? Mr. Clayton is showing me how to take care of a horse."

He went on to tell her about the important chore he'd been given, his excitement causing him to wheeze while spitting out the words.

"Take it easy there, sport." Jared grinned. "You're going to hyperventilate."

"What's that?" Joey asked, still huffing a bit.

"It's when you're talking so fast that you suck in too much air and can't catch your breath."

Had Jared been this excited when Clem and the other hands had taken him riding with them for the very first time?

He shook off a brief moment of concern and slid a glance at Sabrina, at the charcoal-gray business suit she wore. It was a shame she didn't wear skirts and dresses more often. She had a great pair of legs, and the khaki and denim pants she'd chosen before hadn't done them justice.

"Are you ready to go yet?" she asked him.

He was packed. But after taking a look at her, noticing how professional she looked, how carefully she'd dressed and applied her makeup, he had half a notion to stop in town and buy himself some new clothes. He'd only packed jeans and cotton shirts when he left his own ranch. But there was no reason to get fancy. Jared was more interested in meeting Wayne Templeton and letting the man think he was dealing with a run-of-the-mill cowboy and not a college-educated rancher.

Besides, it was always fun to mess with men who thought he was a hick.

As it was, Jared would let Sabrina be the one to go all out. He'd just enjoy having her on his arm. And in his sights.

Damn, she looked good.

A coat of mascara made her eyelashes long and luscious, setting off those pretty blue eyes. And the red lipstick she sported made her lips look plump and kissable. And the fact that he'd already had a taste of them only set his blood pumping and his hormones raging.

Her ebony hair, silky and soft, had been swept up into a neat professional twist. He'd love to see it again, flowing loosely down her back, love to run his fingers through the tresses.

Did she ever let her hair down during the daylight hours—literally or figuratively?

When she blessed Jared with a heart-stopping smile, the thought of their impending trip settled over him, and he couldn't shake a raw thrill himself. And not because he harbored any urges to return to the bright lights and excitement of Las Vegas.

He was actually looking forward to getting away with Sabrina—even if he was determined not to let things get out of hand.

As Sabrina made her way down the aisle of the plane, she scanned the interior of the cabin.

"There's row twelve," Jared said from behind her, his musky, mountain-fresh scent a blatant and stirring reminder of his masculine presence. "We're in D and E."

She looked at the stub of her boarding pass, then at the letters on the overhead compartment, realizing she had the middle seat.

"Are you okay with that?" he asked.

"Oh, sure. It's just that…" She shrugged one shoulder and offered him a wry smile. "It's my first time on an airplane, and I thought it might be nice to sit by the window so I could look out."

"No kidding? You've never flown before?"

She shook her head, then slid into her assigned seat and buckled up.

Jared, who had been pleased with his preferred spot next to the aisle, opened the overhead compartment and put their carry-on bags inside.

Then he sat next to Sabrina and asked, "Have you ever been to Las Vegas before?"

"No. Have you?"

"Yeah." He didn't offer an explanation, but as he

sobered, she got the feeling he was keeping something back. A gambling loss, maybe?

"It sounds as though the place might hold some bad memories," she said.

"You got that right."

She turned, studied his profile. "What happened?"

When he didn't answer right away, she began to wonder if she'd broached some big, dark secret he hadn't meant to share.

Finally, he blew out a sigh. "That's where I met my ex-wife."

"You're divorced?" Mrs. Clayton had mentioned that her boys were all single, so Sabrina had just assumed they'd never been married.

"Since last Christmas."

"I'm sorry."

"Don't be. The marriage didn't last very long. And we didn't have kids."

"Still…"

"It was no big deal—not the marriage or the divorce. I'm glad it's all over."

Was he?

As the flight attendant went over the safety features of the 737, Sabrina took note of the exits, hoping it wouldn't be necessary to know where they were and squelching a rising bit of nervousness.

Then, as the plane backed away from the gate and began to taxi, she realized no one was going to take the window seat next to her, which was nice. So she craned her neck to see the activity on the ground as the plane prepared to take off.

Fifteen minutes later, when the flight was underway,

she returned her attention to her ruggedly handsome traveling companion.

"So what was she like?" Sabrina asked.

"Who?"

"Your ex."

He shrugged. "Just like any old ex-wife, I suppose. Ugly, fat, toothless."

She caught a glimmer in his eye, although she wouldn't have believed him even if she'd suspected he was sincere. "That's not true."

"What makes you think that?"

"There had to have been something about the woman that attracted you to her."

"I was drunk when I met her."

She studied his profile, the high cheekbones, the square-cut jaw, looking for some indication that he was joking. She couldn't possibly imagine him with an unattractive woman. Of course, she wasn't particularly comfortable with the thought of him with a pretty one, either.

"I don't believe you," she finally said. "You couldn't have been that drunk."

"There were times after we split up that I questioned how sober I could have been. Otherwise, I had to wonder about both my intelligence and my sanity."

He made it sound as though there hadn't been any emotion involved. But somehow that was hard to believe. Men didn't have to get married for sex anymore. Not when it was so readily available. And Sabrina suspected Jared wouldn't have to go to any trouble at all to find someone ready, willing and able—without offering any promises.

So she concluded that, in spite of what he was telling her, the divorce couldn't have been that easy.

"Was the relationship that bad?"

"Not at first. But it was a mistake for us to get married. Looking back, I'm not sure why we did." He glanced away, across the aisle.

She sensed that he didn't want to talk about it, so she returned her attention to the window and the white, billowy clouds below them.

For the most part, the trip was uneventful, other than a bit of turbulence over the mountains. It didn't seem to faze either Jared or the flight attendants, who passed out drinks and small bags of peanuts. So Sabrina relaxed and enjoyed the view until the captain announced the plane had begun its descent.

As the flight attendants prepared for landing, Sabrina stole a glance at Jared and caught him studying her in a way that set her pulse racing.

She offered him a smile, yet wondered what had caused the intensity in his gaze.

Las Vegas memories he'd like to forget?

Anticipation of the land deal they'd be negotiating?

Or was it something about *her* that had caught his eye and had him deep in thought?

It was strange, but twice in one day Jared had been on hand to watch someone experience the thrill of doing something for the very first time—Joey feeding the gelding, and now Sabrina sitting beside him on an airplane, her delight almost palpable.

He'd found himself caught up in the excitement with each of them, even though horseback riding and air travel no longer seemed like a big deal to him. But that hadn't always been the case, and it was nice having the chance to relive that first-time buzz through their eyes.

"What's wrong?" Sabrina asked.

"Nothing."

There was something in her expression—skepticism, maybe, or sympathy?

"Really," he said. "There isn't anything wrong."

Not yet, anyway. She'd touched him in a way he wasn't used to, in a place he ought to keep out of reach.

He gave her a pat on her knee…it was bare, soft and warm. The boldness of his move surprised the hell out him, since it suggested an intimacy he hadn't wanted to share again.

"Are you sure it's nothing?" She cocked her head slightly to the side, compassion attempting to soothe him where he'd once been hurt and had already healed. "I get the feeling that something is bothering you. Memories of your ex, maybe."

"Jolene?" He shook his head. "Not at all. I'm not one to stew about a mistake I made in the heat of the moment."

"Good." Sabrina's scent, something floral and breezy, softened the business cut of her suit and proclaimed a gentle femininity a guy could really get used to.

Just sitting next to her was enough to make Jared question what he'd ever felt for Jolene. And to remind him of the heated kiss he and Sabrina had shared in the kitchen of Clem's cabin.

"By the way," he said, trying to steer the subject into safer water, "I called my friend last nigh The attorney I mentioned?"

"The one you were going to consult with on the property sale?"

"Yes. His name is Steve Rankin. I gave him the parcel number of Granny's property, and faxed him a copy of the offer she received. He agreed to meet us at his office as soon as we arrive and promised to have some comps and more information for us."

"Good idea. At least we'll know what we're up against." She rested her elbow on the armrest, turning toward him. Taunting him with that lovely scent again.

So much for changing the subject and regaining his balance.

"Where did you meet Steve?" she asked.

"At Caesar's Palace about five years ago. We were sitting at the same blackjack table. He was at first base, and I was at third. Together, we made a pretty good team, and I think we each walked away with more than five grand. It made for a pleasant night."

"I bet." She grinned. "No pun intended."

He returned her smile. "Steve and I hit it off, and since we were both hungry, we had dinner together. When we found out we both went to Texas A&M, a friendship developed."

"I didn't know you went to college."

There was a lot about him she didn't know. "I nearly dropped out when Clem got sick, but he raised such a ruckus that I filed incompletes. And then he made me promise to go back and get a degree."

"Did you?"

"Yeah. So there's no reason why you can't do the same."

She nibbled her bottom lip, and her eyes seemed a bit glassy. "I know. I plan to."

Jared wasn't at all good at providing emotional support to a woman. Hell, just ask Jolene. So he made another attempt to regain control of the conversation. "Anyway, Steve and I have been friends ever since, and as soon as I hit Las Vegas city limits, I usually give him a call. We try our best to find time to at least meet for a drink."

"How long has it been since you've seen him?"

"Too long." Jared had been steering clear of Vegas ever since he'd found out that Jolene had moved back.

The flight attendant announced that it was time for seat backs to be set in an upright position, and Jared was glad to have the interruption in a conversation he hadn't wanted to pursue.

Forty-five minutes later, after landing and picking up a rental car, they arrived at Steve's office, a smoky-glass high-rise located close to city hall. They took the elevator all the way to the top, where Steve's prominent and respected firm took up the entire floor.

Sabrina seemed impressed with the black leather seats, the chrome-and-glass furniture in the reception area. Jared had been, too, when he'd come here the first time.

"We're here to see Steve Rankin," Jared told the young woman seated behind a raised and curved desk that was crafted out of polished cherrywood and boasted a black marble counter.

"I'll let him know you're here. Please, have a seat."

Jared guided Sabrina to one of the sofas, but they didn't wait long.

Steve called his name, and Jared immediately got to his feet and reached out his arm in greeting.

"This is Sabrina Gonzalez," Jared told his friend. "She's my mother's bookkeeper."

As the man and woman shook hands, Jared noticed that Steve held on longer than was necessary, something that suggested the avowed bachelor had found her more than a little attractive.

But how could Jared blame him? Sabrina was a beautiful woman, even when she wasn't in a thin, cotton gown, barefoot and wearing her hair Lady Godiva style.

"Come on back to my office," Steve said, leading the way.

"So what did you find out?" Jared asked. "Are those guys on the up-and-up? And is that offer anything we ought to consider?"

Steve held open the door and indicated that they ought to take the black, tufted leather desk chairs that sat across from his. "Let's just say that you came to the right place."

"What do you mean?"

"Dazzling Desert Ventures is legit. It's the name of an LLC that was created by some big-name casinos. And their offer was relatively fair."

"What does that mean?" Jared asked.

"In terms of the price per square foot, it wasn't too far off the mark." A slow grin stretched across Steve's face. "But let me be the first to tell you that your mama and daddy made one heck of a good investment. That ten acres is worth millions. And since Dazzling Desert Ventures is trying to put together a major deal, and your mother's land is the prime piece, they'll be willing to pay even more."

"How much more?" Jared asked.

"At least twice the amount they offered."

Jared blew out a long, slow whistle. "Looks like we have something to celebrate tonight. Dinner's on me. Champagne, too."

"I'll have to pass. I have a conference call that will take most of the evening. You have no idea how long it took me to line it up, so there's no way I can reschedule it now." Steve leaned back in his chair. "Where are you going?"

Jared hadn't given it much thought. Dinner and champagne had just been a spur of the moment suggestion. He supposed they could go anywhere; most of the top casinos had a nice steakhouse.

So why he answered, "Serenata" was beyond him.

It was one of the most romantic restaurants in all of Las Vegas.

Chapter Eight

Jared and Sabrina had even more to celebrate than he'd thought.

After Steve had driven them to the property and impressed them with his knowledge of the commercial real-estate market, not just in Clark County, but in all of Nevada, he'd agreed to negotiate the deal as a favor to his friend.

So after checking into rooms at La Trieste, one of the newest and finest casino/hotels on the strip, Jared donned a sports jacket, then took Sabrina to dinner at Serenata, less than a mile away.

Now, as they sat across a linen-draped table from each other, Jared studied Sabrina in the candlelight. She still wore that business suit, which was the dressiest outfit she'd brought, but she'd loosened up and appeared to be more relaxed.

Since their trip was drawing to a close, he wondered if he could get her to let her hair down. Maybe he could suggest going to a show or hitting the casino.

The wine steward arrived at their table sporting a bottle of Cristal, two flutes and an ice bucket. "Your champagne, sir."

"Thank you." Jared watched the man pop the cork and fill the glasses.

"Will there be anything else?" the steward asked.

"No. That's it for now."

The man nodded respectfully, then backed away from their table.

When they were alone, Jared lifted his glass in a toast. The rising bubbles placed a festive mood on the evening. "Here's to a smooth negotiation and to Everett Clayton's foresight when he purchased that desert property."

Sabrina lightly tapped her flute against his, the sound of crystal resonating, then took a sip. "Hmm. I've never had champagne before, but this could become habit-forming. It's really nice."

"This is one of the best, so you have great taste." He tossed her a smile.

"Is it terribly expensive?"

More than she was probably used to spending. "This is a special occasion."

Her lips made a little O, and she nodded. "That means I'll have to save up quite awhile before I have any more."

Sabrina, her blue eyes glistening in the candlelight

and a smile creating dimples, looked like a princess to-night, a woman deserving of all the finest in life.

"What did Mrs. Clayton say when you called her with the news?" she asked.

"She was pleased. But you know, it sounds weird to hear you call her Mrs. Clayton. Almost everyone in Brighton Valley calls her Granny. And the few who don't, call her Edna."

"I don't feel comfortable doing that yet. But maybe someday I will." She took another sip of champagne. "When did you start calling her Granny?"

"Ever since day one."

"When was that?"

Jared didn't usually go in to details with anyone who didn't already know about his early years. But maybe it was the ambiance of Serenata. Or the pretty woman who sat across from him, her smile telling him it was safe to reveal at least some of the past. "I was twelve when Granny threw me a lifeline."

Sabrina leaned toward him, as though they'd reached a level of intimacy. But as the flute listed in her hand, threatening to spill over, he couldn't help wondering if his self-disclosure was also an accident waiting to happen.

"How did she do that?" Sabrina asked.

"She provided me with a home when there wasn't an-other one to be had." Jared was sure that Sabrina could probably relate to that, which was why he continued with the story, sharing what he usually kept close to the vest. "I never knew my mother. And my dad... Well, he had quite a few problems—drugs for one. So when he took off one day and never came back, I was put in foster care."

"Sometimes, when I was growing up, I'd wondered if it might have been better if Carlos and I were taken away from my parents." She took a drink of champagne. "Was being a foster kid a negative experience for you?"

"No one was cruel to me, if that's what you mean." Jared studied his glass, noticing how the candlelight made the bubbling liquid look like a magical elixir. Like a potion that could fix all that had once been wrong in his life and give him a different past. "My first foster father was in the military, and when he received word that he was being transferred to the east coast, he took his family with him, but they had to leave me behind."

"I'm sorry. That must have been tough."

It had been—at the time. But he shrugged it off. "I wasn't a blood relative, so I didn't expect them to take me with them."

"Is that when Granny stepped in?"

"No. After that, I went to live with the Wilsons. They treated me well, and I would have been okay if it had become permanent. But when the parents started having marital problems, counseling hadn't helped, so they threw in the towel and got a divorce."

"And you were uprooted again." It hadn't been a question. Just a conclusion that was easy to come to, especially for a woman who'd experienced a lot of moves herself.

"By the time I hit the teen years, I was placed with a family who got permission to take me to live with them in Brighton Valley. And I finally thought I'd found a place to settle in."

"Was that with Mrs. Clayton?"

"Nope. Hank and Wanda Priestly. But when Hank

developed lung cancer and died, Wanda decided it would be easy on her financially if she moved in with her folks for a while. And their house was pretty small."

Sabrina placed a hand over his, making a connection he wasn't sure what to do with and warming his fingers with hers. Her gentle touch offered a balm—if he wanted one.

He didn't need it, of course. Yet when she removed her hand from his, he wished she hadn't. Still, he continued the story he'd started. "Because of my age at the time, someone at social services decided to send me to the county home for boys."

Jared lifted his glass, savored the taste of the champagne. "Granny has been a longtime friend of Grace Ann Peterson, my foster dad's aunt. So when she heard about me and my plight, she volunteered to take me in even though a social worker said I was a 'rebellious adolescent on the verge of those tumultuous teen years.'"

"Did you give people a hard time?" Sabrina asked. "My brother used to act out a lot when we were growing up. But I always tried to compensate by being good so we wouldn't have to move again."

"Actually, I'd become so distrustful after so many crappy attempts to find a place to fit in, that I'd pretty much given up hope and figured the sooner Granny gave me the boot, the better. So I put on my best surly face and gave her a hard time. But it didn't take long to learn there was something special about Granny. And I soon realized I'd found a home for good. When I was fourteen, she told me she wanted to adopt me, if that was all right with me."

"And obviously," Sabrina said, "it was."

Yeah. It was more than okay. It was the best thing

that had ever happened to him. "It's amazing what a loving mother and a real father figure can do for a kid."

"Did you meet Mr. Clayton? Was he still alive when you went to stay at the Rocking C?"

"No. Clem, Granny's foreman, was a crusty old cowboy who took an instant liking to me and taught me all about horses, cattle and ranching. And for the first time in my life, my future looked happy and bright."

"Clem sounds like a perfect role model for a boy."

Jared couldn't help but laugh. "You've got that right. Clem loved tall tales, good whiskey and five-card stud, and before long, I not only picked up all his good qualities, but most of his vices, too."

"You miss him," she said. "And not just a little. I noticed the way you studied that photograph of the two of you we found in the cabin. And I saw the way you carefully placed it on the mantel."

"You're right. I do miss him. He was unique and a real novelty. They don't make 'em like Clem anymore."

"When did your mother adopt the other boys?"

"First, she took in Greg. Then Matt. But it wasn't easy for me to move over and make room for them. I'd staked my claim and wasn't ready to lose it. So needless to say, there were a few scuffles at first. But we eventually created a family of sorts, something we'd all been missing."

"Did Greg and Matt learn how to play poker and pick up any of Clem's vices?"

Jared chuckled. "Yep. Each in his own way. But since Granny always has been a churchgoing woman and wouldn't have been too happy about our bad habits, we kept them under wraps, believing that what she didn't know wouldn't hurt her."

Sabrina leaned forward again, placing her elbows on the table as though she was finding his tale intriguing. "So how bad were you?"

"Well, I've never been in jail." He flashed her a smile, although she didn't return it.

When Sabrina took another drink of champagne, the steward seemed to appear from out of nowhere to replenish their glasses.

Jared thanked him, and when they were left alone again, he said, "By the time I was twenty-one, I was making regular trips to Las Vegas, where I won at poker and blackjack more often than not. In fact, I was able to put a down payment on a ranch of my own with my winnings."

"So that's what you meant when you said that you'd been to Las Vegas before."

Looking back, probably more than he should have, even though it had given him the financial edge he'd needed to buy his own ranch and become independent. And one trip in particular had been a big mistake—the day he'd met Jolene. Then a few months later, before realizing they weren't the least bit suited, he married her and brought her home to Texas.

They were happy for about a year, but Jared had been busy working his ranch, and Jolene had grown tired and bored.

She left during the holidays—a year ago last November—and it had been especially tough. But rather than rally and join Granny and his brothers in Brighton Valley, Jared chose to drink his way to Groundhog Day.

When Granny learned about the pending divorce and

had revealed her disappointment, Jared had told her they had irreconcilable differences. He was ashamed to let anyone know the truth, that his wife had chosen someone she found more lovable than him.

Jared had been crushed, but in retrospect, he decided it was more from his wife's infidelity and betrayal than by her loss.

"You're a lucky man," Sabrina said.

"I guess I am." Lucky in cards, anyway.

"Mrs. Clayton is a wonderful woman. And you and your brothers were fortunate to have crossed paths with her."

"That's for sure. Granny's love and acceptance were a godsend, although I have a feeling she's the kind of woman who's the exception rather than the rule."

"That sounds like a divorced man talking."

"Maybe so." Jared may have made one mistake, but he wouldn't make another. If he ever got involved with another woman again, he was going be careful about who she was.

One night, after Matt had had the accident and came to live with Jared, the two sat up drinking, commiserating with each other into the wee hours of the morning.

"Jolene was a mistake from the get-go," Matt had said. "That should have been clear to you. But apparently, you don't have a cull shoot when it comes to weeding out the good lovers from the bad. Any fool could have seen that she wasn't the kind of woman a man could trust."

At the time, Jared had gotten hot under the collar, but he'd let it go. Slamming his fist into his crippled brother's nose wouldn't have changed anything.

"Did your mother like your wife?" Sabrina's question came at him like a charging bull, and he didn't quite know how to sidestep it.

"She never said anything negative, although Jolene wasn't very family-oriented."

Thinking Jared was stubborn and a bit on the ornery side, which had probably led to the marital problems, Granny had tried to convince him to go after Jolene, to make his marriage work. But Jared had refused.

"I'm better off now," he told Sabrina, just as he'd told Granny back then. "We both are."

Sabrina offered him a smile. "There'll be someone else someday. Someone better."

"I'm not looking for a replacement."

"Sometimes that's when you find love—when you least expect it."

"And you know that how?"

Sabrina sat back in her seat, taking the glass of champagne with her. "Okay, so I'm not all that experienced with love and marriage. But I do read."

"What do you read? Romances? Self-help books? Articles in women's magazines?" He couldn't help his interest, his curiosity about her take on relationships.

"All of the above, actually."

Romance novels, too? He wondered what she'd learned from them. Or what she thought she'd learned.

"I believe there's someone out there for everyone," she continued. "And you shouldn't settle until the right one comes along."

"You think so, huh?" Jared smiled, thinking her somewhat naive then, signaled for one of the waiters, letting him know it was time to order dinner.

Jared didn't want to keep drinking on an empty stomach. Otherwise, Sabrina's romantic notions might begin to make sense.

For the most part, he'd sworn off women. Not that he wouldn't pursue a sexual relationship now and again. But when he did, he would make sure there weren't any feelings involved or strings attached.

As they waited for the valet to bring Jared's car, Sabrina relished the brisk night air and the clear desert sky. The moon was only a sliver of itself, while the stars winked and blinked as though they were privy to a secret Sabrina didn't know.

She had a buzz from the champagne, but she really didn't care. She and Jared had shared something special this evening. A closeness she hadn't expected.

When she'd first met him, he'd come across as harsh, headstrong and self-righteous. But as the days passed he'd shown her another side of himself—first by reaching out to Joey and giving him a ride on the horse, then by pitching in to help her clean and repair the cabin.

Jared had also gone above and beyond by bringing her wood for the fireplace and making her lunch, all signs of consideration that touched her heart.

And just now, when he shared his past with her, she'd been given a special insight to the man, a glimpse of his childhood that allowed her to understand him in a way others might not be able to.

She suspected there was still a little bit of that abandoned boy inside of him, that child who'd been searching for a place to call home, for a family to love him. It had been an easy conclusion to make, since there was still a bit of the insecure girl in her.

At least he'd found what he'd been looking for.

As she would someday.

A shiver slid over her, and he placed a hand on her back. "Are you cold?"

"Just a little." She offered him a smile, thinking that even though he hadn't actually wrapped an arm around her in a warm, protective sense, his response had been sweet. Affectionate, even.

She wasn't sure what had transpired between them tonight, but after the intimacy of a romantic dinner and the revelations he'd made about his childhood, things had changed.

They'd changed. And so had their feelings.

She wasn't exactly sure how, but she felt it in the desert air, in the musky scent of his cologne, in the heat of his palm as it pressed into the small of her back.

As she glanced again at the sky, and the stars that twinkled like magic overhead, a sudden realization struck. If she weren't careful, she could fall for him.

In fact, that just might happen anyway—no matter how hard she tried to avoid it.

As their rental car swung around to the front of the restaurant, one of the valets climbed out and handed Jared the keys, while another opened the passenger door for Sabrina. Moments later, they were headed back to the La Trieste Hotel and Casino.

"Are you up for a little fun?" Jared asked.

Fun? Both the humor in his tone and the gleam in his eyes made the suggestion enticing. "What do you have in mind?"

"Maybe some blackjack?"

"I don't know how to play."

"That doesn't matter. You're a bookkeeper, so you ought to be able to count to twenty-one. Besides, I'm a good teacher."

It was tempting. And she wasn't ready for the night to end. "I really don't have any money I can afford to lose."

"I'll stake you, and we'll split the winnings." He made it sound like a sure thing, but she knew better.

As they pulled into the circular drive and stopped at the entry in front of La Trieste, Jared again left the vehicle with the valet to park. Then he escorted Sabrina inside, where she found herself just as awed by the bright, blinking lights and the blips and bleeps of slot machines as she'd been when they'd checked in earlier today. Maybe more so, now that she realized some of them were paying off, much to the delight of a couple of lucky gamblers.

As they approached an ATM machine, the man turning away and counting the cash he'd just received nodded at Jared in acknowledgment.

"How's it going?" Jared asked, clearly not expecting an answer.

But the man responded anyway. "Not too good, I'm afraid. That's the only machine that's paid off for me all night."

Jared chuckled, then placed an arm around Sabrina's shoulder and guided her through a maze of people and slots.

"You know," she said, as they walked, "I might feel better getting out of this outfit." She still wore her charcoal-gray business suit and heels. "Would you mind if I went up to my room and changed?"

"Not at all." Jared slowed his steps. "I'll just wait for

you in the lounge near the elevators. I might even play one of the poker machines."

"All right. I won't be very long." Sabrina dug into her purse for the card that served as her room key. When she had it in hand, she told him she'd be right back, then strode to the elevator and took it to the twenty-third floor, where they had rooms next to each other.

Once inside, she kicked off her high heels and tossed her purse on the bed. Then she grabbed a pair of jeans and a white cotton blouse from her carry-on bag and took them into the bathroom.

When she'd freshened up and brushed her teeth, she removed her business suit and hung it in the closet. As she closed the mirrored door, she studied her image.

This morning, she'd woven her hair into a neat and professional bun, but the pins had begun to dig into her head. Now she was ready for something less formal. So she let her hair down and brushed it until it shined. Then she swept it into a casual twist, using a silver clip to hold it in place.

She slipped on the jeans. The blouse had gotten a little wrinkly from the trip, but she wasn't going to stress about it. She'd told Jared she wanted to be comfortable, and that was the truth.

Once she'd slid her feet into a pair of sandals, she returned to the casino floor and looked for Jared.

She found him in the lounge, just as he'd promised. He was having a drink and playing a game.

"How'd you do?" she asked, as he cashed out.

He handed her a receipt and grinned. "I did all right."

She glanced at the figure on the paper, seeing that

he'd won over five hundred dollars. "Does this happen to you on every trip?"

"No. But for the most part, I'm luckier than most."

Before they could take a step, a voice sounded behind them.

"Hello, Jared." The soft, feminine tone rang loud and clear.

They both turned, spotting a tall, voluptuous blonde, her face loaded with makeup. Too much, in Sabrina's opinion. But still, the woman was stunning.

"Fancy meeting you here." The blonde, her long, curly hair spritzed and molded into a blowsy style, eyed Jared carefully. "The last I heard, you weren't coming back to this town on a bet."

Jared stiffened for a moment, then seemed to thaw as he slipped an arm around Sabrina's waist, drew her close and introduced her to Jolene.

His ex?

Catching herself and minding her manners, Sabrina extended a hand. "It's nice to meet you."

It wasn't, though. The meeting was completely unexpected and awkward.

"Likewise." Jolene's gaze drifted over Sabrina, as though she was assessing her and finding her lacking.

Was Jared doing the same thing? Comparing the two women?

Jared held on to Sabrina, as if her presence was keeping his demon at bay. The last time he and Jolene had seen each other had been during their divorce proceedings. They'd had words, he'd said something that had ticked her off and she'd flown off the handle, scream-ing and shouting obscenities.

"It's good to see you," he told her, "but I'm afraid we can't stay and chat. We're headed up to our room."

"Oh… That's too bad." Jolene smiled—one of the fake ones that he'd come to spot a mile away. "I'll have to catch you later."

Not if Jared could help it.

He shouldn't have let her "catch him" the first time.

Jolene might have knocked him on his ass when she told him she didn't love him anymore, that she doubted whether she ever had. And he might have been angry, unbalanced, torn up about it for a while. But in the grand scheme of life, their divorce had only been a minor in-convenience, and he was truly better off without her.

Still, his pride had taken a direct hit.

As he let his hand slide down Sabrina's back, his fin-gers trailed possessively along her hip. He supposed it wasn't fair to drag her into an emotional pissing contest with his ex-wife, but Sabrina was ten times the woman Jolene was. And as far as Jared was concerned, his ex could eat her heart out.

As he and Sabrina strode toward the elevators, neither of them spoke. To her credit, she didn't mention a word about his ex-wife or the blackjack table they were supposed to be heading toward. Nor had she said anything about the fact he still hadn't removed his hand from the perfect slope of her pretty derriere.

Apparently, she not only sensed his need for escape, but was aiding and abetting him at the same time. And that said a lot about her.

Did she understand that he meant to leave Jolene realizing that what goes around, comes around?

When the elevator opened, they waited for it to empty, then stepped inside. As the door shut, leaving them alone, Sabrina turned, causing his hand to fall from her hip.

She leaned against the wall and crossed her arms. "You lied."

About what? he wondered. The hint of a smile took the edge off her accusation, but he wasn't entirely sure what she was getting at.

Did she mean that he'd lied when he'd said they were heading upstairs instead of the blackjack tables?

Or when he'd implied that they were sharing a hotel room?

He raked a hand through his hair. "I'm sorry about that, Sabrina. But the last time Jolene and I ran into each other, there was a scene. I can never trust her to behave civilly, and I didn't want to embarrass you or myself."

"What are you talking about?"

Had he misinterpreted her question? "You accused me of lying."

Sabrina straightened and crossed her arms, but there was more than a hint of amusement in her eyes. "You made it sound like your ex-wife was an old toad."

"As far as I'm concerned, she is."

"That woman *isn't* fat. And she certainly isn't toothless, unless someone paid for an expensive pair of shiny white dentures."

He snorted. "It's pretty standard in a divorce to see the ugliness inside people." Especially when that someone was caught cheating.

"So you're saying that you have a picture of Jolene stored in your mind, and you mentally blackened a couple of her teeth and drew horns on her?"

"She pretty much added those horns on all by herself." Jared punched in number twenty-three, sending the elevator on an upward path.

"How did she do that?"

He clammed up. It was hard to admit that he hadn't been good enough. That the woman who was supposed to stick by his side for life had found someone she liked better.

And even though he suspected he hadn't really loved her, either, that it had only been a terminal case of lust, he didn't like the betrayal. The cheating.

People who made commitments ought to stick by them.

The elevator came to a stop, and the door opened.

"Come on," he said, leading Sabrina to their rooms.

"Where are we going?" she asked.

His steps slowed.

Where the hell *were* they going? He'd been so intent upon getting away from the sight of Jolene, that he'd concocted the excuse to head upstairs.

Jared raked a hand through his hair—again. "I don't know. Are you up for a movie or something? They've usually got some good pay-per-view options."

"What did she do to you?" Sabrina asked.

His gaze met hers, recognizing the compassion that pooled inside.

Downstairs, he'd pretended that he and Sabrina were lovers. It had merely been a game he'd been playing. But standing outside their rooms, looking in those pretty blue eyes, the game took a turn for real.

Her smile threatened to wring out everything in his heart that the divorce hadn't damaged.

She stroked his cheek, her palm grazing the bristles that had been growing since he'd shaved early this morning. "Not all women are like that, Jared. You've got to let it go."

"I have." And he'd never let it go more than he had this very moment.

"Are you sure?" Her gaze locked on his, demanding the truth and pulling it out of somewhere deep inside him.

All he could see was Sabrina, all he could think about was dusting himself off and climbing back in the saddle again.

"Damn straight, I'm sure." He might be sorry later, but every lick of sense he'd ever had went right out the window as he lowered his head for a kiss.

Chapter Nine

The kiss began lightly—a brush of the lips. But soon it intensified, and their tongues began to mate, twisting and tasting until Jared thought he might go crazy.

Their hands roamed, seeking and exploring. With each stroke, each caress, their breathing grew more and more ragged.

Still, the kiss continued.

Right there, in the middle of the hallway on the twenty-third floor of La Trieste, Jared found himself making out with Sabrina like a love-struck, hormone-driven teenager.

And he'd be damned if he even cared.

Apparently, neither did she, because she slid her fingers into his hair, drawing his mouth closer, his tongue deeper.

Jared had never lost himself in a woman's embrace before. Not like this. Sabrina was turning him inside out.

She'd claimed that she wasn't all that experienced with this sort of thing, but he found that hard to believe, now more than ever. She kissed like she'd been schooled in the fine art of seduction, and he suspected she had a few things to teach him.

Damn. If they didn't stop this public display of… lust…she'd be giving him those lessons right in a hotel hallway.

He finally broke the kiss long enough to say, "We need to either head back downstairs to the casino or take this inside one of the rooms."

His pulse thudded in his head, and he found himself holding his breath as he awaited her answer.

"I've never done this before," she said, looking a little nervous.

Done what? Necked and made out in the middle of a public hallway? Entered a hotel room with a man?

Pondered having sex for the first time?

If that were the case, it not only pleased him, but added a ton of pressure. If she was a virgin, he'd have to take extra care to make sure it was enjoyable for her. "We'll take things slow and easy. In fact, we don't have to go any further than we've already gone."

Of course, his hormones were shouting, *Oh, yes, we do!*

He reached into the front pocket of his slacks, pulled out the key card to his room and held it up. All she had to do was say the word.

But instead of saying anything, she took the key from his hand and opened the door.

Once inside, he removed the carry-on bag that lay on

the bed, right where he'd left it after they'd checked in, and tossed it onto the floor in the corner. He hoped she didn't think he was making the bed ready for them. He'd just meant to clear off a place to sit down, although neither of them did.

She continued to stand and reached to the side of her head, feeling a loose strand of hair. She undid the clip, but as she began to work the tresses back into a twist, he stopped her.

"Let it hang loose. Please?"

She studied him for a moment, as though she wasn't sure why he'd made the suggestion. Then she combed her fingers through her hair, leaving it long and free.

He caught the strands that lay along her cheek, letting them slip through his fingers like a veil of silk. "I've wanted to do that since the first moment I laid eyes on you."

"I like my hair long," she said. "But it gets in the way sometimes."

"I like it, too."

Desire stretched between them like a tightrope cable ready to snap. And although he knew better than to let things get out of hand, Sabrina had stirred something inside of him that hadn't been tempted in a long, long time. And if things took a sexual turn, he was willing— if she was.

"Like I said, we don't have to do anything you're not ready for."

There. Now the ball was in her court.

Sabrina looked at Jared, at the way his hair had been mussed by her fingers. At the desire that smoldered in his eyes.

She'd turned down opportunities before. And each time, she'd stuck to her guns. But there had been one guy in college who'd made her reconsider. A guy who'd promised she wouldn't be sorry. Since she'd grown increasingly curious over the years, she'd agreed. She'd also insisted that he wear two condoms—just in case.

Jared ran his knuckles along her cheek, and she found herself curious all over again. More so this time because it would be with a man whose kisses sent her to the moon and back.

"So what do you think?" he asked. "Should we hang out here? Or would you rather go downstairs and play a little blackjack?"

She ought to tell him that she wanted to head for the elevators. But she *felt* something for Jared. Something she hadn't anticipated. Something that had her walking a high wire between love and like. And she suspected he was feeling it, too. The only thing holding her back was fear of pregnancy, although she realized she was older now. Wiser. And better prepared for the consequences.

"I don't suppose you have any condoms?" she asked.

"There might be a couple in my shaving kit. At least, I think they're still there."

Well, there went one excuse, leaving them with very few others to consider.

"I'm not completely innocent," she admitted. "But it wasn't... He didn't... Well, I..."

Jared's gaze snagged hers, wrapping her in a cocoon of warmth and understanding, and her heart took a tumble. She was falling for him. She was sure of it.

"Are you telling me the experience was disappointing?" he asked.

She nodded, cheeks warming enough to let her know she was flushing. "I'd read articles about lovemaking and was curious. I also liked the guy, and we seemed to have chemistry."

But not anything like she and Jared had. His musky scent taunted her nearly as badly as the heat of his touch.

"And?"

She cleared her throat, wanting to get the words right. "Well, sex wasn't all that those women's magazines had led me to believe. And I don't think he enjoyed it much better than I did."

"Was it your first time?"

"Yes. And I guess I was expecting too much."

"Maybe." He tossed her a gentle smile, warming her to the bone. "Sex is something that keeps getting better and better."

"Like our kisses?" she asked.

He slid her a crooked grin. "Yeah. Just like that."

"Then if that's the case, I don't think those books and magazines I've been reading are doing sex justice."

"I'd lay money on that." He didn't step any closer; he just opened his arms, allowing the decision to be hers. Yet it hadn't been a difficult one to make.

She slid into his embrace, ready to take things one step at a time, just as he'd told her they would.

He nuzzled her neck, and she turned her head, providing him better access to the soft spot right below her ear. He used his lips and tongue until she feared she would collapse in a molten puddle on the floor. Then he trailed kisses to her mouth, where he assaulted her sweetly, deeply, thoroughly.

A rush of heat swept over her, and she thought she'd die if they didn't finish what they'd started.

He slid his hands along her back and to the slope of her derriere, then he pulled her flush against a demanding erection. She couldn't help but lean into him, yearning for more.

As the heat mounted, she reached up and ran her fingers through his hair again, fisting it, claiming him as her own.

What they were sharing right now, what they were feeling, was more than lust. More than sex. In fact, she feared that the depth and the power of it would change everything—her hopes and dreams.

She couldn't help wondering if, for the first time in her life, the family and stability she'd always wanted were finally within reach.

A groan formed deep in his throat, and he caressed her breasts, his thumbs skimming her hardened nipples and creating an ache deep in her core. Needing to feel his skin against hers, she began to tug his shirttail out of his pants.

In their haste to work together, a button popped off and flew across the room. But they didn't let that stop them. Moments later, they'd removed her blouse and bra, as well.

Jared knew just what to do, where to touch, how to ravish her with his hands. As her nipples contracted in response, her breath caught. But he didn't miss a beat; he just kissed his way from her throat to her breasts, dropping to his knees to do the job right.

Sabrina hadn't been prepared for any of this, not in her past experience, not even in her wildest imagination.

Still, she wanted more and pulled him to his feet. She reached for the button of his jeans, tugging until his hand covered hers.

He drew back, but his gaze, intense and smoldering with heat, never left hers. "Are you sure this is what you want?"

"Yes." She'd never been so sure of anything in her life. She wanted *him*. And she wanted *this*.

She grabbed his waistband again, fumbling for the metal button until he stopped her.

"I'll be right back."

Jared crossed the room in two steps, then dug through his carry-on bag until he found his shaving kit. Sure enough, he found two little packets.

He'd promised to take things slow and easy, but it was a promise he wasn't sure that he could keep. Only a fool could have fought the desire he felt for Sabrina.

She'd admitted to being curious about sex, so he was giving her what she wanted. Yet for a moment, he almost felt guilty. As if he were taking something he didn't deserve.

When he'd protected them both, when they were both naked and wanting, he joined her on the bed and lay claim to all she offered him. Her body was damn near perfect, and he stroked her reverently.

"You're so beautiful," he whispered.

She brushed a strand of hair from his brow, her eyes caressing his face. "When you look at me like that, I can almost believe it."

"There's nothing *almost* about it." He brushed his lips across hers, then trailed kisses from her chin to her breasts. He suckled one nipple and then the other, tasting and taunting her until her breath caught in pleasure.

Yet he was every bit as mesmerized by her touch, by her taste, as she was by him. And when they were both aching with need, he hovered over her.

Her hair was splayed on the pillow case, her blue eyes glazed with desire.

"I want to be inside you," he whispered.

She smiled. "I want that, too."

Then she opened for him and placed her hands on his bare hips, guiding him to where he needed to go, where he needed to be.

He thrust into her. Her fingernails gripped his back, as he began the rhythmic motions.

She lifted her hips, taking more of him, and he increased the tempo. Her breathing—his, too—increased, as they moved in unison, taking and giving. She wrapped her legs around his waist, and as she peaked, she cried out, just as his own climax exploded inside of her.

His eyes were shut, but an amazing display of fireworks shot through his mind, lighting up in a burst of beauty and awe.

Their joining had been better than even he had expected, the kind of lovemaking that lasted all through the night.

Too bad there was only one condom left.

Jared and Sabrina had made love twice last night, limited only by the number of condoms they had.

Now, as dawn broke over Las Vegas and peeked through a gap between the blackout shades, Sabrina lay in the comfort of Jared's arms, her back against his chest, her bottom cradled in his lap.

She'd slept the last couple of hours spooned in his embrace—and not bothered in the least by insomnia.

Never had she imagined loving someone would be like this, both the physical aspect, as well as the emotional. And for the first time in her life, she felt as though she'd found a place where she actually belonged—even though, on the outside, this particular place was just a hotel room.

Because on the inside, where it counted most, she belonged in Jared's arms, in his bed.

In his life.

He stirred, then ran a hand along her hip, possessively. Lovingly.

"Are you awake?" he asked.

"Yes." And still basking in all that they'd shared last night.

"I'd meant to ask you this morning if making love met your expectations, but I don't have to ask."

A smug little smile stretched across her lips. "Why is that?"

"I have the scratches on my back to prove that it was better than you dreamed it would be."

"You're right," she admitted. "And if I didn't have to get back to work and to Joey, I'd be tempted to stay right here and order room service for the rest of the week."

"Speaking of room service…" Jared lifted his head and braced himself on an elbow. "I'm going to order something for breakfast."

Thirty minutes later, they'd showered—together. And what a surprising treat that had turned out to be.

When Sabrina had lamented the fact that they didn't have any more protection until one of them made a trip to the gift shop downstairs, Jared taught her ways they could pleasure each other without the risk of pregnancy.

Interestingly enough, having Jared's baby didn't seem like a scary thought. In fact, she wouldn't mind having a little boy or girl with his eyes, his smile.

Not right away, of course. But someday.

A knock sounded.

"I'll get that." Jared pulled one of the hotel-provided white robes out of the closet and slipped it on. Then he handed the other one to her. "It's probably room service with our breakfast."

After combing out her hair, leaving it wet and long, Sabrina slipped on the robe and joined Jared at the table in the room, where he'd set out a lavish spread. She'd heard him ordering but hadn't paid much attention. Now, seeing it all piled on the table, she was a bit overwhelmed. He'd chosen scrambled eggs, bacon, waffles, fresh fruit, muffins, coffee and fresh-squeezed orange juice.

"Wow," she said. "You must be really hungry."

"I'm used to having a hearty breakfast, but since coming to Granny's, I've been eating pretty light."

"Connie isn't a very good cook," Sabrina said. "But she tries hard."

"What do you know about her? I'm still wondering how that money could have disappeared from Granny's account."

"Not much." Sabrina reached for a piece of toast. "She hasn't been at the ranch very long, and she's pretty quiet. But I really don't think she's dishonest."

"Some of the best thieves can be pretty sly."

"The bank is still investigating but had no news the last time I asked." Sabrina picked up a knife and smeared a dab of butter on her toast. "I'll give them another call when we get back to the ranch."

Yesterday afternoon, they'd decided to let Steve Rankin deal with Wayne Templeton and Dazzling Desert Ventures. Steve had promised to keep them informed via phone, fax and e-mail. They'd also lined up a flight to take them back to Texas later today.

"You know," she said, "after we eat, I'm going to call and check on Joey. I'll let them know we'll be home tonight."

Jared dug into a plate of scrambled eggs, piling his fork high. "That reminds me. Now that you and I have gotten to be…friends, I was wondering if you were going to answer a question I asked you earlier."

"What's that?" She speared a strawberry from the bowl of fruit with her fork and popped it into her mouth. Mmm. So sweet.

"Why did your brother leave Joey with you? You told me he had a good reason, but you wouldn't tell me what it was."

At the time, Sabrina hadn't trusted Jared with Carlos's secret. But they'd reached a new level of intimacy, and it seemed natural to answer any questions he had.

Yet a part of her wanted to keep it to herself—out of shame, out of fear. Things were too perfect between her and Jared right now, and she didn't want to risk ruining it.

But she owed him the truth.

She placed a half-eaten piece of toast on her plate, set aside her pride and decided to trust this man with everything. "Carlos is in prison."

In prison?

Jared's fork, which was laden with a scoop of scrambled eggs, hung over his plate. He certainly hadn't expected that answer. "What did he do?"

"He was convicted of assault with a deadly weapon."

Damn. That certainly explained why he was AWOL in Joey's life, but it left Jared feeling uneasy about Sabrina, about her family. And it brought to mind the comment Matt had made. The accusation that bore a ghost of truth.

Apparently, you don't have a cull shoot when it comes to weeding out the good lovers from the bad. Any fool could have seen that Jolene wasn't the kind of woman a man could trust.

Had Jared jumped into another physical relationship before learning the true character of the woman he'd slept with?

Instead of beating himself up with the possibility, he focused on her revelation.

"When did he go to prison?" he asked.

"Shortly after Suzy died."

"What provoked the assault?"

"It's probably best if I explain a few things about Carlos to you first. He was young when Joey was born. Only seventeen. And even though he didn't marry Suzy, like I told you before, he got a job so he could support his son. But he was in a Catch-22. With no education or skills, his options were limited. But about a year ago, he lucked out when a national trucking company hired him. And he was thrilled. The pay was decent, and his employer offered health insurance, which was great for Joey. Neither Carlos nor Suzy had been able to provide extras like that in the past, and fortunately, Joey has always been healthy and doesn't need to see a doctor very often."

Jared didn't know anything about kids or their health issues. But Joey didn't have much meat on his bones, and if he ever did get sick, he might have a hard time fighting it off.

Still, Jared understood the importance of health insurance, but a kid needed a dad, too. His own father had abandoned him, and it had taken him a long time to get over the loss and feelings of rejection. Thank God Clem had come along.

But who did Joey have as a male role model?

Trucking was a respectable job, but Jared couldn't help wondering if there was something else her brother could have done for a living. Something that would have enabled him to stay in town and provide for his son.

There had to have been, which is what Jared's mind shouted loud and clear. So for that reason, he didn't share Sabrina's faith in her brother.

Carlos must have enjoyed the vagabond lifestyle, but Jared didn't argue with her. Instead, he waited for her to continue.

"One night, while at a truck stop in Georgia, Carlos witnessed a couple of the locals fighting with another trucker. So he grabbed a baseball bat he kept under the front seat of his rig for protection and tried to scare them off. Things got out of hand, and one of the men charged him. He struck back, and the man was seriously injured."

"That should have been considered self-defense."

"Like I said, they were locals. And they testified that

the other trucker had stolen a wallet from one of them and suggested that Carlos was part of a tag team that had been hitting various truck stops."

"Was he?"

"My brother hasn't always made the best choices. But he wouldn't have been a part of something like that."

Jared wasn't so sure. And he just couldn't find any sympathy for Carlos or his plight. Things just didn't seem to add up.

"What about the other trucker?" Jared asked. "What happened to him?"

"Unfortunately, the police found the stolen wallet on him, so he's in prison, too."

And Carlos had gone to bat—no pun intended— for a thief.

"One of the locals testified that he'd seen Carlos and the other man together earlier, but that wasn't true."

"How do you know?"

"Carlos told me. He tried to explain that in court, too, but neither the judge nor the jury believed him. Now he's serving time in a Georgia prison. I'm hoping that he'll get out in a year or so, but I also hired a private investigator to uncover proof of the lie. So maybe they'll release him sooner."

Private investigators weren't cheap. No wonder she'd had to quit school and go to work. It hadn't been just the day-care situation.

She took a sip of her orange juice, then shrugged. "So there you have it. Now maybe you can understand why I feel so sorry for him. He's gotten a lot of bad breaks in his life."

Jared couldn't buy that. He'd learned that some people just naturally gravitated to the dark side. Carlos was probably one of them, and Sabrina was making excuses for him, which didn't sit right. Her support for the black sheep in her family could only spell trouble, and his uneasy feelings turned to distrust, reinforcing the walls he'd built around his heart, walls Sabrina had been eroding over the past couple of days.

"So what about us?" she asked. "Where do we go from here?"

Was she thinking that they'd shared something more than great sex?

And if so, *had* they?

He'd thought so earlier—before she mentioned that Carlos was in prison. Before he realized that she was offering her brother blind faith and unconditional support, including the cost of a private investigator.

She'd asked him where they were going from here, and he knew she was talking about their relationship. But he really didn't know.

"We're going back to the ranch," he finally responded, his thoughts scampering as he tried to sort through what they'd done, how he felt.

Sure, he was attracted to her. Hell, he was flat-out enamored with her. But he certainly wasn't in a position to make a commitment to her. Nor did he want to set himself up for more heartbreak, more trouble. He just couldn't. Her family situation and her blind support of her brother was too troubling to ignore, even if she was as naive and as sweet as she seemed.

He'd had that kind of faith in someone, too. The kind that convinced a young boy that his father was coming back for him, even when he'd seen the hard evidence of his old man's drug and alcohol addiction, the paternal neglect. And believing in someone who didn't deserve one's faith or love had been a tough lesson to learn.

Heartbreaking, too.

It was bad enough that Sabrina had fallen for her brother's excuses. But she was encouraging Joey to believe in the man's goodness and love, too.

"And *then* what?" she asked, as though probing for a soft spot. For his Achilles' heel.

He found himself weakening for a moment, part of him wanting to throw caution to the wind and see where fate led them. But his logic and defenses won out. The truth was, he didn't know Sabrina very well. For crying out loud, they'd only met days ago.

Hell, maybe she'd been so desperate for money to aid her brother's release from prison that she had embezzled funds from Granny.

It was possible, wasn't it?

There were too many unknowns. He had to think of Granny first.

His own needs, physical or emotional or otherwise, weren't important. He'd come to Granny's ranch to find the thief and needed to get back on track.

"As soon as I return to the ranch, I'm going to find out who's been stealing from my mother. That's why I came to Brighton Valley. And I won't go home until the money is returned and the thief is in jail."

Sabrina stiffened, and he suspected that she'd sensed he'd morphed from a satisfied lover into a suspicious son, a flip-flop that even left him feeling uneasy, awkward and a bit guilty.

As much as he wanted to believe the best about her and completely rule her out as a suspect, succumbing to temptation had left him even more unsettled, more at odds.

Hell, he couldn't trust himself and his feelings right now, let alone Sabrina. And more than that, he just couldn't lay himself bare to betrayal again.

So in spite of what they'd shared, he reached for a familiar defense mechanism and provoked a fight, wanting to do something—*anything*—that would take the heat off him and end a budding relationship he wasn't ready for.

"It could be anyone at the ranch," he said, his gaze targeting her in spite of the lingering uncertainty his heart still felt.

"Anyone?"

No. Not *you,* he wanted to say.

But he couldn't allow himself to be sucked into her world, into her unstable family situation. And he couldn't risk having his trust shattered again.

"Yes, *anyone,*" he said, his head taking charge of his heart and sending him in for the kill. "Even you."

Chapter Ten

It could be anyone, he'd said.

Even you.

Her pulse pounded in her ears, and her temper simmered below the surface, the heat rising until she thought her cheeks might blister.

He'd used her—for sex. His kindness had all been an act—each word, each smile, each touch. Everything that had led up to them making love last night had been an underhanded trick to get what he'd wanted.

Then came the dawn, and Jared Clayton had gone from nice guy to total jerk in zero to sixty milliseconds.

Sabrina wiped her mouth, although there hadn't been any reason to. Then she stood and dropped the linen napkin onto her plate.

If Jared wondered what she was doing, he didn't ask.

She stooped to pick up her clothes and her sandals from the floor where she'd discarded them last night and carried them into the bathroom.

Moments later, she came out fully dressed. Her hair, still wet from their sexy romp in the shower, hung limp and stringy down her back. Under normal circumstances, she would have put some effort into containing it. But there wasn't anything normal about today.

He looked up. A sheepish expression suggested he was going to say something. Apologize maybe, or explain how she'd misunderstood what he'd said and taken it wrong. Yet he did neither, and it wouldn't have helped if he had. He may not realize just how lucky he was that she wasn't throwing things at him.

She patted the front pocket of her jeans, where she'd slipped her key card after leaving her room last night, before running into Jolene and returning upstairs with Jared.

It must have slipped out. Or had she put it in her purse instead?

After a careful search, she came up empty-handed.

"What's the matter?" he asked.

"I'm locked out of my room."

As she headed for the door that led out of the room, he asked, "Where are you going?"

"To the front desk. I'm going to ask for a new key."

He didn't say anything else, which was just as well. He'd shown his true colors.

Once the door snapped shut behind her, the tears she'd been holding back welled in her eyes, and a sense of betrayal clawed at her throat.

She'd known Jared had a suspicious and distrustful side from the first time she'd heard his voice over the telephone line. The night he'd called the ranch asking for Mrs. Clayton and demanding to know who Sabrina was, he'd been rude, which had set her off. But she could almost understand him doing it then, since she'd been a stranger to him, and he was looking out for his mother.

But not now.

How dare he imply that Sabrina might have taken the money? After all they'd shared?

Okay. So it had only been days that they'd known each other. But shouldn't he have seen her true nature?

Like she'd seen his? a small voice quizzed.

Truthfully, she'd made her own assumptions about his character, yet hadn't seen the real Jared Clayton until moments ago, when he'd knocked her to her knees with his accusation, his distrust.

She stood before the elevators and waited for one to stop at her floor. She needed to escape—and not just from Las Vegas. She wanted to get as far away from Jared as she possibly could.

Her options were sorely limited, though. But she couldn't continue working at the Rocking C. Not when Jared might show up at any time.

Seeing him again would only serve to remind her of how foolish she'd been. How starry-eyed and gullible.

A bell-like gong alerted her to the arrival of an elevator. Once the door opened and she stepped inside, she pushed *L* for lobby.

She was alone, yet she continued to fight back the tears, watching the numbers overhead through a blur.

On the fourteenth floor, the car stopped for a couple in their fifties. They were wearing shorts, polo shirts and visors.

Were they going to breakfast? Or maybe out to play a round of golf?

"Good morning," the woman said, her voice too cheerful for a time like this.

Sabrina nodded, but found it impossible to speak. How could she pretend that it was indeed going to be a beautiful day when everything inside her screamed that there wasn't anything good or beautiful or nice about it?

On the way down, the couple smiled warmly at each other, which suggested that some people actually found love and happiness, when others never did.

Sabrina averted her eyes, no doubt red and watery and laden with grief.

All she'd ever wanted was to be loved and accepted, to find a place where she belonged. And last night, she'd been swept away by passion and had fantasized that she'd finally found all she'd been praying for.

But she'd been wrong. Jared wasn't the answer to the home and stability she'd dreamed of having. Instead, he'd turned on her.

It was her own fault, she supposed. She'd put her trust in a man who would never trust her.

As the door opened, she stepped into the lobby in front of the couple and stole away from their happily-ever-after glow.

She strode to the front desk, where she had to stand in line for an available clerk. It seemed that all of her life had been spent waiting for something, for someone.

And she was tired of it.

When it was finally her turn, she told the desk clerk that she needed a new key to her room, then provided him with proof of her identity.

"How many do you want?" he asked.

"Just one." And she wouldn't need it long. Just long enough to get her things.

Minutes later, she had access to the hotel room. She'd placed her makeup in the bathroom when she'd first arrived. She considered taking a minute to put on a bit of lipstick and mascara, but opted to find time to do it later. Right now, she wanted to throw her clothes back in her bag. Then she wanted to get out of this hotel, out of this city, out of Jared's life.

He could wrap up that real-estate deal without her. And as soon as she returned to the ranch for Joey, she'd tell Mrs. Clayton that she was sorry, but that she would have to quit—effective immediately.

By the time Jared got back to Brighton Valley, Sabrina and Joey would be long gone.

Minutes later, she was back downstairs. And once outside, she didn't wait for the bellman to call her a cab. She flagged it herself, then climbed into the backseat.

"Where to?" a heavyset man asked.

"To the airport."

He glanced at her through the rearview mirror. "Running late? If so, I can take a short cut and try to get you there faster."

Yes, she was late. She should have left yesterday. Before she'd pinned her heart and her faith on the wrong man.

* * *

Jared sat alone in his hotel room, trying to convince himself that he'd done the right thing. That he'd ended a crippled relationship in the same way he would have put down a horse with a broken leg.

Yet he mourned his actions, too, just as he had when he'd been forced to put his first horse out of its misery. Old Red had died quickly and without lingering pain, but Jared had moped around for days. And this was worse.

He ought to be happy Sabrina was in her own room and that he'd regained control and balance over his life.

But that couldn't be further from the truth. Not when the evidence of their lovemaking surrounded him. The scent of sex, the tangled sheets mingled with the faint whisper of her floral perfume, haunted him with a memory he wasn't likely to ever forget.

And right now he felt more alone than he ever had before.

He picked up a strip of bacon and took a bite, then tossed it back on the plate. The food no longer tasted edible, no longer looked appetizing. Instead, he carried his coffee out onto the patio, noting that the day, cloudy and dark, was just as dismal as his mood.

From inside, his cell phone rang, so he placed his cup on the table and went to look for it. He scanned the room until he could figure out where it was.

It was right where he left it, he realized—in his pants pocket. And his clothes were lying in a heap on the floor.

By the time he located the blasted thing, the call had ended. He pushed the send button and recognized Steve's home number.

After redialing, he waited for his friend to answer.

"Steve? It's Jared. I'm sorry I missed your call, but I couldn't find my phone."

"At this time of day, your cell should have been charging all night and in plain sight. Or did you get distracted after dinner by that beautiful, blue-eyed bookkeeper?"

Jared had been distracted, all right, but he wouldn't admit it. Not when he didn't want to be quizzed about what he'd done—or how he'd chosen to end it. So he steered the conversation back where it belonged. "What's up?"

"I know that I suggested you and Sabrina could head back to Texas today and that we could hammer out the details of our counteroffer later, but Wayne Templeton would like to meet with you while you're still in town. Are you available this afternoon?"

Jared and Sabrina had tickets to fly home this evening, but he could ask her to go on by herself. He'd just extend his stay if he had to. "Sure. I can do that."

After agreeing to meet at Steve's office, Jared disconnected the line, then knocked on the door that separated his room from Sabrina's. Maybe she would be happy to head back to Texas without him.

When she didn't answer, he knocked again. Louder. Still, no answer.

Thinking she might be in the bathroom, he waited a couple of minutes, then tried the phone. When she didn't pick up, he realized she might not have returned from the front desk.

Did she have a cell? He didn't think so.

Maybe she was avoiding him, and if that was the case, he really couldn't blame her.

If she hadn't taken the money, she'd be deeply offended by his implication. And if she had, then guilt might keep her away.

But was she *really* a suspect? his heart whispered.

The cell phone rang again, and Jared picked it up. Was it Steve calling back? Had there been a change in plans?

A glance at the display told him it was someone from the ranch. He figured Granny was eager to know how the negotiations were going.

He flipped open the cover. "Hello."

"Jared, this is Tori. I'm looking for Sabrina."

"She's not here. I saw her earlier—at breakfast. And I tried her room a while ago, but she didn't answer. She might have gone down to the casino."

"It's important that I find her right away. Can you please look for her?"

Jared stiffened, every fiber of his being going on alert. "Why?"

"I'm taking Joey to the clinic in Brighton Valley, but I have a feeling they'll be sending him to a hospital in Houston."

Jared's gut clenched. Had Joey been injured? Had he gotten kicked or stepped on by Smokey?

There were a million things that could happen if someone hadn't been looking out for the kid.

"What's wrong?" he asked.

"His lips have a bluish tinge, which could mean that he's not getting enough oxygen."

Jared raked a hand through his hair. He remembered the kid trying to catch his breath the day they'd left for Vegas.

"I'm not sure what's going on," Tori said, "but it could mean there's a lung or heart problem."

Heart? Sabrina had said his mother had an undiagnosed heart problem. Was it something genetic?

"You go ahead and take him to the clinic," Jared told her. "And let the doctor know that his mother died from a heart attack when she was in her early twenties."

Tori asked for details Jared couldn't provide.

"You'll have to talk to Sabrina about that," he said. "I'll try to find her as soon as possible. Won't you need her permission for him to be treated?"

"Not if the condition is life-threatening."

"Is it?"

"I don't know. But I'll keep you posted."

"Please do." He hung up long enough to call Steve and tell him there was a change in plans.

"Sabrina and I are heading home as soon as possible," he told his friend. Deal or no deal.

When Steve promised to pass along the message to the prospective buyers, Jared hung up the phone, then banged on the door to Sabrina's room again.

Still, no response.

He picked up the phone and called the front desk. Maybe she was still there.

What time was checkout? He glanced at the clock on the bureau. 9:07 a.m. There shouldn't be a line this early. What was keeping her?

"Front desk," a man answered.

"This is Jared Clayton in room 2314. Sabrina Gonzalaz is in room 2316 and went downstairs to get another key to her room, but she hasn't returned yet. Can you let me know if she's still waiting?"

The man put Jared on hold. When he came back on

the line, he said, "I'm sorry, Mr. Clayton. Ms. Gonzalez has already checked out."

Jared's pulse seemed to fade away, and a cold, clammy chill began at his head and shimmied to his knees. "How long ago was that? Is she still in the hotel?"

"I'm not sure, sir. She had a bag with her, but I have no idea where she went from here."

His heart sank to his gut. "I need to check out, too," he told the clerk. "Use the credit card I have on file and mail the receipt. I'll leave my key in the room."

Jared dressed quickly and threw his belongings into his bag.

Where had she gone?

To another hotel?

Not likely.

To the airport? Hoping to get an earlier flight out? That was his best and only guess.

Fear twisted a knot in his chest, as he hurried out of the hotel and hailed a cab.

He had to find her before she got on board an airplane. If she headed to the ranch instead of to the medical center, where Tori said they would most likely be sent, it would take hours longer for her to get to Joey's side.

A kid needed his mother at a time like this.

And Sabrina was the closet thing Joey had to one.

"Attention please," a crackly voice called through an airport paging system. "Sabrina Gonzalez, please pick up the white courtesy phone."

Sabrina sat up straight and keened her ears. It sounded

as though her name had been announced, but she wasn't sure if she'd heard correctly. Then the message repeated, and she realized someone was looking for her.

She'd told two different airline representatives that she'd like to go standby on their next flights to Houston. Maybe one of them had found her a seat.

Hopeful, she scanned the gate area until she spotted a white, wall-mounted phone.

There was one. By the ladies' restroom.

She hurried to answer the page. "This is Sabrina Gonzalez. I was asked to call."

"Yes," a male voice said. "Ma'am, there's a gentleman in the airport looking for you. He says his name is Jared Clayton, and that it's an emergency."

Jared had come to the airport looking for her?

Was he feeling remorse about the things he'd said, the implications he made? Was he having second thoughts?

Maybe he figured that his apology qualified as an emergency, but she didn't. Not that she wouldn't want to hear what he had to say.

She supposed it wouldn't hurt to give him a moment or two of her time, but that wasn't going to change anything. She wasn't staying in Las Vegas one moment longer than she had to. And she would even leave Brighton Valley as soon as she could pull it off.

Sabrina clutched the receiver until her knuckles ached, reluctant to make this easy for him, yet wanting to get it over with so she could be on her way. "Tell him I'm sitting between gates C-three and C-four."

She hung up the phone and returned to her seat. She doubted there was much Jared would be able to tell her that would make any difference. He'd shown her what kind of man he was. And when it came to seeking a mate, she was looking for so much more than that.

A glance at her wristwatch told her she might want to check again with the customer-service rep at Wild Blue Air. He'd been working behind the desk at gate three had had suggested that she check back with him about the availability of seats on Flight 419. Apparently, there'd been a delay in San Francisco, and it didn't look as though some of the passengers would make their Las Vegas connection to Houston.

She stood, and just as she reached for her bag, she noticed Jared striding toward her. Not wanting to give him the satisfaction of thinking she was waiting with bated breath to talk to him, she looked the other way, focused on the planes that were parked at the gates.

Yet curiosity got the better of her, and she stole another peek.

His hair was tousled as though he'd left the hotel in a rush.

Is that because he was eager to apologize and set things right?

The closer he got to where she stood, the clearer she was able to see his expression—intense, determined…

Maybe she'd been wrong. Maybe what he had to say might matter after all—at least a little. Still, it wouldn't be easy to forgive him for not trusting her.

Yet as he drew near, she realized the expression he wore was more than remorse.

It was grief. And…fear?

As much as she wanted to turn her back, to avert her gaze again, she knew something was wrong.

Terribly wrong.

"Tori called," he said.

She tightened her grip on her bag, her heart pounding as though it might burst. "Did something happen to Joey?"

"Yes. Tori thinks there could be a problem with his heart or lungs. And she's taking him to see Doc Graham in Brighton Valley."

Ringing and buzzing swirled in her ears as she tried to sort through what he was telling her. "Why didn't she call me?"

"Did you bring your cell phone with you?"

"Yes."

"Then it must be turned off. I tried to call you, too." He handed her his. "Her number is the top one, so just hit Send twice."

She did as he instructed, but got no answer. Rather than push End, she waited long enough to leave a voice mail message. "Tori, it's Sabrina. Jared found me. I'm at the airport already and heading home. Please call me as soon as you can. I'm worried sick."

"Try the ranch," Jared suggested.

When she did, Connie answered.

"What happened?" Sabrina asked. "What's going on?"

"Earlier this morning, Joey was out in the barn. Apparently, one of the cats had a litter of kittens. He was so excited, he hurried in to tell Tori and me. But when he got inside the house, he could hardly breathe. And Tori immediately sensed something was wrong."

"Did she say what?"

"No. She didn't want to scare him and make it worse." Connie blew out a sigh. "You can't believe how good she was with him, soothing him and calming him down. Anyway, she and Granny took him to see Doc Graham. She thinks it might be his heart."

"His *heart?*" Sabrina could almost feel the color leave her face. "Oh, my God. No."

"I haven't heard anything more, but Tori wanted me to give you her cell number in case you called in."

"Thanks, I have it. And moments ago, I tried to call her, but she didn't answer."

"Maybe they're in with the doctor."

That was certainly possible. She remembered that there'd been signs posted at the hospital where Suzy had been taken. The use of cell phones was prohibited in some places because it interfered with the medical equipment.

"If Tori calls you," Sabrina said, "will you please tell her that I'm trying to get a flight home as quickly as possible. All she needs to do is let me know where to meet her."

"I'll sit by the phone," Connie said.

Sabrina disconnected the line, then handed the cell back to Jared.

He took it, slipping it onto a clip on his belt, then slid an arm around her. "I'm sorry, Sabrina."

About *what?* His ploy to wangle a sexual romp? His distrust?

Or was that all water under the bridge? Was he trying to pretend that none of it had happened and that the two of them had somehow become good friends? That he actually cared about her and about Joey's health?

"What can I do to help?" he asked.

Nothing, she wanted to say. *Not a damn thing. Just*

leave me alone. Let me stand on my own two feet and take care of my nephew.

But she'd never been one to play tit for tat.

"If you had a hotline to God, that might help. If you had a medical degree… If…" A tear slipped down her cheek, and she swiped it away.

"I can't imagine how tough this is for you."

He was right; he couldn't.

"I don't want you to have to go through this alone," he added.

What was he saying? What was he offering?

He hadn't even apologized for believing the worst about her, so if she accepted his support, how long would it last?

"The only one who would be of any help right now is my brother," she said, a bit of a snap to her tone. "And unless you can spring him from prison, then I'm going to have to face this on my own."

"Where is he?" Jared asked, as though her response hadn't been spoken with an ounce of sarcasm, anger or frustration.

"Grayson State Prison. It's in Georgia."

Jared reached for his cell and dialed a number. When the line connected, he introduced himself and asked to speak to Steve Rankin. Moments later, his friend apparently answered.

"I need to talk to a good criminal-defense attorney," Jared said. "Do you have someone you can refer me to?"

Sabrina couldn't hear what Steve was saying on the other line, but she listened to Jared's side of the conversation.

"I didn't do anything," he said. "And no, that's not why I cancelled today's meeting. The referral isn't for me. Sabrina's brother, Carlos Gonzalez, got into some trouble a while back and is incarcerated in Georgia. His young son may be seriously ill, and I want to see if there's anything that can be done to get him some kind of furlough—if the boy's condition turns out to be life-threatening."

When Jared disconnected the line, he turned to Sabrina. "Steve is going to make a few calls and then get back to me."

She didn't dare put any hope into Jared's attempt to help. But she did appreciate the thought and thanked him.

"You're welcome. Have you managed to get an earlier flight home?"

"I'm still working on it." She glanced at her watch, seeing that it was time for her to check in with the airline again. "I put in several requests. And there's a possibility I can catch the eleven-o'clock flight out on Wild Blue. The man I spoke to thought he might be able to give me a better answer after ten o'clock."

"I'll see if they can find a seat for me on that flight, too."

Sabrina wanted to tell him not to bother, to go ahead and stay in Vegas for whatever meeting he'd scheduled, but she didn't care what he did.

Not anymore.

As she turned to make her way to the desk, Jared followed behind.

She supposed he was just trying to be supportive, but at this point, she didn't care. Last night, she'd thought she'd fallen in love with him, but this morning she'd learned the man she'd once believed him to be didn't exist. And when he'd implied she was a thief, she'd lost whatever trust she'd placed in him.

When it was her turn at the counter, she addressed the airline representative. "Is there an update on my request for a seat on flight 417?"

"You're in luck," the man said.

She hoped so. Lately, it seemed that the cards had been stacked against her.

Chapter Eleven

Just before boarding the plane, Jared's cell phone rang. Sabrina waited long enough to realize it wasn't Tori, then proceeded through the gate.

While she followed the other passengers, she again tried to call Tori, using the number Connie had given her. Once the flight was underway, she wouldn't be able to use her cell.

This time, thank goodness, the call was answered. The background noise at the airport made it difficult to hear, though, so Sabrina covered one ear with her hand and pressed the phone tightly against the other. "Hi, Tori. It's me, Sabrina. What's going on? I've been trying to reach you."

"I'm sorry. We were in the clinic, and I had to turn off my phone."

"How's Joey?" Sabrina asked.

"He's doing okay. He's a great kid."

She blew out the breath she'd been holding and whispered a silent prayer of thanks—short and to the point. "So he'll be all right?"

"Joey's sitting next to me. I'll let you talk to him in a minute. But we're on our way to Houston to visit a friend of Doc's. His name is Dr. Pantera, and he's a cardiologist. In fact, Doc is making the arrangements for us, so all we have to do is walk right in and tell the other doctor that we're there to see him."

It didn't take Sabrina long to realize that Tori was being cryptic on purpose, that she was trying not to frighten Joey. "Is his condition serious then?"

"Yes."

Every cell in Sabrina's body seemed to implode, and it was all she could do to gather her wits and try to make sense of the news.

"How did you pick up on the problem?" she asked.

Tori didn't respond.

"Oh," Sabrina said, "you can't really tell me right now, can you?"

"No, I'd rather not." Tori cleared her throat, then her tone suddenly grew chipper, worry-free. "And do you know what? Granny told us we'd really like Doc Graham, and she was right. He's the nicest doctor I've ever met. And you may not know this, but I used to be a nurse."

"So because of your medical background, you picked up on something I missed?"

"Yes. And before I pass the phone on to Joey, I was hoping you might be able to fill me in on his medical history."

"You mean, the condition that led to his mother's death?"

"Exactly."

"I don't have all the particulars, but her doctor's name was Jaime Ramirez. He has an office on West-heimer. The cardiologist should be able to get the information needed."

"Great. I'll take it from there. We'll be in Houston before you know it."

"I'm headed that way, too."

"Call me as soon as you land. Now, if you'll hold on a second, I'll pass the phone to Joey."

When Joey's voice answered, Sabrina tried to duplicate the same upbeat, nothing-to-be-worried-about tone that Tori had been using. "Hey, buddy. Have you missed me?"

"Uh-huh."

She paused, trying to think of something to say. Something normal. Something that would hide her panic, her aching heart. "Connie told me that one of the barn cats had kittens."

"Yeah. And you should see them, Sabrina. They're really cute."

"Why don't I ask Granny if she'll let us have one."

"Really? No kidding?" Just the enthusiasm in his voice seemed to make him breathe a little harder. Why hadn't she noticed before?

Or was his condition worsening?

She feigned a happy tone, all the while battling tears. "Sure, I'd love to have a cat. They're small and easy to care for. And we'd never have to worry about mice. I probably haven't told you how much I hate those little critters."

"I love the ranch," he said. "First I get to take care

of a horse, and now I get to have my very own kitten. I think I'll pick the little black-and-white one. He's the littlest one, but he's so cute."

"Great." Sabrina cleared the wobbly word from her throat. "Can I please talk to Tori again?"

"Okay."

Moments later, when Tori was back on the line, Sabrina asked, "I'm sure Doc looked at Joey as a favor to Granny. But will the cardiologist treat him without my consent?"

"I'm sure he'll want it—even if it's just a verbal okay since you're en route. But there are times when they don't have to follow protocol."

"You mean, when it's considered a serious emergency?"

"Yes, if it's…extreme."

"Are you trying to say that my consent won't be necessary if this is life-threatening?"

"Yes, but I'm not sure if that's really the case. At least not right now."

Sabrina gripped the cell phone as though that somehow gave her a better handle on all that was happening, on all that could go wrong. "Then you don't think Joey's condition constitutes an imminent emergency?"

"I'm not sure. There are other…modes of transportation, and Doc didn't suggest one."

Like an ambulance? Or a Life Flight helicopter?

"Why don't you call the cardiologist?"

Tori must have passed the phone to Granny, because the older woman asked, "Are you ready? I'll give you the number."

Sabrina tried to talk herself out of crying as she dug

through her purse for a pen and a scrap of paper. "Yes. Go ahead." As soon as Sabrina had the number, she disconnected the line, then dialed Dr. Oliver Pantera's office before the flight attendants could tell her to turn off the cell.

She explained who she was and provided the necessary information regarding Joey's medical insurance. Thank God she'd gone with her gut feelings and made the COBRA payments to continue Joey's coverage after Carlos was incarcerated and lost his job. It had been an expense she hadn't really been able to afford, but it appeared to have been a wise decision now.

Jared, who'd waited in the gate area to finish his own call, was now sliding into the seat beside her. "What did Tori say?"

"Not as much as I would have liked her to. With Joey sitting next to her, it was hard for her to go into any real detail. But it's serious. Dr. Graham sent them to a specialist in Houston."

He reached for her hand, and she threaded her fingers through his before realizing she hadn't wanted his solace or even his presence. Yet something deep inside her craved it anyway.

"Tori seems to know quite a bit about illness and injuries," Jared said.

"She used to be a nurse."

"But not any longer?"

"Apparently not."

"Why is that?"

The anger and heartache Sabrina had been harboring, as well as fear about what was happening to Joey, came crashing down upon her, and what little control she'd mustered over the past hour dissipated. She turned to him and snapped. "Dammit, Jared. Just let it go, will you? For *now?*"

He gave her hand a gentle squeeze, warming it and providing a moment of comfort. "I didn't mean to upset you. I was just curious, that's all."

She unlocked her fingers and pulled her hand away. "Just because you don't know anything about a person doesn't mean they're a criminal or worse. Tori has been very nice to me, very accepting. And she's been good to Joey, too. I don't care what her story is. Nor do I give a rip if she has a motive to steal. She's shown her true colors to me—just as *you* have."

Jared didn't say a word in his defense, although Sabrina wasn't sure if that was to his credit or not. But the words had been said, tossed down like a gauntlet.

Neither one of them picked it up, though, which was fortunate. Sabrina really wasn't up for a fight.

Not until she found out what she was up against in Houston.

Jared was in one hell of a fix. And to be honest, at least with himself, he was also running scared.

Of course, at thirty thousand feet above the ground, he wasn't going anywhere too quick.

Seeing Sabrina worried and hurting caused something inside him to melt, to collapse.

His pride, maybe? His fear of making the same mistake twice?

Either way, she sure had him walking a fine line. Part of him wanted to skedaddle, while the other was determined to stick by her side.

The fact that they'd made love last night had sure complicated things and probably contributed to that "should I stay or should I go?" dilemma he was facing now.

Then again, that really wasn't a decision he was free to make. Not after he'd had that knee-jerk reaction to her question about where their relationship was heading.

All right, in retrospect he wasn't entirely sure that he'd made the right decision to end things this morning. But at this point, he wasn't ready to do anything differently.

They really hadn't known each other very long—just a few days. And he'd yet to decide if he could trust her. Then, when she mentioned her brother being in prison, he'd panicked and decided to cut bait and run.

So what was he doing here with her now, when he had every excuse to remain in Vegas for a business meeting?

He was just trying to…

Well, he didn't actually know what he was attempting to do. Supporting her through Joey's illness, he supposed.

And maybe, at the same time, appeasing his conscience for not being a more considerate lover, at least after they'd climbed out of the shower, bright-eyed and sexually sated.

He'd said he was sorry, though. But he hadn't been clear about what. And he still wasn't sure.

Apologies had never come easy for him. And while he really didn't believe that Sabrina could have taken money from Granny, he wasn't ready to backpedal or try and reverse the direction their relationship had gone.

Damn. The woman had him straddling fences.

But he *would* stick by her for a while. At least until

she got back to Houston and faced whatever it was that Joey was going through.

He figured that was the least he could do.

In spite of all he tried to tell himself, he *did* have feelings for her. And he certainly could understand why she'd been upset with him about what he'd said earlier, about what he'd implied.

For that reason, he'd decided to leave her alone, keep quiet and let her cool off. Maybe she would come to the conclusion that Jared wasn't a jerk, even if he might have behaved like one earlier today.

The flight had been airborne for nearly two hours, when he finally decided that she'd had enough time to cool down, that they could talk without her wanting to bite his head off, although he really couldn't blame her if she did so again. His comments and implied accusation had certainly doused the embers of a warm afterglow following a night of lovemaking he would never forget.

So, hoping to make things right, he tapped her arm with his. "I meant to tell you earlier, but it slipped my mind."

"What's that?"

"Right before boarding, I talked to Darrell Schwartz, one of Steve's colleagues. I told him about Carlos, and he's going to research the case and see if there's anything he can do to get him out of prison, if there's any reason to appeal. And if you'll give me the name and number of the private investigator you hired, I'll pass it on to him. He's also going to contact your brother's attorney in Georgia, so he'll need that information, too."

"Why…?" Her brow furrowed. "I mean, I appreciate your help, but why would you do that?"

Because he owed it to her?

Because he wanted to help in any way he could?

Because he'd come to care for her?

He didn't want that to be true, but he was afraid she might have sucked him into something that he was help-less to fight off, something he was too afraid to think about, let alone admit.

Instead, he said, "I'd like to be your friend. And I want to help you because your brother means a lot to you."

Apparently, she bought his explanation because she reached into her purse, pulled out the P.I.'s business card and handed it to him. "I can't help with the attorney, though. Carlos used a public defender, and I'm not sure who he was."

"I'm sure Darrell has a way of finding out."

She nodded, then bit down on her bottom lip and snared him with those pretty blue eyes. "Do you think he'd be able to get a message to Carlos faster than I can?"

"Let's wait to hear what the cardiologist says first." Jared hadn't meant to imply the two of them were any kind of team. But the suggestive pronoun had rolled off his tongue anyway—just as if they hadn't ended things.

"You're right," she said, skipping right over the "*we.*" "I really don't want to cause Carlos any undue worry. He's been through so much in his life already."

"You've mentioned that more than once," Jared said. "Are you talking about Suzy's death, as well as the as-sault charges and the prison term?"

Or had there been more to it than that, as she'd implied?

Jared wasn't sure why he'd quizzed her about it, why he'd even broached the subject of her brother when she seemed to be so touchy about the guy. But a part of him wondered if maybe she'd been right. Maybe there were things Jared didn't know, things that would make him understand and sympathize—as unlikely as that seemed.

"Carlos is a great guy, and if you met him, I think you'd like him. But he had a tough childhood and more than his share of struggles."

"I imagine you both did."

She picked up the glass of diet soda one of the flight attendants had passed out earlier and took a sip. "My brother's problems were a lot worse than mine. He'd had some health issues growing up, as well as attention deficit disorder. No one understood all that entailed, so it seemed as though he was always getting into trouble for one thing or another. And most of the time it hadn't been his fault. At least, not intentionally."

Jared didn't say anything. He just let her talk, realizing how much he'd missed the soft lilt of her voice, especially when it wasn't marred by the snappy tone she'd been tossing his way ever since he'd implied she was a suspect in the theft of Granny's money.

That possibility, he now realized, seemed more and more unlikely with each passing minute.

"Carlos also had learning disabilities as a kid, so schoolwork was a real struggle for him. Then, on top of that, because we had to move so many times, he and I changed schools a lot, too. The poor kid never could seem to get caught up in class. I remember him crying and begging my mom to let him stay home. And a lot of times she'd give in and let him, just to make it easier on her and whomever we were living with at the time."

"What about you?" Jared asked. "Did you hate school, too?"

"No, I enjoyed getting out of the house. And the work was easy for me. The constant moving was tough, though. But I guess I was more adaptable than my brother."

"Did that affect your relationship with him?"

"In what way?"

"I figure it might have been tough for a guy to compete academically with a bright sister who was able to roll with the punches and who kept bouncing back."

She shook her head. "I don't think so. I never detected any jealousy or resentment. Carlos and I were very close growing up. We looked out for each other. We really had to. No one else paid much attention to us or our needs. In fact, we weren't rewarded for good grades or punished for not doing well in school. It just didn't seem to matter. Everyone was too busy living their own lives." She glanced out the window, her gaze searching the fields below that spread out like a giant patchwork quilt.

"So when Carlos had to drop out of high school to support Suzy and the baby," Jared said, still trying to get a grip on Sabrina's family history, "I imagine he was probably glad to have a reason to quit."

"Yes, in some ways. But he knew the lack of education would always hold him back, too. He never could seem to find a job that paid more than minimum wage. And what made it worse was that he could barely read. Whenever I tried to tutor him, he'd get really frustrated. But never more than when he turned eighteen and tried to take his driving test. The poor guy failed time and again."

"How'd he become a trucker?"

"A couple of years ago, I learned that the Department of Public Safety had a program for disabled people that provided alternate testing methods. In my brother's case, he was allowed to have someone read the questions to him. And that time he made a perfect score."

No wonder she was so sympathetic toward her twin. They'd become a team growing up, parenting each other and becoming a family in and of themselves.

At least, that's the way it seemed to Jared, now that he understood what their lives had been like.

"Carlos would do anything for me," Sabrina added. "And I hate not being able to help him right now."

"You're watching Joey for him while he's in prison."

"Yes, but I would have done that anyway. Joey's a sweet little boy, and I love him." She grew silent for a moment, then added, "By the way, Carlos told me that he enrolled in a prison-sponsored literacy program. He said that he was finally catching on and making some progress. He even mentioned the possibility of getting a GED."

"That's good." But it didn't solve her brother's immediate problem: Joey's heart condition could be very serious.

Sabrina looked out the window again, this time closing her eyes.

"Are you okay?" Jared asked.

She turned, her gaze wistful and teary. "I have to be. That child needs me."

It was true. And Jared realized she intended to be there for the boy through thick and thin. Just as she'd always been for her brother.

His stubborn heart quivered and threatened to

melt, which was too damn bad. Sabrina might never forgive him for what he'd said to her in the hotel room this morning.

And if she didn't Jared could suffer his biggest loss yet.

The moment the plane touched down, Sabrina turned on her cell and called Tori for an update.

The onetime nurse answered on the third ring.

"Hey," Sabrina said, as she walked out of the plane and into a hallway that led to the airport. "We're in Houston now. What's going on?"

"They've taken Joey in for an echocardiogram."

"What's that?"

"It's a test in which an ultrasound is used to examine the heart. It allows the doctor to see a cross-sectional slice while it's beating. They'll be able to check out the chambers, valves and major vessels to see what's going on inside and to determine the best way to treat it."

"And what, exactly, *is* the problem?" Sabrina asked, glad that Tori was away from Joey and could explain and answer all the questions she'd been having.

"When we took Joey into Brighton Valley, Doc picked up a serious heart murmur, which is why he sent us to Houston to see Dr. Pantera. And, of course, Doc was right."

Tori had been the first one to pick up on the problem, and Sabrina realized she hadn't taken any credit for that. She would thank her in person, of course, but right now, she was still trying to understand all she could about Joey's ailment.

"Is this something that just developed?" Sabrina asked. "I don't remember him ever having trouble breathing before. And he never complained about anything feeling weird or hurting."

"Dr. Pantera explained that children with Joey's condition are usually in normal health and don't have any symptoms at all, other than a heart murmur. But in Joey's case, there's a serious obstruction to the blood flow between the left ventricle and the aorta. And while rare, there are documented cases where it was the cause of sudden death during strenuous sports activities."

Like his mother's heart attack while jogging.

"Suzy never mentioned him having a heart murmur," Sabrina said. "Or any health problems at all."

"It's possible that the condition worsened over time. When was his last physical?"

"I have no idea. I'm not even sure who his pediatrician was. Or if he even had one." Sabrina grimaced, hoping she hadn't neglected to do something that could have prevented this. She'd scrimped and gone without so that she could pay for his insurance benefits, but hadn't taken him in for an exam. Of course, she'd only had him a few months....

"The tests they're running will tell Dr. Pantera exactly what's going on and how he can treat it."

Jared, who was walking beside her now, slid an arm around her and guided her through the airport, following the throng of people heading for baggage claim and on to their destination. And as much as she wanted to lean into him, to accept his strength and his presence, she knew better than to depend on him for anything at all.

She and Joey were in this alone.

"So it's correctable?" Sabrina asked, holding her breath.

"Hopefully. We'll know more after they finish running all the tests."

"Okay." Sabrina blew out a sigh. "I'll get to the hospital as soon as I can. We only have carry-on luggage, so it won't be long. Where can I find you?"

"We're in a waiting room near the cardiac wing."

Sabrina thanked her, then disconnected the line. Maybe she wasn't all alone after all. Tori had been a godsend, and so had Granny.

She glanced at Jared, who'd now ushered her outside and toward the parking garage.

"Do you mind giving me a ride to the hospital?" she asked.

He looked at her as though she had a giant cuckoo bird perched on her head. "Of course, I don't mind. And I'm going with you. I plan to stay until we find out what's wrong with Joey."

We?

She knew better than to read anything into his statement. He had, after all, grown close to the boy, going so far as to give him a horseback ride around the ranch and promising to give him lessons when they returned from Las Vegas.

But Joey wouldn't be getting any lessons anytime soon.

And Sabrina and Jared were a long way from becoming a "we."

Chapter Twelve

Just before four o'clock, Sabrina entered Whitman Memorial Hospital with Jared at her side. He seemed to know just where he was going, and she let him lead the way.

As he took her past the information desk and straight to the elevators, she finally asked, "Have you been here before?"

"Yes. Hank Priestly, my foster dad, stayed here a couple of times before he died. Wanda used to bring me and their kids to visit, and sometimes I'd feel like a fifth wheel. So I'd say I had to find a bathroom, then I'd slip out and roam the halls, checking out the place."

She tried to think of Jared as a young boy, as a kid who hadn't quite fit in—just as she hadn't when she'd been a girl.

"I know you're in a hurry to see Joey," he said, "but if you'd like a tour later, there's a pretty cool broom closet I can show you on the fifth floor and a stairwell on the sixth that has a great echo. All you have to do is say the word."

She glanced up at him, and even though they continued on their way at the same pace, their gazes locked and something warm and fluid passed between them. She ought to hate him, to etch his distrust in stone on her mind, but during Joey's crisis, she appreciated his presence, his attempt at support.

He tossed her a boyish smile that turned her heart on end, and she realized he wasn't really offering her a tour; he was just trying to lighten things up, to make her feel better.

"It sounds like a fabulous adventure," she told him, "so I'll keep it in mind."

He escorted her to the elevator, and when the doors slid open, they stepped inside. Then he pushed the button that would take them to the second floor.

His musky scent, fading as the day wore on, permeated the air she breathed, causing her to want to take another whiff, to lean against him and absorb some of his strength. But she couldn't trust him to offer that support forever. And that was that kind of loyalty and commitment she would require from him.

Ever since learning of Joey's medical condition, he'd been especially thoughtful. Yet she realized his kindness was merely an outpouring of concern for the child he'd grown to care for. It had nothing to do with her, with *them*.

Still, as much as she wanted to remain at odds with the rugged rancher, that was growing more and more difficult to do with each passing moment.

Falling out of love with him, she feared, wasn't nearly as easy as falling in love had been.

The door opened, and they took a left, following the corridor.

"You really do know your way around this place," she said.

"Yep. It seems like only yesterday when I was a twelve-year-old explorer trying to avoid adult detection." He tossed her another heart-thumping, boyish grin. "But since we haven't reached our destination yet, I'd better not gloat."

Their soles clicked along the squeaky-clean linoleum until he slowed in front of a waiting area just off the cardiac unit. The small room with pale blue walls and connecting brown tweed chairs was nearly empty, except for a middle-aged couple and Sabrina's silver-haired employer.

Mrs. Clayton stood as they entered, then offered Sabrina a warm embrace. "How are you holding up, dear?"

"All right." Thanks in part to Jared, she ought to add, but she wasn't ready to admit it. "How's Joey doing?"

"He's fine. And not the least bit worried. Everyone's been very nice to him, especially Tori."

"She used to be a nurse," Sabrina added, as though it all made perfect sense.

"Yes, I know."

Mrs. Clayton didn't explain, and Sabrina didn't question her. Interestingly enough, Jared didn't jump on that tidbit of information, either, like he'd done on the plane. Maybe he was afraid she'd snap at him again.

Should she credit him for that?

Maybe, but there still hadn't been an apology or any remorse.

"Tori's with Joey now," Mrs. Clayton said. "I thought it would be best if I waited here until you two arrived."

Good. Sabrina didn't want Joey to be alone or scared.

Granny arched her back and stretched, as though trying to work out a crick. "You know, Tori is going to make a wonderful wife and mother someday."

"I'm sure you're right," Sabrina said. "I really appreciate her taking such a personal interest in Joey. In fact, you've both been wonderful. I don't know how to thank you."

"There's no need for that. Joey is a precious little boy, and I can't imagine being anywhere else." Mrs. Clayton again took her seat. "From what I understand, they've run all the necessary tests. And we're just waiting for the cardiologist to come in. Doc says he's tops in his field."

"Maybe I should find Joey and let him know that I'm here now."

"That's a good idea," Mrs. Clayton said.

But before Sabrina could make a move, a man in a white lab coat poked his head into the room. "Ms. Gonzalez?"

Sabrina stiffened and turned to face him. "Yes?"

"I'm Dr. Pantera."

She joined him instantly.

The doctor, a slight man with dark hair and compelling brown eyes, reached out to shake hands and introduced himself as the cardiologist. "Joey has a condition that causes obstruction to the blood flow between the left ventricle and the aorta."

"It sounds serious."

"Yes, it can be. I talked to Dr. Ramirez, the attending physician who treated his mother in the E.R. before her death, and it appears that the condition is genetic. I realize you've just become Joey's guardian, but I suspect he hasn't been seeing a doctor for regular checkups. If he had, the heart murmur would have been picked up during a routine physical. It's the kind of murmur that would have been followed up on, even by someone who wasn't a cardiac specialist."

Sabrina couldn't remember Suzy mentioning anything about Joey having a pediatrician, just that it had been a blessing that he'd been exceptionally healthy.

"Will he need open-heart surgery?" she asked, her stomach clenching at the thought.

"No. We should be able to do a balloon dilation through cardiac catheterization."

"Is that dangerous?"

Dr. Pantera placed a hand on Sabrina's shoulder. "There's always some risk, and I know how frightening all of this is to parents and guardians. But we've made tremendous strides in these treatments over the years. Sometimes we do them as an outpatient procedure, although I'd like to keep Joey overnight, just as a precaution."

Knowing he wouldn't have to stay in the hospital for days made her feel slightly better. "And the procedure will correct the problem? Permanently?"

"Well, it won't correct the valve itself, which sometimes needs to be replaced with a donor valve or an artificial model. But it does decrease the obstruction from severe to mild in a large majority of the patients."

"When will you do it?"

"Actually, we may be able to do it later tonight. I'll let you know for sure in a few minutes. In the meantime, you can see Joey now. He's been asking about you."

"Can I come, too?" Jared asked.

"Certainly." Dr. Pantera led them into the cardiac unit, along with Mrs. Clayton, then asked a nurse to take them to Joey's room, where he lay in bed, the TV set on the Discovery Channel, the volume turned down low.

Tori, who'd been seated in a rocker near the boy's bed, stood when they entered.

"Hey," Sabrina said, as she approached Joey. "I leave for one day, and look at you lounging around and reaping all kinds of attention."

Joey grinned. "Cool, huh? And this bed goes up and down. All I have to do is push this button."

"That's pretty fancy," Sabrina said.

"I told Granny that you said we could have the little black-and-white kitten," Joey said.

Sabrina was about to remind him that he shouldn't refer to her employer as Granny, but decided to let it ride. They had been through a lot today, and the formality no longer seemed all that important.

Joey, who'd been resting his back against the raised mattress, shot up straight and looked at the elderly woman. "And if it's okay with Sabrina, I can have the little orange one, too. Right?"

"As far as I'm concerned," Granny said, "you can have the entire litter as soon as you get out of here."

"Oh, no," Sabrina said. "One little cat will do."

"But with two, they won't get lonely," Joey countered. "And they can catch more mice."

"What a deal." Jared chuckled. "I can tell you from experience that you don't want to be within ten feet of your aunt Sabrina when she sees a rat or a mouse. You'll be holding your ears while laughing your head off."

"Hey!" Sabrina bumped his arm with hers, as though she didn't want to be the butt of a male joke. But in reality, she was happy to see Joey smiling, to know that— God willing—he would pull through and not suffer the same fate his mother had.

Dr. Pantera entered the room. "Well, we're in luck. I've got things lined up, and we can take Joey in for the procedure shortly."

It all seemed to go quickly, although Sabrina suspected it was more like an hour or so. Someone from pediatrics came in with a puppet and explained things to Joey in a way that made him feel comfortable with what was about to happen.

"When it's all over," Jared said, "and I get a chance to talk to Dr. Pantera, I'll ask him about those horseback-riding lessons I'm going to give you and find out how soon we can start them."

Joey grinned. "Cool."

Sabrina had yet to tell anyone she planned to quit working for Granny, that she and Joey would be moving, but she supposed that would have to wait until Joey had recovered.

And until he'd received at least one riding lesson. She suspected he'd never forgive her if she put the kibosh on that.

After they wheeled Joey out of the room, Tori suggested they head to the cafeteria for a bite, and Jared, of course, led the way.

Even though Sabrina hadn't eaten anything since breakfast, she didn't have much of an appetite.

She was too worried about Joey and how he would fare.

Once in line at the cafeteria, Jared followed Sabrina, noticing that while she looked at each selection, she neglected to put anything on her tray.

"What's the matter?" he asked. "You've got to be hungry."

"I know, but at the same time, nothing really looks that good to me."

Jared picked up a bowl of fruit and placed it on her tray. "Try this." Then he stopped by the sandwiches. "Turkey, beef or ham?"

"Will you split it with me?" she asked.

No, he wanted a thick, juicy burger, although he figured they'd give him one of the healthy versions here. But she didn't need to know that. Nor did she need to finish whatever sandwich she picked. Just a couple of bites would do. Something to keep her stomach from growling and to provide some nourishment.

So he told her he'd share, hoping that would convince her to take the whole thing, even if she only wanted half.

"How about turkey?" he asked.

When she nodded, he placed a plastic-wrapped sandwich on her tray.

They neared the cash register, where a middle-aged brunette was totaling the items Tori and Granny had chosen.

Jared pulled out his wallet and addressed the cashier. "I'll get all of this."

"You don't have to do that," Sabrina protested. "I can pay for my own."

"I know that I don't *have* to. But I want to."

After he paid the tab and accepted the unnecessary appreciation of all three women, he joined them at a table in the rear of the cafeteria. They sat near a window that overlooked the grounds. In the distance, the city lights sparkled, providing evidence that the rest of the world were going on with their lives while Jared and Sabrina struggled with their own problems. And not just because of what Joey was going through right now.

They had a relationship that needed mending, although he wasn't quite sure exactly how to go about it. Or when it would be appropriate.

Jared chose the seat next to Sabrina, but she merely studied her food.

Tori reached across the table and placed her hand over the top of Sabrina's. "I know how hard this must be for you, but Dr. Pantera has an excellent reputation. I'm sure everything will go well. We need to be thankful that the problem was diagnosed before we found out the hard way."

Sabrina blew out a soft sigh. "I know."

Tori's comments seemed to ease Jared's worries, too, and he wondered again what the pretty redhead's story was, where she'd come from.

He knew better than to ask, though. No way would he risk upsetting Sabrina, who was pedaling as fast as she could to stay on top emotionally.

All he wanted to do was to see her smile again. To

catch that glimmer in those pretty blue eyes and know they were sparkling just for him.

He stole a glance at her, watched as she took her fork and poked at a strawberry in her bowl of fruit. She lifted it, but didn't put it into her mouth.

"You know," she said to everyone at the table, "I really need to tell Carlos what's going on. Do you think they'd let me talk to him if I called the prison?" She glanced first at Tori, then at Granny.

Her gaze finally landed upon Jared, as though he were the last word on the matter—the one who had all the answers.

At one time, he'd thought that he had. But Sabrina had him tossing aside his well-worn, know-it-all attitude and convinced that he needed to stop and think things through. To smell the roses…

Or rather, in her case, the hint of the floral scent of her shampoo.

"If it would make you feel better," he said, "you could call the prison and ask what the protocol is. Then, if they'll let you get a message to him, you can leave one that's upbeat. You know, like, 'Good news. We picked up on a problem with Joey's heart, and the doctors are correcting it now. I'll keep you posted.'"

"That's a great idea, Jared. I can tell him without making him worry too much." The relief that flooded her face turned his heart topsy-turvy and made him feel like some kind of hero.

Damn, that was nice.

He was glad that he'd finally done something to please her. Something to set things right. But he knew it wasn't going to be enough.

She popped the strawberry into her mouth, then placed the fork back on the tray. Taking her purse into her lap, she dug through it until she found her cell phone. "She dialed information and waited for a bit. Then a grimace stretched across her face. "I'm not getting any reception here. I'm going to go outside and try again."

As Sabrina strode out of the cafeteria, Jared watched her go. Ever since learning of Joey's condition, he'd stayed by her side. He'd tried to offer his support, even though at times she seemed to look right through him.

There was no reason for him to hang out and wait, but he couldn't leave.

He was concerned about Joey, of course, but it was more than that. If Sabrina needed a shoulder to lean on, he wanted it to be his.

Tori lifted her soda, and the lid shifted, splattering cola down the front of her white T-shirt. "Darn. Would you look at that? I'd better try and wash this before it stains."

When she excused herself, Jared watched her walk toward the ladies' room, leaving him and Granny alone.

With both young women out of hearing range, he couldn't help pursuing his curiosity. "Do you have any idea why Tori gave up nursing?"

Granny picked up her napkin and blotted her mouth. "She mentioned something to me while we were waiting for them to run one of Joey's tests, but I think she ought to be the one to talk to you about it."

"Then maybe I ought to ask her."

"No. Under the circumstances, I think you should wait and let her tell you when she's ready."

Which might be never, Jared realized, and that only

made him all the more curious. Before he could conjure another question that would provide a hint, his cell phone rang.

When he answered, a woman sniffled on the other end. "Jared?"

"Yes?"

"It's Connie." Her voice sounded waterlogged, as though she'd been crying or was suffering from allergies. "How's Joey?"

Damn. He should have called her to keep her posted. "The doctor is performing some kind of procedure he expects will clear up the problem. And if all goes well, they'll discharge him tomorrow."

"Good," she said. "Will you be coming back to the ranch tonight?"

He doubted Sabrina would want to leave Joey at the hospital. Something told him she'd be staying, which meant that he'd be here for the duration, too. "I'm not sure yet. Tori and Granny will probably be heading home tonight. Sabrina is outside trying to talk to her brother. When I see her, I'll ask her to give you a call."

"Okay, thanks." Connie released a wobbly breath. "I'm glad he's doing okay. He's a neat kid."

"Yes, he is." Jared had no more than disconnected the line when his cell rang again.

"Hey," Matt said. "How's Joey doing?"

"I think he's going to be all right. We hope to talk to the doctor soon and will know more then."

"Good."

Silence.

When there was no attempt on Matt's part to end the call, Jared asked, "Is everything okay at home?"

Matt grumbled, then swore under his breath.

"What happened?"

More silence.

Finally, Matt let out a heavy—guilt-riddled?—sigh. "I snapped at Connie, hoping to make her angry so she'd leave me alone, but I didn't realize she was so damn sensitive."

Jared knew the cook was pregnant, which probably didn't help.

"God," Matt said, "I *hate* it when women cry."

"Have you been drinking?"

"Some. Why?"

"You can be a real jerk sometimes, Matt. Especially when you're commiserating with a bottle of Jack Daniel's."

More of the damned silence stretched across the line, which made Jared realize his assumption had hit the mark.

"I'll let you go," Matt said. "I'm going to bed."

"That's probably just as well. Your apology might mean more to Connie in the morning."

"You mean, if I'm sober?" Matt swore under his breath. "Maybe you ought to mind your own business."

Determined to not argue with a man who'd been drinking, Jared disconnected the line.

"Is there a problem at the ranch?" Granny asked.

Jared didn't want to upset his mother, so he said, "Nothing out of the usual."

Tori, who was sporting a wet splotch on her white blouse, returned to the table and took a seat beside Granny. "What was that all about?"

"Matt's been grieving," Granny said. "And he's been

drinking, which can make him thoughtless. I don't really know the details, since Jared clammed up, but I think Matt made Connie cry."

Jared hadn't realized she'd put two and two together so quickly.

"Is he an alcoholic?" Tori asked.

"No, although he's been drinking more these past few months than usual." Granny opened a packet of ketchup and squeezed it onto her paper plate, right beside a pile of golden-brown French fries. "He was the driver in a fatal car accident. His fiancée and her son were killed, so he carries a lot of guilt. There's also a question about whether he'll walk again."

At this point, Jared wasn't sure if Matt really cared if he'd get up out of that wheelchair or not. If so, he would have gone back to physical therapy, like he was supposed to.

"How sad." Compassion splashed across Tori's face. "That poor man. Maybe I should talk to him."

"I wish you would," Granny said, as if she believed Tori had some kind of magic potion that would make Matt jump out of his wheelchair and be the man he once was.

Jared knew better, though. But it wasn't his place to discuss his brother's past or future with a stranger, no matter how good Tori had been to Sabrina and Joey.

"I have an idea." Granny dipped the tip of a long fry into the ketchup. "Maybe you can talk him into helping you plan a surprise birthday party for me. I'll be eighty next month."

"I love parties and would be happy to organize it," Tori said, "but we can't call it a surprise if you already know about it."

"I don't see why not." Granny popped the fry into her mouth and ate it. "Each year there's a couple of folks who put their heads together and try to plan a surprise for me, but then someone always spills the beans."

Tori chuckled and a grin tugged at Jared's lips. Granny was right. She'd done so much for so many in Brighton Valley that people just naturally wanted to do something nice for her.

But the subject of the party dissipated in the air, as Sabrina returned and took her place at the table.

"Any luck?" Jared asked.

"I was able to talk to Carlos for a few minutes and told him I'd call back later and let him know what Dr. Pantera had to say." She took a couple of bites of her sandwich, but then set it down and grabbed her napkin. "I'm eager to get back to the waiting room in case the doctor comes looking for me. I don't want to miss him."

"I'll go with you," Jared said.

They strode along the corridor to the elevator, arms brushing against each other. He felt compelled to take her hand in his or to slip his arm around her and draw her close, yet did neither.

As far as being a couple or a team, he'd shot himself in the foot this morning. Now, as the day progressed to night, he'd become more and more aware of how wrong he'd been about her.

When the elevator door opened, they stepped in, joining an older woman and a dark-haired teenage girl. No one spoke until the next stop, which was his and Sabrina's.

Jared took her arm and led her to the waiting room. It seemed as though his whole life—or at least the future—rode on whatever happened next.

"I need to tell you something," he said.

"What's that?"

"I realize you didn't take Granny's money, that you wouldn't have done something like that."

Her steps slowed, and she turned to face him, her gaze snaring his. "What changed your mind?"

You did.

What we shared last night.

What you've been revealing to me about yourself over the past few days.

"I was a jerk," he said. "And I'm sorry. Will you accept my apology?"

She looked at him for a moment, those sky-blue eyes searching for something. Sincerity, he supposed.

"All right," she said. "I forgive you."

Was it enough? Did he need to say more?

Before he could think of a response, a voice sounded from the doorway. "Ms. Gonzalez?"

They both turned to find Dr. Pantera entering the room. A smile broke across his face. "Joey's doing just fine. In fact, his condition wasn't as serious as I'd anticipated, and the procedure went better than expected. We'll keep an eye on him, but I see no reason why he can't go home sometime tomorrow."

"Oh, thank God." Sabrina grabbed the side of the nearest chair to steady herself.

"We'll take him into recovery for a while, and someone will let you know when you can see him. In the meantime, do you have any questions?"

"He's really going to be all right?" Sabrina asked.

"Yes. There will be some limitations, but nothing that will hamper him growing up to be a happy, healthy adult."

Sabrina blew out a soft sigh, and Jared slipped an arm around her. They'd become a team in all of this, and it felt good. Right.

They both watched as the cardiologist left the room.

"That's great news," Jared said.

"Yes, it is. I can't wait to tell my brother."

"I'm sure he's been worried. And when you make that call, tell him I've got an attorney trying to get him released."

"Thanks, Jared. I appreciate that. And Carlos will, too."

Of course, the poor guy would probably go back to driving a truck, which was fine. But Joey needed more of his time, especially while he was recovering from surgery. Too bad her brother couldn't find something…

"You know," Jared said, "why don't you tell him that once he's out of prison, I have a job for him on my ranch—if he wants it. And there will be a place for Joey, too."

Her lips parted, and her eyes glistened as she searched his face. "Why are you making that kind of offer?"

"Because I've come to admire you. And if you tell me your brother is a decent guy and conscientious, I believe you."

"He *is*. And I appreciate your faith in him." She turned, facing him full-on.

"It's *you* that I have faith in, Sabrina. And I'll go to bat for Carlos because I believe in you."

"Does that mean you trust me without question?"

Days ago, he might have had doubts about believing in people in general. But not *her*. Not any longer. The only thing she'd stolen was his heart. "Yes, I trust you."

She smiled and brushed a kiss on his cheek.

His heart swelled, and his lips quirked in a crooked grin. Yet for a moment, the little boy who lived deep within him, the child who'd been deserted, protested.

Jared had jumped into a relationship with Jolene before getting a chance to know her. And look where that had gotten him.

But Sabrina wasn't like Jolene. She didn't ditch her commitments or abandon loved ones—not Carlos, not Joey. And if she had a lover or a husband, Jared realized, she was the kind of woman who would vow to love a man until death parted them, and she'd stick it out, no matter what—even during the bad times.

Unlike Jolene.

After his divorce, Jared had vowed not to get involved with another woman for a long, long time—if ever.

But that was before he'd met Sabrina, a woman who was sure to bring out the best in him, if he'd let her.

And he had every intention of doing just that.

"This morning I made one of the biggest mistakes I've ever made, and I can't tell you how sorry I am. I want another chance. I want our relationship to grow."

She studied him for a moment, her lips parted, her eyes searching his for signs of deceit. But she wouldn't find it.

"I can't see how this will work, Jared. With you living a hundred miles away, we'd be hard-pressed to be anything more than lovers. And I want more. A lot more. The next time I sleep with a man, I'll be laying my heart on the line. And I'm not going to risk doing it with someone who won't take that same risk."

"What makes you think I wouldn't be doing that, too?"

"Would you?" she asked.

Jared raked his hand through his hair. "I've been burned before, and I damn sure don't want to make another mistake. And that makes this scary for me because I'm feeling so much more for you than I ever felt for Jolene."

"How much more?" she asked, a grin putting a sparkle in her eyes.

"I could fall head over spurs in love with you, if I haven't done so already."

A tear slipped down Sabrina's cheek, then another.

He brushed them away with his thumbs. "What's the matter? Am I screwing up again, saying all the wrong things?"

"No. You're saying all the right things." Then she wrapped her arms around him and lifted her lips to his.

They shared a promise-filled kiss that dazed him with wonder. And when it ended, they stood in the middle of the hospital waiting room, holding on to all they'd found—a chance at love and the home they'd both been wanting.

"Why, there you are," Granny's voice said from the doorway, drawing their attention from each other.

Seeing that Granny was alone, Sabrina asked, "Where's Tori?"

"Just as I was getting into the elevator, she got a phone call and said she'd meet me up here." Granny's grin broke into a full-on smile. "But this is a lovely surprise."

"This?" Jared asked, afraid he knew what she was getting at.

"I had a feeling that you two would make a good match."

"You *did?*" Sabrina asked.

"Well, I was *hoping* you would. That's why I sent you both to Vegas. I thought you'd find out you had something in common besides looking out for my best interests." Granny crossed her arms and shifted her weight to one foot. "And if either of you had told me that property was worth one dime less that five million dollars, I would have insisted that you sit tight and wait for me to get there and square those casino bigwigs away myself."

"You knew the value of that property all along?" Jared asked.

"Of course, I did. You don't think I fell off a turnip truck, do you?"

"Actually, I *was* a little worried. But I'm happy to find out you're just as ornery and cagey as ever."

Granny laughed.

Moments later, Tori joined them, and Sabrina filled them in on the news Dr. Pantera had just announced.

Granny blew out a huge sigh of relief. "Oh, thank goodness."

"By the way," Tori said to Granny, "that was Connie who called me a few minutes ago. She said someone from the Brighton Valley Savings and Loan came out to the ranch looking for you. One of their tellers was arrested for pilfering funds from elderly account holders, and you were one of them."

"Why steal from senior citizens?" Granny asked.

"Apparently, the teller carefully selected older account holders he thought would be less likely to catch on to what he was doing."

"Well, shame on him," Granny said.

Jared had a few choice comments he could make

about the thief, but he held most of them back. "I hope he gets all that's coming to him and more."

"Me, too," Granny said, yawning. "Boy, oh, boy. This has certainly been a long day. But I'm glad everything has worked out well."

"So am I," Tori said. "But we'd better go. We've got a long drive back to the ranch."

"You're right, and I'm winding down fast." Granny looked at Sabrina, then at Jared. "I suppose I don't need to worry about you two finding your way home."

"Nope." Jared slid his arm around Sabrina and held her close. Not when home was where the heart was.

"Give Joey our best," Granny said, as she and Tori turned to go. "We'll see you all tomorrow."

As they left, Jared turned to Sabrina. "Now, where was I?"

"In my arms," she said, "and in my heart."

"You got that right." Then he drew her close and kissed her.

There was no telling how they'd work this out, but Jared didn't care.

Love would find a way—one sweet day at a time.

* * * * *

Don't miss Tori and Matt's story,
Healing the Cowboy's Heart,
the second book in Judy Duarte's new mini-series
THE TEXAS HOMECOMING, *on sale October 2009,*
wherever Mills & Boon® books are sold.

THE DIAPER
DIARIES

BY
ABBY GAINES

Abby Gaines wrote her first romance novel while still in her teens. Encouraged by her incredibly supportive parents, she wrote her novel longhand in school notebooks, supplying new pages daily to her biggest fan, her younger sister. When she'd finished, she typed up the manuscript and sent it to Mills & Boon and was shocked when they rejected it. To this day, no trace remains of that original work.

Yet after five years of submitting she sold her first Superromance. A few years ago Abby and her family moved out of the city to live on an olive grove. It's beautiful, peaceful – and a long way from the mall. Contact Abby on abby@abbygaines.com.

For the Novelchicks: Karina Bliss, Sandra Hyatt and Tessa Radley. Wonderful writers and wonderful friends – I couldn't have done it without you, gals.

CHAPTER ONE

THE LETTER ENDED the same way they all did. *Thank you for caring.*

"I'm too damn busy to care," Tyler snarled at his secretary, who'd just deposited today's stack of heartrending pleas for cash on the corner of his steel-and-glass desk.

"You always are," Olivia Payne agreed cheerfully. With her graying hair held back in a bun, she looked staid and professional—an appearance that was entirely deceptive. She nodded at the letter Tyler held in his hand. "Anything interesting?"

Tyler fanned out the four pages of closely written text dotted with exclamation points. "Some guy wants two hundred grand to save the red-spotted tree frog. If we don't act fast, we might never see the frog again."

He picked up another letter—a single-page e-mail asking for thirty thousand dollars to buy computers for a preschool—and weighed it against the frog letter, as if he could somehow gauge the relative worthiness of the two causes.

The Warrington Foundation, whose purpose was to give away some of the multimillion-dollar profits earned by Warrington Construction, had hired extra staff in the new year to do the preliminary evaluations. It was their job to send polite rejections to the men who wanted bigger breasts for their wives and the people seeking donations to surefire lottery schemes.

But that still left anywhere up to a hundred potentially genuine requests for the chairman—Tyler—to read each day. Many of them ended with what seemed to be that mantra: *Thank you for caring.*

Tyler folded the first page of the frog letter into a paper airplane.

All he cared about right now was convincing the powers that be in Washington, D.C., that he was the right person to head up their new think tank, established to determine how charities and government could work together to support families. They were looking for someone who understood the concerns of ordinary American families. And Tyler had ended up on the shortlist thanks to the foundation's good work with various children's charities.

Presumably, he was at the very bottom of that shortlist. Yet he wanted the job to an extent that surprised him and would have amazed his family, who would doubtless say he was more suited to a think tank on how to get more fun into people's lives.

Tyler flipped his hand-forged-silver Michel Perchin pen between his fingers as he contemplated his possibly irredeemable reputation. Every news report about his work at the foundation was countered by a juicy piece in the gossip pages about "playboy bachelor Tyler Warrington." He'd made a major lifestyle adjustment—dating the same woman every night the past two weeks—but he wasn't sure that act of heroism was enough. Correction: after the headline in this morning's *Atlanta Journal-Constitution,* he knew it wasn't.

He smoothed out the paper plane, slapped the two letters together, handed them to Olivia. "The frog's a no go. Invite the preschool to pitch at the next committee meeting."

What could be more *ordinary* and *American* than preschool?

Maybe his PR team could write an opinion piece about early-childhood education and submit it to the *Journal-Constitution* in Tyler's name.

Olivia tucked the letters into her folder. "I'll deal with these right after I go downstairs. Joe called to say there's a delivery for you. He sounded pretty excited."

"Just as well our security guy doesn't make the allocations." Unlike Tyler, Joe was a sucker for the attention-getting ploys to which some people resorted when they asked for money. "If it's balloons, cake or cigars, tell him to take them home to his kids." He raised his hands in self-defense against Olivia's daggered look. "Okay, okay, hold the cigars."

OLIVIA RETURNED carrying a faded green duffel bag in a fierce grip, the straps wrapped around one hand, her other arm underneath the bag. She cradled it with a delicacy that suggested its contents were at least as valuable as the Venetian-glass sculpture she'd spent hundreds on last week.

Tyler shoved his chair back from the desk, got to his feet. "What is it?"

Very gently, she slid the bag across the surface of the desk; Tyler saw the zipper was open. "Take a look," she invited, her voice curiously high.

He parted the top of the bag, peered in. And met the un-blinking blue gaze of a baby.

Wrapped in a whitish blanket and wearing a soft yellow hat so that only a little round face showed…but definitely a baby.

"What the—" Tyler leaped backward, glared at his secretary. "Is this a joke?"

Olivia blew out a breath as she shook her head. "A young woman came in, told Joe she had a delivery for you. She excused herself to go to the bathroom and left the bag on Joe's desk. After a couple of minutes, the baby sneezed—gave Joe a heck of a fright. That's when he called me."

Tyler raked a hand through his hair. "For Pete's sake, the woman's probably still in the bathroom. Or by now, back out with Joe and wondering where her kid's gone. Take it back down."

Olivia handed Tyler an envelope, his name written on it in blue ink. "This was in the bag."

It had already been opened—Olivia read all Tyler's correspondence. The paper crackled: thin, cheap, almost weightless. Yet it felt far heavier than those requests he'd been reading a few minutes ago. Tyler unfolded the page.

The handwriting was young, or maybe just uneducated, and the message brief.

Dear Mr. Warrington,
I know you are kind and generous and you help lots of people. Please can you adopt my baby? I just can't do this. Thank you very very very much for caring.

No signature.

So much for the she's-still-in-the-bathroom theory. Tyler read the letter again. *Damn.*

With a caution that would have amazed the college buddies he played football with every month, he advanced on the duffel. The infant was still there, still staring. It had worked one little hand loose and was clenching and unclenching a tiny fist against the blanket.

Hey, kid, if you're frustrated, how do you think I feel? "What the hell am I supposed to do with you?" he said, the words rougher than he'd intended.

The baby blinked, and its mouth moved. If it cried now Tyler would be screwed. He patted the small hand as gently as he could, while he tried to think of words that might soothe. Snatches of nursery rhymes flitted through his head but were gone before he could catch them. "I meant heck," he said at last.

The kid still looked worried, so Tyler moved out of its line of vision. He looked out the window, over Peachtree Street, where courier bikes scraped between cars and vans with no margin for error, and the crosswalks thronged with business-people. No place for a baby.

"We have to find the mother," he told Olivia. "Ask Joe to send up the security-camera footage."

"I already did, but he doesn't think it'll help," she said, cheerful now she'd handed the problem to Tyler. "The woman wore a woolen hat pulled right down, and she had a scarf wrapped around her face. It's cold out, so Joe didn't think anything of it."

"Someone has to know who she is," Tyler persisted. "We'll give the tape to the police. And you'd better call social services—they can take the baby until the mom turns up."

"And they say you're just a pretty face," Olivia marveled. "I don't know why that young woman didn't go to social services in the first place." She chuckled. "I mean, do you know anyone less suited to looking after a baby than you?"

"You," Tyler returned sharply. Stupid to let her "pretty face" comment needle him. He might not be an expert on diapers and drool, but he knew he could do whatever he set his mind to. And that made him good for a whole lot more than simply doling out the money his brother Max made in the family's "real" business. Which he was about to prove by winning the job in Washington, D.C.

Olivia, who'd never married, never had kids, and as far as

Tyler knew, was having too much fun to regret either omission, laughed at his insult.

She didn't know about Washington. She and Tyler's mom were close enough that there was no chance she wouldn't spill the beans. No one knew, not even Tyler, officially. The news that he was under consideration had come from his cousin Jake, who had reliable political connections. But the whole thing was so sensitive, so confidential, there was no way Tyler could do what he knew would work best—jump on a plane to D.C. and talk them into giving him the job.

All he could do was continue his strategy of raising his profile in the media—his political profile, not his social profile. He glared at the duffel from his safe distance.

"The press will be all over this," he told Olivia, "no matter how fast we palm the kid off to social services."

"It can't be as bad as today's story." She ruined the comforting effect by snickering.

Two women Tyler had dated in the past had gotten into a tipsy argument at a nightclub a couple of evenings ago, apparently over which of the two he'd liked best—he barely recalled either of them. In a misguided attempt to emphasize her point, one had slugged the other with her purse.

None of that would have made the newspaper if one of the women's pals hadn't posted the purse for sale on eBay. The purse had been of supreme disinterest to most of the world, but the bidding in Atlanta was fierce and the story had spread in the media as one of those quirky "I sold my grandmother on eBay" tales. Tyler could only hope it hadn't reached Washington.

He needed damage control, and he needed it now. Pacing in front of the window, he tried to think of a political angle he could play up with the baby that might counter the gossip. How about a photo opportunity of him handing the baby to social services, commenting about the challenges facing young mothers?

Then it hit him—or, rather, smacked him in the head with a force that left him dizzy.

There wasn't just one political angle to the baby story, there were *dozens*—the foster system, parenting, money, infant health, who knew what else?—that he could tap into. This was his chance to show the world how well he understood the concerns of families.

"On second thought, don't call social services," he told Olivia. "Nor the police." He grinned at the duffel, suddenly feeling a whole lot warmer toward its occupant. "We need to get the baby out of the bag."

"*We?*" she said, horrified.

"You," he amended.

She backed off. "Uh-uh, no way."

Tyler directed his most cajoling smile at her. "Please."

She rolled her eyes, but came back and reached into the bag. He steadied it while she lifted the baby out. Olivia held it in a grip that he judged possibly too tight, but the baby didn't protest, so Tyler bowed to its superior knowledge. He looked around his office, all hard surfaces, sharp corners, glass and metal. "How about we spread the blanket on the floor," he suggested, pleased with his own parental-improvisation skills.

He managed to get the blanket out from around the baby, who turned out to be encased from head to toe in yellow terry. "We'll use your office," he told Olivia.

"My floor has slate tiles." With the unnaturally pointed toe of her shoe—and with undisguised triumph—she nudged the plush rust-colored carpet that enhanced Tyler's luxurious work space. "Yours is much more suitable."

Too bad she was right. He spread out the blanket, smoothed

it confidently—because looking after a kid wasn't rocket science—then nodded at Olivia, who knelt down to lay the baby on its back. She rubbed her own back as she got to her feet. "Now what?" she said.

Tyler looked down at the infant. Two short, pudgy arms waved at him, but there was still no crying. *Thoughtful of the mom to give me a well-behaved kid.* "You'd better organize a crib or whatever it is babies hang out in."

"You can't be thinking about keeping this child," Olivia said, shocked.

"Of course not. Just until we find the mom." At least a few days, he guessed, even if he put a private investigator onto it today. Maybe as much as a week or two. He would call his PR manager, tell her to arrange some media opportunities for him right away—just as soon as she found someone to get him up to speed about kid-parent issues.

"But—" Olivia shook her head, nonplussed "—you don't know the first thing about looking after a baby."

"That's what sitters are for. Call an agency, see if you can get someone immediately."

"I didn't even know you *liked* children." She was practically wringing her hands with worry, which Tyler considered an overreaction.

"I only have to like this one." He didn't even *have* to do that, but he was willing to try.

Olivia picked up a pad and pen off the desk. "Then I guess we need to think about food. Special baby formula." She jotted that down. "And diapers. They go through those pretty fast." She shuddered.

The baby hiccuped, its face contorted. Hell, was it about to puke? They did that all the time, didn't they?

"We should call a doctor," Tyler said. "Find out if the kid's

okay before I make any plans." He pulled out his handkerchief in case of an emergency wipe-up situation. "Call that
woman we gave money to last year. The pediatrician doing
the kidney research."

"Great idea." Olivia's voice warmed. "She's a real peach."

Tyler frowned. "Are we talking about the same woman?"

"Dr. Bethany Hart."

"That's her." He would have described Bethany Hart as
more frosty than peachy. And she was quite possibly the most
ungrateful woman he'd ever met. The Warrington Foundation
had granted her a generous sum for her research into childhood kidney disease which was part of a wider research
project at Children's Healthcare of Atlanta, attached to Emory
University. Instead of the thank-you letter most people wrote,
she'd sent Tyler a curtly worded missive to the effect that if
he was at all serious about helping young kidney patients he
would give a lot more money.

Unlike everyone else, she'd accused him of not caring.
Tyler had found her ingratitude refreshing.

Just a couple of weeks ago she'd written to him again. The
money, intended to cover her salary, along with admin support and the use of lab facilities and equipment, was almost
gone: she'd asked him to renew her funding. She'd enclosed
a comprehensive—in his opinion, *boring*—report on her work
to date, and had invited him, rather insistently, to visit a bunch
of sick kids in the hospital.

"She may not be your biggest fan," Olivia said with rare
diplomacy. She'd read the pediatrician's letters, too. "But she
sure loves kids."

Tyler had noticed the way Dr. Hart's blue eyes lit up when
she talked about the children she worked with. "Then she'll
want to check out this baby."

He didn't plan to give her a choice. Bethany Hart might have complained about the amount of money she'd received, but no one else had offered her a dime. The foundation had given more than her presentation to the Philanthropic Strategy Committee had merited.

Tyler had swayed the PhilStrat Committee in her favor. Not because she'd wowed him with her presentation—despite her obviously high intelligence, she'd been inarticulate to the point where he'd been embarrassed for her. Definitely not because of that spark of attraction that had flared between them, despite her frostiness—he never let that kind of thing get in the way of business.

When she'd bumbled to the end of her appalling pitch, she'd shot Tyler a look of angry resignation that said she might have messed up, but it was his fault.

He shook her hand as she left, and couldn't help smiling at the furious quiver in her otherwise stiff fingers. Which enraged her further. She looked down her nose at him as she said, "You haven't heard the last of me."

He sighed. "I was afraid of that."

She reeked of do-gooder earnestness, coupled with the kind of instinctive, misguided courage that led people to pursue hopeless causes without, unfortunately, actually losing hope.

So Tyler had believed Bethany when she said he hadn't heard the last of her. During the PhilStrat Committee's deliberations, he'd cast his vote in her support largely to shut her up.

Now, as it turned out, that might have been a smart move. He needed her discreet cooperation over this baby and he expected her to give it, however reluctantly.

Because Bethany Hart owed him.

CHAPTER TWO

BETHANY WAS IN THE SHOWER sloughing off the fatigue of three straight shifts in the E.R. at Emory University Hospital when the phone rang in the studio apartment she rented near the campus.

It was Olivia Payne, Tyler Warrington's secretary, asking if Bethany could come to the Warrington Foundation offices right away. "Tyler would like to meet with you." Olivia paused. "At this stage I can't tell you why."

He wants to give me more money. Jubilation surged through Bethany; adrenaline transformed her exhaustion into energy. She punched the air with the hand that wasn't holding the phone, then had to clutch the towel she'd wrapped around herself before it slipped to the floor.

After she'd hung up, she celebrated with an impromptu dance around her living room singing, "I aaaaam a reeesearch geeenius" to the tune of Billy Joel's "Innocent Man." But the room was too small for her to burn off this much excitement: as she danced, she grabbed the phone again and dialed her parents.

"Mom, it's me. Bethany." She slowed down, suddenly breathless. Crazy that she still felt compelled to identify herself—it was fourteen years since her sister's death, there was no chance of confusion. Without waiting for a reply, she said, "Looks like the Warrington Foundation plans to extend my research grant."

Her mom squawked with delight, none of her usual listlessness evident. "Darling, that's wonderful. Just wonderful."

"I'm seeing Tyler Warrington this morning. The foundation can extend the grant for a second twelve months at its discretion, without me having to pitch again."

"That's the best news—let me tell your dad."

Bethany heard her mom calling out to her father, heard his whoop of excitement. Then a muffled question she didn't catch, and an "I'll ask her" from her mom.

"Uh, honey," her mother said into the phone, "is there any chance they'll give you more money than last year? You always say you could get so much more done if you could afford to pay your assistant for more hours."

The familiar defensiveness—the urgent need to impress upon her parents that there just wasn't enough money around to fund all the research into kidney disease—constricted Bethany's chest. She puffed out a series of short, silent, relaxing breaths. Her parents weren't worried about other projects, only about hers. She understood; she even sympathized. Brightly, she said, "Of course I'll ask for more, but I may not get it."

Mentally, she doubled the figure she would propose to Tyler Warrington. If she started high, even ridiculously high, chances were she'd end up with more than if she went in low.

"I know you'll do your best," her mother said warmly.

Bethany basked in that praise. No use telling herself she was too old to be grateful for the crumbs of parental approval that came her way; some things never changed.

The moment she'd finished the call, her phone rang again. It was Olivia. "I forgot to say, you'll need to bring your medical bag."

Bring her bag so Tyler could hand over a check? *Uh-oh.* A

chill shivered through Bethany, the kind that either meant she was ill or something bad was about to happen. And in her own expert opinion, she wasn't ill.

Should she call Mom now and admit she might have been hasty with her talk of more money? Her finger hovered over the phone's redial button.

Then her natural optimism took over, binding itself to the remains of that energy surge. Okay, so Tyler likely had a nephew or niece with a chest cold, and His Egoness figured he had dibs on Bethany's time now that he'd contributed to her research. But if he didn't plan to renew her funds, surely he wouldn't dare summon her help? And that report she'd sent a couple of weeks ago had made an excellent case. Whatever he wanted today, she could still talk to him about money.

Provided, of course, she could string together more than two coherent words. As always, the recollection of how she'd mangled her last pitch to the super-smooth Tyler mortified her. No matter how often she prayed for selective amnesia—either for her or Tyler—her memory stayed depressingly clear. His was doubtless just as sharp.

But with any luck, he was so hopelessly in love with his new girlfriend—according to the newspapers, he was embroiled in a hot-and-heavy romance with Miss Georgia—that he'd see everything, including Bethany, through rose-tinted lenses.

"All you have to do is stay calm," she told herself out loud as she fished through her wardrobe for something to wear. Last time, she'd borrowed a suit from a colleague, but Banana Republic navy chino hadn't stopped her messing up.

She tugged a burgundy-colored woolen skirt off its hanger. Maybe she'd have better luck with this—unmistakably homemade, it was a gift from a young patient's grateful grandmother. If anything could fire Bethany up to get more money from Tyler it would be a reminder of the kids she hoped to help. She pulled the skirt on, added a long-sleeved black T-shirt, then inspected herself in the mirror.

Hmm, maybe the skirt was a bit too peasant style, with those large felt flowers appliquéd around the hem, and—she twirled around—maybe said hem wasn't entirely straight— the old lady's eyesight had been failing—but Bethany's high-heeled pumps would dress it up.

Besides, she didn't have a lot of choice. Thanks to her huge student loans, her wardrobe consisted of scrubs, lab coats and a bunch of stuff she could hide beneath them.

Bethany waved the blow-dryer briefly at her shoulder-length reddish-brown hair, then, in deference to the importance of the funds she was about to request, not to the man who was to bestow them, she applied some mascara and a pinky-red lipstick.

"Calm," she reminded her flustered, wild-eyed reflection as she rolled her lips together to smooth the lipstick.

She couldn't afford to screw up again. Last time, Tyler hadn't bothered to hide first his boredom, then his amusement at her inarticulateness. Then, of course, he'd done that *stupid thing* that had left her feeling like the joke of the day.

Maybe she'd been oversensitive, she chided herself. There was probably a good explanation for his behavior. A nervous tic. Tourette's syndrome. Thirty-something years of silver spoon–slurping, privileged existence that had blinded him to the needs of—

Okay, now she was being uncharitable, the very thing she'd accused Tyler of in the letter she'd sent after her pitch. Besides, Miss Georgia was apparently committed to working tirelessly for world peace. Clearly Tyler's charitable instincts were in full working order.

Bethany would give him the benefit of the doubt and ask him politely—and coherently—for more money.

OLIVIA PAYNE GAVE Bethany a warm welcome, then phoned through to tell Tyler she had arrived.

When he appeared in the doorway of his secretary's office, Bethany was struck anew by his good looks. The camera loved him—she knew that from the newspaper photos—but real life suited him even better. She might not like the guy, but she'd have to be blind not to notice he had dark hair just too long for decency and when he smiled, as he was doing now, his eyes gleamed with a dare that plenty of women might be tempted to accept.

She doubted anyone could consistently achieve a smile like that without hours of practice in front of a mirror.

"Good morning, Dr. Hart." His voice was part of the package, low and warm, as if she was the person he most wanted to see right now.

Poised, calm, smooth, she cautioned herself. She shook his hand firmly, noted the gold links that punctured the crisp white of his cuffs. In his immaculately tailored charcoal suit he looked more put together than a *GQ* cover, and for some unspecified, illogical reason, Bethany disapproved. "Good to see you again, Mr. Warrington—Tyler."

"How is your research going?" he asked courteously.

"Quite well, given the funding shortfall." Not subtle, but definitely articulate.

His lips twitched. "That shortfall would be my fault, I assume?"

"Nothing you can't rectify," she said encouragingly, and he chuckled outright. Was he laughing at her again? She plowed on. "As you'll have seen from my report, I'm on the verge of a breakthrough into therapies that interfere with antibody production. If the foundation would consider—" she thought of her parents, drew a shaky breath "—*tripling* its investment in my work, there's every chance—"

"I didn't ask you here to talk about your funding." His interruption confirmed her fears, sent her spirits into free fall. Bethany clenched her toes inside her shoes to counter the sagging of her knees. Less abruptly, Tyler continued, "But if you want to call Olivia next week and ask her to set up a time in my diary…"

Bethany's hopes shot back up again. Her first instinct was to grab the opportunity he offered. Then he favored her with that calculated smile that seduced socialites and beguiled beauty queens. And distracted Bethany? *Not this time.* She folded her arms and said deliberately, "And what will Olivia say when I call?"

Tyler blinked. Olivia made a strangled sound. Bethany waited.

Then he grinned, something much more genuine—as if to say, "You got me." "She may say there's no room in my diary," he admitted.

"Just like there was no room for you to visit the kidney patients I work with?"

"I have a lot of demands on my time." He spread his hands disarmingly. "You wouldn't believe the number of people who want a piece of me."

Most of them female. Even before Miss Georgia, the newspapers had reported his dating exploits so comprehensively, Bethany wondered how he found time to make it into the office. But evidently he did, because lately the press had been covering the foundation's charitable activities, and in that sphere, at least, it seemed Tyler was a saint. Albeit one untroubled by anything so pesky as a vow of celibacy.

"I want a piece of you, too," she said. Tyler raised his eyebrows, and she stuttered, "I—I want you to guarantee me that appointment to talk about my funding. Please."

For a long moment Tyler stared at her. Then he said, "I like a woman who knows what she wants." Before she could decide if he was being provocative, he turned to Olivia. "Give Bethany some time next week. And when I tell you to fob her off, don't listen to me."

That frank admission of his lack of interest in her work floored Bethany…and, amazingly, made her want to laugh. Which she was not about to do: she took her work seriously, even if he didn't. She compressed her lips, picked up her bag. "Olivia asked me to bring this. I assume there's a patient you want me to look at?"

"In my office." He held the door open for her.

Tyler figured it was the oddness of Bethany's skirt that drew his attention to the neat round of her bottom as he followed her into his office. That, and the same kick of awareness that had surprised him at their last encounter.

He couldn't think why he found her so intriguing. Yes, that polished-cherry-wood hair waved nicely around her heart-shaped face. But her nose was too pointy, all the easier for her to look down it at him, and her mouth a trifle wide for that stubborn chin. She was pretty, but Tyler dated beauties.

He was still puzzling over his attraction to her when she stopped; he almost bumped into her. She'd seen the baby.

"Oh, you gorgeous little thing." She sounded awed, breathless, as she dropped to her knees on the carpet. "Hello, precious," she crooned. The baby's face split in an enormous smile, and Bethany laughed out loud.

Humor widened her mouth to even more generous proportions and revealed a dimple in her chin. All trace of obstinacy vanished, and she was much more the peach Olivia had suggested. A cute-but-not-his-type peach. Women who went gaga over babies usually had him hightailing it out the door.

She looked up at Tyler, confusion wrinkling her brow. "Who's this?"

He shifted on his feet. Now that he had to explain, he realized just how weird this was. "Someone left it downstairs for me."

"It?" Her eyebrows drew together, and the effect in combination with that skirt was of a disapproving pixie.

"Uh…her?" Damn, he should have had Olivia check.

Bethany unsnapped the terry garment. She hooked the front of the baby's diaper with one finger and peered inside. "Him," she corrected as she refastened the snaps. "What do you mean, someone left him?"

Tyler handed her the note. Watched curiosity turn to shock to alarm, all telegraphed across her face. She stared at him, mouth slightly open, apparently dumbfounded.

"This woman…" She groped for words. "This child's mother thinks *you* would make a good parent?"

As if her intimate knowledge of children's kidneys put her in a position to judge him. "I'm one of Atlanta's favorite sons—and its most generous."

Bethany sat back on her heels. "You hadn't even figured out he's a boy."

"I believe in equal-opportunity parenting. Gender is irrelevant."

She pffed. "You need to call social services."

"My lawyer says I don't." He was glad he'd clarified the legality of the situation in the forty-five minutes that he'd waited for Bethany. "The mother's letter effectively appoints me the baby's guardian. According to my attorney, that may not carry weight long term, and I'll need to meet with social services. But if they're satisfied he's well looked after and that efforts are being made to find the mother—which I'll hire a private investigator to do…"

Bethany leaned over to scoop up the baby, then scrambled to her feet. As she hoisted the infant to her shoulder in a casual, practiced movement, Tyler caught a glimpse of slim, winter-pale midriff where her T-shirt pulled away from her skirt.

"You mean, you plan to keep him?" she said. "What about your incredibly busy schedule? Babies take time and attention."

"I'll organize a sitter."

"You can't tell me you care about this baby." She sounded suspicious and she was doing that looking-down-her-nose thing, one of his least favorite memories from the first time they'd met.

"I care about families, about children." What the heck, he might as well try out some of the lines he planned to use in media interviews. "Children are our future."

"Wonderful," she said brightly—to the baby. "Your new guardian is a graduate of the Whitney Houston School of Philosophy." She looked at Tyler and her eyes sparked, not with the tenderness she'd directed at the baby, but with something more…electric.

Tyler's senses stirred in response to that spark, and he struggled to keep his mouth from curving, his wits from deserting him to go frolic with his imagination in a place that involved him and Bethany and not much clothing. Definitely not that skirt. "Are you saying children *aren't* our future?" he asked with spurious confusion.

She shifted her hold on the baby, and the movement emphasized the high, full curve of her breasts. "You made it plain you're not interested in my kidney patients, so why should I believe you have any real concern for this child?"

But he hadn't invited her here to examine his motives. All he needed was for her to check the baby over and leave. Then he could get Operation Family Man under way. Still, he couldn't resist saying, "You're carrying a grudge because I didn't give you all the money you wanted, and it's clouding your judgment. You need to admit that was your own fault."

Bethany's face heated. So much for Tyler being either amnesiac or love-struck to the point of forgetting her humiliation. Yes, she'd brought it on herself…but he hadn't helped. She'd been sucked in by his charm—the charm she'd been too naive to realize was hardwired into him and freely dispensed to every female he came across—and in the misguided belief she'd already won him over, she'd wandered away from the scientific facts to support her case and detoured into anecdote.

Halfway through her pitch, she'd realized she'd lost Tyler's attention. He'd still been giving her that encouraging smile, but he'd glanced at his watch a half-dozen times, yawned more than once. She'd scrambled to get back onto the solid ground of medical fact, lost track, dropped her notes and been too nervous to take a break and sort them out. She'd garbled her way through, and just as she hit the crux of her case, Tyler—

"You winked at me!" she accused.

"I did not." He widened his eyes, as if to prove there was no winking going on. At the same time, his brows lowered in a puzzled frown that hinted she was being irrational.

"When I pitched to your committee." The baby hiccuped and she rubbed his back in a circular motion. "You sat there not listening to a word I said and then you winked."

"*That's* why you're so touchy? Because I winked?" Tyler ignored the way Bethany stiffened at being called touchy. "I could see you felt awkward and I guessed it was because of that thing between us…"

"What thing?" she demanded.

"That…awareness, that—" he flung a hand wide to encompass the full spectrum of sexual attraction "—*edge*. It's here again, right now, even when you're mad at me."

Her face was blank. "I have absolutely no idea what you're talking about."

Tyler snorted. No way was this all on his side. There'd been a real and definite connection between them and it hadn't abated. He was used to women finding him attractive and, less often, to experiencing a mutual chemistry. If the situation wasn't appropriate, he could shrug it off and get on with the job. But he could see Bethany inhabited a less sophisticated planet than the women he dated. That big doctor brain of hers was probably a handicap when it came to something as simple as sexual attraction.

"You winked," she said again, a note of revelation creeping into the words.

Being an egghead was no excuse for not understanding the basics. "I told you," he said impatiently, "I did it because you—"

"While I was putting my heart into that pitch, you were *flirting?*"

CHAPTER THREE

"I WAS READING your signals," Tyler corrected her. "And I acknowledged them. I was being *polite*."

Just when Bethany had thought she'd reached the pinnacle of embarrassment, he'd thrown this at her. Why didn't he just come out and say he thought she was an all-round loser, and sex-starved to boot?

"I was pitching for the most important thing in my life," she said in a tight, strained voice. If she hadn't been holding the baby, she would have yelled.

The baby whimpered. Through his hat, she nuzzled the top of his sweet little head with her chin, a caress intended to soothe herself as much as him.

No wonder Tyler hadn't taken her pitch seriously, if his rampant ego had decided she was making a pass at him.

"If you weren't giving me any signals—"

"I wasn't," she snapped.

"Then my...wink was out of order. I apologize."

Bethany saw the opening and dived for it. "You need to let me pitch again, right away."

He grinned. "Nice try."

The baby wriggled against her, and automatically she noted his good neck control—he had to be at least a couple of months old. "You can't have made an objective decision, if you thought I was flirting."

"Women flirt with me all the time. I don't take it seriously," he said, half laughing, half irritated. "Look, Bethany, I promise the reason you *only* got fifty thousand dollars was because that's the maximum the team thought your work deserved. I didn't underpay you because I thought you were flirting."

"And you're certain you weren't—" it sounded stupid, but she had to say it "—so distracted by your attraction to me that you failed to grasp all aspects of my presentation?" Because that happened to her all the time. *Not.*

"I swear I wasn't." His face was so grave she just knew he was laughing hysterically inside. "It wasn't even an attraction. It was an awareness, a spark. Not that you're not very attractive," he added hastily, as if she was about to take offense on a whole new scale. "But…you must know your presentation didn't do you any favors."

The fire left Bethany, and suddenly she was cold. "No," she agreed quietly. And now that she'd accused him of being in the thrall of an overwhelming attraction to her, how likely was it he'd give her more money when they met next week?

She'd blown it again.

"Can we start over?" he said, evidently deciding he'd neutralized her.

Start over. That's what she'd have to do with her research funding. Nausea churned in her stomach.

"I asked you in here to examine the baby, to check if he's healthy," Tyler said.

"Of course." She could at least do something for this child, get that right.

"There's a meeting room that adjoins this office." Tyler pointed to a door halfway along the far wall. "You can use the table in there." He looked at the baby, now dozing against her shoulder. "I'll carry your bag."

She followed him into a room that, like his office, had expansive views over midtown. Instead of a desk, it held a long table flanked by leather-upholstered chairs.

"How about you hold this little fellow while I set up?" Bethany said.

Tyler took the infant from her, held him at arm's length, like a puppy that had rolled in something nasty and needed a good hose-down.

"He won't bite," she said.

"It's more the barfing I'm worried about." He glanced down at the fine wool of his jacket, which fitted his shoulders snugly enough to reveal their breadth, while still allowing fluidity of movement.

"That's why I don't buy custom-made suits," she sympathized. "I don't mind dropping a thousand dollars on a new suit, it's the twenty bucks for the dry cleaning that kills me."

He gave her a hard look, but he took the hint, held the baby closer. The little boy's head flopped against Tyler's chest, a tiny thumb went into his mouth. Then a fist curled around Tyler's lapel. Tyler looked less than thrilled.

Bethany tore open a plastic pack and pulled out a sterile mat. "I hope you've baby-proofed your house, because these critters get into everything." The baby was several months away from that stage, but why not give Tyler a scare?

"Luckily I had that done last year, on the off chance someone abandoned a baby on me."

She frowned so she wouldn't smile.

"But even if I hadn't," he continued, "this guy looks too young for me to worry about him digging out the magazines from under my bed."

Her head jerked up.

"Car magazines," he said blandly. "I only buy them for the pictures."

From her bag, Bethany took out the items she'd need for her examination. She rescued the baby from Tyler, laid him on the mat. Instantly wide-awake, he gurgled up at her. "Can you imagine how desperate his mom must have been," she mused aloud, "to abandon a cutie like this?"

"Why do you think she did it?" Tyler perked up.

"It's more common to abandon babies at birth if the pregnancy was a secret or if the mom had no support. At this age...possibly if he had a birth defect or a serious illness she couldn't handle..." She unsnapped the yellow sleeper and began to remove the garment. "But there's nothing obviously wrong with this guy." She appreciated the healthy pink tone of the baby's skin. Too often the youngsters she saw in the E.R. were either pale or flushed from illness. "I'm wondering if there'll be some clue to his name, maybe a wristband or ankle band under these clothes."

"Uh-huh." Tyler was looking at the baby, but the tapping of one black loafer on the carpet told her his thoughts were elsewhere.

A thought struck Bethany. "You don't know his name, do you?"

That brought his gaze back to her. "It wasn't in the note, so how could I?"

She waited before she replied, listening through her stethoscope to the baby's heart. He'd flinched when the cold metal touched his chest, but he didn't cry. Heart rate of one-fifty, perfectly normal.

"It occurs to me," she said carefully as she coiled her stethoscope, "that this might be your son."

He jerked backward. "Mine?"

"I mean—" she put a thermometer to the baby's ear, relieved she didn't have to meet Tyler's gaze as she elaborated
"—your...love child."

She didn't expect the silence. It was unnerving, so much
so that even after the thermometer beeped a normal reading,
she kept looking at the display.

"Tell me that's a joke," he said.

She swallowed. "I have to ask. I'm a doctor, I have my
patient's best interests in mind."

"You're not just a gossip with a juicy story to spread?" he
asked silkily.

"Certainly not." She put the thermometer away.

"Because if a rumor like that got around, it could do me a
lot of damage."

Bewildered, she said, "Tyler, according to the newspapers,
you've dated half the women in Atlanta and the other half are
eagerly awaiting their turn. Miss Georgia must know she's the
latest in a long line."

"Professional damage," he elaborated. "And for your information, dating a lot of women doesn't mean I'm siring *love
children*—" he embellished her euphemism with sarcasm "—
all over town, then neglecting them until their mothers
abandon them."

"Only one love child," she corrected reasonably. Then,
when his face darkened, "If you say he's not yours, I believe
you. But like you said, you're Atlanta's favorite son, you
could get away with—"

"Forget it," he said with flat finality.

Bethany pressed her lips together and conducted the rest
of her checks on the baby in silence. She put a finger in his
mouth, ran it over his gums. Next, she pulled a brightly
colored rattle from her bag, held it above and in front of the

baby. His eyes focused on the toy, and when she moved it to her left and then her right, his gaze followed. When she put the rattle down on the table, the little boy turned his head to see it. His hand reached out, found only air, and he gave a squirm of frustration.

Bethany picked up the toy, held it to the tips of his fingers. He curled his fingers around it, held it for a moment, then dropped it. "Hmm, I'd say he's hit three months."

"How do you know that?"

She'd forgotten momentarily that she wasn't talking to Tyler after he'd accused her of being a gossip. Nonetheless, she magnanimously decided to share her conclusions with him. "He's able to follow an object with his eyes and grasp it, but he's not rolling over, though he's in good health, with plenty of fat, plus good muscle development. And there's no sign of teething."

There was a knock, then Olivia stuck her head around the door. "I have diapers. And something called baby wipes."

"Perfect timing." Bethany pulled the tapes on the diaper the baby wore. "Bring them in."

She tugged the wet diaper out from under the baby. She gave his private parts a quick check, then Olivia handed her a fresh diaper and a wipe. The secretary left the room double quick.

"On all the obvious measures he's fine, a healthy little guy," Bethany said as she fastened the clean diaper. She glanced at Tyler. "I still think it's best if I call social services and have them pick him up." She began to dress the baby again.

Tyler shook his head. "I can't throw him into the welfare system when his mom asked me to take him. Who knows what might happen to him."

"*I* know." She gathered the baby in her arms. "Social services will send someone to get him. They might be satisfied with my medical assessment, or they might take him to another doctor. While they try to find his mom, they'll place him with a foster parent *who knows how to look after a baby*," she said with heavy emphasis. "Someone who'll *care about him.*"

He looked at her for a long moment, then his gaze flicked down to the baby in her arms. "Thanks very much for your professional advice, Dr. Hart. Be sure and send Olivia your bill."

Just like that he was dismissing her. He even had the nerve to offer her that meaningless smile, the one he'd given when he'd dismissed her pitch.

He would do the same at their meeting next week. It wouldn't make any difference if she was coherent, babbling or speaking Swahili.

Bethany's future flashed before her eyes, and it wasn't a pretty sight. She'd have to pull out of the research team at Emory; she'd been a late addition to the team, accepted on the basis of her funding from the foundation. Every cent was allocated, they couldn't carry freeloaders. She would have to start traipsing around the charitable foundations, submitting applications, presenting her case. And every time, she'd be up against dozens of other worthy projects.

This could mean the end of the goal she'd worked toward since she was thirteen years old.

She could find a way to deal with the recriminations from her parents—she just wouldn't answer her phone for a year—but knowing she'd failed to do the one thing that would make any sense of Melanie's death…that would haunt her.

Now Tyler stood before her, frowning with faint confusion, as if he couldn't understand why she was still in his office, still holding "his" baby. He didn't give a damn about the children she hoped to save. Did he care about anyone, other than himself?

Bethany's mouth set in a determined line. "I'm not leaving until I'm certain you've made acceptable arrangements for this baby."

"For Pete's sake." His hands came together in a throttling motion that she hoped was involuntary. "I told you, I'll find a sitter. I'll have Olivia call you later and let you know how I get on."

"Does that work the same as, 'Call Olivia and have her slot you into my diary'?"

A smile tugged at Tyler's mouth. Surprise, surprise, he wasn't taking her seriously again.

"Do you know how to choose a sitter?" she demanded. He probably planned to ask one of his girlfriends. Goodness knew what sights the poor baby might be subjected to. "You need someone qualified. And I mean capable of more than sashaying down a catwalk."

He laughed out loud. "Modeling is a very demanding profession," he chided. "I've been told many times."

"I'm trying to say—"

"I *am* saying, this is none of your business," he interrupted. "I assure you, though I don't have to, and I really don't know why I'm bothering, that I'll hire a qualified, professional sitter, the best that money can buy."

Everything came back to money.

He had it, she needed it.

Which seemed so monumentally unfair, Bethany wanted to cry.

"We're done here." Tyler took a step toward the door. "I'll be happy to update you about the baby at our meeting next week. If you'll hand him over to me…"

"No," Bethany said. Because an idea was glimmering in the recesses of her mind, and she just needed a minute to tease it into the open.

"You don't want an update?" He added hopefully, "Or you don't want to meet next week?" It obviously didn't occur to him she wasn't about to hand over the baby.

It was coming closer, her idea, coalescing into a plan. A plan to get money out of him, without her having to beg, or rob him at gunpoint, both of which had occurred to her in the course of this encounter.

"I want," she said casually, confidently and—best of all—coherently, "you to hire me as your babysitter."

The allure of Bethany's feisty brand of cute was wearing off fast, Tyler decided. And the way she was holding on to the baby as if he was a bargaining chip was decidedly alarming. "No way."

"I've worked with social services in the emergency room," she said. "They know me, they trust me. When I tell them you're not a fit guardian for this baby, they'll be around here faster than you can proposition a supermodel."

"I doubt that's possible," Tyler said coolly. "But, humor me here, why exactly would you want to tell social services that?"

"Because it's true." Her tone said, *Duh,* and he could see she believed it. "I'm not going to let you risk this child's well-being because you want, for whatever reason, to keep him—" She stopped. "I bet you see this baby as some kind of chick magnet."

"*I'm* a chick magnet. And I don't need you telling lies to social services." Just the thought of her carrying out that threat made Tyler go cold. He imagined the resulting furor when the news hit the headlines. He might as well go out and have *Don't choose me to run a family think tank* tattooed on his forehead right now.

"If this is about the handbag incident," he said, "I swear I was nowhere near that nightclub, and I haven't seen either of those women in a long time."

"What handbag incident?" She shifted the baby to her other shoulder.

Great, why didn't he make things worse? "Just kidding. Look, how about I let you choose a sitter—one who meets whatever standard you want to set." He reached for the baby. "Here, he looks heavy, why don't you pass him over."

She squinted at him and held the infant tighter. "The standard is, it has to be me."

"You're overqualified," he said. "And you have lives to save. Your research, remember?"

"The research I've run out of money for," she pointed out. "I've been pulling shifts in the E.R. for weeks now, so I can use some of the foundation's grant to extend my assistant's hours. But as of this week, she's working for someone else until I get more money."

The money. Again. "I find it difficult to believe you have a burning ambition either to work for me or to be a babysitter."

"I admit I have an ulterior motive—access to you." She turned her cheek to avoid a sudden grab by the baby. "I'll use up the vacation time I'm owed looking after this little guy until his mother is found, and I'll spend every minute I can educating you about my research."

The days and weeks stretched before Tyler in a *Groundhog Day* nightmare of lectures about kidneys and caring.

"Did you think of demanding a renewal of your funding in exchange for your butting out of my business?" Not that he would have paid her off, but it would in theory have been simpler than this Machiavellian scheme.

"That would be blackmail," she said, shocked. "All I want is a fair hearing." The baby blew bubbles, and she wiped gently at his mouth with her finger. "I'll work for you—" the hardness of her voice, at odds with that tender gesture, startled Tyler "— and I'll make you listen."

She couldn't *make* him do anything. But he couldn't afford to have her bad-mouthing him to social services. And he did need a qualified sitter. Plus, her knowledge, not just of how to look after this baby, but of wider child-related issues, might come in handy.

Tyler made a decision—*his* decision, for *his* reasons. "You can have the job." Her eyes lit up, so he said hastily, "But if you think that's going to make me listen to you…all I can say is, hold your breath."

She blinked. "I believe the expression is *don't* hold your breath."

"Ordinarily," he agreed. "But in this case I'm hoping you'll suffocate yourself."

"And then this poor baby will have no one who cares." She patted the little boy's back. "Let me tell you how much I charge for my services." Bethany named a sum that had Tyler's eyebrows shooting for the ceiling.

"I had no idea babysitting was such a lucrative profession."

"One of a thousand things you have no idea about," she said loftily. "Now, when can I move in?"

"Move in?" Tyler felt as if his brain was ricocheting around his head, trying to keep up with her twisted mind. What was she planning next?

"You're aware that babies wake in the night?" she asked. "That they need feeding and changing 24/7?"

Tyler had been vaguely aware of the unreasonable nature of infants, but he hadn't yet translated that to having to violate his privacy by having someone move in. He'd never even had a live-in girlfriend. "You're not moving in."

"Okay, if you think you can handle the nighttime stuff…" She shrugged. "I guess with your dating history you're used to not getting much sleep. But those middle-of-the-night diapers are the worst. Just make sure you buy a couple of gallons of very strong bleach and three pairs of rubber gloves. Oh, and have you had a rabies shot?"

Was she suggesting he could get *rabies* from the baby? He stared at her, aghast. She looked back at him and there was nothing more in her blue eyes than concern for his well-being. Which made him suspicious. But he wasn't willing to take the risk.

"Fine," he said, "you can move in."

She didn't blink. Only a sharp breath betrayed that she hadn't been certain he would agree. Immediately, he wished he hadn't. "But don't get too comfortable. I don't imagine I'll have custody of him for more than a few weeks, max, before either his mom is found or social services take over."

"That's all the time I'll need," Bethany said.

"I'll have Olivia get me some earplugs," he said. "When you're nagging me about your research, I won't be listening."

"While she's out buying those, she can buy or rent some baby equipment and supplies," Bethany said. "I'll write you a list—do you have a pen?"

Tyler handed over his silver pen with a sense of impending doom.

Bethany scribbled a list of what looked like at least two dozen items, and handed it to him.

"If you like, I can take the baby to your place right now and—" She stopped. "We can't keep calling him 'the baby'— how about you choose a name for him?"

"Junior?" he suggested.

"A proper name. One that suits him."

Tyler rubbed his chin. "Okay, a name for someone with not much hair, a potbelly, incontinent… My grandfather's name was Bernard."

Bethany laughed reluctantly. "Bestowing a Warrington-family name on him might create an impression you'd rather avoid."

Good point. Tyler looked the baby over. "Ben's a nice name for a boy."

"Ben," she repeated. "It suits him." She dropped a kiss on the infant's head, as if to christen him. "Okay, Ben, let's get you home." To Tyler, she said, "I don't have a car. Are you going to drive me, or call me a cab? Better order one with a baby seat."

"How did you get here today?"

"By bus," she said impatiently.

"Everyone has a car," he said.

"Underfunded researchers don't."

Pressure clamped around Tyler's head like a vise. He massaged his aching temples.

Bethany had promised to give him hell, and she didn't even have the decency to wait until she'd moved in.

CHAPTER FOUR

BETHANY PULLED her knitting out of its bag, propped herself against two large, squashy pillows and checked out the view. Of Tyler's bedroom. From Tyler's bed.

This was so undignified, being forced to wait for her employer on his *bed.* No doubt he'd be less than impressed to find her here.

"It's his own devious, underhanded fault," she muttered as she untangled a knot in her wool.

She'd been full of self-congratulatory delight at having inveigled her way into Tyler's multimillion-dollar home in Virginia Highlands so she could brainwash him into giving her money. Her sense of triumph had lasted through three nights of interrupted sleep, fifteen bottles of formula and thirty thousand dirty diapers.

At least, that's how many it felt like. It was now Thursday evening, and Bethany hadn't seen Tyler since the meeting they'd had with social services on Monday afternoon, at which it had been agreed that Tyler would have temporary custody of Ben. Correction: she hadn't seen him in the flesh. Beside her on the bed was today's newspaper, featuring a photo of Tyler and Miss Georgia at the opening of an art exhibition in Buckhead on Tuesday.

She tossed the newspaper across the deep crimson bedcover.

Who would have thought crimson could look so masculine? It must be the combination of the white walls, the dark polished floorboards, the Persian rug woven in rich reds and blues.

Her cell phone rang, breaking the silence and startling her. Bethany fumbled her knitting, reached for the phone's off button. She'd spent the past few days dodging calls from her mother and stalling the head of the emergency department at Emory with vague promises that she'd be available for work "soon."

The one person she wanted to talk to was Tyler. But she hadn't even said two words to him about her research.

Because the man was never here.

So now, when Ben was napping and Bethany should have been sleeping—the dark circles beneath her eyes were growing dark circles of their own—she was instead relying on the irregular clack of her knitting needles to keep her awake. If she wasn't careful, Tyler would make one of his lightning raids on the house while she dozed.

She didn't know how he managed to figure out exactly when she'd be out taking Ben for a walk, or catching forty winks, or at the store stocking up on diapers. But at some stage every day she'd arrive home, or come downstairs into the kitchen, and there'd be…no actual evidence of his presence, just an indefinable sense of order shaken up. And, occasionally, the scent of citrus aftershave, freshly but not too liberally applied.

Tyler wouldn't elude her today, she promised herself as she hunted for a dropped stitch with little hope of rescuing it. No matter how much Bethany knitted, she never improved, probably because knitting was a means of relieving tension rather than a passion.

Since she'd arrived at Tyler's home, she'd knitted most of a sweater.

Today, she would relieve her tension by delivering Tyler a brief but salient rundown on childhood kidney disease. Waiting on his bed meant he couldn't sneak past her; she wouldn't let him out of the house until she'd said her piece.

Bethany yawned and leaned back into the pillows, letting her eyelids droop just for a moment. Her bed in Tyler's guest room was very comfortable, but this one was in a different league. It was like floating on a cloud....

THE NEAR-SILENT SWISH of a well-made drawer sliding stealthily closed woke Bethany. She jerked upright.

And saw Tyler standing frozen next to the dresser, holding a plastic shopping bag, watching her watching him.

Bethany roused her wits. "Who are you, and how dare you barge into this house?"

She had the satisfaction of confusing him, but only briefly. Those full lips curved in irritated appreciation of her comment.

"Sorry I haven't been around, I've been busy." He crossed the room, a picture of relaxed grace, and dropped the shopping bag onto the end of the bed. He stood, clad in Armani armor, looking down at her as if she were a territory he had to conquer before dinner.

"I've been busy, too," Bethany said. Unlike him, she bore the ravages of her day, evidenced in the baby-sick that blotted the shoulder of her sweater, in her lack of makeup, in the hair she hadn't had time to wash this morning.

"You mean, busy doing something other than snoozing on my bed?" He took a step closer. "Or are you here because you want...something?"

"I *want* to talk to you." She scowled. "You were hoping to sneak in and out without waking me, weren't you?"

"You looked so sweet," he said blandly, "it seemed a crime to disturb you. Where's Ben?" He glanced around with casual interest, as if she might have stowed the baby under a pillow. For all he knew, that was exactly what she did each day.

"He's sleeping."

Tyler sat on the other side of the bed from Bethany, and farther down so he was facing her. Still too close for her liking. She'd have liked to stand up, but one foot was still asleep, and she'd probably topple over if she tried. She settled for edging away from him.

"That kid's amazing," he said. "Every time I come home, he's fast asleep. I feel as if I've hardly seen him." He must have noticed the anger kindle in her eyes, for he continued hastily, "So, how are you?" His gaze flicked over her from top to toe. "You look tired."

Didn't every woman love to hear that?

"I," she said deliberately, "am exhausted. The reason Ben is asleep whenever *you're* around—" she pointed her knitting needles at him for emphasis "—is because he's awake every other minute of the day. And night."

"Careful, Zorro." Tyler reached out and deflected the needles, which were almost stabbing him in the chest. "It's not my fault if I don't hear Ben at night."

"The only way you wouldn't hear him is if you're wearing those earplugs Olivia bought you."

He shook his head. "Uh-uh."

Bethany narrowed her eyes. "Maybe you can't hear him because you're sleeping somewhere else."

He appraised her through thick lashes. "I've been right here every night. In this bed."

She didn't need to think about that.

"Alone," he added mournfully.

With that newspaper article visible from the corner of her eye, she couldn't help saying, "Things not going well with Miss Georgia?"

"That would be your business...how?"

"It's the whole city's business, if you read the newspaper. Besides, if she dumped you," Bethany said hopefully, "and you're looking for an excuse to see her again, you can set me up to brief her about my research. She gets a lot of media coverage, she might be a useful spokesperson."

"Nice idea, but I think she has her hands full with world peace. And in the unlikely event of a woman dumping me, I won't need your help in patching things up." He leaned forward and grabbed the plastic shopping bag, which bore the logo of a local independent bookstore. He pulled out several books, stacked them on the nightstand on his side of the bed. Among them, Bethany recognized one that many of her patients' parents recommended: *What to Expect the First Year.* He crowned the pile with *Real Dads Change Diapers.*

He caught her watching him. "Obviously I'm philosophically opposed to this last one."

"I noticed," she said. "Still, it looks as if you're willing to be educated. So you'll be interested to learn that if researchers could figure out how to control antibody-producing cells, kidney patients might be able to accommodate transplanted organs from incompatible donors."

"Who do you think Ben's dad is?" Tyler asked.

Bethany counted to five and managed an ungracious "How would I know? Has the private investigator come up with something?"

"Nothing yet. I was just wondering... What if his dad is looking for him?"

Bethany blinked. Tyler had noticed she did that whenever

he disconcerted her…which wasn't as often as he'd like. Too often it worked the other way around.

"Good question, I've been thinking more about his mother," she admitted.

"That's because you're a woman," he said smugly. "It's hard for you to acknowledge that Ben's dad has just as much claim on him." It was a line he'd found when he'd skimmed *Real Dads Change Diapers,* a somewhat political tome, in the bookstore. He'd also skimmed the index of *What to Expect the First Year* and found no reference to rabies, which gave him another score to settle with Bethany.

She frowned. "In my experience, fathers love their kids just as much as moms do, though they're not always as good at showing it. But every kid needs a dad he can rely on. Maybe not so obviously at Ben's age, but in a few years' time he'll need someone to show him what being a man is all about."

Tyler was sorely tempted to pull out a pen and make notes. Bethany was more useful than any number of books when it came to getting up to speed on baby issues.

Bethany continued. "I'm not a guy—"stating the obvious, he thought, scoping out the fullness of her breasts in her thin, ribbed sweater "—but I'd bet being a father is the most rewarding, fulfilling, hope-giving experience a man can know. It'd beat those other coming-of-age experiences—first car, first girlfriend, graduation—hands down."

Enthusiasm lit Bethany's face, emphasizing its pixieish quality. Very cute. Then she added, "If you talk to some of the fathers of children in the kidney ward at Children's Health-care of Atlanta—"

Okay, now she'd gone past quotable and was riding her hobbyhorse into earnestness.

"Fascinating though this is," Tyler interrupted her, "I'm due at dinner in half an hour. You're welcome to stay, but I need to get changed."

"Miss Georgia again?" she said coolly, ignoring his invitation.

He folded his arms. "You seem overly interested in Miss Georgia."

Bethany flushed. "I'm interested in the fact you're never here with Ben."

"Right," he said dryly. They both knew she wanted him here so she could spout kidney facts. "The fact is, I pay *you* to care for him." Damn, he could sense another of her lectures coming. He said quickly, sympathetically, "You know, you wouldn't be the first woman to be jealous of Miss Georgia."

Her outraged gasp had him stifling a smile. "I'm about as jealous of Miss Georgia as I am of that table leg." She waved at the nightstand.

"That's a very shapely table leg," he conceded, "but you shouldn't put yourself down." He eyed her sweater again, noticed that it had worn perilously thin in places. "You have a great figure."

She drew herself up, and her indignation had the interesting effect of swelling her bosom. "My figure has absolutely nothing to do with—"

"There's every chance you'll find a boyfriend one day," he continued.

"I have a boyfriend," she snapped.

That was unexpected. Even more out of left field was Tyler's sudden urge to tear a telephone directory in half with his bare hands—he'd never indulged in primal-male competitive behavior. Finding Bethany curled on his bed asleep, one arm flung behind her head, her lips parted, must have struck a chord with some unconscious fantasy, and it had obviously unbalanced him. He forced himself to say lightly, "Is he deaf?"

"Of course he's not deaf!"

"I just wondered how he puts up with you." He dodged vengeful knitting needles. "What does he think about you living with me?"

"He's not *exactly* a boyfriend," she admitted. Tyler's testosterone surge ebbed slightly. "Kevin is just…someone I see sometimes."

"Ah." Tyler put all the knowledge of a man who knew every nuance of dating into the syllable. "Someone convenient. I've had plenty of those."

Bethany raised an eyebrow. "Convenient boyfriends?"

He grinned. "Plenty of convenient girlfriends."

She sniffed. "Emphasis on the plenty."

"Emphasis on the convenient," he corrected. "Did it occur to you that you might get further convincing me about your funding if you were nice to me?"

"You have more than enough people being nice to you," she said. "I plan to stand out from the crowd."

No matter that even sitting on the bed she was discernibly shorter than him, she was giving him that superior look down her nose. He said, "I don't have any trouble noticing you."

No trouble at all.

His gaze locked with hers across the bed, and there was a connection that Tyler figured even Bethany couldn't deny. It made no sense that he should find her so attractive—she dressed like a color-blind bag lady, she persisted in judging him according to her own overemotional standards and she was a pain in the backside.

But since when had sex and sense had anything in common, beyond the fact that they were both one-syllable words starting with S?

He leaned closer to her, which prompted her, gratifyingly, to lick her lips. His gaze zeroed in on that full mouth.

"Tyler," she warned, "I am *not* sending out signals. Not now, not ever."

He shook his head. "You are so deluded. One day you're going to wake up to this attraction, and when you do, I'll be here."

"Never," she insisted.

"You're making this hard on yourself," he chided her. "The longer you hold out, the more there'll be egg all over your pretty face when you have to admit it."

Bethany put a hand to her face involuntarily, then scowled when he laughed.

"Tell you what," he said. "I'm going to make this easier on you."

"You're going to walk out that door and have dinner with your *girlfriend?*"

"Uh-uh," he chided her. "Miss Georgia is fun, but she's not my girlfriend. Now, Peaches, I'm going to figure out a signal you can give me so you don't actually have to say out loud that you want me." He added kindly, "I understand that might just about choke you."

He took his time pretending to think, all the while enjoying the sight of her on his bed. Obviously sensing he planned a hands-on demonstration, she backed up against the headboard. "Don't touch me." Her voice held irritation, panic...doubt.

"Just this once," he said, "so you'll know what I mean."

In one graceful movement, Tyler shifted so close to Bethany that she could see the gold flecks in his blue eyes. Just as plainly as she could read the amused condescension in them.

He stretched a finger toward her, and Bethany forced herself not to flinch. *Let him play his stupid game.*

"This is what you need to do," he said softly. His finger found the tender skin just below her left ear, traced the line of her jaw. He tilted her chin so she was looking directly into his eyes and smiled down at her. Appreciatively. Seductively. And Bethany, dammit, was only human. She smiled back. If more world leaders were women, she thought, the USA would have a secret weapon right here in Tyler Warrington.

"That's all you have to do, Peaches, to tell me you want me."

Reason found her again, and Bethany jerked away from his touch. "Never going to happen." To her horror, she sounded breathless. And her jaw, where his finger had traced, felt tight, tingly.

Tyler laughed. "Never say never." His mission of throwing her off her stride apparently accomplished, he got off the bed and said briskly, "By the way, if I don't see you when I get in tonight, I need you to bring Ben to my office tomorrow afternoon. Four o'clock."

Now he was done toying with her, he was dismissing her.

"Tyler," she said firmly, "I need to talk to you about my research. Now."

"Go ahead," he invited, surprising her. Then he unbuckled his belt. His hand hovered over the button of his pants. "You don't mind if I get changed while we talk, do you?"

If she'd been braver, or at least less prone to blushing, she would have told him to go right ahead. But with her face in flames, Bethany scrambled off the bed and almost ran from the room.

AT THREE-THIRTY on Friday, Olivia was typing the latest batch of rejection letters Tyler had asked her to send out, when the door to her office opened. She looked up.

And thought, *Call Security.*

A hobo stood framed in her doorway. A giant hobo, more than six feet tall, enormous shoulders made broader by a grubby overcoat. His hair, an unkempt salt-and-pepper mix of brown and gray, grazed his collar, and Olivia judged the matching stubble on his chin to be at least three days' growth.

She reached for the phone.

"I'm Silas Grant," the hobo announced.

Two things stayed Olivia's hand. First, his name seemed familiar. Second, the words were uttered in a voice that was slow to the point of sleepiness, gravelly…and unquestionably educated.

As she puzzled over that riddle, he walked toward her with a silent, purposeful tread at odds with his sleepy voice. That lithe, almost graceful gait would have worried her if she'd been walking down a darkened street, but here she couldn't believe he posed any threat. Other than to her discriminating taste in fashion. His brown corduroy trousers were pale and worn at the knees, and over them he wore a heavy shirt in brown and green plaid, buttoned to the neck, but untucked. But while they may have been more suited to gardening, the clothes did appear clean. Unlike the overcoat.

"I'm here to see Tyler Warrington," he said.

Now that he was up close, Olivia saw he had gray eyes, but they weren't at all cold. They held the deep, dormant heat of ashes, beneath which lurked the potential, if stirred by just a hint of breeze, for fire.

"Do you have an appointment, Mr. Grant?" She knew he didn't—neither she nor Tyler believed in Friday-afternoon appointments. Tyler invariably had a hot date to prepare for, and, often enough, so did Olivia. Today she planned to be gone by four; she'd promised Gigi Cato she would come by to approve

the floral arrangements for this evening's soiree. It was incon-
venient—she'd have to drive home from Gigi's to change,
then turn around and go straight back to the Catos' again—
but what were friends for?

Silas Grant frowned. "How could I have an appointment,"
he asked gently, "when Tyler Warrington can't see a conservation crisis when it's right in front of him?"

Conservation crisis? Olivia remembered where she'd read
those words.

"You're the man with the red-spotted tree frog," she said,
pleased with herself. She couldn't quite remember if the spots
were red or yellow.

"Hyla punctatus," he said sternly.

It took Olivia a moment to realize he wasn't uttering some
dreadful curse over her, but rather was giving her the Latin—
or was it Greek?—name of the frog.

"It's on the verge of extinction," he said. "And Tyler Warrington just signed its death warrant."

He spoke slowly, even for a Georgian. The pace lent an
unlikely authority to his words, went some way toward coun-
tering his oddball appearance. But not far enough.

"I'm Olivia Payne, Mr. Warrington's secretary. I'm afraid
he's unavailable," she told him with the dismissive, well-
bred Atlanta-belle tone that had served her through her years
as a debutante, then as a single woman. Olivia was an expert
at giving men their marching orders. Over the years, she'd
broken off no fewer than six engagements. Possibly seven, if
you counted Teddy Benson, who'd popped the question three
years ago. She'd seen the light faster than normal, and broken
it off even before the engagement announcement hit the newspapers.

"Thank you so much for stopping by," she added pleasantly to Silas. Because one should always be polite in one's dismissal.

He planted both hands on her desk, which might have intimidated her if he'd done it any faster than a hedgehog crossing the road. The movement put his eyes level with hers, close enough to break through the professional distance she'd set with her voice.

She dropped her gaze, and observed that his hands were clean, his fingernails cut so neatly they might be manicured. She recalled that the tree-frog funding application had come from an address in Buckhead—could this man really live in the most expensive area of Atlanta?

"I won't take no for an answer," he said, and there was a hint of steel behind the soft drawl.

While his announcement might be tiresome—at this rate she'd be late to Gigi's house—it was nothing Olivia couldn't handle.

"Mr. Grant, as you were told in the letter you received, the foundation does not enter into correspondence about its endowment decisions." The same clean-break policy worked well with fiancés, she'd found. "I understand you're disappointed, but I can assure you, Mr. Warrington will not see you."

He straightened, but only so he could reach one long arm to pull up a chair. "I'll wait," he said, and sank into it, legs stretched out in front of him.

This had happened before, so she said, "As you wish," and returned to her typing.

Most people started to fidget within two minutes. After five minutes, they'd bluster some more. But when they saw she wouldn't be moved, they'd leave. The longest anyone had stayed was fifteen minutes. Something about silence unnerved them.

Today, it was Olivia who was unnerved. Silas didn't fidget,

not once, for fifteen minutes. He sat with his arms folded, quite still.

She kept her gaze fixed on her screen and wished the phone would ring with a summons to collect something from another part of the building, so she'd have a reason to move. But for once, no one called.

"Who else have you refused money to lately?" Silas's abrupt question startled her, so that she mistyped a word and looked at him before she remembered not to.

"It's not my money to give," she said politely. She added, "Nor is it Mr. Warrington's."

"What are your views on conservation and the environment?" he asked.

He really did have an attractive voice, one that almost made her want to say those things mattered to her. But, in this respect at least, she was always honest. Better to admit an unnatural lack of sentiment than to pretend to care.

"I don't have any." She was concerned, of course, that the planet shouldn't be flooded or burned up as a result of global warming. But that wasn't going to happen in her lifetime, so she didn't lose any sleep over it.

"*Hyla punctatus* is a Georgia native, not found anywhere else in America."

"I'm aware of that. From your funding application."

He ran a considering gaze over Olivia. She half wished she'd had her roots done this week. She wasn't out to impress him, she scolded herself. And if she was, her hair, worn loose today in its sculpted bob, her artfully applied makeup and the emerald-green cashmere polo-neck that made her neck look longer and slimmer would surely withstand his scrutiny.

"You know what this world lacks?" he said.

She pressed a hand to her mouth and gave a ladylike yawn.

"People who care." Sharpness tinged his words.

Of course she knew that! She said lightly, "If you can't beat them, join them."

Fire sparked into life in his eyes, and his jaw jutted beneath the mouth that she now noticed was firm and well shaped behind all those whiskers.

Olivia had the same keen appreciation for good-looking men that she did for silk lingerie and French champagne. Each of her seven fiancés had been gorgeous by anyone's standards. So she could only look at Silas Grant and rue the waste of such a fine specimen.

She wondered why his bizarre appearance didn't exempt him from her appreciation. Discomfited by the thought that perhaps, now that she'd turned fifty-five, she might be desperate enough to let her standards slip, Olivia looked away.

"It's exactly your kind of apathy that's sending this world to hell in a handbasket," he growled.

She'd obviously pressed one of Silas's buttons, because he began to decry, albeit in an undramatic way, the parlous state of the world, the shallowness of materialism and the loss of life's simple pleasures.

Olivia, who collected designer handbags, liked to dine on Wagyu beef and had two real fur coats in her wardrobe that she resented being unable to wear, struggled to sympathize.

Yet still, Silas Grant mesmerized her, whether with that unexpectedly cultured voice or with his sheer size. When she found herself wondering what he would look like with a shave and a tuxedo, she realized this had gone far enough.

"What will it take to convince you to leave?" she said abruptly, heatedly. She'd never reacted like this before, not to any of the cranky rejectees who'd turned up here.

"Your promise that you'll ask Warrington to meet me."

Either Silas had the good sense to say no more, or he'd run out of steam.

Olivia was so relieved to hear the end of that gentle diatribe that she agreed. "I'll let you know Mr. Warrington's response."

"Thank you." The two syllables stood stark, and for one moment, Silas sounded alone, as alone as Olivia.

CHAPTER FIVE

BETHANY PAUSED on the threshold of Olivia's office. Tyler's secretary was locked in a death glare with a bum in a dirty coat. Should she fetch help? She tightened her grip on Ben's car seat in case she had to run and said, "Olivia?"

The bum didn't acknowledge her arrival. He said to Olivia, "I'll be back," with about as much menace as a low-on-batteries Terminator. He swung around, loped past Bethany with his coat flapping.

Before Bethany could ask Olivia what that was about, Tyler opened the door of his office. "Olivia, have you seen my silver pen? I can't think where I—" He stopped, distracted by the disheveled appearance of the departing visitor, now out of earshot but still visible. "Who's that?"

Olivia cleared her throat. "Silas Grant, the guy who's saving the red-spotted tree frog. He wanted to see you."

"Was he bothering you?" Tyler took a step forward as if he might head down the corridor and grab hold of the man.

Olivia shook her head. "He's all right. Just…odd. I told him I'd find out if you're willing to meet with him."

Tyler cast another look at the guy, then turned to Bethany. He scanned her outfit—black leggings and a taupe crochet sweater, a by-product of the stress-relief technique that had preceded knitting, worn over a black slip. A taupe cardigan completed her layered look.

Bethany liked to think of it as Bohemian.

"Why is it that most do-gooders dress so badly?" he demanded. "It's like a badge of honor with some of you." He glanced down at his own clothing, which Bethany observed was unusually casual, yet as crisp and new looking as if he had a Calvin Klein store tucked in his office. "Nope," Tyler said complacently. "I don't see any reason why you can't look good *and* do good."

Bethany gaped. "You call yourself a do-gooder?"

He rubbed his chin. "Let me see...my job involves giving millions of dollars away to people in need, I'm an acknowledged expert on philanthropy, and now I'm fostering an abandoned baby." He nodded at Ben in his car seat but made no move to take him. "You're right, I'm evil."

"You spend money," she said, "but you don't care."

He groaned. "If you mean I don't respond emotionally to every problem, you're right. But if you mean providing practical assistance that makes a difference..."

"I mean," she said, "giving something of yourself, caring in a way that changes you as well as the other person."

He looked mystified. "Why would I want to change, when everyone loves me the way I am?"

Bethany was about to deliver a few choice words on that topic, when she saw laughter lurking beneath the innocent inquiry in his eyes. Tempted though she was to laugh—something she felt surprisingly often around Tyler—she chose not to indulge him. "That pen you're looking for," she said, referring to the question that had brought him out of his lair. "Would that be the one I borrowed the other day to write out a list of baby equipment?"

"So you did," he said.

"I took it," she admitted. "By accident."

He held out a hand. "May I have it back?"

"I haven't seen it in a couple of days." She frowned. "I know I used it to sign a check at the supermarket. I'm not sure if I put it back in my purse…"

"Could you think a little harder?" Tyler said. "It's my favorite."

Oops. Bethany grimaced. "I think I left it in the store."

"You're kidding, right?" His shock sounded out of all proportion to the loss of a pen.

"Keep your hair on," she said. "I'll buy you another one."

He folded his arms. "You're going to buy me another twelve-hundred-dollar Michel Perchin pen?"

She clattered Ben's car seat onto Olivia's desk before she dropped it. Olivia leaned back in her chair, looking askance.

"You didn't say twelve *hundred* dollars, did you?" Bethany pleaded. "You said twelve dollars."

Tyler glared at her.

She felt sick.

"That money's coming straight off your next research grant," he said. "Or it would, if I had any intention of giving you more cash."

In an instant, her fighting spirit was resurrected.

She planted her hands on her hips. "Twelve hundred dollars is an obscene amount to pay for a pen. You should be ashamed of yourself."

"*You* have an attitude problem." Tyler's effortless urbanity had vanished, and he spoke with the fulminating tension of a man goaded beyond endurance. "You've lost my handmade pen, which for all you know could be of great sentimental value, and somehow you've made this all about *my* flaws."

"*Could be* of sentimental value," she mocked. "But it's not, is it, because for that, you'd have to have a heart."

Into the seething pause, Olivia said, "What shall I tell Silas Grant? Will you see him?"

Bethany saw Tyler grapple to regain his control as he turned to his secretary. "I'm a family guy, not a frog guy," he said to Olivia with a passable replica of his normal ease, though Bethany's snort had his fists clenching at his sides. "I'm not interested."

Olivia looked relieved. "I'll let him know." She pulled a file out of her drawer. "In fact, I'll call and leave a message on his voice mail before he gets home."

Tyler frowned. "If you're worried about dealing with him, I'll do it."

His offer surprised Bethany. As far as she knew, Tyler didn't do anything for other people.

Olivia's face flushed. "It's no problem."

"Don't say I didn't *care* enough to offer," he said, with a pointed glance at Bethany. So that's what his sudden consideration was about. Then he said to her, "You'll be pleased to know I'll be *caring* for Ben personally tonight. I'm taking him out with me."

"Taking him where?" Bethany picked up Ben's car seat again. Somewhere that didn't involve Tyler's usual suit and tie, obviously. He wore designer-faded jeans, a long-sleeved fine-knit polo shirt, casual shoes. He looked like…like… Bethany struggled to define the annoyingly alluring blend of preppy and rugged. She failed.

"Babies don't go out at night," she told him. "You'll have to find another drinking buddy."

"My drinking buddies are all female, and believe me, there's no shortage of them." He grasped the car seat, one hand at each end, and tried to tug it from her. She held on. She wasn't about to pass Ben over until she was certain he wouldn't end up at some nightclub—she'd belatedly caught up with the eBay purse scandal, and it had reinforced her view that Tyler wasn't a suitable guardian.

"I'm taking him to a meeting of Divorced Dads International," he said.

Surprise loosened her clutch on the car seat, and he seized it. Bethany pretended she'd let him have it, and folded her arms. "That would be because you're divorced, or because you're a dad?"

His new look suddenly made sense. *He looks like a dad.*

A million-dollar dad, sure, but Tyler definitely looked like a guy who might have been woken by a baby at five this morning, who might have heated formula, who might even have changed a diaper.

Who knew appearances could be so deceptive?

"I'm the guest speaker at their quarterly meeting," he said.

"What the heck can you talk about?"

His gaze slid away from hers. "Motivational stuff. I figure I'm not qualified to offer actual advice." He added, "I know that doesn't stop some people."

She sent him a withering look. "What's in it for you?"

"Excuse me?" He put Ben's car seat down on Olivia's desk, which drew a resigned groan from his secretary.

"Like you said, you prefer to sign checks. What makes you want to motivate a bunch of dads?"

"The press will be there, it's good publicity for the foundation. The more people know about our work, the more partners like government and other charities will want to get involved in joint ventures with us." He spread his hands. "Which means bigger checks for all those people I love to help."

The challenge in his eyes dared her to object to his noble purpose. She longed to—something about this didn't add up.

But his argument was technically sound. With something approximating good grace, she handed Tyler the bag containing Ben's diapers, bottle and other essentials. "Here's all his stuff. He'll need a diaper change before you go."

He frowned. "Can't you do it?"

"I would," she said sweetly, "but it'll help you empathize with the divorced dads."

"I don't do empathy," he said. "I do checks."

She smiled sunnily and headed for the door.

"Olivia," Tyler cajoled behind her.

"If you ask me to change that diaper," his secretary said, "you'll be looking for a new assistant. There are only two certain things in this world, Tyler—you're selfish, and I'm even more selfish."

Maybe it was the shock of hearing the truth about the adult who'd taken responsibility for him, but Ben started to cry. Olivia began typing as if her life depended on it.

Tyler cursed. "Bethany!"

She'd just made it out the door. Though she told herself not to, she stuck her head back around.

"He's crying."

She gave him a thumbs-up. "Well done—you're a natural at this parenting stuff."

"Can't you do something?" And when she would have pulled the door closed and left, he added, "Please?"

Darn it, he was projecting the kind of male helplessness that called to a woman's maternal instincts, then subverted those instincts, thanks to the addition of a sexy smile, into something far less wholesome.

Drawn by a force too strong to resist, Bethany eased back into the office. "I'm doing this for Ben. Not for you."

"Of course." She could tell herself that if she liked, Tyler thought, but he was the one she hadn't been able to turn down.

"If this was about you, I'd be out of here so fast you wouldn't see me."

"Dust," he agreed.

Her blue eyes turned calculating. "And you understand that I have never, ever given you any kind of signal? You agree that I am not attracted to you in any way?"

Tyler was aware of Olivia's bristling speculation. What was the bet his mother would hear about this conversation within the hour?

Ben's cry turned to the kind of howling wail that would have someone at the far end of the building dialing 911.

"I agree," he lied. He sent Olivia an intimidating look. She winked in reply.

"Sweet baby," Bethany cooed to Ben as she unclipped his harness. She lifted him out of the seat, and for one second the sobbing stopped, but then it was back full force. She grimaced as Ben got too close to her ear.

She had pretty ears, Tyler noticed, with her red-brown hair tucked behind them.

Bethany swayed with Ben in her arms, her attention so focused on the baby that Tyler felt as if she no longer saw him or Olivia. Softly, sweetly, she sang, "Rock a bye baby, on the treetop, when the wind blows the cradle will rock."

"With lyrics like that, it's no wonder I don't remember any of those old rhymes," he said. "Who would put a baby up a tree?" Ben's cries had quieted somewhat, but Tyler figured any guy might shut up and listen with Bethany crooning at him, no matter how psychotic the words.

"When the bough breaks—" Bethany frowned at Tyler as she sang on, lowering her voice to a murmur as the baby's sobs turned to wet hiccups "—the cradle will fall, and down will come baby, cradle and all."

"You'll give him nightmares," Tyler protested.

"He doesn't understand the words," Bethany said in the same low voice she'd used for the song.

"You don't know that for sure. This is probably why you're having so much trouble with his sleeping."

"If you think you can do better..." Eyes sparking, she offered the baby to Tyler. He got the message loud and clear: if he didn't shut up, she'd walk right out of his office.

He shut up. Bethany held all the aces when it came to Ben, though, fortunately, she didn't seem to realize that.

Suddenly, taking Ben to the divorced-dads meeting didn't seem like such a great idea. What if he started yelling again? But without a kid in tow, Tyler would look too much like his old playboy self, despite the clean-cut, low-key outfit he'd adopted for the occasion.

He propped himself against a filing cabinet, made no effort to take Ben from her arms. "No way can I do better than you," he soothed her. "How would you like to come along to this meeting and show the single fathers how a pro does it?"

"No, thanks, this is my night off." With Ben now settled, she headed into Tyler's carpeted office. Tyler picked up the change bag she'd left on Olivia's desk and followed her.

Bethany spread a changing mat on the floor and whipped off Ben's wet diaper.

As Tyler watched, Ben's soft unfocused gaze found him, then sharpened into a kind of bemused recognition. It struck Tyler just how vulnerable this little boy was, bare bottomed in a roomful of strangers, with the office door open so even Olivia could see the whole process.

"Give the kid some privacy," he told Olivia, who was observing with a kind of fascinated repulsion.

Olivia rolled her eyes. "I saw your cute baby bottom more times than I can remember when you were this age. Doesn't seem to have done you any harm."

"Great." Tyler moved to block her view of Ben. "My secretary has not only seen my butt, she talks about it."

"Don't they all?" Bethany asked in surprise, and it took him a second to realize she was joking. He glared at her, and heard Olivia snicker.

"How about I give you a whole day off on Sunday, instead of tonight?" he said. To remind her how irresistible he was to women, he added, "Miss Georgia's always saying she loves kids, I'll invite her over on Sunday for some hands-on experience."

Bethany knew she should refuse to help him out, should make him fend for himself with Ben tonight. And she didn't feel a need to humor Miss Georgia's desire to play mommy.

But something had shifted in the dynamic between Tyler and Ben just now. Something had clicked.

One minute she'd been changing the diaper, with Tyler looking and yet not looking, with his usual disinterest.

Then everything had changed.

She'd seen it in his sudden straightening, in the flaring of compassion in his eyes, in his admonishment to Olivia and his not-so-subtle shielding of the baby.

Bethany didn't know why it had happened, but she knew what it meant. As of right now, Tyler saw Ben as a person, with dignity in his own right.

She wasn't naive enough to believe Tyler had suddenly developed a fully evolved conscience in place of his throw-money-at-the-problem attitude. And certainly Ben's need for privacy was not one of the more pressing issues.

But maybe that moment of recognition had been a first step—a baby step, if you will—on the journey to becoming a less selfish human being.

And once Tyler Warrington learned to care, who knew how much help he'd give her for her research?

THE RATIO OF MEN to women in the ballroom at the Excelsior Hotel was pretty well what she'd expected. After all, this was a convention for single dads. Among the fathers chatting in clusters, taking their seats in ordered rows or handing babies and preschoolers over to the woman running the daycare area in the back left corner of the room, Bethany counted just two female hotel workers, the daycare woman, plus herself.

Everyone else had a Y chromosome. A couple of hundred divorced dads, a handful of male reporters—Divorced Dads International had a reputation as a vocal and sometimes aggressive supporter of fathers' rights—and Tyler.

Tyler insisted on putting Ben in the day care so he could "meet some other kids," once again showing his skewed prioritization of Ben's needs. Bethany suspected Tyler wanted to fit in with the other dads.

The meeting was called to order. The organization's chairman introduced Tyler as the man they'd all seen in the news this week as the remporary guardian of baby Ben. He used terms that couldn't have been more glowing if Tyler had delivered Ben himself while surrounded by raging fire in the middle of an earthquake, rather than just opening a duffel bag and finding the little boy lying there. Tyler wore a self-deprecating, and very appealing, smile that said he was just your regular hero, no need to make a fuss, folks.

He eased into his speech with a couple of jokes about diapers and sleepless nights. So what if he knew nothing about either? He had the kind of charisma that made people—even tough, tattooed men, as some of these guys were—pay attention, laughing when they should, murmuring in sympathy or agreement in key moments.

As he moved into what Bethany guessed was the main part of his speech—as unfazed as his audience by the occasional squeal of laughter or cry of frustration emanating from the day care area—Tyler acknowledged he didn't have a lot of experience with babies.

"But," he said, "I'm starting to figure that being a father is the most rewarding, fulfilling, hope-giving experience a man can know. It beats those other coming-of-age experiences—first car, first girlfriend, graduation—hands down."

Now that was impressive.

And familiar.

The rat was repeating exactly what she'd said last night.

"Heck," he said, "I'd go so far as to say it's better than sex."

Okay, that was original. Obviously he didn't mean it, but it got a big laugh from the audience.

"In my experience, fathers love their kids just as much as moms do," Tyler continued. "They're just not as good at showing it. But every kid needs a dad to be a role model. Maybe not so obviously at Ben's age, but in a few years' time he's going to need someone to show him what being a man is all about."

The audience cheered, a couple of cameras flashed white lights at the stage. Bethany seethed. Once again, the master manipulator had played her. That softening she'd seen back at the office had doubtless been a ploy to persuade her to come along tonight, just so Tyler wouldn't have to get his hands dirty actually looking after the baby.

"I may not be in Ben's life then," Tyler said soberly. "But I'll do my best to make sure he's got someone—some guy—to look up to."

Empty words.

Tyler issued a couple of insightful suggestions that hadn't come from Bethany, so she assumed they were straight out of *Real Dads Change Diapers*. Then—surely by now he was skating at the extreme limits of his capacity to talk about parenting—he began to wrap things up.

"In the few days that I've had responsibility for a baby, I've realized just what hard work parenting is," he said.

Bethany snorted. A man in the back row whose muscled forearms and low-riding pants suggested he might be a construction worker turned to frown at her.

"You guys have my respect," Tyler said. "Give yourselves a round of applause." There was a stutter of self-congratulatory clapping, which at Tyler's urging grew more solid, then thundered through the ballroom. When it died away, Tyler leaned forward at the lectern, fixed his gaze on the audience with an intimacy that suggested he was making eye contact with every man in the room.

He lowered his voice, but in the silence his masculine presence commanded, his words carried to the farthest corners. "Guys, I don't know much about looking after a baby, but if there's one piece of advice I can offer from my limited experience, let it be this…"

He paused, and the suspense just about killed Bethany, so she could guess what it was doing to people who actually believed this garbage. "Please, guys, no matter how busy you get with your precious kids…please, I know it's hard…but take some time for yourselves."

The room erupted into applause, punctuated by whoops

and hollers. The tough-looking construction worker in front of Bethany blew his nose into a none-too-clean handkerchief.

The man who took more time for himself than anyone Bethany had ever met stepped down from the stage. His progress toward the back of the room, where she knew he'd arranged to chat to a couple of the reporters while the meeting continued, was slowed by men wanting to clap him on the shoulder, shake his hand or discuss their child-rearing issues. Tyler accepted the first two with buddylike equanimity and managed to deflect the last with a charming admission of ignorance that somehow came across as authoritative.

Bethany stepped forward. "I had no idea you knew so much about being a father," she said coldly.

On a high from the applause and the adrenaline rush of having spent twenty minutes talking on something he knew nothing about, Tyler grinned. "Nor did I, Peaches. It's amazing how it all just came to me."

He took advantage of Bethany's speechless outrage and moved on to greet the reporters who were his only reason for being here. One of them was a stringer for the *Washington Post.* Tyler had no doubt the think-tank crowd would soon be reading about tonight's success.

He managed to hold up his end of the interview by talking common sense—no, he didn't think men should resort to illegal methods to see their children, and yes, he thought mediation between estranged parents was a great idea—and by throwing in a few more of Bethany's pearls of wisdom.

He could tell from her pursed lips that his parenting muse wasn't happy…but too bad, what could she do?

The interview moved on to the search for Ben's mother.

"Social services is trying to locate her, and we're boosting those efforts with the help of a private investigator I hired," Tyler said.

"What consequences will the mother face for abandoning her child?" asked the *Post* reporter.

Tyler would bet the divorced dads would have some suggestions. "We don't know yet how old she is…what her circumstances are. Until we do, none of us can judge her," he said. "The priority will be to make sure Ben ends up in a loving, supportive environment. It's too soon to say whether that will be with one or both of his parents."

Both reporters had brought photographers, and both wanted to take a picture of him with Ben.

Interrupting his own reply to a question about joint-custody agreements, Tyler turned to Bethany. "Could you fetch Ben from the day care?"

Her infinitesimal pause should have warned him.

"No," she said. A battle light glinted in her eyes, and something in her tone had both the reporters turning to her.

Uh-oh. No way did Tyler want them copping her views about him as a parent. "The number-one problem facing a lot of dads who share custody," he said to the reporters, "is finding a good babysitter. Sometimes you end up scraping the bottom of the barrel." He twitched his head in Bethany's direction, then winked to show his audience he was teasing.

But he knew how sensitive Bethany was—she had no sense of humor when it came to him winking—and, true to form, she got mad. So mad that she stalked off, red-faced, almost frothing at the mouth. Even if she'd stayed, he figured she would have been incoherent with anger.

Of course, that meant he had to get Ben himself. He excused himself from the reporters with a promise he'd be back in a minute, then headed for the day care.

"You were great, Mr. Warrington," the woman in charge said.

"Thanks." He gave her his warm, playful Superdad smile, and her hand moved involuntarily to cover her heart. "I'd like to take Ben out for a photo."

"Sure, I'll just—"

"Excuse me." Bethany spoke from beside Tyler, startling him.

So she'd caved, huh? He might have known her do-gooder instincts wouldn't let her butt out where Ben was concerned. She didn't look quite as mad as before, but she held herself stiffly, as if her calmness was the product of rigid self-control. Tyler rewarded her with a full-on dazzling smile.

But she wasn't looking at him. She said to the day care woman, "You see that little girl over there?" She pointed to an angelic-looking girl wielding a pink fairy wand to deal punishing blows to two smaller boys. *The innocent-looking girls are the worst,* Tyler thought, remembering how Bethany had blackmailed him. She deserved whatever grief he gave her.

"I'm a pediatrician and I noticed she's showing signs of an allergic reaction," Bethany continued.

The day-care woman's forehead crinkled. "You're a doctor? Not a babysitter?"

"A doctor *and* a babysitter," Bethany said. "Mr. Warrington insists on nothing but the best care for Ben." Understanding dawned on the woman's face, and Bethany went on, "The girl's allergy doesn't look too serious, but you might want to notify her father."

The day-care woman looked horrified. "Of course I will. Thank you so much for letting me know." As she leafed through her list of names, looking for details of the girl's father, she said distractedly to Tyler, "Can you get Ben yourself, Mr. Warrington, I need to deal with this."

She found the information she was looking for, and scanned the crowded room.

"You go and find the dad," Bethany encouraged her. "I'll keep an eye on the kids for a minute."

The woman gave Bethany a look of such gratitude that for an instant, Tyler could see how rewarding it must be to have a job like Bethany's. If you liked that kind of thing.

He left her chatting to a couple of toddlers and made his way over to the infant section, where half a dozen babies snuggled in their car seats.

Half a dozen *identical* babies.

In half a dozen car seats as near as dammit identical.

Hell. Which one was Ben? Panic gripped Tyler and he forced himself to slow his thoughts. Ben was wearing a white romper. That eliminated the baby in the red sailor suit and the one in the yellow dress—which was probably a girl, though you couldn't be sure these days.

Four babies wore white rompers, obviously some kind of must-have infant fashion. Perspiration beaded on Tyler's brow. The baby second from the left had much more hair than Ben, he was certain. Darker, too. The one next to it looked too fat. That left two—one at either end—to choose from.

Tyler looked from one to the other. Now he could see they weren't identical at all, but he still had no idea which one was Ben.

Bethany spoke at his elbow. "Need some help?"

Relief flooded him. Then he saw the glitter in her eyes.

"I'll show you which baby is Ben," she said coolly, "but it'll cost you."

Blackmail, her weapon of choice.

"How much?" He couldn't afford to blow an interview with the *Washington Post* and if the reporter, or anyone in the audience here, suspected Tyler didn't have a clue which baby he was responsible for, his family-man image would be shot to pieces.

He figured her price would be something to do with those kidney kids. Not the research money, for some weird reason she considered that unethical, though she didn't hesitate to make other demands.

She drew a deep breath, and Tyler braced himself for whatever new way she'd devised of making his life difficult.

"Two hours of your time, every day, to be spent with Ben."

She surprised a laugh out of him. "What's the catch?"

"No catch." Her blue eyes were serious.

"Two hours a day doing whatever I want with Ben?" he said skeptically.

"Two *waking* hours," she amended, "for both of you."

Tyler couldn't believe his luck. He would probably need to spend that much time with Ben anyway, with all the media appearances his PR manager had lined up over the next couple of weeks. For once, Bethany's naiveté was working in his favor. She'd be sick to know how much better a deal she could have scored if she'd been tougher, if she'd realized how important this interview was. He didn't let his inward smile show on his face, just stuck out a hand. "Deal."

Satisfaction glinted in Bethany's eyes. Ignoring his hand, without another word, she bent to pick up one of the infant car seats, passed it to Tyler.

She'd chosen the fat baby that hadn't even made his short-list. Dubiously, he inspected the pudgy white bundle. "Are you sure this is Ben? I didn't think he was so, uh, round."

"Of course I'm sure," she said scornfully.

Tyler's departure from the baby area was hindered by the

arrival of the day-care lady and an anxious-looking man in a suit.

"This is Lucy's father," the woman said to Bethany.

Bethany's brow creased in perplexity. Then it cleared. "I'm so sorry to have worried you," she said to the guy. "From a distance I thought your daughter looked a little flushed and swollen, but I can see now there's nothing wrong with her. My mistake." The reassuring smile she gave the girl's father might not have dazzled on the scale of Tyler's, but it was sweet enough that the guy—who Tyler now saw was good-looking, in a weedy kind of way—perked up.

Her *mistake?* Tyler pinned Bethany with a glare, willing her to look at him. The connection between them was as telepathic as it was sexual. It took only a second for her to glance his way. The bland innocence of her countenance didn't fool him for one second. Then she couldn't help herself, and a pleased-as-punch smile broke out.

The manipulative little witch.

Though, he had to admit, that had been pretty quick thinking for a babysitter scraped from the bottom of the barrel. It bespoke the same almost poetic cleverness he liked to think he possessed himself. His mouth twitched, and he clamped it back into line.

"Don't apologize." Lucy's father put a hand on Bethany's arm. "I appreciate you taking so much care." *Care, that word again,* Tyler thought sourly. The guy darted a lightning-quick glance at Bethany's left hand, pushed his trendy rimless glasses higher up his nose and said, "Maybe I could buy you dinner soon. Just to say thank you."

Someone should warn Bethany that divorced dads had more than gratitude on their minds when they asked a pretty woman to dinner. Tyler coughed significantly. All three of them—Bethany, Lucy's dad, the day-care woman—turned to stare at him.

"I'd love to," Bethany said. "But my employer is very unreasonable and I don't get a lot of time off."

Which didn't stop her giving the jerk her cell-phone number along with an invitation to call her.

He could be an ax murderer, for Pete's sake.

"Do you realize you just put Ben's safety at risk, inviting a stranger into your life?" he demanded as they headed back to the journalists.

Her nose went up in the air. "I am so not talking to you."

"You can't go out with that guy," he persisted.

She stopped suddenly, but her force field of self-righteousness prevented him from bumping into her. "What's your problem, Tyler?" she demanded. "Are you jealous that despite this supposed attraction that's rampant between us, I gave my number to another man?"

He narrowed his eyes. "I'm as jealous of Mr. Specs as you are of Miss Georgia."

"Okay, you're not jealous," she agreed. "You've got the right baby, thanks to me, and all you had to do was agree to spend a lousy two hours a day with him. I'd say things are going pretty well for you."

She flounced away.

CHAPTER SIX

BETHANY WATCHED from a distance as the photographers did their work and the reporters threw in a couple more questions that seemed designed to make Tyler look good. She couldn't decide if she was furious with him—the cretin, not even recognizing Ben—or elated that she'd pinned him down to that daily two hours.

It might not seem like much, but Bethany was certain that she was on the right track.

Tyler might have faked that moment of connection with Ben back in his office this afternoon, but once he was spending more time with the child, there was no way he wouldn't fall for him. Then he'd be more open-minded about her research and a whole host of other issues where he could do some good.

She was going to *make* him care.

As they drove home in Tyler's BMW M6, Bethany's cell phone rang, breaking the loaded, wary silence that so far not even Ben had dared breach.

Overwrought by the tensions of the day, Bethany answered the phone without checking her display. And immediately wished she hadn't.

"Where have you been?" her mom said. "I've been calling. The hospital said you're on vacation."

Bethany closed her eyes. Her parents had to know sooner

or later. "I'm taking a short break from my research to look after Tyler Warrington's baby." From the corner of her eye, she saw his head jerk around. "Although it's not actually his baby," she amended.

"The little boy who's been in the papers?" her mother said, flabbergasted.

"That's right," Bethany enthused. "He's such a cutie, you'd love him." They both knew that wasn't true. Mom was all out of love.

"But what about your work?" Her mom's voice turned high and thin, and Bethany's conscience pricked. "You said you were getting more money."

"I—I wasn't quite right, as it turned out. But, Mom, Tyler Warrington, the guy I'm working for, is the man with the money."

Next to her, the money pot's eyebrows knitted in disapproval. Bethany shifted in her seat so she couldn't see him.

"This job puts me close enough to Tyler to convince him to fund my work for another year." Anxious silence down the phone. Bethany pictured her mother twisting the cord in her fingers, trying not to blurt out her disappointment. "Another *two* years," she said desperately. She ignored Tyler's snort. "Believe me, by the time he's had me living in his house a few more weeks—"

"You're *living* with him?"

"It's a live-in job, Mom. Nothing's going on."

The sound from Tyler might have been emphatic agreement.

"Sweetheart, you know we love you." Her mom's voice dropped to a coaxing note.

Did they? In their own way, perhaps. But never as much as they'd loved Melanie.

Mom said, "But I'm worried you're losing sight of what you're working for."

Her work was all Bethany ever thought about, so the unfairness of that comment stung. She ended the call as fast as she could, then let out a long, slow breath.

"Good thing I was under no illusions about how you feel about me," Tyler said. "Discovering you only wanted my money could have been quite a shock."

She stuck out her tongue.

"You've been spending too much time with juveniles," he said.

"You haven't been spending enough time with them." She folded her arms. "But that's about to change."

She held on to that single bright spark.

TYLER WOULD HAVE SPENT his promised two hours with Ben on Saturday, but he'd already arranged his monthly football game with his pals before he'd made that commitment to Bethany. He couldn't let the team down on such short notice. He told Bethany so, and explained that although the game didn't take long, they always went for a few beers afterward, then ended up at one of the guys' houses to watch a game on TV. Obviously, he couldn't mess with tradition.

She made a big show of counting to ten, hands behind her back, gazing at the ceiling, then grudgingly accepted his explanation with the rider that he had to start with Ben tomorrow.

On Sunday, his almost-genuine intention to spend time with Ben was derailed when Tyler remembered that today was the two-weekly lunch at his mother's house.

He canceled the planned visit from Miss Georgia and left for Mom's. Unfortunately, he wasn't able to take Ben with him because Bethany had taken the baby out for a walk, even though it was her day off. Tyler had to admire her work ethic.

He left her a note to say where he was, and in a fit of generosity that he'd probably regret, added a P.S. promising to spend extra time with Ben on Monday.

It was a sunny day, though cold, so lunch was set up in the conservatory. As always, Tyler was the last to arrive, right behind Olivia, who was an honorary member of the family. Max, his brother, would have been first there, followed by their cousin Jake. Jake's mother had died some years ago and he was estranged from his father. Susan Warrington, Jake's aunt and godmother, treated her late husband's nephew as a surrogate son.

"I can't believe you didn't bring the baby with you," Susan complained as they started in on the appetizer of smoked-salmon roulade.

"If you smelled him you'd know why." Tyler broke open a hot, freshly baked bread roll and savored the aroma.

His mom rapped the back of his hand with her fork. "That's mean, and so are you for not bringing him."

"Are you sure you didn't put him in the trunk and forget about him?" Max said.

It was a referral to an incident from their childhood. A friend of their parents had given Max and Tyler, aged six and four, respectively, an enormous chocolate teddy bear each. Tyler had eaten his in about an hour. Max, possessed of much greater self-control—which he still was, now that Tyler thought about it—planned to eat his bear over the course of a month.

By day three, Tyler's bear was a distant memory—he didn't fully believe he'd ever had one, let alone eaten it all himself—so he began pestering Max for a share of his. Max had a strong sense of what was fair and right—again, he still did—and refused.

After a week, Tyler convinced himself that not only was Max the greediest kid alive, he must also have taken Tyler's bear and eaten it. From there, it was a short step to finding a way to right this terrible wrong.

When Max was having his piano lesson, Tyler took the remaining three-quarters of chocolate teddy, and hid it in the trunk of their mother's car. Amazingly, it took Max two days to notice the theft. By which time Tyler had forgotten where he'd put it.

Now, twenty-seven years later, Tyler figured his guilty conscience had blotted out the whole incident. No one had believed he couldn't remember, and he'd had the sore backside to prove it. They found Max's chocolate, or what was left of it, the next time Mom opened the trunk—on a scorching July day about a month later. They'd never gotten the trunk completely clean. And Max had never let Tyler forget the incident.

But these days it was a subject of humor, not acrimony, so when Max made that comment about leaving Ben in the trunk, Tyler laughed along with him. "I have a babysitter who'd never let me get away with that."

He wondered if Bethany was home yet, what she was doing.

"I can't imagine you looking after a kid," Max said.

Tyler spread butter on his roll. "He's kind of cute."

"Yeah, but—ouch!" Max lifted the tablecloth and glared under the table. "Mom, that mutt of yours bit me."

"Don't be silly, darling," Susan said. "Mitzy is the sweetest-natured dog in the world."

"She sure is," Tyler agreed, happy to let his mother's unreasonable devotion to her aging Cavalier King Charles spaniel deflect his brother's curiosity. He grinned in response to Max's scowl.

His respite didn't last long. Jake was gazing past him out the window of the conservatory with an abstracted expression, twirling his wineglass between his thumb and forefinger.

"It's been a while," his cousin said thoughtfully, "since an enraged female has descended on this place with the intention of amputating a sensitive part of your anatomy, Tyler."

Yet another youthful memory that kept the family amused. "Those were my wild-oats days," Tyler said. "I've grown up."

Jake gave him a pained look, then focused back out the window. "Funny how those things can come back to haunt a guy."

All eyes followed Jake's. Tyler had to turn in his seat.

"What the—?" He inhaled a crusty flake of bread roll and began choking.

Bethany was walking—no, stomping—up the driveway, Ben strapped into his front-pack. Tyler had an awful feeling she'd taken a bus here from his place, which doubtless involved two transfers and a long walk in between. He imagined it wasn't the sort of journey that left one in a happy frame of mind. He couldn't actually see a knife, but even from this distance, he could read in Bethany's black look the intention to emasculate him.

"Hell." He coughed, managed to dislodge the rogue bread crust, swallowed. Cutlery rattled as he shoved his chair back from the table.

"She's pretty, but she's not your usual type," his mother said, interested.

"She's the babysitter." Tyler threw his napkin onto the table. "I'll go see what she wants."

Jake snickered. "Apart from the obvious."

Tyler hurried out into the hallway so he could head her off at the pass.

When he opened the heavy front door, Bethany's teeth snapped together and she began unclipping the front-pack. Seemed she was too mad to speak.

"Let me help," he said, and was rewarded with a filthy look from flashing blue eyes. He was fairly sure Bethany wouldn't actually throw the baby at him, but just in case, he kept a tight grip on Ben while she wriggled her arms free of the harness. That achieved, she dropped the diaper bag on Tyler's foot. Manfully, he didn't flinch.

"Take your baby and look after him," she said through gritted teeth.

"Would you like to come in?" He knew she wouldn't, but he was intent on scoring points for hospitality.

"Do I *look* like I've had a lobotomy?" she demanded. "If I step through that door, you'll have me feeding Ben, changing his diaper, putting him to bed…"

"You mean, all the things I pay you to do?"

She rammed fisted hands onto her hips. "You promised me two hours a day."

"And you'll get them. Soon. Look, I'm sorry about today, but I promised my family I'd be here, and Ben wasn't around when I left." As he explained himself, which he *never* did to, say, women he dated, Tyler's sense of personal grievance grew. She'd blackmailed him into this two-hours-a-day thing, and hadn't made any allowances for him needing to carve out that time. "I can't just drop everything to suit you—do you have any idea how busy I am?"

"Too busy to have taken a good enough look at Ben's face to remember what he looks like."

Damn.

"Too busy to visit a bunch of sick kids who might die if researchers don't figure out how to help them."

Double damn.

"Too busy to—"

"You've made your point," he snapped, before she convinced even him he was lower than…whatever the lowest bug was in the bug hierarchy.

"*You* made a promise. And I'm yet to hear a decent excuse for breaking it. Don't give me busy." She shoved a sticky-out piece of hair behind one ear. "*I'm* so busy with Ben, I haven't had a proper meal in a week. You're a—a—"

"He's a brute," Tyler's mother said from behind him.

Just what he needed.

Bethany blinked, adjusted her focus. "Yes, he is."

"It's my fault," his mom said.

Bethany blinked again.

"I gave birth to him," Susan apologized. "I inflicted him on the world, then I brought him up to have no regard for anyone other than himself."

"Thanks, Mom," Tyler said.

"Why would you do that?" Bethany asked, so mystified that Susan laughed.

"We all make mistakes. In my defense, he does have very good manners." She clasped Bethany's hands. "My dear, I'm Susan Warrington, mother to this wretched creature."

Belatedly, Tyler remembered his famous manners. "Mom, this is Dr. Bethany Hart."

"I've heard all about you from Olivia," Susan said, and Tyler knew that had to be bad. "The research you're doing into kidney disease is so important, it quite captivates me."

Just like that, Bethany melted. She made an indistinct sound that left her lips parted, so Tyler could see the pink tip of her tongue, and she swayed slightly toward his mother.

"My dear, you're clearly in need of a decent meal," Susan said. Tyler rolled his eyes. "We just happen to be sitting down to a salmon roulade, followed by citrus-roasted goose, then peach cobbler with homemade ice cream."

Bethany's stomach growled, and she clamped her hands over it. "I can't come in," she said reluctantly, "because *he*—" she jerked her head at Tyler "—won't do a thing for Ben if I'm here."

"I'll insist that he does," Susan said. "Besides, who could refuse this gorgeous baby anything?" She leaned down to goochy-goo at Ben, which immediately sent her to the top of Bethany's approval list—no easy feat, Tyler knew.

"He'll con you into doing it instead," Bethany said morosely.

Susan tugged on Bethany's hands. "Absolutely not. You're right, my son should face up to his responsibilities. Did you knit that sweater?"

Tyler was certain no reputable store would stock anything as odd as the open-knit blue sweater with the asymmetrical hem that Bethany had teamed with a long skirt and boots.

Bethany put a self-conscious hand over a particularly large hole in the weave. "I'm not very good."

"The wool is lovely and the color is gorgeous on you," Susan said diplomatically. She pulled Bethany over the threshold. "Come in, and I'll show you the shawl I'm knitting. But first I'll just shut Mitzy—that's my dear little dog—away, not that she would *ever* hurt Ben. And you must tell me more about your work." She spoke so rapidly, darting from subject to subject, that Tyler could see Bethany caving in under the gentle, inexorable force.

"We'll set an extra place for lunch," his mother said, "and I promise Tyler will be solely responsible for the baby while you eat."

Tyler scowled at his mom's treachery, but she just laughed over her shoulder as she led Bethany to the conservatory.

Tyler carried Ben, still in the front-pack. With a jerk of his head, he requested Jake to hold on to the pack so he could release Ben from his confinement. It took half a minute of wrestling the little wriggler, but at last he got the baby out. Tyler was holding Ben from behind as Jake tugged the front-pack away. His cousin started to laugh.

"What's so funny?" So what if Tyler wasn't a natural when it came to holding a baby?

Max took one look at Ben and guffawed. Tyler turned the little boy around so he could share the joke.

Ben had an oval sticker plastered to his navy blue romper. One of those stickers they hand out at conferences.

Hello, my name is Ben.

Tyler slammed Bethany with his glare.

"I wanted to avoid any confusion," she said snootily as she accepted the chair Susan proffered.

Before Tyler could wreak revenge, Bethany was sitting down, eating the smoked-salmon dish with a knife and fork and with a leisurely bliss that suggested she wasn't even thinking about the baby.

Tyler, on the other hand, held Ben in one hand and a fork in the other, and struggled constantly to ensure the two didn't meet. Ben's wandering hands—this kid had a great future as a horny teenager—made it almost impossible for Tyler's fork to connect with his meal.

Max couldn't stop chuckling every time he caught sight of that name sticker, Jake was flirting with Bethany, and Susan was going all out to ensure Bethany's comfort. The only person who had any evident sympathy for Tyler was Olivia, who winced every time she looked at him, but nonetheless steered a wide berth around Ben.

Bethany's instinct was to shovel her food in as fast as she could, before Tyler handed Ben back. But the atmosphere in Susan Warrington's house was so genteel, her hostess so gracious, that she couldn't bring herself to abandon good manners. She found herself delicately forking food, laying her knife aside, transferring salmon to her mouth with a sense of relaxation that felt otherworldly.

"Give us the scoop, Bethany," Max said. "Is Tyler the world's worst dad?"

Max wasn't as handsome as Tyler, but he had a commanding presence and a hard charm that probably attracted a lot of women.

Even though Bethany knew Tyler would win a Least Likely Father contest hands down, she replied with a noncommittal "He's adjusting."

She caught the flash of surprise in Tyler's eyes before Ben stuffed four fingers up his temporary dad's nose, and the surprise turned into a yelp of pain.

"He's certainly the best-looking daddy a boy could have," his mother said fondly. When Max groaned, she patted her older son's hand across the table, "So would you be, dear, it's just you don't have a baby."

Max sent her an impatient look. "Neither does Tyler. This is just his latest fad."

"Hey," Tyler protested. "This kid's mother left him with me."

"The Warrington Foundation strikes again," Max said dryly. "Leaving us to make millions of dollars, while you change diapers."

By "us," he meant Warrington Construction, Bethany presumed. Max's joke fell flat. Tyler got a resentful look in his eye, but he obviously wasn't about to admit he'd never changed a diaper, which limited the responses he could make to his brother's comment.

Just when the silence threatened to get awkward, he recovered his equanimity and said with a self-righteousness that made Bethany giggle, "It's sad how you rate the ability to make money so much higher than the ability to look after an abandoned child."

"Now, boys, you know I don't like to hear you arguing about business." Susan smiled at Bethany. "The foundation is my baby."

"Oh," Bethany said politely.

"Ten years ago, it didn't exist. My husband and I used to get a lot of personal letters asking for money, so I decided to set up a charity to help people."

"It was a hobby, like her knitting," Max said, which Bethany read as an older-brotherly attempt to put Tyler in his place.

"In those days we were giving away small amounts to hundreds of people," Susan said. "After my husband died, Tyler moved out of Warrington Construction and took over the charity. He created the Warrington Foundation." She reached over and ruffled Tyler's hair before he could duck. "It was perfect for you, darling—all that schmoozing you're so good at."

Tyler's smile was tight.

Jake, who had an easy, relaxed manner that Bethany imagined would encourage women to lower their guard way too fast, spoke up. "Auntie Sue didn't explain, Bethany, how Tyler transformed the whole concept of a family charity. The Warrington Foundation has one of the best returns on funds given away, by any measure—it's a business in its own right."

"Do you have any involvement in the foundation?" Bethany asked Max.

He shook his head. "I'm the chairman of Warrington Construction. Jake's the vice president for major projects. The foundation fits around Tyler's social commitments." He raised his glass to his brother in a toast.

"Which reminds me," Susan said, "I'm hosting the Save

the Children afternoon tea next Tuesday. Do you think you could come along, Tyler? The old ladies give so much more money when you do the asking."

"Mom, I have work to do," Tyler said. Bethany read exasperation beneath his casual tone. "And you know those women give me their daughters' phone numbers, then complain to you if I don't call them."

"It's for a good cause," Susan said reproachfully, but Tyler shook his head.

"I might have some time on Tuesday," Max said. He sounded disinterested, but Bethany saw the alertness in his eyes, which were the same blue as Tyler's.

His mother shook her head. "It's okay, darling, I'll manage."

Max's jaw firmed, almost imperceptibly. How strange that he should be annoyed he wasn't needed for a charity afternoon tea.

"But I do need someone to look after Mitzy when I'm away next weekend," Susan said.

Horror was uniform across the three men's faces.

"Forget it," Max said flatly.

Jake muttered something about a date who was allergic to dogs.

"Ugh, this baby stinks," Tyler said.

"Couldn't you have saved this until Bethany's back on duty?" Tyler asked Ben as, one-handed, he spread the changing mat on his mom's guest bed.

The baby smiled and made a razzing sound.

Tyler pulled the tabs on the diaper and a choking smell filled his nostrils. "Go easy on me, kid," he muttered.

Half a box of wipes and three diapers later, he had the baby clean and changed. He was exhausted.

When he got back to the lunch table, the appetizer had been

cleared away, though Tyler hadn't finished his, and Max was carving the roasted goose.

"Can I put the baby down somewhere?" Tyler asked Bethany.

"There's a blanket in his bag. You can lie him on the floor with a rattle to play with, if you want to ignore him for a few minutes."

Once Ben was installed on the floor, Tyler wolfed down his goose in case he didn't get to finish it. But Ben dozed off on his blanket, and Tyler ended up with plenty of time to observe Bethany with his family. For someone who made no effort to be nice when he was around, she was sweet-natured, even cute. Neither Tyler nor Jake had ever been attracted to sweet women, so that sour feeling Tyler was experiencing had to be surprise at the amount of attention his cousin was paying his babysitter.

IT WAS FOUR O'CLOCK by the time lunch broke up. Susan escorted her guests out to the antebellum home's pillared front porch.

She cooed at Ben, kissed Bethany on the cheek and caught Tyler in a tight squeeze. "Anytime you have an errand and you need to leave Ben somewhere, bring him to me," she told Bethany.

"Thank you," Bethany said. Tyler's mom's willingness to get involved with Ben was a welcome contrast to her son's reluctance.

At the same time, Tyler said, "I pay Bethany to look after him."

His mother swatted him.

"Mom, who's that guy loitering outside your gate?" Max asked.

Susan stepped forward, as if moving a few inches might make all the difference in her ability to see what was happening a hundred yards away. "I'm not sure."

Olivia said something inarticulate and started down the steps.

Tyler shaded his eyes against the late-afternoon sun. "It's the wacko frog guy."

CHAPTER SEVEN

OLIVIA STUMBLED on the bottom step.

Tyler brushed past her. "I'll get rid of him."

"No." Olivia caught his arm. "Let me do it."

Tyler's brows drew together. "He's already harassed you once."

"I—I feel sorry for him." Silas Grant was looking up the driveway, right at her. She gave him a merry wave, so as not to alarm Susan. He didn't wave back. "He's harmless, I'll be fine," she assured Tyler.

Tyler looked confused, and she knew why. Like him, she didn't generally do anything that wasn't in her own immediate interest—the two of them worked so well together because they understood each other. She wasn't about to admit to him that Silas did interest her. After he'd left her office the other day, she'd read his funding application right through, and been quite intrigued.

Olivia hopped into her sporty little Mazda RX-7, wondering if she had time to apply a fresh coat of her Chanel Crimsonite lipstick before she reached the gates. She didn't take the chance because she was worried that, if she didn't keep an eye on him, Silas might barge into Susan's property.

But it was Olivia he was looking at. Her stomach tightened. A quick run of her tongue over her lips confirmed her lipstick had indeed been wiped away by that delicious lunch. But she'd had her hair styled yesterday, and she was wearing one of her nicest outfits, a soft pink dress with a matching belt and a large gold buckle that showed off her still-trim waist.

Silas, on the other hand, looked every bit as disreputable as he had the last time. That overcoat hadn't got any cleaner, and she was certain those were the same pants and shirt. Just maybe, she thought, he'd washed his hair—it looked springier, shinier. But if he had, he'd forgotten to comb it.

She pulled over to the curb, got out of her car, beeped the remote lock.

"Hello, Olivia." His deep, well-modulated voice sparked a sense of inevitability and excitement that set her heart thudding. Too silly at her age. And at his—she'd learned he was sixty years old, five years older than she was.

"You shouldn't be here." She tried to sound cross but didn't quite pull it off. The men she'd met recently had all been so underwhelming, even the handsome—and definitely interested—cardiologist Gigi had introduced her to at Friday's soiree. In contrast, a powerful undercurrent of excitement pulled her toward Silas. "As I said on your answering machine, I did ask, but Mr. Warrington won't see you."

As if to reinforce her words, Tyler's BMW M6 swept out of the gates behind her, and turned in the opposite direction.

"How did you know I was here?" she asked Silas.

He frowned and said slowly, "I didn't. I came looking for Tyler Warrington."

Of course he had. Embarrassment heated Olivia's cheeks.

Silas gave her a measuring look. "But since he's gone and you're still here, I suppose I could talk to you instead."

You'd never guess from his slow talk that this man had one of the state's finest scientific minds. The excitement in the air must all be on Olivia's side. She told herself the cardiologist's overt appreciation was looking more appealing every second.

Silas looked around, took a hesitant step in the direction of Susan's house.

"Not here," Olivia said. "There's a café around the corner."

She glanced at her car, and regretfully dismissed the idea of driving to the café, no matter that walking would do a distressing amount of damage to the hand-lathed leather sole of her Italian pumps. If Silas got in the Mazda, not only would his coat likely permanently stain her custom white leather trim, but if someone saw him...

In her fanciful imaginings about him, she'd decided he was a trust-fund kid from impeccable stock, who'd dropped out back in the seventies—but you couldn't explain all that in the half second it would take for anyone Olivia knew to look at Silas and decide she'd lost her mind.

"Let's walk," she said. He was probably too tall to fit comfortably in her car anyway. This way, if she saw someone she knew, she could put enough distance between them to make their proximity look accidental.

AT THE PEPPERMILL CAFÉ, Olivia led the way to a table tucked right in the back. She ordered a double espresso; Silas asked for a filter coffee.

At first, they waited for their drinks in silence. When the scrutiny of those gray eyes set beneath bushy eyebrows became too unnerving, Olivia spoke.

"Mr. Grant, or should I say—" she paused delicately "—*Professor* Grant, I understand you're very passionate about those frogs. But you need to realize everyone who applies to the foundation is passionate about something." She thought about Bethany and her research—a lovely girl, but far too serious.

Silas didn't acknowledge her use of his title. He reached into his shirt pocket and pulled out a pair of spectacles, which he slid onto his nose. When he leaned forward, Olivia had the uncomfortable sensation those glasses were magnifying the lines around her eyes and mouth. She smoothed the edges of her lips with her index finger.

"What are you passionate about?" he asked, his voice betraying no more than academic curiosity.

"Er, excuse me?"

"There must be something that keeps you awake at night."

Good grief! The thing that had kept her awake at night over the weekend had been the memory of Silas's voice. Olivia glanced around, but no one at the nearby tables appeared to have heard that leading question.

"Something you want to fight for," he prompted.

She drew a blank.

Their coffees arrived. Olivia added half a sachet of sugar to hers. Silas topped up his cup liberally with cream. Then he launched into a meandering monologue about the red-spotted tree frog. If he was right, the amphibian's situation was certainly dire. But by the time he'd finished, Olivia cared no more about the frog than when he'd started.

She wished she did. Wished something in her life fired her up to the extent that nothing else mattered. Imagine being willing to be seen in public dressed like a bum. Imagine not minding that people thought you were crazy.

Olivia wanted to feel passionate about something more than shoes and dresses and custom white leather trim.

But it was hard to care so deeply for anything—or anyone—when no one had ever loved you like that.

"There's nothing." She flung the words at him to put an end to her own thoughts.

"Humph." Silas's eyes bored into hers, disbelieving.

Something prickled in the air between them, and Olivia felt as if she'd just had one of those facial treatments that use electrical pulses to tighten the skin. She rubbed her cheeks with her palms. She shouldn't let this mad scientist provoke her into dissatisfaction with her life. Whatever instinct had prompted her interest in him, she no longer wanted to pursue it. No matter how many letters Silas Grant got to put after his name.

She brought the conversation back to the reason they were here. "Silas—" she liked his name, it was strong and honest "—the foundation's rejection wasn't personal."

He smiled, a sudden movement of the mouth that lit his eyes, then vanished before she could add it to her impressions of him.

"Not for Warrington, no," he agreed. "But sometimes, things matter for reasons that are intensely personal, don't you find?"

For the umpteenth time in her life, Olivia felt as if she'd been measured on some depthometer and been found lamentably shallow.

"I can't say I do," she said haughtily, seeking refuge in the knowledge that she was a scion of Atlanta society, who over the years had given her time to numerous worthy causes. Not a gala ball, not a charity fund-raiser, had taken in place in this city without some involvement on her part.

Silas assessed her. "You're an interesting woman." He nodded, as if to reinforce his assessment, picked up his cup and drained the contents. "Guess I'd better go." He stood, stuck out a hand.

Having already ascertained it was every bit as clean as it had been the first time they'd met, Olivia didn't hesitate to shake it. His fingers were as strong as the rest of him looked, and his hand dwarfed hers.

"I'd appreciate if you can do what you can for me with Warrington." Briefly, he tightened his clasp.

"I already told you," she said, frustrated, all tendency to simper evaporating. "There's nothing more I can do."

"Goodbye, Olivia," he said.

She told herself she was relieved when he and his coat flapped out of there. Leaving her to pay the check.

THAT NIGHT, Ben woke at 2:00 a.m. wanting his bottle. As Bethany bent over the crib to pick him up, Tyler stopped inside the nursery doorway.

"Nice panties," he said with the air of a connoisseur.

Bethany scooped Ben up with one hand, and with the other she tugged down the back of the butt-skimming Medical College of Georgia T-shirt she slept in, covering up her skimpy pink-and-white lace panties.

He ran a hand through sleep-tousled hair. "What's wrong with Ben?"

"He's hungry, I usually give him a bottle around this time."

Tyler's interest in her underwear was apparently of the "out of sight, out of mind" variety. Which made it vastly unfair that he should turn up wearing only a pair of blue silk boxer shorts. Bethany had to work hard to keep her gaze on his face, well clear of his bare torso, which the briefest of glances had told her was solid, muscular and very sexy. Didn't he know it was winter, for Pete's sake? She ignored the fact that Tyler's house was so warm she herself hadn't bothered to pull on a robe.

"I thought he must be in mortal pain, he was yelling so loudly." Tyler moved closer to look down at Ben, as if to check he was really okay.

Bethany stepped backward. "It's the same noise he makes

every night." She pulled the bottle out of the electric warmer. "He'll drink this pretty fast, then he'll drop right back to sleep."

Tyler watched as she settled herself and the baby in the armchair he'd moved into the nursery at her request. Ben latched on to the bottle the way Tyler latched on to a beer after a game of football. As the baby chugged the white stuff, his eyes traveled from Tyler to Bethany.

He smiled around the teat of the bottle, and there was a strangely adult tentativeness to it. Then his eyes fastened on Tyler's face, and one hand flapped in a half wave. Feeling stupid, Tyler waggled a couple of fingers back…and felt an unexpected tug somewhere inside him.

Ben's smile widened, so that milk dribbled out of his mouth.

"You're distracting him," Bethany griped. But as she wiped the baby's chin with a piece of flannel that Tyler had learned was called a receiving blanket, her eyes were warm with something unfamiliar—he was startled to realize it was approval. She said, "You did an okay job with Ben at your mom's today."

He put a hand on his heart. "No, please, you're gushing."

Bethany laughed and, maybe because it was the middle of the night and she was tired, or maybe because Tyler had only just walked in and so hadn't had time to say anything to annoy her yet, she seemed more relaxed than usual.

He soon tired of watching Ben, but it was no hardship to watch Bethany, intent on her task, her mouth soft and curved in a half smile. A lock of russet hair had fallen over one cheek, pointing toward the tip of her nose. Her T-shirt was stretched wide at the neck and as Tyler watched, it slowly slipped to bare one smooth shoulder.

That glimpse of silken smoothness was somehow even more enticing than that peek at her panties.

She tugged the bottle out from between Ben's gums, and hefted him to the shoulder still protected by her T-shirt. Right away, the baby emitted an enormous belch. "Good boy," she crowed.

"My mother would have smacked my behind if I'd done that," Tyler said.

She laughed as she settled Ben in her arms to drink some more. "Not at this age, she wouldn't have."

When she laughed, the dimple in her chin showed up. Tyler wanted to kiss it. How bizarre that his first specific thought on how he would act on the attraction between them should be so tame. And that his desire to kiss that dimple should be so strong. Maybe Tyler was only capable of G-rated fantasies with Ben around. It was an alarming thought, which he banished by reminding himself that the dimple was just a starting point. From there, he'd move to other, more exciting places. Mmm, yes, that was better.

As if he'd floated the idea into the ether, Bethany leaned down and kissed the baby's forehead.

A resentful noise escaped Tyler.

Her puzzled gaze met his. "Did you just…growl?"

"What if I did?"

"*Why* did you growl?"

"Maybe I didn't." But she wasn't about to accept that, so he said, "Maybe I thought you're spoiling Ben with all this attention."

Which probably was the lamest thing he could have said. Laughter gurgled out of her, confirming it.

"You're jealous because I kissed him." Mischief warmed her eyes, and she taunted, "Jealous of a little-bitty baby."

He scowled. "No way. Now, if you were breast-feeding him maybe…"

She wrinkled her nose, pixie style. "Ugh, that's sick."

"Not from where I'm sitting."

Bethany realized his gaze had dropped down, and the way she was leaning forward, he could see right down the gaping neck of her T-shirt.

She spread a hand over the expanse of bare skin, and Tyler's smile widened. "Grow up," she said.

A few minutes later Ben was drawing only air from the bottle, so she sat him up and patted his back until he belched again. She glanced at Tyler. "Do you want to do his diaper?"

He scowled his answer to that, and she sighed with theatrical disappointment. She made swift work of the wet diaper and soon had Ben snugly taped up again and back into his pajamas patterned with space rockets improbably piloted by teddy bears.

Bethany eased him down, tucked the blankets around him. Ben lay with his eyes open, but he blinked with a frequency that suggested he would soon be asleep.

"Guess he had a long day," Tyler said. "Meeting all those new people."

She nodded. "He liked your mom."

He shot her a glance. "You mean, *you* liked her."

"That too," she agreed. "She was really charming."

"Mom's a sucker for a cute smile."

About to reply, she realized he'd said her smile was cute. And, of course, no matter how hard she fought it, no matter that he'd made what was doubtless an autopilot flirty comment, she couldn't help smiling right then. And smiling automatically lowered her guard and allowed her to check out his torso again. *No fair.*

Tyler's eyes followed the curving of her lips with enough interest to suggest that he did actually think her smile had something going for it. Then his gaze dropped lower, into territory that was clearly beyond anywhere Mrs. Warrington might find cute, and strictly within the expertise of Atlanta's favorite playboy.

Aware of the responsive tightening throughout her body, Bethany folded her arms across her chest. "Your brother is kind of bossy."

"He plays to his strengths."

"And Jake is fun."

He frowned. "He's a workaholic."

"I had the impression he plays hard, too. He invited me to a ball game."

Tyler scowled. "I need you to look after Ben that day."

"I haven't told you when it is yet," she said, annoyed.

"Doesn't matter."

She gave a hiss of irritation, and Tyler smiled.

"What I don't understand," she said thoughtfully, "is how come when your dad died, Max and Jake ended up at Warrington Construction, and you ended up at the foundation?"

It was a reasonable question. One Tyler wasn't fond of answering. "My compassion and do-good instincts made me a shoo-in for the job."

She snorted.

He wondered what she'd say if she knew the truth. That no matter how highly the rest of Atlanta regarded him, when it came to anything important, his own family had no faith in his abilities.

"How long ago did your father die?"

"It'll be four years next month." He glanced at Ben, whose eyes were still open. "Dad was flying his chopper, he came down in bad weather."

"I'm sorry," she said.

He nodded. "He was such a larger-than-life character, his

death left a big hole in our lives. Mom's only been herself again the last year."

"You and your brother must miss him, too." She plunked herself into the armchair, tugged her T-shirt down. She looked as if she was settling in for a chat Tyler didn't want to have. He should just walk out, but to do so while Ben was still awake felt as if he'd be leaving a job half done.

Tyler eyed her bare legs—might as well get some enjoyment out of this. "Max and I haven't been on great terms since Dad died. I used to work in the construction business, but the first thing Max did after Dad died and the board appointed him chairman and president of Warrington Construction was fire me."

She gaped.

"Not so much fire me," he admitted, "as insist I take up the job at the foundation."

"But…why?"

He leaned against the changing table. "Dad and I got on pretty well, he knew my capabilities, he had me in the company as VP of marketing." He shrugged. "Turned out all everyone else, including Max, thought I was good for, was charming customers and making stockholders feel secure. Max decided those skills didn't justify my inflated salary."

Bethany looked troubled, and Tyler guessed his history had tapped into that deep vein of compassion that ran through her.

He braced himself for a whole lot of questions he didn't want to answer. And was saved when Ben belched again. There was a wet quality to it, and when Tyler looked at the crib, he saw the boy had been sick over his sheets.

"Poor baby." Bethany lifted him up. "Can you hold him while I change his bed?"

Tyler took Ben; he smelled of sick, but it wasn't offensive.

As Tyler watched Bethany strip the crib and put new linen on, he reflected on how helpless the little boy would be if Tyler and Bethany walked out of here right now…if no one fed him…if his mom had abandoned him in the street, rather than bringing him to Tyler's office…

He shook off the unpleasant thoughts. Ben was safe, he had Bethany lavishing love on him, and Tyler providing for his material needs.

"Maybe I should start a trust fund for him," he pondered aloud.

Bethany looked up from the sheets she was tucking in with precise hospital corners and chuckled.

"You find his lack of financial security amusing?" Tyler said loftily.

"That's so typical of you. Ben starts to look as if he might need something, and you think of money."

"Money's good," Tyler said.

"I know why you woke up when Ben did tonight." Her smugness would have been irritating if it hadn't been so cute.

"It was the nightmares I had from changing that stinking diaper at Mom's place today."

She tsked. "It's because when you were forced to look after Ben today, you bonded with him."

He recoiled. "No, I didn't."

"You feel something for him."

"Only disgust at his stinkiness." Tyler didn't know why, but he felt he had to convince her of that.

She sent Tyler that disapproving look he knew so well. But for some reason, most likely because of her preposterous theory about him bonding with Ben—how could he bond with someone who couldn't talk, couldn't understand and probably didn't have a clue who Tyler was?—the look was mellower than usual.

"He'll need clean pajamas, too," she said. While Tyler held Ben, she removed his clothing. When the cool air hit him, the baby instinctively snuggled against Tyler, who equally instinctively cupped the back of Ben's head with his hand.

She rummaged through the dresser drawer, pulled out a pale blue terry sleeper, turned around. "Here we—"

Bethany stopped, mesmerized.

"What?" Tyler said defensively.

"You and Ben," she said. "You're cuddling him."

He rolled his eyes. "I'm keeping him warm. I am *not* bonding."

"I wish I had my camera," she said. "I'd make a killing in the greeting-card business."

His dark eyebrows drew together. "Excuse me?"

"You know. Gorgeous near-naked guy holding gorgeous, near-naked baby. On second thought, it's an advertiser's dream. We could sell aftershave."

"I have no idea what you're talking about." Except she suspected from the quirk of his lips he *had* gleaned that she thought he was gorgeous.

"It's the sort of thing that turns women on," she explained, and added hastily, "Emotionally."

"Emotional turn-on, huh?" His tone said, *Right.* His gaze held hers.

"Only very late at night," she said, and suddenly it seemed neither of them was talking *emotional.*

Without warning, he leaned forward and planted a quick, hard kiss on her mouth. Its very brevity made it demanding, hot. She wanted more, wanted to protest she hadn't had time to register the exact firmness of his lips.

She stepped backward, mustered coolness. "Don't do that again."

"Why not?" His eyes narrowed. "You liked it."

Was *liking* it what made her mouth burn, made her feel as if she hadn't eaten in weeks, made her want to reach out and—

She did reach out, but only to take Ben from Tyler. "You told me you wouldn't act on your one-sided—" her voice shook, making a liar of her "—attraction to me unless I gave you a signal." She took refuge in self-righteousness. "Did I give you any kind of signal?"

"Not consciously," he admitted. "But you were talking about turn-ons."

"I was talking about emotions." She laid Ben on the changing table, slipped him into his clean pajamas. Without looking at Tyler she said, "For someone who's supposedly good with women, you can be pretty dense."

Tyler's chuckle carried all the confidence of a man who knew everything about women's responses to him. "Whatever you say."

She slipped Ben back under his covers. His eyes closed immediately.

"Looks like my work here is done," Tyler said. He took a step toward Bethany, his eyes on her mouth.

"I told you…" Bethany warned.

She was ready to jerk away from an attempted kiss—she didn't expect him to reach around and pat her bottom. His touch made her leap forward, so she bumped into him.

"See, Peaches, you can't keep away from me." Tyler tapped her nose with his finger, then sauntered from the room, his bare shoulders golden in the dimmed light.

Bethany sat down heavily in the armchair, touched an experimental finger to her lips. It couldn't be true. No way could one kiss, followed by one pat on her bottom, have pulled together all the pieces of a puzzle she hadn't even known existed.

Tyler had been right all along. She wanted him.

By Wednesday, Tyler was sleep deprived and sex starved. Every night since Sunday, he'd been woken by Ben crying for his middle-of-the-night meal.

Every night, he tried hard to ignore the wailing. But even after it stopped, even when he was certain Bethany must be with Ben by now, something compelled him to go and check.

Of course, she was there every time, always dressed in some horrible item of nightwear bearing the logo of an academic institution or pictures of fast food. There was that panty-baring MCG T-shirt, a longer and thus less appealing—to Tyler—Emory University Hospital sweatshirt, a pair of shortie pajamas with rather phallic hot dogs on them. They all led Tyler to one conclusion. Bethany had great legs.

Only for looking at, not for touching. Because no matter how conscious Tyler was of that attraction, her extreme cussedness meant she continued to deny it was mutual. She'd told him not to kiss her again, and he'd decided to respect that, mainly with the intention of driving her crazy with longing for him.

But he was the one who couldn't forget that brief, sweet sensation of her lips beneath his. He was the one whose imagination had bought a season ticket to a quite extraordinary variety show. He was certain Bethany was having the same thoughts—he saw it in her skittishness every time he showed up in the middle of the night. She went out of her way to avoid bumping into him, and since he'd planted that kiss on her, she'd barely met his eyes. He just had to get her to admit the obvious.

Then they could all get some sleep. And some other things, too.

On Thursday morning, Tyler called Bethany from work.

"The investigator just came by. He thinks he's found Ben's mother."

Tyler explained that an old lady had informed the investigator that her young neighbor had looked pregnant but had denied it repeatedly. "She's a whole lot thinner now," the old woman reported, "and there's no sign of a baby."

Bethany thought about the footage she'd seen so many times of Ben's mother leaving him at the Warrington Foundation. Although the mother's face was almost entirely concealed by her black woolen hat and a long knitted purple scarf, Bethany had decided she was young, mainly on the basis of her loping walk.

Why had she given Ben away? Did she want him back?

I don't want to give him back.

The possessiveness that gripped Bethany shocked her. Ben wasn't hers, wasn't Tyler's.

"Is social services going to check her out?"

"I haven't talked to them yet. I thought," Tyler said, unusually hesitant, "maybe you and I should visit her first."

"But social services—"

"She's not necessarily his mother," he said. "And if she is, and if she's just a kid who's been in a difficult situation, we may be able to help smooth things with the authorities."

Bethany approved of his compassion. That just left one hitch. "You want us to go together?"

"Of course together," he said, irritated.

Apart from those inevitable—and oddly intimate—midnight sojourns in the nursery, Bethany had been trying to stay out of his way. He'd been putting in his two hours a day with Ben, and on each occasion she handed Ben over, then left him to it. Because now that she'd realized she…liked him, every contact fanned the attraction.

How could she *like* someone as selfish as Tyler? If she was ever to fall for a guy—*this is sexual attraction, I'm not falling*—it would be someone who would put her first. Who would, when the time came, put their children first.

"If she's a kid, she might need reassuring she's not in trouble," Tyler said. "And she might prefer to talk to a woman."

"We'll go together," Bethany agreed.

She tried to imagine handing Ben back to his mom. Maybe it wouldn't be that straightforward, depending on the circumstances. Maybe Ben would stay a little longer—

What was she thinking? Tyler didn't want to keep Ben, he wasn't father material. Bethany had only been here ten days, but she had the sudden feeling it was high time she got back to her real work. High time she got away from Tyler's increasingly captivating presence.

As she loaded Ben's dirty clothes into the washing machine, Bethany decided she was thankful they'd found Ben's mom. She was looking forward to resuming her research.

What research? She realized with a shock she hadn't pushed Tyler about the money at all these past few days. That she didn't have any work to go back to unless the foundation paid up, and she was doing a miserable job of making that happen.

She'd let his kiss deflect her, take her mind off what really mattered. *I need to persuade Tyler to give me the money, then I need to get out of here.*

CHAPTER EIGHT

TYLER AND BETHANY'S visit to a surprised, scared sixteen-year-old in Augusta proved a false alarm. The girl had been pregnant, and her parents had forbidden her to reveal the pregnancy to anyone. They'd convinced her to hand the baby over to some childless cousins, who'd filed a formal application to adopt the baby.

Tyler was silent most of the long drive home; Bethany had no clue how he felt about still being Ben's guardian. She, herself, felt only relief.

The kind of relief experienced by someone who jumps off a sinking ship and hauls herself into a lifeboat, only to find the lifeboat is leaking. She and Tyler were back to square one.

Only it was a whole lot hotter in here now.

OLIVIA'S MAZDA RX-7 was far too conspicuous for the errand she had in mind, so she'd borrowed her friend Margie Biedermeyer's maid's Toyota.

Olivia couldn't quite believe she was disguising herself so she could cruise the streets of Buckhead, Atlanta's most elegant neighborhood—where she'd lived all her life—and check out Silas's home.

She had chosen this time of day, four-thirty, because it was just starting to get dark, which left her enough light to get a good look, but minimized the chances of Silas looking out a window and recognizing her.

Her hands tightened on the steering wheel at the thought of him seeing her skulking. But how else could she find out more about him?

"You're acting like a lunatic," she told her reflection in the rearview mirror. She'd had two dates with Gigi's cardiologist, a charming, *normal* man, and yet here she was, pursuing a crank. Maybe her lunacy had nothing to do with Silas, who on every measure other than his good looks wasn't her type. Maybe it was menopause's parting shot.

She flicked her turn signal, headed left onto Armada, Silas's street. Like much of Buckhead, the homes were large, prepossessing. Some of them had been divided into apartments, and she envisaged Silas living in one of those. Alone.

She didn't know for sure he wasn't married, but he didn't wear a ring, and no woman would let her husband go out looking the way Silas did. No woman in Buckhead, at least.

When she got to the two hundreds, she slowed down. Silas had given 280 Armada as his address on his funding application. She left her headlights off to aid her anonymity…274, 276, 278… Olivia eased her foot off the gas, let the automatic transmission move the car forward at a snail's pace. Number 280 had a high brick wall across the front, which meant she wouldn't see much until she was right outside the gates.

There was only one letter box set into the wall—no indication that the house was apartments. The gates were beautiful black wrought iron, elaborately patterned. Most unusual. Olivia came to a stop across the road from the house.

And stared.

She buzzed down her window to get a better look.

Silas's home was stunning. A huge, gracious Federal-style brick house, three stories, shutters at the windows. The wide, paved driveway had a fountain in the center, and bisected rolling green lawns on its path from the gate up to the grand front steps that ran the length of the house, then back around to the gate.

It was Olivia's dream home.

As she sat there, lost in wondrous contemplation, the gates swung open. Even with her window down, Olivia couldn't hear any intrusive mechanical operation. They moved silently, as if by magic.

Too late, she realized *why* they were opening.

A car whose approach had been obscured by the brick wall appeared in the driveway. A black Maserati, sleek and gorgeous, its powerful Italian engine purring like a well-fed tiger.

The driver paused at the gates, checking for traffic in the street. Even in the half-light Olivia recognized the tall, broad figure behind the steering wheel.

Silas drives a Maserati.

She was so glad she'd come.

He moved forward and the car's headlamps swept the road, bathing Olivia in their glow before she could duck down.

She froze.

Silas stared right at her.

ON SATURDAY MORNING, Tyler took Ben on a protest march in support of cheaper day care for low-income families.

"You've got to be kidding," Bethany said when he told her where they were going.

"You said I could spend my two hours with him any way I like." He jiggled Ben, who was getting fractious, against his hip. "You can come too, if you like."

"I'm going back to bed. I was up three times last night."

"Let the record reflect that you put your beauty sleep ahead of the crisis in day care," he said.

"Let it," she said, and went upstairs.

Naturally, it turned out Tyler wasn't just attending the march. When Bethany switched on the TV news during Ben's dinner that night, she saw him at the front of the protest— one of the leaders. He carried Ben in the front-pack, and held a placard that proclaimed, Poor Kids Need Day Care Too.

"If that was all you were worried about, you'd have been happy to walk at the back of the line," she lectured Tyler as he grabbed a beer from the fridge.

"I would have been delighted to, but that wouldn't have done the foundation any good," he said virtuously. "It's no picnic being constantly in the public eye, you know."

"That's why you're taking Miss Georgia to the red- carpet premiere of that new show tonight." She put her TV dinner in the microwave and set the timer. "I'm surprised she has time to date you when she's so busy working for world peace."

His eyes gleamed at the edge in her voice, which sounded, she had to admit, like jealousy.

He sighed. "She needed cheering up. Poor girl, I fear she's losing heart over the peace thing."

Right after he left, Bethany's mother phoned to ask if she'd secured the new funding yet.

"I'm working on it." Bethany decided it was an aspiration rather than a lie.

BETHANY WAS SURPRISED to hear Tyler let himself in before midnight. Had he and Miss Georgia had a fight?

Normally, she would have been asleep at this hour, but

Ben had picked up a cold. This was the second time he'd woken already.

Tyler appeared in the nursery doorway. "Everything okay?" He propped himself against the doorjamb, relaxed and self-assured in dark pants and a gray shirt. He didn't look as if he'd had a bust-up with his girlfriend.

"Your protest march gave Ben a cold." Bethany wiped away a trail of mucus from Ben's nose.

"Hell, I'm sorry." He came into the room, and she saw real remorse in his eyes. "Will he be okay?"

"Tyler, it's a cold, not the bubonic plague."

"You may not appreciate this," he said, "but guy colds are much more serious than girl colds."

"I'd heard." She smiled—it was much easier to talk to him when he was fully clothed.

"Just so long as you're aware." He looked down at her, took in her shortie pajamas decorated with rainbow-pastel soft-freeze cones. "Did I ever tell you that you have great legs?"

"No, but you look at them often enough, I figured it was either that or you're trying to creep me out."

"Both," he said.

There was a moment's silence. Then Bethany said, too loudly, "Ben's asleep, I'm going back to bed."

BEN WOKE at one o'clock, fretting, unwilling to be pacified.

Tyler watched Bethany walk the baby up and down the small nursery. He started to walk alongside her, matching his steps to hers. Eight steps down, turn, eight steps back. It soon grew tedious. "I prefer circuit training."

"Then why don't you carry the weight?" She passed Ben, still wide-awake and peevish, to him.

They resumed their pacing. The room wasn't that wide, so

they were forced to walk close together. Maybe this exercise was more strenuous that he'd thought, because heat prickled all over Tyler.

"I forgot to ask how the show was tonight," Bethany said.

Tyler grimaced. "It was one of those interminable family dramas—a whiny bunch of people who didn't like each other much."

"A pretty ordinary family, then."

"You've been talking to your mother again," he said.

She stopped midpace. "How did you know?"

"Maybe I'm not as self-absorbed as you think," he said smugly. "I noticed last time you spoke to her you kept scratching your neck afterward. You've been doing that tonight."

Since at that very moment Bethany's hand was curled at her nape, she wasn't in a position to deny it.

"I'm not allergic to my mother," she muttered.

"No, but you're tense." He clasped Ben with one hand so he could jog her elbow. "Keep walking."

She did as she was told. After a moment he said, "Where do your folks live?"

"In Madison."

He'd never been there, but he knew the town was around an hour from Atlanta. "Any siblings you're allergic to?"

She sucked in her cheeks and said reluctantly, "I had an older sister, Melanie. She died when she was fourteen."

Tyler waited.

Bethany screwed up her face, revealing her struggle not to say more. Eventually, the pause became so pregnant it threatened quintuplets.

"Of acute kidney failure," she blurted.

What the—

Bethany kept moving, staring straight ahead at the teddy-bear height chart on the wall. Tyler wondered why the baby planner he'd enlisted to stock the nursery had decided he needed a height chart for a baby he would have only a few weeks.

He halted Bethany with a hand on her arm. "How old were you when she died?"

"Thirteen. We were born fifteen months apart."

"That's tough," he said. "I'm sorry." He resumed walking, and Bethany followed. "Any other kids in the family?"

"My younger brother, Ryan—he was just a year old when Melanie died."

Tyler exhaled against Ben's head, and the little boy batted Tyler's chest. "So that's why you chose kidney disease as your specialty?"

"I guess."

He searched her face. "Is it why you became a doctor?"

Bethany shifted. "Maybe…indirectly."

Tyler was still trying to process what he'd learned. There had to be more to it. "I think it's strange you didn't say anything before, about your sister."

"It was a long time ago."

He reached over and tucked a strand of hair behind her ear. "Strange."

"Is HE OKAY?" Tyler asked at 2:00 a.m. Once again, with an uncanny sense of timekeeping, Ben had woken almost on the hour. "He's…snorty."

"He's blocked up. I need to get these saline drops into him." Bethany squeezed the contents of a dropper into Ben's nose, much to his outrage. She soothed the screaming baby with her usual lack of perturbation; as always, Tyler was impressed by the way she got on with the job without complaint. "He'll be fine, we'll just have to wait this thing out."

She peered at Tyler. "Or, rather, I will. You look tired, you don't need to get up to him every time."

"Oh, yeah," he said. "If I sleep through, I'll have you accusing me of selfishness."

She actually looked guilty. "I won't," she promised. "You've been great tonight."

That unqualified praise hung in the air between them.

"Why don't you go to bed." She sounded as if she really, really didn't want Tyler there.

Which had to mean he was getting to her.

Deliberately, he eyed her legs. "I don't mind staying."

So that's what he did. He stayed, and let his mind wander to how Bethany's legs would look and feel wrapped around him.

THREE O'CLOCK WAS TIME for Ben's feed. Bethany hoped like heck Tyler hadn't heard him crying, but he got to the nursery at the same time as she did.

"After you." He sketched a bow in the doorway.

Ben was both ravenous and ill, his face was redder than a tomato. Bethany hastened to heat his bottle.

Tyler picked Ben up. "His diaper is full." A pause. "Shall I change it?"

"I must have fallen asleep for a second," Bethany said. "I just dreamed that you offered to change—" Tyler's darkening expression made her cut her little joke short. "Yes, please."

He grumbled something about ingratitude as he untabbed Ben's diaper, threw it in the trash can.

"Uh, Tyler, you might want to have the new diaper ready before you—"

Too late. Ben shot a steady stream of pee into the air. Tyler leaped backward, but not before the full force of the spray hit his bare chest.

"Damn." Several other curse words followed as he grabbed a couple of baby wipes and began rubbing his chest with such distaste that Bethany burst out laughing. She fastened the clean diaper on Ben and put him back in his crib, which he protested loudly.

"Need any help?" she asked Tyler, still chuckling.

"No, no, my life's goal is to keep you amused and I seem to be doing fine."

She plucked the wipes from his hand and picked up a clean receiving blanket. "Let's dry you off."

The second the blanket made contact with his chest, she realized this was a bad idea. The soft flannel fabric afforded her hands no protection against the heat of his torso. Involuntarily she uncurled her fingers from around the cloth, then spread them wide in a futile attempt to span the firmness of all that muscle and sinew. Her wiping motions slowed, slowed. Stopped.

Tyler covered her hands with his own, securing them against his chest. Bethany felt the thud of his heart, felt his gaze on her, willing her to look up. She kept her eyes locked on their joined hands.

Then Ben squawked, and Tyler released her. They both turned their attention to the baby. Bethany gathered him in her arms; Tyler patted the back of Ben's head, his fingers brushing across Bethany's. Static electricity snapped between them, and she jumped back, fixed him with an accusing look.

He smirked. "Told you there was a spark."

Bethany rubbed her fingers against her thigh. "That was science, not sex."

AT 4:00 A.M., Bethany could hardly stand up straight, she was so tired. Yet one part of her—the sad, pathetic part that held out for any glimpse of Tyler seminaked in the middle of the night—was wide-awake. Each time he appeared in the nursery, she noticed something new about him. The shadow on his jaw, the whiteness of his teeth as he smothered a yawn, the cording of his biceps as he ran a hand around the back of his neck to ease his exhaustion.

Was it her imagination, or was he standing closer to her each time they leaned over Ben's crib together? Like now, as she stroked Ben's head to help him get back to sleep, she felt as if Tyler was only an inch behind her. To test the theory, she leaned back, and instantly encountered the hard warmth of his chest. When she would have pulled away, his hands descended on her shoulders, keeping her there. His chin dropped onto her head. "Tired?"

"Uh, yeah." Best to let him think that was why she was leaning on him.

"Me too." He turned her around to face him, and his eyes were unfamiliarly compassionate. "But this has got to be tougher on you than on me. You're doing all the work."

"Not all," she demurred. She added mischievously, "Ninety percent, tops."

He laughed. "I don't know where you get the energy to joke at this time of night."

"You think I'm joking?"

He laughed again, and it chased away Bethany's fatigue. Her whole body went on alert, every corpuscle pulsing with energy. His fingers burned into her shoulders, ten points of radiant heat. Even though he'd had as little sleep as she had, Tyler looked so strong, so vital, so red-blooded, that Bethany could stand it no longer.

She'd said this moment would never come, that she would never give him a signal. But she'd been wrong. Just plain wrong. *Nothing to be ashamed of in that.*

She lifted her hand, reached to a point just below Tyler's left ear, ran a finger from there along his jaw to his chin.

She waited.

Tyler gazed down at her, intense, unreadable.

And yawned.

He ran a hand over his eyes, cutting her off from that intensity. "Guess I'll hit the sack."

He was turning her down! Bethany braced herself against the wave of mortification, somehow managed not to let it topple her.

"Good idea," she muttered. Blindly, she turned back to the crib. "I think Ben's asleep now."

She waited, frozen in her humiliation, until she heard Tyler's bedroom door click shut; then she made her way back to her own room.

WAS IT POSSIBLE to feel more tired, Tyler wondered as he sank into bed. His head swam, red and black spots hovered before his eyes like demented ladybugs. He hadn't slept a wink tonight—he'd been unable to drift off between stints in the nursery, partly because he was worried about Ben, mainly because he was hyperaware of Bethany.

How did she manage to look so good when she must be every bit as exhausted as he was?

She smelled good, too. Tyler had given up the fight to keep his distance and moved closer to her, just so he could absorb that fragrant blend of lemon and mint and something floral that he'd come to associate with her. Then there was the feel of her, her shoulders satiny smooth beneath his fingers.

And somehow she retained the energy to backchat him at every stage of the night. He liked the way her eyes sparkled with humor when she tried to stomp on his ego—she'd doubtless be disappointed to know it wasn't as fragile as she thought.

Then there were those touches. He didn't know what it was about that woman, but every time she touched him, he felt as if he'd been set alight. It had taken all his willpower just now not to react to the featherlight touch of her hand against his jaw.

Her hand…his jaw…

Tyler sat bolt upright. Dammit, Bethany had given him the signal.

He leaped out of bed, fatigue forgotten, only one thought in his mind.

Get to Bethany. Now.

He barged into her room without knocking, cursed when he stubbed his toe on what felt like a book. It was pitch-dark; he heard scrambling movements as she sat up in bed. "Tyler? Is it Ben?" She sounded alert, worried.

He reached the bed, fumbled for the lamp on the nightstand, snapped it on. She blinked at him, her face flushed, tilted toward him so that a minimal movement would join his mouth to hers.

"You gave me the signal," he said.

She dropped her gaze. "What signal?"

"I was tired, it took me a couple of minutes to click. I'm sorry."

"Oh…that." A forced laugh. Her fingers plucked at the duvet. "I'd forgotten already."

"I'm here to take you up on your offer."

Panic widened her eyes. He might have known she'd get cold feet. She'd had such difficulty getting this far, when from day one Tyler had seen it as their obvious destination.

"It wasn't an offer." She pulled the bedclothes higher, up to her neck. "I changed my mind."

He tugged the duvet so sharply that the unexpectedness made her let go. "Oh no you don't." He sat down on the edge of the bed, stopped her moving away from him by simply putting a hand at either side of her. "I've been waiting forever for this."

Bethany snickered nervously. "I've been here not quite two weeks. That's hardly forever."

"It feels like ten years."

"That's because I nag you."

"It's because I want to do this," Tyler corrected her. He leaned in, kissed her, wanted desperately to devour her. But that would likely scare her off, so instead he took it easy. Which had the unexpected and very pleasant benefit of allowing him to fully savor the sweetness of her lips in a way he didn't remember doing since he was a teenager. He murmured against her mouth, "You don't get to change your mind now."

All the same, he pulled back a little.

"I suppose it would be rude," she agreed, her eyes fixed on his lips.

Yes! He kissed her again, harder, felt the response of her mouth to his. Her lips parted and he went in. This was what he'd been waiting for; it felt even better than he'd imagined...and he only realized now just how much imagining he'd done.

She made a mew of pleasure as her tongue met his. He pushed her back against the pillows and lay down so he was half on top of her, pressing into her delicious curves, soft against his hardness. Her arms went around his neck.

Bethany abandoned herself to the delight of Tyler's kiss. His hands stole beneath her pajama top, caressed the skin of her waist, sending her arching against him. His thighs were hot against hers, combustible.

If she didn't stop right now, she wouldn't be able to stop at all. She didn't want to stop. Then she remembered, and suddenly, stopping was easy. She shoved hard against Tyler's chest.

"Hey." He pulled away, surprised. "What's wrong?"

"You went out tonight. With Miss Georgia." She pressed

her palms to her cheeks, but her hands were as hot as her face and didn't cool her.

"And?" he said impatiently.

"Did you think you'd go straight from her bed to mine?" Bethany swiped the back of her hand across her mouth, to erase the imprint of his two-timing lips.

His eyes narrowed. "I don't treat women like that. I told you, Sabrina's not my girlfriend."

So, Miss Georgia had a name.

"Do you really think I'd kiss you like that if I was dating her?" he demanded.

Who would have thought playboy Tyler Warrington had a streak of decency? He looked so offended, Bethany decided it would be impolitic to answer. "So you're certain she wouldn't be upset about…what we just did?"

He laughed, incredulous. "You're worried about her feelings?"

Bethany shifted up the bed, so she was semi-upright. "I don't steal other women's men." Not that she'd ever been in a situation where that was even a remote possibility. But it seemed like a sensible rule.

Tyler wanted to laugh at the seriousness with which Bethany was treating a kiss. A great kiss, a hot kiss…but just a kiss.

Trouble was, Bethany didn't take anything lightly.

"So," she said, "you're not dating her, and you're kissing me like that…"

She wanted to know if she and Tyler were dating.

Did he have to decide that right now? Before he'd even finished kissing her?

Typical of Bethany to complicate matters.

One part of him wanted to say yes, then take her to bed to seal the deal.

But maybe having a baby in his life was making him more cautious, because what stopped him from acting on that impulse was the thought of tomorrow and the day after.

If he was honest with himself, he'd admit that his attraction to Bethany was just a little out of control.

He thought about her all the time. About kissing her. And other things. Disturbingly, not all of those things were physical. He wasn't used to being preoccupied with a woman, and it didn't seem a smart place to be.

Especially not with Bethany, when they were living under the same roof. Things could get tricky.

He measured her lips with his gaze, resigned himself to the fact he probably wouldn't taste them again anytime soon. He shuffled down the bed a bit. "I'd rather not overanalyze what just happened," he said. "We kissed, it was nice." *Understatement.* "Let's not suck all the fun out of it."

Her eyes narrowed. "You think talking takes the fun out of a relationship?"

Definitely. "You think we have a relationship?" he countered.

She opened her mouth, then closed it again. "We have an attraction," she said tentatively.

"Agreed." He watched her face in the lamplight, the progress of her thoughts across her face.

"But in your mind that doesn't lead to a relationship, not even if we kiss and…stuff?"

Tyler shifted at the thought of *stuff.* "A relationship is based on more than attraction." He felt the way he had when he'd talked to the divorced dads about parenting—out of his depth.

"That's true," Bethany said. "And the fact is, I'm here to ask you for money, nothing more than that."

Couldn't she forget the damn money?

"Getting close to you emotionally could screw things up."

She bit her lip. "And chances are, you and I don't have anything in common, apart from that attraction. A relationship would be an unnecessary risk."

"You could be right." Had he misread her question about relationships? Was she saying she was up for no-strings sex? Tyler's entire body went on alert. He moved so he could see inside her pajama top, the first few buttons of which were undone. He got a glimpse of an enticing, pale swell of breast.

"I mean," she said, "you're rich and famous."

He dragged his gaze up from her cleavage just long enough to shoot her a wary look.

"And I'm intelligent, hardworking and caring. So, Tyler—" she paused and the silence made him look up again "—I don't think this is going to work, do you?"

She held his eyes as, with deliberate movements, she refastened all the buttons on her pajama top.

CHAPTER NINE

ON MONDAY MORNING, Olivia set an unsolicited cup of coffee on Tyler's desk. Since he usually had to ask her to bring coffee at least three times, her consideration inspired suspicion rather than gratitude. He sat back, waited.

"I've met someone I like," she said.

Tyler stuck his fingers in his ears. "I don't want to know."

"It's complicated."

"It always is," Tyler said bitterly. He couldn't believe Bethany had ended up giving him the brush-off on Saturday night. No matter that common sense told him it was the right thing to do. "You're always meeting men you like," he reminded Olivia. "You're worse than I am. With women," he clarified.

"I like this guy more than the others," Olivia said.

Tyler looked at his secretary. She was very attractive, slim, always well groomed, her graying hair carefully highlighted. Olivia was a class act. "I'm sure he'll like you back."

"I doubt I'm his type. I think he's looking for someone… deeper."

"Ouch," Tyler said. Because neither he nor Olivia was good at deep. He had the same problem with Bethany, who was— He pulled himself up. "Don't you have girlfriends you can have this conversation with?" he said. "Like my mom?"

"I don't want your dating advice," she snapped. "I need a favor."

"I'm not going to ask him if he likes you."

She laughed, but without enthusiasm. "It's Silas Grant."

It took a moment. Then: "The frog weirdo!"

Olivia didn't object to having her romantic crush referred to as a weirdo. Tyler figured that was for obvious reasons.

"Olivia, have I been putting too much pressure on you?"

She plunked herself down in a chair with none of her usual elegance. "As if I'd let you. I know it's crazy, Tyler, but I like the guy. Now, are you going to do me this favor, or do I have to call your mom and have her order you to help me?"

"You've told Mom you like Frog Guy?" he said, incredulous.

"Of course I haven't." She shuddered. "Please don't make me."

He sighed. "What's the favor?"

"Let Silas pitch to the PhilStrat Committee."

She'd never tried to influence how the foundation spent its money before. They both knew she was overstepping the mark. But Tyler couldn't get angry. Sometimes, you met someone who made you want to act out of character. He was strong enough to resist that temptation, but Olivia obviously wasn't.

"You think that'll impress him?" he asked.

"It's the only thing I've got." The words fell out of her, startling both of them.

"Take it easy, Olivia," Tyler said.

She grimaced. "I can't believe I'm telling you this. It seems like only yesterday you were—"

Tyler held up a hand. "This had better not be about my bare baby bottom again."

She clamped her lips together. But only for a moment.

"Did you know Susan asked me to be your godmother when you were born?"

"No," he said, surprised.

"I refused, told her it wasn't my thing."

He nodded. Olivia had doubtless been too busy partying.

She crossed her legs, flexed one black patent-leather shoe "It wasn't true. I just didn't think I'd be a very good godmother."

"Of course you would," he said automatically. He couldn't see that godmothering was too difficult a task.

Olivia took his assurance more seriously than he intended. Her smile might have been skeptical, but her eyes lit up. "You really think I could have done it?"

"I wish you had," he said, and realized he meant it. "Instead, I had Lyddie Hudson telling Mom that, 'dear Tyler would look so adorable wearing a suit and tie to church, you really must have him fitted.'"

Olivia shuddered. "You were only six—I never saw a kid look so uncomfortable. I couldn't convince Susan to get rid of that suit until after you put a hole in the pants, climbing a tree."

Tyler narrowed his eyes. "You dared me to climb that tree."

"Did I?" she said innocently.

He grinned. "I definitely wish you'd been my godmother."

"If I'd known how fond of you I would eventually become, I might have accepted," she said, surprising him again. He had a lot of affection for Olivia, and he'd assumed she felt the same, but it wasn't something they talked about. "Truth be told," she added, "I didn't like you much at first."

"Even with my cute little…?" He waved in the direction of his behind.

"Even with that," she said dryly. "Your mother was so besotted with you, it was painful. She loved Max, of course, but I've never seen anyone as potty about a baby as she was about you." She laughed. "Susan couldn't think or talk about anything else after you were born."

"Sounds horrible." One thing about Bethany, no matter how devoted she was to Ben, she had plenty of time and energy to tell Tyler where he was going wrong. He chuckled at the thought.

"I was jealous," Olivia admitted. "I've known your mom longer than I've known anyone else—she's the person I'm closest to in the world."

Tyler shifted in his seat. "I guess we've all matured since then."

Her smile was wry. "Right now, I feel about twelve years old. I don't know what to make of this thing with Silas. I'm so confused."

"Sounds like it." He couldn't imagine what the attraction was.

"When you're twelve years old," Olivia said, "you're so *hopeful.* Dreadfully naive, but there it is."

Tyler sighed, spread his hands on the desk. "Fine, tell your boyfriend he can pitch to the committee. As long as he gets a haircut."

Olivia beamed, and for a second she did look like a girl, a hopeful, happy kid.

"Maybe you should trust your instincts," he said abruptly.

She stood, considering him. "Maybe *you* should trust *yours.*"

What the hell was that supposed to mean? He wasn't the one who felt like a twelve-year-old. "This conversation is not about me."

She tutted, but she was still smiling. "That makes a nice change."

Troubled, Tyler watched her walk out of the office. Olivia had fallen for Silas hard and far too fast, which she had a habit of doing, as he knew from her multitude of past engagements.

But he'd never seen her put herself out for someone before. He'd never heard her talk about her fears, her hopes.

The world was turning upside down, and Tyler didn't like it.

WHEN OLIVIA CALLED Silas with the good news that he could pitch to the PhilStrat Committee, he didn't say anything about her presence outside his house last Friday.

So maybe he hadn't seen her. Had he been wearing those glasses?

She made herself believe he hadn't, because otherwise she'd be too embarrassed to proceed with her plan. It would be so blatantly obvious that she'd checked out his material wealth before she took this step.

"There's not a lot of time before the pitch meeting," she said casually, "so I thought I might…help you."

"Hmm," he said, neither encouraging nor discouraging.

"I know how the committee makes its assessment, so I can make sure you cover all the bases," she said. "And I'm a whiz with PowerPoint."

She was learning not to rush him through the silences he seemed to enjoy.

"That's very kind of you," he said at last.

Was it Olivia's imagination, or did a thread of amusement run through the words?

She was glad she couldn't see him. She clutched the phone tighter. "Would you like to come to my place on Wednesday night so we can plan your campaign?"

He thought about it. "Yes," he said, "I believe I would."

TYLER HAD BEEN out of sorts the past couple of days. Ever since that kiss.

Since Bethany felt the same, though in her opinion she was

doing a better job of hiding it, they didn't talk much. And they definitely didn't touch. They passed Ben from one to the other without the slightest contact.

As she fed the baby his dinner late Tuesday afternoon— Ben had graduated to rice cereal or pureed vegetables served in his high chair for his evening meal—Bethany admitted that, as far as the baby was concerned, Tyler was shaping up better than expected. He gave his two hours every day, without argument. He took Ben out with him, often to a media interview. Bethany never heard him speaking to Ben in a way that was anything but kind, if disinterested. And he changed diapers, if not with enthusiasm then with tolerance.

"I think he likes you," she told Ben.

Tyler had shown less tolerance toward the pamphlets about kidney disease that she'd taken to leaving around as part of her new stealth campaign. She found a bunch of them in the wastepaper basket in his den. And the Your Kidney and You poster she'd pinned to the back of the bathroom door was unceremoniously torn down within hours. She never found it.

The head of Bethany's research team had called her yesterday to see if she would be rejoining them anytime soon. But while he was hopeful the team's budget might be expanded in the second half of the year, right now there was no money to pay her beyond what she could get out of the Warrington Foundation.

Which was big fat nothing. Nagging Tyler hadn't worked. Not nagging hadn't worked. And her strategy of getting him to fall in love with Ben and throw cash at her research was...well, that wouldn't succeed overnight.

The doorbell rang, interrupting the dismal inventory of her progress.

"Just a minute, sweetie," she told Ben.

On the porch stood the most gorgeous specimen of woman-hood Bethany had ever seen. A blond, bronzed bombshell. Tall, slim, but with curves. Enticing curves, by anyone's standards.

"You must be Miss Georgia."

The smile was wide, warm, wonderful. "Sabrina Merritt," she said. A magical name for a magical creature. "Also known as Miss Georgia. And you're Bethany. May I come in?" She held up a small Tupperware container, as if it was some kind of admission token.

Doubt—and guilt—assailed Bethany. Could Tyler really not be dating this woman? And what if Miss Georgia was in love with him? What if she'd guessed about that kiss and wanted to confront the woman who was after her man? Maybe Bethany should just confess now that she'd forgotten the beauty queen's existence when she'd issued that reckless invitation to Tyler to kiss her. Let the woman club her to death with the Tupperware, and be done with it.

From the kitchen, Ben squealed, then hiccuped.

"Come this way," she told Sabrina. The presence of a baby would surely distract even the most jealous of lovers. Six feet of stilettoed beauty queen sashayed behind Bethany to the kitchen.

Miss Georgia caught sight of Ben in his high chair. "Isn't he adorable."

He'd made hay in Bethany's absence, dipping his hands into the bowl of rice cereal she should have removed from his tray, and was now squeezing the gooey mixture between his fingers.

Sabrina brought her face close to Ben's and made clucking noises. Bethany had read that even babies recognize beauty; Ben took one look at Miss Georgia and paused in his play. His wide eyes roamed her perfect face, then a chubby hand reached for that spun-gold hair.

"Careful," Bethany warned her, just as Ben tugged hard.

"Ouch!" But nothing disturbed Miss Georgia's apparently flawless temper, and she was still smiling as she disentangled Ben's hand from her hair. "You little cutie, you're going to be irresistible to the ladies."

Ben chortled and waved with excitement at having the attention of this vision of loveliness. Bethany supposed making a fuss over babies was high on the list of a beauty queen's essential job skills, so she didn't take the usual pride she might have in Sabrina's praise of Ben.

Some contrary impulse stopped her mentioning that the woman had a large glob of rice cereal stuck in her hair. She picked up a spoon and began trying to coax the remains of Ben's dinner into his mouth.

"I told Tyler I'd call around this afternoon. He said he'd be home early—" Sabrina shook her head indulgently at Tyler's tardiness "—but maybe you and I can make girl talk until he gets here." As if there was nothing Bethany would rather do than be made to feel like a total frump.

The other woman slid onto a stool at the granite island, every movement as smooth as a performance of *Swan Lake*. She set the Tupperware container in front of her with a precise movement. The clump of rice cereal swung as she moved, attracting a few more strands of hair.

Bethany should say something. But right now, that lump of cereal was the only thing that made Miss Georgia human enough to talk to. She'd mention it soon, she assured herself as she put the kettle on to boil. She offered her guest a drink; Sabrina chose herbal tea.

"Tyler tells me you're doing a great job of looking after Ben."

"He's a wonderful baby, anyone would want to help him," Bethany said.

"How did you end up getting involved?"

At Sabrina's urging, Bethany told her about her kidney research. The other woman was interested and compassionate but not, Bethany guessed, turned on by the cause. It seemed unlikely she could enlist Sabrina's help in persuading Tyler to spend more money.

She was surprised to find herself enjoying their conversation. The "girl talk" stayed at a level Bethany could follow—moisturizer, sunscreen, lipstick—rather than soaring into the realms of Botox, collagen, or, worse, men.

"Oh, I forgot—" Sabrina slapped her cheek in a charmingly ditzy way "—I made some food for Ben." One long, lilac fingernail tapped the Tupperware container. "Tyler told me you prepare Ben's food yourself, rather than buying cans."

Tyler talked about baby food with Sabrina? And he'd actually noticed Bethany pureeing carrots? "Uh…thanks, that's really thoughtful of you."

"It's coq au vin," Sabrina said. "I pureed it thoroughly so it's total mush, and there's no salt in it. I know salt's bad for babies."

Bethany peered at the container. "Um, did you say coq au vin?"

Sabrina chortled. "I'm Cordon Bleu trained, so I can't help cooking fancy meals. But there's no alcohol in it. I mean, there's a tiny bit of wine, but the alcohol evaporates during cooking."

As far as Bethany knew without consulting a textbook, Sabrina was right. There shouldn't be a problem giving a baby food that had de-alcoholized wine in it. But something about the thought of feeding a baby coq au vin seemed just plain wrong.

"He's only having rice and vegetables at this stage," she said. "Chicken won't be on the menu for another month or so. I'll put this in the freezer."

Before she could do so, Ben banged his spoon on the tray

of his high chair and gurgled with such purpose that she and Sabrina turned to see the source of the fuss. Tyler had arrived.

He greeted Bethany, ruffled Ben's nonexistent hair, then moved on to their guest.

"Sabrina." After a swift glance at Bethany, he dropped a kiss on Miss Georgia's beautiful mouth. "I forgot you were coming over."

"Do you have other plans?" She didn't seem miffed at the thought of being forgotten, and Bethany liked her for it.

"No. Yes." He stared at the cereal in Sabrina's hair. A few more tendrils had been drawn into the sticky mess, and it looked larger. Without commenting on it, he looked back at Sabrina, and Bethany saw concern in his face. Concern about something more than the state of Sabrina's hair. "Jake said he might call in for a drink."

Sabrina bit her lip, but not hard enough to mar her lipstick's perfect finish. "I'll stay a little while," she said, "then get out of your hair before he arrives."

That phrase, *get out of your hair,* had Bethany painfully aware she should say something about the rice cereal. Because when Sabrina looked in a mirror, she wouldn't have to be the sharpest file in the manicure kit to realize the mess had originated with Ben and that Bethany had seen it and not told. "Uh, Sabrina…"

The peal of the doorbell had Sabrina stiffening.

Jake let himself in, called out a hello as he made his way to the kitchen. "Hey, buddy, I know I said six o'clock, but—" He stopped at the sight of Sabrina, whose fingers had curled around the Tupperware container and were clenching it as if it was a talisman to ward off evil.

"Hello, Jake," she said coolly.

"Sabrina." His eyes swept her. "You have puke in your hair."

Bethany cringed. "It's not puke," she said, "it's rice cereal."

As if that somehow made it better. Well, it did. Given the choice of having her hair clogged with rice cereal or puke, anyone would choose cereal.

Bethany couldn't figure out why the easygoing Jake had been so rude.

Sabrina colored, rummaged in her tiny, elegant Chanel purse, pulled out a mirror. After a quick inspection she stowed the mirror again, her expression neutral.

"I'd better get home and fix this mess." She pushed herself off her stool. Lightly, she said to Bethany, "It's funny, once you've been onstage in a swimsuit and a diamanté crown, no one ever tells you if you have lipstick on your teeth, or a smudge on your face, or—or puke in your hair." Her voice wobbled, but she brought it under control quickly.

Bethany felt lower than an earthworm, and Tyler was squirming too. Sabrina turned to Jake and said, "So, thanks, Jake. I guess this means right now you're my best friend in the world."

He flung her a look of such loathing that Bethany flinched on her behalf.

But Sabrina seemed to find that oddly cheering, and her smile warmed up as she said goodbye to Tyler.

"Thanks for bringing the puree." In a last-ditch effort to redeem herself, Bethany said urgently to Jake, "Sabrina made a meal for Ben. She cooked chicken." She wasn't about to specify coq au vin, she had a suspicion Jake would have a field day with that. As it was, he rolled his eyes rather than commending Sabrina for her thoughtfulness.

Sabrina acknowledged Bethany's feeble, belated effort to intervene in an obviously damaged relationship with a smile. But there was a distance in it that hadn't been there before. Bethany still felt like a heel.

When the beauty queen had left, Tyler grabbed a couple of beers from the fridge, handed one to Jake.

"Would you like a glass of wine?" he asked Bethany.

She had him pour her a glass of merlot.

Jake clinked the neck of his bottle against Tyler's. With Sabrina gone, he seemed his usual relaxed self. "I have news for you, buddy. I had a call from a pal in Washington, D.C."

Tyler glanced at Bethany, and said, "Let's go to the den."

TYLER SAT DOWN on the button-backed leather sofa that had seen him through years of TV ball games, dozens of Chinese takeouts and an immoderate amount of making out. "You have news on the think-tank job?"

"First, my usual disclaimer, none of this is written in stone," Jake warned. But he was well connected—his father, Tyler's uncle, had been governor of Georgia—and his information was seldom wrong.

"Understood," Tyler said.

Jake took a swig of his beer, eyeing Tyler over the rim of his bottle. "Those guys in D.C. should be the last to believe what they read in the press, but that article in the *Post* about you at the single-dads conference made a big impression. As of this week, you're the front-runner."

Nervous excitement dried Tyler's mouth. He gulped down beer. "I'm up against some big names," he said, trying not to get excited. "People who've had years of working with families and kids."

"I hear there's some pressure to choose a candidate from the South," Jake said.

"There's plenty of competition down here, too. Carson, Lavelle…"

"You're the golden boy."

"That doesn't mean anything to those guys. Hell, it didn't mean anything to my own family."

Jake folded his arms, didn't disagree.

"If I get this job it'll be on my own strengths." Tyler didn't know if he could pass the test.

"Looking after the baby was a smart tactic." Jake was clever enough to figure out where Tyler's interest in parenting stemmed from, and cynical enough not to object.

Tyler didn't have to pretend with him. Still, he found himself saying, "Ben's a nice little guy."

"A bonus."

Which was true. Even if Ben had been the baby from hell, Tyler would have gone ahead with his plan.

"If you can swing another media coup on the scale of the *Washington Post*," Jake said, "you might just have yourself a job." He frowned. "I hope my family doesn't handicap your chances."

Jake's father had exited the governor's office in disgrace, and Tyler knew the shame still rankled with his cousin. "If they wanted to hold your father against me, they'd have ruled me out a long time ago."

"I guess." Jake stretched his arms behind his head. "How are you getting along with the cute kidney doctor?"

Tyler shrugged. Then suspicion hit. "Why do you call her cute?"

Jake laughed. "She have a boyfriend?"

"Yes," Tyler said, remembering the "convenient" guy he'd never actually seen. Plus the divorced dad who'd asked for her phone number. Had he called yet?

Jake looked skeptical. "You wouldn't have a problem if I ask her on a date, would you?"

"I heard you already did."

Jake grinned, unembarrassed.

Tyler couldn't explain the sudden coldness that settled into his spine. "If she's out with you, I'll have to look after the baby. So, yes, I would have a problem."

Jake gave him a knowing look.

"I'm not interested in her," Tyler protested. He thought about that kiss, the memory of which still sneaked up on him at least a dozen times a day. "Not beyond the 'she's a pretty woman, I'm a red-blooded man' level. You know I don't go for the wholesome do-gooder type." He folded his arms and found himself staring his cousin down in a way that was vaguely reminiscent of years ago, when he and Jake both had crushes on Sabrina.

Back then, Jake had won, and it hadn't bothered Tyler. But Jake damn well wouldn't get to date Bethany. The strong surge of possessiveness caught Tyler by surprise, and he had to struggle to stay polite.

Maybe sensing that struggle, Jake didn't stay long.

"Remember what I said," he told Tyler as he climbed into his Alfa Romeo. "Find yourself another opportunity like the *Post* one, and do it fast."

After his cousin drove away, Tyler tried to enjoy the thrill of knowing he might soon win that job in D.C. But he kept thinking about Jake dating Bethany.

It wouldn't hurt to figure out exactly what Bethany thought of his cousin.

CHAPTER TEN

"Do you cook?" Tyler asked Bethany when he walked back into the kitchen.

She looked up from the newspaper she was skimming as she stood at the counter. "I do a nice pureed carrot."

He tapped the tile floor with his foot. "I'll make us dinner."

"Aren't you going out?" she said, surprised.

"I don't go out every night."

She raised her eyebrows.

"I stayed home one night last year," he said, and she laughed. "Most boring damn night of my life."

"And that's what you're offering me?"

Tyler could think of any number of ways to spice up an evening in with Bethany. In fact, the breadth of his imagination startled him. "I've got to be better company than Ben."

"If you say so," she said dubiously. "But you don't have to cook. I usually eat one of the microwave meals out of your freezer."

Her hand reached over to Ben, still in his high chair. She stroked his head, and Tyler wished it was him she had her hands on.

"I'll cook," he said.

BETHANY PUT BEN to bed before they ate, and when she came downstairs, Tyler had set the table in the formal dining room with cutlery, condiments…and candles.

She reminded herself he was hardwired for seduction and that this meant nothing. He'd made it clear he wasn't after a relationship, and she wasn't after sex. Or a relationship, she added hastily.

The table was huge, so they sat at one end, opposite each other. Tyler had cooked steaks with artery-clogging but delicious garlic butter, home-fried potatoes and—a nod to the health lobby—green beans. Bethany's steak was perfectly medium-rare, tender and juicy.

With the candle flickering between them, the atmosphere was way too romantic.

Bethany broke the mood. "My brother called, he wants to stay over on Friday, is that okay?"

Tyler shrugged, distracted. "I'll be out at a concert, do whatever you like." He put down his fork. "Did Jake tell you when that ball game is yet?"

"I thought I wasn't allowed to go."

"I can't stop you dating," he acknowledged. He didn't sound happy about it, which given he wasn't interested in her himself smacked of pettiness.

"Good, because I had a call from Scott, the father of that girl who didn't have an allergy."

He hissed his annoyance, and because her ego needed pampering, she added, "Maybe I'll go out with him next week, then Jake the week after, now that I have your permission."

He eyed her with disfavor. "Jake's not your type."

Bethany sighed as her ego took another tumble. "You mean, he wouldn't want an ordinary woman like me?"

"Don't put words in my mouth."

That drew her attention to his lips and the memory of that kiss.

"Jake's not a one-woman guy," he said. "You'll get hurt."

Nice of him to care. "What's with Jake's hostility toward Sabrina?" Bethany asked.

"They go back a long way," Tyler said vaguely. His gaze sharpened. "Why didn't you tell her she had that gunk in her hair?"

Bethany felt her face redden. "Why didn't you?"

He fixed her with a curious stare, and drummed his fingers on the table.

She held out as long as she could, then said, ashamed, "It made her seem more…human."

"Sabrina's lovely."

"I know that now. But, believe me, when you look like I do and you meet a woman like her, it's intimidating. She wasn't so frightening when her hair was a mess."

"You're not frightened of anyone," he said. "Besides, you're pretty, you have no reason to feel insecure."

As compliments went, it wasn't a top-ten, all-time great one.

"So why didn't *you* tell her about the rice cereal?" Deliberately provocative—not to mention pathetically insecure—she added, "You're her boyfriend."

Annoyance shadowed his face. "For the last time, I'm not. Sabrina and I like to spend time together. Having me around boosts her profile, and when I need a date who's not going to cause a scandal, she's my first choice. We're friends. Old friends."

"All the more reason for you to have mentioned her hair."

"I couldn't. Blame it on my mom—she raised me to always be polite to a lady. Never to point out her faults."

"It doesn't seem to work that way with me."

He rubbed his chin. "You're right, there's some kind of mutant instinct at play where you're concerned." He splayed his hands on the table, his fingers strong, capable. "I still think you were mean not to tell Sabrina."

"You were mean, too."

"We were both mean," he said.

The awful thing was, Bethany enjoyed the comfort of that shared failing. She buried her face in her hands. "I can't believe I've sunk to your level."

"Or I've come up to yours," he suggested helpfully.

She glared. "I would *never* have been that selfish before I met you."

He shook his head sadly. "I'm just glad Ben's too young to understand how you've fallen."

She sighed in agreement. "You're probably a better role model for him than I am right now."

He reared back. "That's going a bit far."

"I'm paid to look after him," she pointed out. "You've been spending two hours a day with him without fail, and you've been great with him."

"I had to be blackmailed into it," he reminded her.

"There is that," she said, relieved.

He folded his arms across the powerful chest that she realized she'd seen naked more often than clothed. A smile played on those firm lips. "You really think I'm great with Ben?"

"Occasionally," Bethany said, because he didn't need a bigger ego.

He surprised her by looking thoughtful instead of pleased with himself. So she added honestly, "I might even have misjudged your commitment to the foundation."

"Is that so?"

"At first I thought you didn't take it seriously, that you enjoyed the social aspects and didn't care about the people you help."

"What's changed your mind?" he said cautiously.

"You've worked so hard on publicity, all those media interviews you've done the last couple of weeks. You're becoming almost as boring on the subject of family issues as I am about kidneys."

"No way," he said, shocked.

She smiled. "And there's nothing in it for you, you're doing it all for the foundation. I...admire that."

Tyler shifted in his seat. "Let me guess, this is a ploy to get me to listen to your Kidneys 101 lecture." He sure as hell hoped it was—the last thing he wanted was Bethany seeing him as some kind of hero.

Naturally, she wasn't able to pass up the opportunity.

"I'll keep this lecture short," she said, "out of deference to your attention span for any subject other than yourself."

She didn't seem to be able to pass up the chance to have a dig at him either, Tyler thought, amused. Her foot brushed his under the table, gaining her his full attention.

"How would you feel if Ben had kidney disease? If, unless the doctors were able to learn more about his condition, that disease would kill him?"

Pain slammed through Tyler, winding him. Was she trying to break some bad news? "He's not sick, is he?"

She shook her head. "That's the situation my patients and their families are in."

Tyler regrouped his emotions. "That was a low tactic," he said coldly. "Don't do it again."

She looked down her nose at him, unrepentant. "I've said all I wanted to say. Think about it."

TYLER DIDN'T THINK about kids with kidney disease that night, not once. But he did think about Bethany.

She'd sneaked into his mind subtly, infuriatingly, at first only with the odd stray, usually negative, thought, but now she'd launched a full-scale invasion of his mental space.

There was no reason for it, Tyler thought as he stared unseeing at the computer screen on his desk the next morning. Except, maybe, that by not telling him much about herself, she'd intrigued him enough to make him want to know more.

Many of the women Tyler dated were Atlanta socialites whose families he'd known for years, their pedigrees a matter of public record. And as most women were keen to talk about themselves, he usually ended up knowing way more than he ever wanted to about them.

What did he know about Bethany?

That she was prickly and defensive about her work, yet ready to laugh at her own expense about anything else. That she was small-minded enough not to tell Sabrina about the gunk in her hair, yet compassionate to the point of self-sacrifice for sick kids. That she attacked Tyler's ego with all guns blazing, yet she lavished tenderness on Ben. That she kissed like a dream.

Get a grip. Tyler hauled his wandering mind back to the facts he knew about Dr. Bethany Hart. She'd studied medicine at the Medical College of Georgia. She worked at Children's Healthcare of Atlanta, on the Emory University campus. He cast around for more hard facts. He had no idea about former boyfriends, lovers…and decided ignorance was much better for his peace of mind. He knew she had parents in Madison, a brother, and a sister who'd died. Of kidney disease.

Which must have been a big deal, big enough to set the course of her life. Yet she'd never mentioned it again, not even when she was haranguing Tyler for money. He needed to find out more.

OLIVIA HAD GIVEN the cardiologist his marching orders. He was showing alarming signs of thinking long-term, and she'd resolved she wouldn't get engaged again until she found a man who would love her above all else.

Of course, she'd made the mistake before of thinking she'd found such a man—seven times—but she was starting to realize that was because she'd been looking at the wrong kind of man. She dated men who liked to be seen with a beautiful woman, one who fit right into their expensive homes and wealthy lifestyles.

She needed a man who would care more about her than he did about life's accoutrements. A man like Silas, who was not only incredibly attractive, but also a physics professor at Georgia State, who thought deeply about things and, more important, cared deeply. Yet who still had a reassuringly large fortune, to judge by his house, his car.

Olivia couldn't think why she hadn't dated a man like him before.

The things she didn't like about Silas—his dress sense, his droning on about frogs, his tendency to stare into space saying nothing—could be fixed in a jiffy.

He arrived at her place at six on Wednesday night, right on time.

"Hello, Olivia." He stepped into her home without looking left or right, no curiosity about her environment discernible.

But as she led him through the house, she felt his eyes on her back, on her hips as they moved in her slim-cut black velvet skirt, as surely as if they'd been his hands, and was glad she'd dressed up.

It was more than he'd done. Although his plaid shirt looked clean, his jeans had the beginnings of a hole in one knee and his overcoat was as disreputable as ever.

But—she hugged the knowledge to herself, didn't betray by so much as a smile that she'd noticed—Silas had shaved.

In place of that rough stubble was smooth male skin that tempted Olivia to reach out and touch.

Instead, she wrapped her hands around a hundred-dollar bottle of merlot and offered him a glass.

He accepted, to her relief. She'd worried his eco-warrior attitude might extend to most of life's pleasures, though the Maserati had afforded her some hope.

Since this was supposed to be a business meeting, she steered him to the dining room table. Silas opened his battered briefcase—his battered *Gucci* briefcase—and withdrew a rough outline for his pitch, along with some of the background material.

He spread the documents across the table and invited Olivia to take a look. He stood next to her, explaining, in his sexy voice, which photos, charts and statistical information he considered most useful.

It had to be the contrast between those polished vowels and his rough appearance that made Olivia's insides curl in on themselves with excitement. He left her short of breath, long on giddy anticipation.

As she gave him her views on the presentation and what he should be covering, it was impossible to tell if she had the same impact on him. Once or twice, she thought she saw him glancing at her legs when she moved and the slit at the side of her dress parted. And his gaze rested on her cleavage for several seconds as she leaned over the table to look at the state map that showed the location of the red-spotted tree frog's habitats.

If only she could be certain he was actually thinking about her cleavage, rather than those blasted frogs.

She poured him a second glass of wine, but when it was

only half-full he reached out, covered her hand with his and tilted the bottle upright.

"No more for me."

His fingers interlaced with hers around the bottle—his thick and roughened, hers pale, pink-tipped.

Olivia couldn't drag her gaze away from the contrast. She sensed him looking down at her, and a strange shyness stopped her from looking back, even though she longed to show him how much she liked him.

Then his hand twisted, broke the contact, and he took the bottle from her. He stood it on the table, moved away so there were several feet of space between them, and she wondered if she'd imagined the whole charged moment.

She cleared her throat. "How did you get interested in the frog?"

"Through my wife," he said.

Her stomach caved in. "You—you're married?" Everything changed in the blink of an eye, leaving her feeling naive and very foolish.

"Widowed," he said. "Anna died two years ago."

"I'm sorry," she said, ashamed of the relief she felt. "Was she sick?"

He shook his head. "She had an accident out at the frog sanctuary she'd established—the preservation of the red-spotted tree frog was her life's work. She slipped and fell at the edge of a pond. Hit her head on a rock and drowned."

"Silas, that's awful." Olivia swallowed. "Was she a scientist too?"

"A biologist."

"She must have been smart." Olivia had spent her three years in college organizing sorority parties. She'd passed one exam, more or less by accident. She'd quit before they threw her out.

"Anna was smart," he agreed. "And kind, and good." He added, almost belligerently, "I loved her very much."

"Of course you did." It was the depth of Silas's feelings that had first attracted Olivia to him. "You must have been very happy."

For the first time since they'd met, he didn't look her directly in the eye. "Before the accident, I was involved in an international physics project, which meant a lot of travel. I…neglected Anna. She was unhappy when she died." He sounded wretched.

Olivia didn't know how best to comfort him. Awkwardly, she reached for his hand, clasped it between hers.

"That's why I'm on sabbatical from Georgia State." He lifted his gaze. "I'm taking a year out to secure the future of the Anna Grant Frog Sanctuary."

Olivia knew she absolutely should not feel jealous of a woman she'd never met, a woman who'd died tragically. "It's a beautiful gesture," she managed to say.

His mouth twisted. "It's better than nothing. Though my kids don't see it that way."

"You have kids?"

"A son and a daughter, Paul and Jemma. But," he said heavily, "they don't speak to me. They haven't forgiven me for upsetting their mother. I don't blame them."

He looked so remorseful, Olivia wanted to shake him. She couldn't believe Anna had been unhappy. Not with a husband who loved her enough to take over her cause after her death.

Silas moved around the table, gathering his papers. "Thank you for your help tonight, I appreciate it."

"Would you like to stay for dinner? It's just leftovers." Actually, it was a freshly cooked chicken-and-mushroom casserole.

He looked at her, looked away. "I don't think so." He sounded distant, distracted again.

She followed him out to the entryway, where he took his coat off the hook, pulled it on. He shoved his hands into its pockets.

Olivia said, "Silas, do you ever have that coat cleaned?"

He looked down at her in surprise. "Not much point. I go out to the frog sanctuary fairly regularly, just to think about things, and I often end up with a frog or two in my pocket."

She shuddered.

A beat-up Chevy truck sat outside her front door, alerting her neighbors to his presence. She'd have to say she was interviewing a new gardener. She wondered why Silas hadn't brought the Maserati. Hopefully, of course, he had no idea she knew of its existence.

As he climbed into the truck, he said, "Can we do this again? Maybe at my place on Saturday morning? I should have a clearer idea of this presentation by then. We could start on the PowerPoint."

"Of course." Olivia's heart skipped and her mouth developed the irrepressible curve of a sixteen-year-old with a crush. "Uh, what's your address?"

The corners of his mouth moved in the tiniest smile. "I haven't moved since Friday night."

Drat.

BETHANY'S BROTHER, Ryan, arrived at Tyler's house at five o'clock on Friday.

She hugged him, delighted to see his awkward, angular face.

"Nice place," he said with a fifteen-year-old's casual interest as he looked around Tyler's open-plan living and dining room.

"Nice enough," she agreed. "Come and meet Ben." The

baby was in his high chair, and she set Ryan to feeding him while she made a start on the hamburgers she'd planned for their meal.

An hour later, they were just sitting down to eat, when Tyler walked into the kitchen.

Bethany's knife clattered onto her plate. "What are you doing here?"

"I live here." He headed for Ryan, who'd stood and was wiping his mouth with his napkin. "I'm Tyler Warrington, you must be Bethany's brother."

"Ryan," Ryan agreed. He shook hands with Tyler.

"I thought you had a concert," Bethany persisted.

Tyler said to Ryan, "This must be what it's like to be married. So glad I never took the plunge."

She glared. "Unfortunately, marriage does require one to think of someone other than oneself. I doubt you're suited to it."

"I always thought it was for people who'd run out of ideas," Tyler returned.

Ryan was glancing from one to the other, looking slightly shocked.

"Sorry, Ryan," Tyler said, "your sister is such an interesting conversationalist, I sometimes forget my manners."

"Sometimes..." Bethany muttered. More loudly, she said, "There are extra hamburgers if you'd like some."

Tyler loaded up a plate with burger and salad, then joined them. Between mouthfuls, he asked Ryan a few questions, eventually eliciting the information that Ryan was on a weekend away from his boarding school near Atlanta.

"Why do you go to boarding school?" Tyler asked. "Aren't there good schools in Madison?"

Ryan's mouth turned sullen. "Mom and Dad don't want me around."

Bethany got over her surprise that Tyler had remembered her hometown and tried to forestall a conversation that could only give him too much information. "That's not true," she scolded Ryan. To Tyler, she said, "Mom hasn't been well for a long time. I boarded through most of high school, and now Ryan's doing the same."

Ryan made a gagging noise. "You don't believe that crap any more than I do. They sent me to an elementary boarding school when I was eight. They'd have sent me to boarding pre-school if they could."

"Ryan..." Bethany sent Tyler a helpless look, pleading with him to drop the subject.

Tyler didn't even consider complying. When had she ever paid the slightest attention to his requests that she drop the subject of her work? "What exactly is wrong with your mom?"

"Nothing," Ben said. "I get on her nerves and so does Bethany. So does anyone who's not Melanie."

Bethany closed her eyes, evidently giving up the fight.

"You were only a baby when Melanie died, weren't you?" Ryan hadn't been much older than Ben.

Some of the resentment drained out of Ryan at Tyler's reasonable tone. He sagged back in his chair, nodded. "I don't remember her, I only ever saw photos."

"Do you look like her?" There was a clear resemblance between Ryan and Bethany, in the russet color of their hair and in the shape of their faces, though Ryan had brown eyes.

"Some," the boy said. He fidgeted with his fork, flipping it between his fingers. "I never really knew Mom and Dad not the way they were before Melanie got sick. They probably used to be okay."

"Melanie had a rare blood type that made a kidney transplant almost impossible," Bethany said. "Dad had the same blood type, but he couldn't donate because he had only one kidney." Seeing Tyler's shock, she said, "A single kidney isn't that unusual—most people born that way never realize they don't have two. Anyway, Mom and Dad had some very stressful years." To Ryan, she added, "But they love you. And me."

"They loved Melanie more." Ryan's tone was so flat, even Bethany didn't argue further. She threw Tyler a glance that said, *Thanks a lot.*

Tyler felt an out-of-character obligation to repair the damage. He tried to steer the conversation into safer waters. "What brings you here, Ryan?"

Ryan looked at his sister, dropped his gaze, then muttered, "I ran away from school."

"You *what?*" Bethany jumped to her feet.

"I hate it there," Ryan said. "If you're no good at sports, no one likes you. And then you get bullied."

"You're being bullied?" Her face whitened.

Her brother nodded abruptly, as if he was ashamed.

"Have you told Mom and Dad?"

He waved a hand at her. "I tried, but they said I should tell the teachers."

Tyler knew that wasn't a solution any teenage boy would welcome. "Maybe your parents could talk to the principal, in confidence."

"They'd have to care first," Ryan said.

Bethany held up a hand. "They do care. And right now, I need to phone the school and tell them you're with me. You'd better hope they haven't already called Mom."

"They won't know I'm gone," Ryan said. "I had a pass into town and I'm not due back until ten."

He was right—when Bethany spoke to the housemaster, Ryan's absence hadn't yet been noticed. That put the man at a disadvantage, and Bethany was able to insist she keep her brother for the weekend. When she suggested she would tell her parents she'd invited Ryan to stay, the man agreed with obvious relief.

Ryan grinned when she told him the news. She warned him sternly, "But Sunday night, you're going back to school, no arguments."

She felt awful when his elation evaporated.

"Will you talk to Mom and Dad about the bullying for me?" he begged.

Bethany didn't want to say yes. Her relationship with her parents was fragile enough that she didn't want to risk damaging it. She didn't want to put another brick in the wall that separated them from her.

"I'll try," she told Ryan discouragingly. Tyler shot her a surprised look.

It was all very well for him. He had a mother who doted on his every word. He'd never had to earn his parents' love.

He'd never disappointed his parents the way she'd disappointed hers.

CHAPTER ELEVEN

TYLER DECIDED on Monday morning that he needed to stop thinking about Bethany as a woman, turn the clock back to those days he'd thought of her as nothing more than a pediatrician and a pain in the butt.

He shouldn't have invited her and Ryan to Zoo Atlanta with him and Ben on Saturday. He'd justified it to himself on the basis she could help with Ben at the zoo, but instead, he'd just had a good time with her. He'd compounded his error by taking Bethany and Ryan to Mom's for lunch on Sunday, which had produced speaking glances from the family.

From now on, he would take less interest in her body, because that was what kept him making overtures to her, and more interest in her work—guaranteed to turn him off big-time. Which meant he had to make a great personal sacrifice, and start learning about kidney disease.

Bethany was the last person he wanted to talk to on the subject. Any whiff of interest on his part and he'd never hear the end of it. Not only that, she'd assume the foundation was going to extend her research grant, and if that didn't happen, she'd be devastated.

He called Olivia into his office and asked her to find out who the main research teams were in pediatric kidney disease. She cocked her head, inquiring. But Tyler turned back to his computer screen, so after a moment she left to do as he'd asked, tutting under her breath.

Two hours later, Tyler placed a call to Dr. Robert Harvey at Toronto's Hospital for Sick Children.

The doctor was patient and courteous in explaining kidney disease and the main areas of research. Among those, Tyler recognized Bethany's area of specialty—overcoming antibody barriers to kidney transplants.

"It's a very exciting area that several research teams, including ours, are following up," the doctor said. He made a whistling sound through his teeth. "Like everyone, we're limited by our funding as to what we can do." He paused. "What would be our chances of a grant from the Warrington Foundation?"

Alarms clanged in Tyler's head. "Anyone in North America can apply," he said cautiously. "You can use the application form on our Web site, or format your own application, and from there we'll contact you if we think it's worth your pitching to us."

He ended the call with a far greater understanding of the issues surrounding pediatric kidney disease…and with a fervent hope that Dr. Harvey wouldn't apply for funds.

THREE DAYS LATER a FedEx package arrived from Toronto.

Dr. Harvey must have stayed up all night, judging from the comprehensiveness of the material enclosed in support of his application. The foundation would have to take it seriously. Tyler told Olivia to contact the doctor and invite him to pitch at the next PhilStrat meeting.

"Another kidney project?" she said.

"Yep."

"But it's against the foundation's policy to fund more than one project in a specific area."

"You don't say."

She sucked in a breath, but didn't comment further. Now that he thought about it, Olivia hadn't been butting into his affairs much lately.

"How's your romance with Frog Guy?" he asked.

She sniffed. "It's not a romance, it's a working relationship."

"Bad luck," Tyler said. Then he realized her situation was similar to his with Bethany. The difference, he told himself, was that he wasn't looking for more than a working relationship.

BETHANY'S CONSCIENCE, aided by Ben's erratic sleep patterns, was keeping her awake at night. It was definitely her conscience, not thoughts of Tyler sleeping across the hall, so she asked Tyler to invite Sabrina for lunch on Saturday.

Sabrina's acceptance of the invitation, coming as it did from Bethany rather than Tyler, said a lot about her graciousness. Bethany was determined to make amends.

The sooner she said what had to be said the better. As they enjoyed a glass of wine with hors d'oeuvres in the kitchen before lunch, she announced, "I owe you an apology."

Sabrina's perfectly shaped eyebrows rose. "You do?"

Tyler stopped stirring the pumpkin soup Bethany had on the stove and came to listen. Bethany wasn't sure she wanted an audience.

"That day, when you had cereal in your hair." She blushed at the memory. "I'm so ashamed I didn't tell you. I was... relieved you could mess up like the rest of us. I was jealous," she said honestly, "that you're so beautiful and so put together. And I'm really sorry."

Tyler had an odd look on his face. Sabrina stared. *Great, I made a complete idiot of myself.*

Sabrina started to laugh. It didn't sound malicious, and

Bethany couldn't help smiling. "Glad you find my base emotions so amusing."

"I knew you felt bad," Sabrina said. "You were so sweet the way you never told Jake that I made coq au vin for Ben which I later mentioned to a friend of mine who's a nurse and she hasn't stopped laughing since."

"You made coq au vin for a baby?" Tyler said, aghast.

Sabrina raised her wineglass to him in ironic salute. "As if you would have known it was a dumb idea… But, Bethany I do appreciate your apology. When I saw that stuff in my hair I couldn't figure out why you wouldn't have said something and then I wondered if maybe you thought I wanted Tyler and you were in love with him—"

"No!" The horrified cry came from both Bethany and Tyler.

"But now, well, let's forget all that and just be friends."

"I'd love to," Bethany said. There was an awkward silence then Tyler said, "What the heck," and kissed both of them Typical of him to turn the situation to his advantage, Bethany thought, even as she noted that he lingered a lot longer on her lips than he did on Sabrina's.

"We must have lunch one day next week," Sabrina said "I'll be in Washington, D.C., on Monday and Tuesday, briefing Senator Bates about the peace initiatives in Kurdistan. But any other day is fine."

Which gave Bethany another chance to feel like a worm just in case she needed it.

While they were eating the pumpkin soup, along with the bread Bethany had made in Tyler's bread machine, Sabrina offered to visit some of the kidney kids Bethany worked with Bethany jumped on the invitation, and they agreed on the following Thursday.

After lunch, Bethany and Tyler stood on the porch to wave

Sabrina off. As soon as her car turned out of the driveway, Bethany smacked Tyler on the arm.

He grabbed her hand, held it in place. "What was that for?"

"Why didn't you tell me she really does work for world peace? You knew I thought that was a crock of beauty-queen babble."

His gaze alighted on her fingers, crumpling the crisp cotton of his sleeve. Then he looked right at her. "I didn't want to spoil your illusion that unless you wear odd clothes and beg for money you're a shallow, worthless person."

Bethany drew a sharp breath. Was that how she came across? Worse, was that what she believed deep inside? She pressed a fist to her mouth, gnawed on a knuckle.

Tyler shook his head, exasperated yet amused. "If it makes you feel any better, it's only peace in Southwest Asia."

Oh, yeah, she felt much better.

OLIVIA AND SILAS had had several more meetings, but they'd all, for one reason or another, ended up taking place at Olivia's house. Today, finally, she got to go the big Federal-style house on Armada.

The cynical side of Olivia couldn't think why she was excited about visiting a man who was so devastated by his wife's death that he'd dedicated his life to saving her precious tree frog.

Ironic that when she at last found a man who knew how to love a woman above everything else, he'd already given that love away.

The foolish, romantic side of her wondered if it was possible to love that way twice. Because if he loved her, she could definitely love him back.

But she still had no idea how he felt about her.

She'd dressed to impress regardless, in a knee-length green

skirt that showed her shapely calves, and a lighter green blouse, classy and just the tiniest bit transparent.

Silas opened the door before she got there. A different plaid shirt today, this one blue and gray, worn with faded jeans that looked almost normal. Apart from the fact that he was barefoot, he could have been a dressed-down version of any man she knew.

Then he said, "Good evening, Olivia," and the words brushed her skin like a hot summer breeze, and she knew he was a man apart.

Inside, the house was as beautiful as the exterior promised. Her gaze flitted around the paneled entryway, up the wide, curving staircase to high ceilings as she followed Silas into an enormous living room.

She gasped.

Every wall was plastered with posters of frogs, aerial photographs of wetlands, charts showing population statistics. The coffee table bore several stacks of papers, and more covered the sideboard along the far wall.

"May I take your coat?" Silas asked.

She shrugged out of her ivory wool peacoat. When his fingers touched her shoulders, Olivia shivered.

He frowned. "I guess I forgot to put the heating on." A pause. "I'll do that now."

When he returned, Olivia was reading one of the red-spotted tree frog fact sheets on the wall, still trying to feel the passion that Silas did. Still failing. She turned, and found Silas right behind her. Up close, he was so big she longed to lean into him.

His thick lashes made his eyes his best feature, she thought. Or maybe that was his mouth, with that thinnish top lip and full bottom lip. She'd never paid much attention to the tiny details of a man's face before. She was more a pocketbook girl, she liked to evaluate her dates' material assets.

Silas cleared his throat. "Perhaps it would be best," he said, "if I just kissed you and got it over with."

That's how deranged this man made her—she thought he'd just said something about kissing her. "Excuse me?"

"I can't stop thinking about kissing you—" he spoke faster than she knew he could "—and don't tell me you can, because I can see you can't."

"I—I—"

"I haven't kissed another woman since Anna. Haven't wanted to, until I met you." He'd slowed down again and he sounded so subdued, not at all enthusiastic, that Olivia just stared at him, mute, wondering if she was hearing right.

"How long since you kissed a man?" he asked with about as much energy as if he was asking if she thought it might rain.

"A couple of weeks." Now she wished she hadn't gone tongue-to-tongue with the cardiologist.

His craggy eyebrows shot up. "Any good?"

"I beg your pardon?"

"Was it any good?"

"Not really," she admitted.

He humphed. "We'd better give it a try."

"Surely some enthusiasm would be appropriate," she said.

Then his arms closed around her and she was incapable of speech, just filled with relief that at last it was happening.

His kiss was at once tender and rough, seeking and taking. Olivia opened to his firm, warm lips, pressed herself against him. She should be alarmed at how wanton he made her feel.

His large hands roamed her curves, making Olivia, taller than most of her friends, feel delicate. He was strong enough that he could probably sweep her up in his arms, carry her upstairs.

Then the kiss was over, as suddenly as it had started. Silas moved away from her, and she grabbed hold of the back of the couch for support. He looked pleased and annoyed at the same time.

"You're a good-looking woman," he said.

She nodded.

"Did you ever get married?"

"No," she said discouragingly.

"Why not?"

"Not for lack of offers," she said tartly, and pushed herself off the couch, steadier now.

"Never thought it was." Silas leaned against the sideboard, his gray eyes inquiring.

"I've been engaged seven times," she admitted.

His laugh cracked the air. "Just altar shy, huh?"

"Perhaps." She busied herself with tucking in her blouse, which had come away from her skirt.

His eyes followed her movements. "What was wrong with those men?"

Her hands paused. "Maybe there was something wrong with me."

He looked skeptical.

"They were good men," she said. "But any man I married would need to prove he'll always put me first."

"Selfish," he commented.

"I suppose I am. My parents led very busy lives, separate from each other and from me."

"I've heard of them." Her family had been prominent Atlanta benefactors.

"Nothing I did, good or bad, got their attention for more than a few minutes." She didn't want him to see how that hurt, so she fixed her gaze on the one piece of non-frog-related paraphernalia in the room. A silver-framed photo of a smiling, dark-haired woman, a child seated either side of her. This must be Anna. Olivia's focus blurred. "I hated that I could never be sure my parents loved me. I want a man who loves me so much he proves it every day, by choosing me above everything."

"Hard for any man to measure up."

You could. Olivia pushed her hair behind her ears. "I'm lonely, Silas. I have friends, I have a lot of fun, but I've always been lonely, every day of my life. But at least I know what to expect and can live my life around it. I'm terrified of marrying someone and having it not last, and I'll have forgotten how to survive on my own."

"Sometimes you have to take a risk."

She shivered, hugged her arms around her, turned slightly so she couldn't see that photo of Anna. "Finding someone, knowing that love, then ending up lonely again, would be worse than never knowing it at all."

"Chicken," he said. "I miss Anna every day, I'd give anything to have her back. But I'll never wish I hadn't loved her."

Olivia swallowed a salty lump in her throat.

His brow creased. "So you never met a man you loved enough to take the risk?"

"Never."

The wheezy sound from the back of his throat was a laugh. "You want a man who loves you enough to take a risk on you, but you don't want to give him the same."

She stepped back. "That's not true."

He didn't say anything, and Olivia considered the subject dropped. They moved into work mode: she busied herself with reading his presentation, made a few comments and suggestions, then refused his invitation to stay for supper.

"Come back tomorrow," he said as he showed her out the front door.

Silas watched her leave, driving that toy car of hers too fast down the driveway. Today he'd been to the deli for the first time in years, to buy the fancy foods he knew Olivia would like. He'd hoped she would stay; a small part of him wanted her never to leave.

Maybe, like her, he was lonely. Yet while he missed Anna, he didn't hate being on his own. Olivia was a special temptation. The taste of her, the feel of her in his arms, had been sweeter than anything he could remember.

He ran his knuckles across his mouth, fancied he could still feel her lips on his.

If Olivia knew the truth, that kiss would never have happened.

THE TYLER WARRINGTON publicity machine was an unstoppable beast. Tyler had only to decide he would come along on Sabrina's visit to the kidney ward, and his PR team swung into action. They had no trouble lining up a group of journalists to accompany him: Atlanta's favorite playboy was now Atlanta's favorite daddy.

Bethany had to assume all this publicity was doing the foundation some good, though she'd never fully understood the link between media coverage and its ability to boost the foundation's work. But it was nice to think that needy people were benefiting.

Sabrina looked stunning in a pale blue wool wrap dress and decked out in her Miss Georgia crown and sash. To Bethany's mind, Tyler was equally gorgeous in his black suit, pale gray shirt, and black-and-gray tie threaded with silver.

First on the agenda was a tour of the ward. The kids were ecstatic to see Miss Georgia, and so were their fathers. The mothers took more interest in Tyler, and Bethany saw a couple of appreciative glances from women she knew to be happily married.

"Tyler, this is Molly." She introduced him to a ten-year-old who was waiting for a transplant, and gave him a brief rundown of the girl's condition.

In less than a minute he'd charmed Molly out of her anxiety-induced moodiness.

That set the pattern for the rest of the visit. With every child, he requested details of his or her condition, first from the patient, then supplementing those shyly given but often painfully honest replies with technical information from Bethany. Then he'd chat until the child was relaxed and smiling. For a guy who never thought about anyone other than himself, he did a great job.

Bethany couldn't stop the hope that bubbled up inside her. Tyler was taking an interest in her work—if this visit convinced him to spend more of the foundation's money, the last month would have been worthwhile.

It already was worthwhile, she realized as, having introduced Tyler to a young boy who'd recently had surgery, she stepped back to let the man work his magic. Regardless of the outcome for her research, it had been a pleasure to look after Ben. She'd made a new friend in Sabrina. And then there was Tyler.

The man who'd argued with her, flirted with her, kissed her.

The man who was starting to mean something to her.

Not that.

"Bethany, how did Jason's surgery go?" Tyler called her attention back to the moment.

She bustled forward. "He's doing great."

It was almost an hour before they left the ward. One of the nurses came to "borrow" Ben to show her colleagues, while Sabrina and Tyler hosted an informal question-and-answer session with the media. A crowd of spectators gathered, among them Susan Warrington, presumably here to watch Tyler at work.

Tyler, well briefed as always, talked about sick kids and the strain illness put on families, and how the foundation was here to support families.

One of the reporters asked if he had a particular interest in kidney disease. Tyler grabbed Bethany's hand, tugged her forward.

"This is Dr. Bethany Hart. Her research into antibody production is funded by the Warrington Foundation. The foundation is committed long term to supporting advances in understanding and treating pediatric kidney disorders."

To the journalists it might have been just a quotable quote. But Bethany's ears latched on to the words *long term.*

Tyler must plan to renew her funding. What else could he mean? Of course, she wasn't rash enough to whip out her cell phone and call her parents—she'd wait until she knew exactly how much she was getting. But she had to struggle not to break into a skip.

One of the reporters asked for an update on Ben. Tyler described Ben's latest development with an accuracy that surprised Bethany—he must have been reading those books.

The crowd had questions about Ben, too. Tyler fielded queries about his sleeping and eating habits with aplomb. When he said he only had time for one more question, a teenage girl with blond dreadlocks raised her hand.

"Do you think the baby would rather be with his mother?" she asked. She sounded distressed on Ben's behalf, and Bethany wondered if maybe she'd been fostered herself.

Dismay flashed across Tyler's face, as if the thought of Ben's mother hadn't occurred to him in a while. Bethany took that as a good sign. A sign that he couldn't easily relinquish Ben, because he was fond of him.

When Tyler didn't answer, she stepped forward and said carefully, "I don't think Ben is consciously upset that he doesn't have his mom. But I'm sure he has a bond with her that he doesn't with anyone else." The girl nodded doubtfully. Mindful of the listening media and the chance to reach out to Ben's mother, Bethany added, "We would love for his mom to come forward, for her sake as well as his."

Deliberately, she shut down the voice that warned it wouldn't be easy to hand Ben back. Then shut down her own speculation as to what Ben's mother's reappearance would do to Tyler, to her and to their relationship.

AFTERWARD, THEY moved into the staff cafeteria for a coffee get-together with some of the nurses.

At Tyler's invitation, his mother joined them in the cafeteria, along with his brother, Max, who arrived just as they were on the move. Susan hugged Bethany in greeting.

"Nice to see you." Bethany hugged her back. "You too, Max."

"Darling," Susan addressed her older son, "shouldn't you be at work signing the multimillion-dollar contracts that are going to support me into my old age?"

"And miss out on seeing Tyler being fawned over by all these nurses?" Max protested mildly.

"He *is* rather popular." Fondly, Susan watched Tyler charming the half-dozen nurses clustered around him.

"Tyler did a wonderful job with the media," Bethany said. "He's so good at getting to the essentials of an issue and putting it in terms anyone can understand."

It wasn't her job to make sure Tyler's family appreciated him, but she couldn't help herself.

Susan and Max gave polite agreement, but didn't show any interest in continuing to discuss Tyler's accomplishments. But Bethany's words had carried to the man himself, and he turned to look at her.

She met his gaze…then she winked at him. Tyler laughed out loud, and excused himself from the nurses.

"Don't you know that winking at someone can ruin their concentration?" he complained as he reached her.

"You're a pro," she reminded him with a smile. "Nothing I do could hurt you."

"Maybe not." His gaze turned brooding. "Come out for lunch with me after this. Mom can take Ben back to her place." He sent his mother a questioning look. Susan nodded.

Bethany shrugged. "I guess lunch would be fine."

Tyler grinned. To judge by Bethany's lack of enthusiasm, you'd think she wasn't hot for him. He knew better. "I'll find Ben, and we'll hand him over to Mom."

The nurse who'd taken Ben originally no longer had him. She pointed Tyler in the direction of a group of nurses. Several of them held babies. He groaned inwardly. Not this again.

"Ladies, how are you?" He edged into the circle with a smile and hoped someone would offer him Ben. They returned his greeting and politely tried to involve him in their conversation.

Tyler replied to a question while he surreptitiously checked out the babies.

Then he said to the nurse on his left, "May I take Ben now?" And held his breath.

Maybe she replied right away, but to Tyler it felt like hours.

"He's so cute," the woman said as she handed Ben over.

"He is," Tyler agreed mechanically, barely processing her words through his relief. He hugged Ben to him—*hey, pardner, we did it!*—and headed back to Bethany, who was now chatting to a doctor she evidently knew.

"Why the goofy grin?" she asked.

"I got the right baby." He recounted what had happened.

"I told you you're bonding with him," she said in her superior tone.

"I'm not bonding," Tyler growled. But his heart wasn't in it.

The familiar unmistakable aroma wafted from Ben's diaper.

"I'll change him before we give him to Susan," Bethany said.

Tyler went with her. In the corridor, they found a parent-and-child bathroom.

"You don't get any less stinky as you get older," she told Ben as she wiped him clean.

He said something that might have been "Ah goo."

"Goo indeed," she said severely as she bundled the mess into a plastic bag. "He's been saying that sort of thing for a couple of weeks," she told Tyler, "which suggests he's four months old."

Ben batted her face with his little hand. When she'd fixed the new diaper in place, she spent a couple of minutes playing peekaboo, a game that involved Bethany holding a receiving blanket between her and Ben. She slowly lowered the blanket, and when Ben saw her eyes and started to smile, she said, "Peekaboo," and blew a raspberry on his bare tummy, which had Ben squirming and laughing.

"Can anyone play?" Tyler asked.

"Sure." She offered him the blanket.

"I wanted Ben's part," he said.

"Don't be silly." But her eyes wandered over him, and Tyler would bet she was thinking about what she could do to him naked, just as, increasingly, he was thinking that about her. It had to happen soon.

CHAPTER TWELVE

TYLER WAS AWARE he'd gotten carried away during today's informal press conference. He'd talked to half a dozen sick kids, and the next minute he was committing the foundation to long-term support of kidney disease. His usual strategy of noninvolvement—or as Bethany would say, non-caring—suddenly made a whole lot of sense.

He knew exactly what Bethany would be thinking after this morning's visit.

He couldn't let her.

He took her to Magritte, one of Atlanta's most expensive restaurants. When the maître d' helped Bethany out of the coat she'd worn all the way around the hospital, it turned out she'd actually dressed sexy today, though he doubted she knew that. Skinny black pants emphasized the length of her legs, and her faded green scoop-necked T-shirt had a shabby-chic, shrunk-in-the-wash look that sat a half inch above the waistband of her pants and enticingly low on her breasts.

Bethany looked around at the restaurant's soaring ceilings, the chandeliers, the plush banquette seating.

Her interest in her surroundings meant she didn't notice the curious appraisal of several male diners, all accompanied by much more glamorously, elegantly dressed women. Tyler found himself taking her hand possessively as the maître d' led them to the table that would be unavailable to most people arriving without a reservation.

"This place is incredible," Bethany said after the waiter had handed them menus and poured water into their glasses. She scanned the leather-bound menu. "So are the prices."

Tyler held up a hand. "I don't want to know how many kidney transplants you could do for the price of the lobster entrée."

She feigned disappointment. "You're so shallow."

They ordered their food and two glasses of wine. Tyler sat back, watched her from beneath lowered lids. "Do you realize this is the first time we've been out on our own, without Ben?"

Bethany spread her fingers on the banquette's taupe microsuede. "We'll probably have nothing to say to each other."

"Probably," he agreed.

Then he asked her a question about one of the less friendly doctors he'd met today, and that led to a conversation about people with Napoleon complexes.

The time flew until the waiter arrived with their appetizers.

Tyler watched Bethany savor her tomato-and-basil soup with grilled prawns. He found it oddly satisfying to observe her enjoying herself. *That's because if she's enjoying herself, she's not nagging me.*

"Thanks for sticking up for me with Mom and Max today," he said.

She put down her spoon. "I only told the truth."

"You had to see the truth first," he said. "My family has never gotten beyond the playing around I used to do."

"*Used* to?"

He laughed. "Used to do a lot more. The foundation is big business these days, I have to take it seriously. But I doubt Max will ever see that."

"His jealousy won't let him," Bethany agreed.

Tyler choked on his water. "Max isn't jealous of me."

"Of course he is." She took a ladylike sip of her wine.

"Why?"

She sighed as if he was too dense for words. "Because you're Susan's favorite."

He recoiled. "Garbage."

Bethany put down her wineglass, leaned in. "Tyler, your mom hangs on your every word and dismisses most of what Max says, unless it's about the business."

"Mom thinks of me as someone to help out at afternoon tea," he said.

"That's because you're her precious boy." Bethany grinned at his revulsion. "She adores you. I'm not saying she doesn't love Max, but you're the one she dotes on."

It was true, Tyler realized. His mom was much more indulgent toward him than she was to Max. "And you think Max sees that?"

The bitter edge to her laugh reminded Tyler what her brother had said about his and Bethany's parents loving Melanie the most. "Believe me, he sees it. And believe me when I tell you that if you said this to your mom, she wouldn't accept it and she'd be hurt."

"I won't say anything." Tyler sat back for the waiter to deliver his entrée.

They ate in silence for a few minutes. Then Bethany said, "Tyler, about the foundation's support for kidney kids." She put down her cutlery, fixed him with a searching look. "Was that just heat-of-the-moment stuff to impress the journalists? Or did you mean it?"

He'd been expecting the question, and he had his answer ready. "I didn't intend to say it, but now that I have, I'll stick with my word."

She shook her head, her smile tremulous. "I can't believe it."

He reached across the table, laid his hand on hers. The warm heat of her skin felt like home—he couldn't have drawn back if he'd tried. "Bethany, it's not as simple as you think. I want you to pitch to the PhilStrat Committee again, for however much money you need. The next meeting is in two weeks, does that give you enough time?"

Her eyes shone. "It's fine. Better than fine, it's wonderful."

Now came the difficult part. "I need to tell you I've had an application from another research team in the same field—from the Hospital for Sick Children in Toronto."

Bethany opened her mouth, then closed it again. She chewed her lip. "I'd have thought the Warrington Foundation was off their radar, I wonder how they—" She shook her head. "Of course, Sick Kids has a great kidney team," she said abstractedly. "But, Tyler, I am going to do such a great job of my pitch, you won't recognize it."

The excitement in her face softened him inside in a way he didn't recognize. But he couldn't afford to go easy on her. "You'll need to." He lifted his hand from hers. "You know, Bethany, this isn't all my decision. The committee decides who gets the funds."

"Of course," she said quickly. "But I know I can do a great job, and as an incumbent project, I must have some advantage."

That was true. It was easier for someone who already had funding to get more than to break in from scratch. The other truth was, although the decisions were made by committee, Tyler had the casting vote. He couldn't even claim a conflict of interest; the foundation's charter stipulated that applications from Warrington Group employees and related parties were to be encouraged. One big, happy family…he groaned inwardly.

As they ate their entrées, chatting about everything and nothing, Tyler realized he hadn't had so much fun in a long time. It wasn't his usual kind of fun. In fact, it was so suspiciously close to *good clean fun* that it had him wanting to hightail it out of here and seduce a pastor's daughter.

The thought slammed home that the only woman he wanted to seduce was Bethany.

OLIVIA HAD SPENT almost every evening with Silas since that first time he'd kissed her. Ostensibly, it was to help with his presentation, but every day their kisses grew more heated. They started the second she walked in the door, occurred at regular intervals through the evening, and severely delayed her departure at the end.

They ate together most nights and, on weekends, they had whole days to revel in each other's company. With Silas's lack of interest in small talk, those were quiet days—but Olivia found she didn't miss talking about food, books, mutual acquaintances. On the occasions Silas had something to say, it was serious. At first she had to stretch her mind to accommodate the conversation and found herself praying it would be over before she made a fool of herself. But Silas's patience meant she never felt under pressure, and somehow they always connected. Olivia had never talked so little yet felt as if she'd said so much.

When she was with Silas, nothing existed except the two of them. And the frogs.

They didn't go any further than those kisses and increasingly intimate touches. Physically, Olivia was frustrated. Emotionally, she was almost willing to wait. Silas had lost his wife, he had some irrational sense of guilt over whether she'd been happy or not. He wouldn't rush past those obstacles, but ultimately he'd get there. And then…

For the first time, Olivia had none of those doubts about whether a man could love her enough. Once Silas made up his mind to move on from his old life, he would be hers, for always. And then, she would love him back.

In the meantime, she made maximum space for him in her life. She'd bowed out of her book club meeting, a friend's daughter's bridal shower and a bachelorette party for an acquaintance embarking on her third marriage. But when she tried to cancel dinner with Susan Warrington, things got sticky.

"Who is it?" Susan demanded. "I know you're seeing someone."

"What did Tyler say?"

"You told *Tyler* and you didn't tell me?"

Drat, she'd given herself away. "I'm...interested in a man who's pitching to the foundation."

"A doctor?" Susan asked excitedly. "What charity is he with?"

"He's a professor, actually. Physics. His name is Silas."

"I want you both here for dinner on Friday," Susan ordered.

Olivia tried not to reveal her alarm in her voice. "We're not really dating."

"I'll invite Tyler and Bethany. You can tell Silas it's a chance to get to know Tyler before he pitches." Susan's tone held the implacability that compelled even her two strong sons to accede to her demands; Olivia didn't stand a chance. "If you won't invite him, I'll have Tyler do it."

Olivia could just imagine Tyler's response to that. "I'll invite him," she said. "But, Susan..."

"Yes, sweetie?" Susan was nice as pie now that she had her own way.

"Silas isn't the kind of man I usually date. He's not very sociable."

Silence. "I'm sure we can draw him out," Susan had finally said.

OLIVIA WARNED Silas the evening at Susan's might not be to his liking.

"Take a risk," he told her, smiling.

"I'm not afraid," she lied. "I just thought you might not enjoy it."

"I'll risk it," he said with gentle irony.

Olivia picked him up from his house because she couldn't guarantee that he'd bring the Maserati rather than the truck. By the time they got to Susan's, the others were already there.

Silas and Tyler had never met before. They appraised each other in the way strong men do—the handshakes were overly firm, the greetings were respectful but not too friendly. Both appeared to be reserving judgment.

Olivia tried to see Silas through Tyler's and Susan's eyes... and quailed. He'd made an effort, but it wouldn't be obvious to anyone else. His chinos were wrinkled, his white shirt was missing a button. He fell far short of the sartorial standard set by Tyler, impeccable in dark pants and ironed shirt.

Susan looked mystified from the moment Silas walked into her living room. Olivia could understand her initial reaction, but half an hour later Susan was still nibbling on her bottom lip every time Silas spoke. Admittedly, he was getting somewhat carried away in his discourse about conservation.... But couldn't Susan see he had more emotion, more depth in his little finger than all the other men they knew put together?

Bethany made a valiant effort to talk to Silas, asking him intelligent questions about frogs. Which, perversely, annoyed Olivia, who'd never pretended a genuine interest in the red-spotted tree frog. Silas hadn't seemed to mind, but Olivia didn't need Bethany being *so* curious about the thing.

They shouldn't have come; she wasn't ready to expose her relationship to scrutiny.

They sat at the oak dining table to eat. Susan, at the head of the table, directed Olivia and Bethany to sit on either side of her. Silas and Tyler were opposite each other farther down.

The two men were engrossed in a discussion of how the foundation worked, when Susan leaned close to Olivia. "Silas is unusual, isn't he?"

Olivia nodded, though she knew Susan used the word as a euphemism. She meant *odd*.

"He's wearing sneakers," Susan said. "I'm not even sure they match."

Olivia was certain they didn't. "There are worse things than wearing sneakers to dinner."

Susan put down her silverware and hissed, "You're making a mistake, Olivia."

"Just because Silas doesn't dress well," Olivia began defensively.

"It's not just the clothes. Nothing about this makes sense."

"I like him." Though that didn't make much sense, either.

"He's the wrong man for you," Susan said. "And you know I'm always right about you and men."

It was true. Olivia normally welcomed Susan's opinions of the men she dated—her friend had excellent instincts.

"Maybe you're wrong this time."

Susan had always been the bossy one in their friendship, and she didn't like being contradicted. "Listen to me, Olivia, or you'll end up making a fool of yourself."

Too late, both women realized the men had stopped talking, and everyone had heard Susan.

Silas put his hand over Olivia's on the tabletop.

Susan blushed slightly. "I'm sorry, it was rude of me to let you hear that."

"Whereas saying it behind my back wouldn't have been?" Silas asked mildly.

Susan's color deepened. "I'm not saying you're not a nice man, Silas. I just don't think you're right for Olivia. And—" she drew a sharp breath "—I can't help wondering if you're using her to get to Tyler."

Strangely, the thought had never once occurred to Olivia. But now Susan said it, doubt pierced her on all sides. It was entirely possible that Silas was exploiting her attraction to him. She swallowed, looked at him, waited for him to say in that deep voice that he found her a "very interesting woman."

If she could just hear that sturdy, Silas-style endorsement, she would be fine.

He was staring at her. She read his mind as clearly as if he'd spoken aloud. *Take a risk.* He wanted her to trust him— he deserved to have her trust him. But he'd never said he loved her....

"Olivia," Tyler said from across the table, and she tore her gaze from Silas, "remember those instincts we were talking about?"

It was all very well for Tyler to tell her to trust herself— he wasn't the one who stood to lose…everything.

Olivia shut her eyes, aware she was at a crossroads. She knew Susan's intentions were pure. Others would say far worse. If she thought they had no future, now was the time to end it.

Silas still cupped her hand. Olivia turned hers over, so their palms met. "Silas," she said, "will you come to the Biedermeyers' ball with me next week?"

Susan looked shocked. Stu and Margie Biedermeyer were staunchly correct. Tyler gave Olivia a thumbs-up.

"Yes," Silas said.

Usually Olivia loved that he either said yes or no, no conditions, no questions, no procrastination. But her invitation was a significant milestone, and she'd have liked him to acknowledge that. But this was Silas, the man she'd decided to take on trust.

SILAS DIDN'T SAY anything about her decision on the drive home. But he did tell her he had met the Biedermeyers. In fact, as they talked about Atlanta society, the kind of thing they never talked about, she learned that Silas knew many of her friends. She'd been aware his family had had plenty of money—which was how he lived in this beautiful home on an academic salary—but she hadn't realized how far their circles overlapped with hers.

Olivia felt as if she was being rewarded for her brave decision. All she had to do now was make sure Silas was presentable on the big night.

"Silas...sweetheart," she said, as she drove through his automatic gates, "would you mind if I choose something for you to wear to the ball?"

"Sure. Do you want to take a look at what I've got?" He gestured toward the house.

She'd only been in his bedroom once, when he'd given her a tour of the place. She'd admired the cherrywood four-poster, the beautiful silk taffeta drapes. She had a feeling she wouldn't admire the contents of his closet.

"If you don't mind," she said, "I might find something... somewhere else."

The look he gave her was long, harder than she expected, and Olivia felt her face grow warm. But his kiss good-night was as thrilling, as powerful, as demanding, as always.

Two days later, Tyler and the rest of the Warrington Foundation's Philanthropic Strategy committee heard this month's six shortlisted applications for funding.

Silas turned up in an impeccably cut navy suit, pale blue lawn shirt and a red striped tie. Tyler had to admit that his case for the preservation of the red-spotted tree frog hit all the right buttons and was as professionally prepared as any pitch could be.

Next up came the team from Toronto's Hospital for Sick Children. It would have been hard to find a bunch of more dedicated and able medics. Their presentation was fluent, comprehensive, compelling.

"Those guys are good," Jake, who'd sat in as Warrington Construction's observer on the committee, said afterward. He slid a glance at Tyler. "How's the cute kidney doctor going to stack up?"

"She'll be fine," Tyler said shortly, and prayed it was true.

Bethany had refused to let him hear her presentation ahead of time, even though he'd offered to coach her. He'd had to be content with asking Olivia to schedule Bethany's pitch for two o'clock, right after lunch. The team would be fresh, and if she arrived early, she could chat to the committee less formally before she began her presentation. He figured it might relax her. Bethany had been wary of being too relaxed, so he wasn't sure if she would get there ahead of time or not.

By ten to two, he'd given up on her early arrival.

At five to two, she stepped into the foundation's boardroom. She bore no resemblance to the woman in the ill-fitting suit who'd pitched a year ago.

She wore a dress Tyler had never seen—copper-colored wool crepe, high waisted to emphasize her bust, then slim fitting to her knees. Her heels were higher than normal, making her calves look even more slender. Bronze lipstick made her mouth shimmer beneath that pert nose, and those blue eyes were mesmerizing beneath lashes that had been lengthened by mascara.

She looked calm and confident, except for her white-knuckled grip on the folder tucked under her arm.

Tyler had planned to treat her like any other candidate. But he couldn't keep away from her.

He reached her almost before she made it over the threshold. He stood close so no one would overhear, and said, "You look incredible."

Her cheeks colored prettily. "I asked Sabrina to help me choose a new outfit when we had lunch yesterday."

New perfume, too, he guessed. She smelled of peaches and honeysuckle; instinctively he moved closer. "You should have told me you could look like this," he murmured.

"Because looks are so important?" Humor lit her eyes. "I was afraid you might not be able to control yourself."

His body tightened. "You're probably right."

Behind them, people were starting to sit down, and Tyler heard water glasses being topped up, the shuffle of papers. It was time to start.

Certain no one could see, he touched a hand to her cheek. "Good luck, Peaches."

She didn't need luck. Tyler silently cheered her as she smiled a greeting at the committee, introduced herself and her work, and launched into a polished presentation.

Tyler tossed in insightful and intelligent questions that allowed her to show off her knowledge. He could see her confidence grow by the minute as his colleagues took their lead from him and gave her their full attention. She didn't stumble once, and her presentation hit every one of the foundation's criteria.

It was hard to believe this was the same Bethany Hart he'd listened to a year ago.

When she left the meeting, Tyler could tell she was walking on air. He watched her go, the swing of her behind in her new dress. And knew he had to make one of the toughest decisions of his life.

BETHANY KEPT the promise she'd made her brother. She told Tyler she needed a day off on Saturday to visit her parents.

"What am I supposed to do with Ben for a whole day?" he demanded.

"The same as you do for two hours, only more."

He frowned at her as she folded Ben's clean laundry. "Ben and I will come with you."

"No, you won't." She started in on her own laundry. "Find your own family freak show. I need to talk to Mom and Dad about Ryan."

"I assume you'll be driving there in the car I bought you?"

He'd bought her a Honda Accord to take Ben around town. "Are you saying because you bought the car you get to go everywhere with me?" she said. "Because I need to make a trip to the store to buy diapers."

"I'm merely suggesting I might be able to help." Tyler eyed the panties she was folding with interest.

"You can't," she said with absolute certainty as she stuffed the panties beneath Ben's rompers. "Besides, you don't know how to help if it doesn't involve signing a check." Not that she actually believed that these days, but it wouldn't pay to let him see that.

"I'm coming with you," he said stubbornly.

It occurred to her he might be planning an extravagant gesture—announcing in front of her parents that the foundation would renew her funding. But that was the stuff of dreams. More likely, he didn't want to change diapers for a whole day.

Of course, there was a faint chance Mom and Dad might be more reasonable with a stranger present.

"Okay," she said, "you can come."

"PRETTY PLACE," Tyler said as they drove past the antebellum houses that made Madison one of the state's tourist attractions.

"Yep," Bethany said glumly.

"Wasn't it the only town around here that Sherman didn't burn down in the Civil War?"

"Yep." Her gloom seemed to deepen.

Where was the intrepid battler who never hesitated to come out fighting? "Your parents can't be that bad," he told her. "You just need to stand up to them."

Her lips flattened. "Thanks for that useful tip."

That's what a guy got for trying to help.

Bethany's parents lived in a quiet cul-de-sac. From the way Bethany dragged her feet up the cobbled path to the front door of the Arts and Crafts–style home, you'd think she was on her way to an execution. Her own.

She pushed open the door, called out a greeting. After a moment's stifling silence, her parents came into the hallway.

Mrs. Hart had the same coloring as Bethany and her brother, but unlike her daughter she enhanced it with well-chosen clothes. She was still pretty, with big, tragic eyes. Her husband was tall and spare, and one long arm curled protectively around his wife's shoulders.

Bethany kissed her parents. "Mom, Dad, meet Tyler Warrington. Tyler, these are my parents, Joanne and David Hart. And this is Ben." Her parents made a perfunctory fuss over the baby.

Tyler shook hands with her parents, while Bethany carried Ben, asleep in his car seat, to a bedroom.

They sat down to coffee in a living room dominated by photos of a girl who looked like Bethany but wasn't. She was pretty; Bethany was prettier. Melanie Hart had had serious eyes, a thin frame and a mouth that looked as if it might quiver. There was a lot of her mother in her.

The conversation focused on incidentals for all of fifteen minutes. Then Bethany put her mug down on the coffee table and said, "Mom, Dad, I'm here about Ryan."

"What's wrong?" Her mother started to flap and flutter. "Did something happen? Why didn't the school call me?"

"It's nothing," Bethany soothed her. Then she said firmly, "No, it's not nothing, it's important. Ryan's being bullied."

David tsked. "Not this again." He took his wife's hand in his. "Your mother and I have spoken to Ryan. We concluded he doesn't like being away from home, and that's led him to exaggerate a couple of minor incidents in his own mind."

"He's upset," Bethany countered. "I think you should talk to the principal."

"It's not true," her father insisted.

"Maybe he needs to come home and go to a local school. He's not as independent as I was," Bethany said. "I think he's lonely."

Joanne's hands tightened on the arm of her chair. "You know I'm not strong enough to have him here, Bethany." Her reproachful look suggested Bethany was unspeakably cruel to even suggest it.

"Your mother hasn't been well lately," David said.

From what Tyler remembered Ryan saying, Joanne hadn't been well for some time. He wondered exactly what the matter was.

"How about we talk about something else," David said to Tyler. "I saw in the paper the other day that the Warrington Foundation is committed to supporting kidney patients— that's great news."

Tyler made a noncommittal reply. He couldn't see anywhere this conversation could head that wouldn't be a problem for Bethany.

"Does that mean you'll renew Bethany's funding?"

Bingo.

"Dad, I pitched to the foundation yesterday, but I won't know the outcome for a while." Bethany slid an apologetic glance at Tyler. "And it's not just Tyler's decision."

Both her parents looked suspicious, and rightly so, Tyler thought.

"Dear," her mom said, "did you make sure these people know exactly what you can achieve with that money?"

There followed an interrogation and an impromptu—and totally useless—coaching session, that had Bethany tying herself in knots.

When Tyler couldn't stand it any longer, he said, "Ryan seems a nice kid." Why not exchange one touchy subject for another?

There was a brief pause while the combatants adjusted.

"You've obviously done a great job bringing him up," Tyler said to fill the silence. "But I think Bethany's right. He's lonely."

One good thing about speaking so plainly, he wore out his welcome fast. Bethany's parents were stiff and suspicious, no matter how deeply he drew on his reserves of charm. When Tyler told Bethany it was time they headed home, her folks didn't argue.

Back in the BMW, Bethany sat hugging herself, despite the car's excellent heating system.

"Thanks for your support back there," she said as they hit the freeway.

"I did more harm than good," he said ruefully.

"It was nice to have someone on my side." She sounded almost shy.

"Did your mom ever take you shopping for clothes?" he asked.

She blinked at the change of direction. "Not after Mel died."

"You need to dress a lot better than you do."

She bristled. "My clothes are none of your business."

"You looked fantastic at yesterday's pitch. I realized the crap you normally wear is a sign of a lack of self-respect."

"That's idiotic." Her eyes flashed. "My work is very important."

"I know you respect your work," he said. "But you're more than your research, Bethany. Having met your parents, I can see why maybe you don't know that, but trust me, it's true. You're smart, kind, determined—you're as persistent as a damn leech." She started, and he said, "That's a compliment, by the way. If you don't know where to find that self-respect inside yourself, then start building it on the outside. Dress properly, show everyone how beautiful you are, and then you might start to realize you're just as incredible on the inside."

No one had ever said anything so blunt, so personal, so insightful to her before.

Bethany dropped her chin to her chest before Tyler could see the shock in her face. Her hair swung forward, concealing the unexpected, illogical tears that scored hot, salty trails down her cheeks.

"Bethany?" A hand touched her hair, and she shied away. "Peaches, I'm sorry, I didn't mean to upset you."

Sorry she was so pathetic? Sorry to have held up a reality check that threatened to unbalance her? Or sorry because he'd already figured out what Bethany had only just realized: that sometime in the last few weeks she'd added Tyler to the list of people she loved and who didn't love her back.

CHAPTER THIRTEEN

BY THE TIME they got back to Atlanta, Ben was grumpy, Bethany subdued and Tyler edgy in a way he didn't recognize, but it felt vaguely like a storm was brewing.

"What exactly is the problem with your mom's health?" he asked Bethany as he dished up the Chinese takeout they'd bought on the way home. Thankfully, she'd recovered from that little upset in the car before he'd even figured out what he'd said to cause it.

Kneeling on the rug, she buttoned Ben's rocket-and-teddy pajamas. "In my professional opinion, she's suffered severe depression since Melanie died. In fact, since Melanie first got ill."

"Have you told her that?"

"I have, but she's of a generation that sees depression as weakness."

"So instead she wallows in it, and drives her other children away because she can't cope."

Bethany tsked. "If you knew how long, how hard, Mom and Dad fought for Melanie's survival you might be more sympathetic. Mom had Melanie when she was thirty-two. She and Dad had been trying for a baby for ten years. Mel was their miracle."

"So your mom was…how old when she had Ryan?"

"Forty-five. Another miracle, though I'm not sure they saw

it that way. By the time Melanie died, I think Mom and Dad had exhausted their stock of parental emotions."

"And you were the miracle in the middle." The words slipped out. Tyler wasn't even sure what he meant by them, but he knew they sounded...serious. He hurried on. "Your folks are pretty tough on you about your work."

She smiled distractedly, and he guessed she was trying to unravel that crap he'd blurted about miracles. "I made the mistake of saying right after Melanie died that when I grew up I'd become a doctor and make sure other kids didn't die, too. It gave them something to hold on to, and they started saving for me to go to medical school."

"A mistake?" He latched on to the word. "You think you made a mistake in your choice of career?"

"I—" She looked confused. "Of course not. I love my work. The mistake was letting Mom and Dad get so hung up on it." She shrugged. "I can understand they don't want other parents to go through what they did with Melanie. They have high expectations of me."

He handed her a pair of chopsticks and sat down on a stool at the island. "Whereas my family would be amazed if I achieved anything."

Bethany smiled, happy to move the conversation away from herself. Tyler's comment had been made without rancor, and she knew he was mindful of what she'd told him at the restaurant the other day about his mother and Max.

She lunged at a mouthful of chop suey that was about to slide off her chopsticks, slurped it into her mouth.

"Nothing like a well-mannered woman to turn a guy on," he said.

She slurped louder with the next bite, just to make it clear she wasn't trying to turn him on. And she wasn't. After that moment of illumination earlier, she'd pushed the realization that she loved Tyler out of her mind. There was a danger she might inadvertently give her feelings away before she decided what to do about loving him.

Were her feelings something to bury, to forget about? Or something to pin her hopes on?

She couldn't explain why she loved him—apart from the fact that he was great with Ben even when he didn't want to be…that no one could make her angrier or make her laugh more…that in little more than a month he knew her better than anyone else did… Okay, maybe there were a few reasons to love him. But he didn't love her, she knew that, and she couldn't think of a single reason why he would.

AFTER DINNER Bethany sat on the couch with her knitting. She seemed to have lost half a row, because this section was definitely wonky. Or maybe it was a tension problem. The tension in the wool, not in her. Tyler sprawled next to her with a book, which meant she had to divide her concentration between her stitches and trying not to notice the solid length of him, the hard line of his jaw, the dark wave of his hair.

Clearly, she wasn't succeeding.

"What are you knitting?"

"A sweater." A fleeting glance satisfied her craving for the sight of him. For now.

"Are you sure you have the size right? It looks too small."

"This is a sleeve." Already, she wanted to look at him again. She focused on her work.

"You look good in those jeans."

"Thanks." Sabrina had helped Bethany with a couple of other purchases, made at an outlet center. The jeans sat low on her hips and hugged her derriere.

Tyler tweaked her knitting, which made her look at him. "Are you going to wear this sweater with those jeans?" he asked.

"Not after what you said today," she admitted reluctantly.

He smirked. "Good. Because that thing you're knitting now is the worst yet."

He was right. She jammed the knitting down between the sofa cushions, out of his sight and hers. "I don't know why so many women like you."

"Don't you?" he said softly.

The air between them thrummed with awareness—Bethany couldn't think how she'd ever had the gall to deny it existed.

"You're too quiet tonight," he said. "I'm used to you jabbering at me until I can't take it anymore." An odd tenderness belied the blunt words.

"I'm surprised you're here then, rather than out on a date," she said, breathless.

"Me too. But since I am…" Tyler leaned toward her. Then: "Ouch." He'd put a hand down on the exposed tip of a knitting needle. He tugged the whole mess out and tossed it to the floor.

"Hey," Bethany protested as she saw a bunch of stitches unravel.

He grasped the hem of her body-hugging cerise skinny rib. "I'll buy you a new sweater, better than anything you could knit in a dozen lifetimes, if I get to take this one off."

"What?" Instinctively, she put her hands over his to prevent any upward movement.

His eyes gleamed with laughter, but also with unmistakable heat. He might not love her, but he wanted her. Bethany's heart beat faster under her sweater.

She dropped her hands and said slowly, "Okay."

Her agreement obviously surprised him, and for a moment he didn't move. Bethany swallowed, threw him the most challenging look she could muster, then raised her arms above her head.

Her boldness elicited a hum of appreciation from Tyler. His eyes held hers, intense, glittering, as he lifted her sweater. It wasn't until he pulled it over her face that the eye contact was broken.

"Damn."

Inside her cerise cocoon, Bethany heard the curse. She giggled. Tyler tugged the sweater over her head in one sharp movement. "Very funny," he said.

"I don't know what you mean." Innocently, she folded her arms beneath her breasts—over her turquoise stretch cotton tank.

"I could have sworn you didn't have anything on under this thing." He waved the cerise sweater in her face. "I would have bet money on it."

"You did bet money," she pointed out. "You owe me a new sweater."

Tyler lost interest in the bet, his gaze arrested by the way that figure-hugging tank molded to Bethany's generous curves.

All the way to Madison and back, the whole time he'd been in her parents' house, he'd wanted her. It made no sense, he couldn't remember ever feeling so *hot* for such an extended period.

"Now, if you've had your fun..." She took the sweater from him, and he realized she was about to put it back on.

Not going to happen. In one seamless movement reminiscent of his glory days in college football, he tossed the sweater to the floor, hauled Bethany into his arms and kissed her.

First, a quick kiss that did an effective job of silencing her automatic protest. When that reminded him of the ambrosia he'd found on her lips before, he went back for more.

Their last kiss had been incendiary. This one was hotter, needier, a conflagration.

Bethany's passion kindled under Tyler's instant heat, and she responded with something embarrassingly close to desperation. Her hands found his shoulders, clutched, then moved up and around, burrowing into his dark hair.

The pressure of her fingers against Tyler's scalp drew a groan from him, and he plunged into her mouth, his tongue seeking her warmth.

Bethany explored his mouth with the same searching thoroughness, with a hunger so great she couldn't imagine it ever being satisfied.

When he broke away, a cry of protest sprang to her lips. But he trailed a path with his mouth, with his tongue, until he found her earlobe.

He nibbled, sending darts of pleasure through her so she quaked with longing.

Tyler moved down to her neck, nuzzled the frantic pulse. Against her skin, he murmured, "I've been wanting to do this for a long, long time."

"How—how long?" That couldn't be her voice, all throaty and raw.

He lifted his head, and his eyes blazed into hers. "If I said since the day you first pitched to the foundation, would that sound tacky and unprofessional?"

"Totally," she breathed, more turned on than she'd have thought possible.

Turned on not just by the mouth that kissed her and by the hands that lifted her derriere to pull her closer against him, but by his sense of humor, by the laughter they'd shared in getting to this point.

This is love, she thought, and the knowledge that he didn't love her back—yet—didn't hurt the way it had earlier.

Because she'd felt and seen the tenderness that warred with the outright desire in his kiss, in his eyes. She knew this was about more than sex for him. Just as she knew he loved Ben, even though he hadn't figured it out yet.

"Tyler." She tugged his head back down to her, kissed him again. Restless, she pressed herself into him.

Tyler wanted to make love with Bethany more than he could remember wanting anything else. Ever. That she wanted the same thing made this moment perfect.

His hands slipped beneath the stretchy fabric of her tank, found the warm skin of her waist. She shivered at the contact, her whole body brushing against him until he thought he might explode.

Easy, he warned himself. If this perfect moment was to be as incredible for Bethany, he couldn't rush it.

And he did want it to be incredible for her. She was the most giving person he knew, she deserved his best.

He took her mouth again, and was stunned to find that his sensual pleasure was increased by the strength of his desire to give to her.

He wanted to put his mouth to the softness of her waist, her stomach, to make her shiver again.

He slid down her, grazing her curves with his hands, pushed her tank up.

"You're so beautiful." He pressed a kiss to her navel, and her hips jerked in instinctive demand. He unsnapped those sexy jeans, tugged them down a little, then pulled away so he could see more of her. Oh, yes, he could take his time right here.

His tongue traced the bottom of her rib cage, then moved lower to the soft roundness of her stomach. Bethany writhed, then giggled, as he found a ticklish spot. He kissed her there until she yelped, a sexy, frustrated sound. Tyler moved on, discovered two tiny scars, one just to the right of her navel, the other way over to the left. He kissed one, then the other.

"What happened here?" The tip of his tongue probed one of the scars. "A knitting accident?"

She half gasped, half laughed, soft and breathy. "Keyhole surgery."

"Poor baby." He used the excuse to kiss both scars again. "Anything major?"

She stilled. "I, uh, had a nephrectomy."

He chuckled. Even in the throes of lovemaking, she was an egghead doctor. "Are you going to tell me what that is, or do we have to play Twenty Questions?"

"It's…a kidney removal."

"What?" The haze of desire had Tyler befuddled, but it was dissipating fast. He lifted his head to stare at her. "You had kidney disease, as well as your sister?"

"I donated a kidney to Melanie." Bethany's fingers kneaded his shoulders, and she squirmed against him. "Tyler, can we get back to where we were?"

"How old were you?" he demanded.

She sighed. "Thirteen, does it matter?"

Does it matter? *You bet it does.* Tyler sat up, raked a hand through his hair. "That's got to be illegal, for a child to give away a kidney."

With an exasperated huff, she scrambled into a sitting position. "Okay, we can have this conversation, but then I want to get back to what we were doing." She'd left her jeans unsnapped, and Tyler fought to keep his eyes on her face.

"In the USA you have to be eighteen to donate an organ, but in England they'll use a younger donor in exceptional circumstances," she said. "Melanie's rare blood type meant she was highly unlikely to find a match from the general donor pool, and she had no chance of survival without a transplant. I was a perfect match. Our doctor here in the States put us in touch with a private surgeon in London—he considered our situation exceptional enough to allow me to donate."

Fury rose within Tyler. "Your parents made you do it."

"Of course they didn't," she said, shocked. "I wanted to. We all wanted Mel to get better."

"What happened?" he asked.

"The surgery was initially successful. But T cell–mediated responses were generated to the transplanted organ and Melanie suffered acute rejection a week later." Bethany spoke as if reading from a medical report. Then her calm fractured, leaving still-raw pain exposed. "It shouldn't have happened, but it did. And she died."

"So it was all for nothing," Tyler said flatly.

Bethany nodded. She couldn't begin to express the despair she'd felt when Melanie's body had rejected the transplant.

"You think it was your fault," he said.

She stuck her nose in the air. "I know perfectly well it was not my fault."

"You know it wasn't, but you think it was," he said.

Bethany scowled at him, but Tyler barely noticed. He was shaken to the core.

Two minutes ago he'd been congratulating himself on his generosity in wanting to show her a good time in bed. Bethany had trumped that feeble gesture by revealing she'd given away a kidney, a part of herself, when she was just a kid. At an age when Tyler had been so self-absorbed he'd barely known anyone else existed.

Bethany would say he was still that way.

For the first time, it occurred to him she was right. Because he couldn't imagine making the decision she'd made, then or now. And even if he admitted to himself that he could be—should be—a more giving person, he knew he didn't want to give that much.

Her selflessness terrified him.

He eased away from her. Saw understanding, then hurt, flash in her eyes.

"We're not going to pick up where we left off?" Her flippancy sounded forced.

Tyler shook his head. Without looking down, he refastened her jeans. His fingers brushed her abdomen—*near those scars*—and she quivered.

"I don't get to be your first one-kidney lover?" She might have made that a quip, but he read the pleading in her eyes, and it scared him even more.

"You and I are very different people, Bethany." He didn't need to tell her that—she'd never believed he was one of the good guys. "This—" he waved a hand to encompass her tousled hair, her swollen lips, the skewed straps of her tank "—would mean nothing to me."

And everything to her. He could see that now, could only be thankful he'd seen it in time.

CHAPTER FOURTEEN

OLIVIA HAD TAKEN a taxi to Silas's house, and from there they would go to the ball.

"You look gorgeous," he told her. She smiled. It was by his standards a flowery compliment, one he would have been incapable of a few weeks ago.

She leaned forward slightly in her red silk dress so that it showed off her breasts. Which had Silas pulling her into his arms for one of those exquisitely thorough kisses, while his hands checked out exactly how well that dress fit her.

But they were due at the Biedermeyers' at eight, so Olivia broke off the kiss. She picked up the suit carrier that had fallen to the floor when he'd taken her in his arms. "I brought your clothes."

She'd spent a lot of money on him, but he didn't need to know that, and going by how little he knew about fashion, he'd never guess. "Let me show you." She started to unzip the bag.

His hand closed over hers on the zipper. "Why don't I just go put these on."

That took some of the fun out of it, but she didn't argue.

She wandered into the living room. And found it transformed. The frog paraphernalia was gone, leaving the deep cream walls bare, except for five striking modern-art canvases that Silas must have stowed while he worked on the frog project. The coffee table and the sideboard bore nothing but the gleam of polish, and the scent of wax hung in the air.

What did this mean? Confusion churned into hope. Olivia told herself to stay calm, but her fingers shook as she repaired her lipstick in the gilt-edged mirror above the mantelpiece.

Silas rejoined her just fifteen minutes later.

"You look wonderful," Olivia exclaimed, knowing her excitement wasn't attributable solely to the perfect fit of the tuxedo, the delicious contrast the white shirt provided against his healthy skin tone. His bow tie sat exactly as it should, tied from scratch by Silas. She'd expected to have to help him.

He wore the cuff links she'd tucked into the pocket of the tuxedo jacket. Gold with a very discreet diamond stud. Freshly shaved, he was every inch the debonair kind of man any woman would be proud to be seen with.

She put her hands on his arms, went up on tiptoe to kiss him. His kiss felt reserved.

"Is something wrong?" She hadn't left the price tag on the tuxedo, had she?

"I don't want to ruin your lipstick."

My, he was turning into quite the gentleman. Olivia couldn't contain her curiosity another moment. "Silas, what happened to everything?" She waved at the bare walls.

He looked around the room as if, like her, he was seeing it for the first time. "I packed it all up after the pitch to the foundation."

"Why?"

"It's time," he said slowly, "to move forward."

It was what she'd been waiting for, but Olivia hadn't expected the flood of joy that left her feeling as if she was floating.

Silas grabbed her hand, as if to anchor her. "Let's go."

IT TURNED OUT Silas knew around half the people at the Spring Fling, which was held at the Biedermeyers' country estate just out of town.

Olivia loved having him on her arm, loved the widening of her friends' eyes as they took in her handsome escort. Silas was the best-looking man there—and the best dressed.

He got quieter as she chatted gaily to as many people as she could. She suspected he was overwhelmed—hardly surprising, given there must have been five hundred people at the ball. Early on, they met up with Charlie Gooding, who was apparently an old friend of Silas's.

The two men shook hands, clapped each other on the back. Charlie kissed Olivia's cheek. "I couldn't believe it when Silas told me you and he are an item," he said. "Never thought you'd go for a dull dog like him."

Silas had told people about her? She darted a glance at him. He was looking at her with mingled amusement and…surely not disappointment?

She took his hand in hers, and stepped forward to kiss him, right there in front of Charlie. There, that should prove… whatever it was that needed proving.

Silas smiled so tenderly it made her want to cry. Then he leaned down and his lips skimmed her ear.

"I love you, Olivia," he murmured.

He straightened again. "Before you answer that," he said, so calmly that if she hadn't seen that blaze of emotion in his eyes, she'd have thought she'd imagined those words, "we need to talk."

"You two look far too cozy compared with all us married folks," Charlie complained. "I insist you dance with me, Olivia."

Before she had a chance to tell Silas she loved him back, Charlie tugged her onto the dance floor. She threw Silas a

beseeching look over her shoulder, but he just smiled his
usual imperturbable smile.

She didn't see him again for half an hour, by which time
he was talking to Mary-Jane Dayton. Olivia loved that Silas
was the kind of man who'd never give her any reason to be
jealous when he spoke to another woman. Then she realized
he looked upset.

She hurried over to him. "Hello, sweetheart." Concerned
by his pallor, she laced her fingers through his. He squeezed
her hand, but the gaze he turned on her was troubled.

"I just heard that you and Silas are together," Mary-Jane said.

Olivia nodded.

"Silas's wife was my best friend."

Olivia hadn't thought about the fact that if Silas knew
some of her friends, his late wife, Anna, would have known
them too. "I'm sorry, you must miss her."

"Apparently more than he does." Mary-Jane brushed a tear
from her eye with an angry swipe.

Olivia drew in a sharp breath. Silas pulled her hand against
his chest. "Excuse us, Mary-Jane, but Olivia and I have things
to talk about."

That was what he'd said earlier. Olivia had envisaged
declarations of love, plans for the future. Now, a chill blew
down her spine.

They left immediately, drove to Olivia's house. Silas didn't
talk, but he kept one hand on her thigh the entire journey. As
if he was trying to make her stay.

"Silas," she said as she snapped on the lights in her living
room, "you're worrying me."

He didn't take her in his arms, as she wished he would. His
hands hung at his sides, his fingers loose and open.

"Olivia," he said slowly, "I lied to you. I didn't tell you the truth."

"About Anna," she guessed.

He nodded. "This will hurt you, and I'm sorry." He closed his eyes, as if he couldn't bear to witness her reaction. "Olivia, I cheated on her."

A knife of pain stabbed her, deep, deep. "No."

"Just once—just one night. But Anna found out."

"No," she said again. She groped behind her for the sofa, and collapsed onto it.

Silas stayed where he was. "She was devastated, nothing I said could convince her how sorry I was. After one of our arguments, she left to visit the frog sanctuary, said she had to get away."

Olivia moaned. "That's when she fell."

"It was my fault," he said.

If he thought she would disagree, he was wrong. An ache seized Olivia's chest, spread through her until she wanted to double over.

"The kids blamed me for her death, that's why they don't speak to me."

Olivia blamed him, too. "You should have told me." She would *never* have let herself feel anything for a cheater.

Two steps brought him to the sofa. He hunkered down, took her hands. "I'm asking you to forgive me, to love me back, the way I love you. *No matter what.*"

This isn't fair. "You know," she said shakily, "you know I can't."

He nodded, as if he had indeed known, and she felt a stab of irrational resentment that he thought so little of her.

"You need to leave now," she said.

BETHANY AVOIDED TYLER for two days. At the start of their time together he'd managed to slip in and out of the house without encountering her; now she became a master of the same art.

It wasn't that difficult. Given that he didn't want to see her any more than she wanted to see him.

His rejection the other night had hurt so much, she'd been convinced she would wake up the next morning to find her love for him had disappeared.

Instead, she'd woken numb. And when the numbness wore off, the love was still there. So strong that Bethany found herself trying to understand his reaction, which she was certain wasn't physical revulsion at the thought of her having only one kidney.

He was scared, she'd concluded. It had taken her a couple of days to realize that, but now, as she sat stirring her coffee in Tyler's kitchen at ten o'clock on Tuesday morning, she was convinced she had it right.

Tyler was afraid that loving her might mean he had to make some grand sacrifice—not a physical sacrifice, like a kidney, but something in his life or his nature he didn't want to change. And he didn't know if he could do it.

Bethany added a third spoonful of sugar to her coffee— she hadn't felt like eating much, and was maintaining her energy with regular doses of syrupy caffeine. She tossed the spoon into the sink.

"Scaredy-cat," she said out loud.

Because no one knew what sacrifice they were capable of making until the need arose. She hadn't started out intending to give Melanie her kidney, but when they'd reached the stage where that was the only option, she hadn't thought twice.

Not true. She remembered several nights lying awake, wondering what would happen if she ever got really sick and needed that kidney back. But in the daytime, the fears receded, and when she made her decision—on her own, unpressured by Mom and Dad—it hadn't felt like a huge sacrifice.

She held her coffee mug up to her face, cupped in her hands, and let the steam warm her.

Tyler had never been tested, so it was no wonder he didn't trust himself to do the right thing.

WHEN TYLER'S BMW M6 roared up to the house an hour later, an illogical hope kicked Bethany's pulse into overdrive. He'd never come home during the day before.

But any thought that he might be here to put things right between them was dispelled by the grim set of his face when he strode into the kitchen, where Bethany, uncharacteristically inactive, still sat.

"Where's Ben?" he asked.

"Having his morning nap." Ben had at last settled into a routine of two major naps a day, which made Bethany's life easier.

Tyler stopped in front of her, hands fisted carelessly in the pockets of his suit pants. "Ben's mother has come forward."

Whatever she'd expected, it wasn't that. "How? Who is she?"

"She's been watching the coverage in the media. The investigator says she can't bear to be without him any longer."

Of course she couldn't, Bethany thought. Ben was so precious. The poor woman must have been in desperate straits to give him up in the first place.

"Social services will want to talk to her," she said. "*I* want to talk to her. We can't give Ben back unless we're sure she's able to care for him." Not that she or Tyler would have any say in the matter once the authorities took over.

For once, Tyler didn't question her emphasis on caring. "I already told the investigator to set up a meeting for us at her

home, so we can check out the environment Ben will be going
into. Then if it's appropriate we can help with social services."
He sounded like an expert on child custody.

"And if everything's all right," Bethany said, "Ben will go
back to her." And Bethany would go back to work. She reminded herself she needed to do that, tried to feel enthusiastic.

A tiny pause. "It's not our decision. But she is his mother."

He was right, but Bethany couldn't find it in herself to be
glad. She would miss that little boy so much...she'd fallen in
love with him every bit as much as she'd fallen in love with
Tyler. Her love for Ben was an entirely separate thing, and yet
it made her love for Tyler more meaningful.

Which it shouldn't, because Ben wasn't Tyler's child any
more than he was hers.

"How will you feel," she asked, "about giving him back?"

His eyebrows drew together. "This isn't about how I feel.
Ben should be with his mother."

She'd lifted a hand, intending to comfort him with a pat on
the shoulder. Now she let it fall back to her side. "Thanks for
coming to tell me in person," she said awkwardly.

He tipped his head back, scanned the rack of gleaming pans
suspended from the ceiling above the counter. "That's not the
only reason I'm here."

Now he would talk about the other night.

When he lowered his gaze to hers, his eyes were as unyield-
ing as flint, his *GQ* cheekbones thrown into sharp relief by
the severe slash of his mouth.

Bethany gulped.

"The PhilStrat Committee met first thing this morning to
finalize its recommendations." He spoke fast, without expression. "We agreed your pitch was excellent...but Toronto's
was better. We're giving them the money."

She felt a pit open up somewhere inside her, hope gushing out, draining away. "No."

Bethany clamped down with her teeth so hard on her lower lip, Tyler thought she might draw blood. She breathed in, out, in, out as she battled to contain her emotions.

Just as, in the end, she'd contained them the other night. He knew he'd hurt her, had been grateful for her restraint. Now he had hurt her again.

He told himself it was a good idea to reinforce the message that he was a selfish jerk.

"The committee—" her voice was scratchy, she cleared her throat "—how does the vote work?"

He knew what she was asking. If he'd voted for her but been outnumbered. He thought about lying. But why leave her with any illusions? He'd recognized when he first met her that Bethany had a rare courage, though he'd had no idea just how rare. He would honor that courage by having the guts to tell her the truth.

"It was unanimous."

She flinched, and he knew he couldn't leave it there. Maybe he could never be the man she needed, but he didn't want her to hate him. "The Toronto team does amazing work. Their presentation convinced me they're the best people to achieve your goal."

She swayed on her stool. "You know how hard I've worked for this, how much it means."

"That's assuming," he continued, as if she hadn't spoken, "your goal is to save those children. Not just to assuage your guilt over Melanie's death."

Her chin snapped up as if he'd hit her with an uppercut. "How dare you."

"Bethany, my decision was in the best interest of kids with

kidney disease." He watched as the inevitable inarticulateness overtook her, and she clammed up, red-faced, mouth tight, shoulders shaking with emotion.

"I imagine you don't want to be around me right now, so I'll stay at Mom's place tonight," he said. "Shall I take Ben?"

Bethany found her voice, but it was thick, waterlogged. "All his stuff is here, best leave him with me."

He nodded, scooped up his car keys from the counter. "I'll pick you up tomorrow afternoon for the visit to Ben's mother." When he reached the kitchen doorway, he stopped. Without turning around, he said, "Bethany...I'm going to miss the little guy."

"I don't believe you," she choked.

NEXT MORNING, Tyler got some news he'd been waiting for. One of the scheduled guests had canceled out of the *Marlene Black Show,* a live TV program based in Atlanta but syndicated all over the United States. The show, a mix of hard news and magazine-format stories, was one of the most respected in the country. This was the media breakthrough Tyler need to clinch the job in Washington, D.C.

The timing would be tight, but he could do the interview before they went to see Ben's mother.

STILL SO ANGRY she hadn't been able to talk to Tyler, Bethany stood by as talk show host Marlene Black introduced herself to him. Bethany sneered when he said he'd been a fan of Marlene's for a long time, but no one was looking at her. Predictably, when Tyler turned that smile of his on Marlene, her voice grew more animated, her eyes brighter.

"I'll introduce the segment, then we'll cut away to the footage of the mother leaving the baby at your office," she said. "Then, Tyler, I'll talk to you about the baby." She turned to Bethany. "Maybe I'll ask you about the baby's health and development."

She signaled to one of the crew to attach a microphone to Bethany.

"But I don't want—" Bethany said.

"Actually, Marlene, I'd rather we spent as much time as possible talking about how the foundation helps parents and children," Tyler said. "Do you think we could do that?" He gave her a smile so hot, Bethany half expected the woman to combust. Dammit, he was such a manipulator.

"Absolutely," Marlene breathed, and laid a hand on Tyler's arm. "I think the work you do is wonderful."

"If you think that's wonderful, you should see him naked," Bethany said snarkily. Because that's what the woman *meant,* Bethany would bet her entire research budget on it.

Tyler choked. Marlene whisked her hand off his arm faster than the speed of light.

"Not that I have," Bethany said chattily, "but his secretary assures me it's an impressive sight." Olivia hadn't used that exact word when she'd mentioned seeing Tyler naked as a baby, but Bethany was extrapolating.

"Uh…" Marlene darted a confused glance at Tyler.

"Let's just stick to business, shall we?" He glared at Bethany. "I'll hold Ben for the start of the interview, then I'll pass him to you before he starts crying or puking."

That's right, duck out of the hard yards, she fumed.

After his introduction Tyler handed Ben over to Bethany. He presented a compassionate yet authoritative persona to the camera as he talked about how rewarding his time with the baby had been.

The interviewer still looked wary every time she caught Bethany's eye. Then the woman said, "We're going to talk to pediatrician Bethany Hart about Ben's health and development."

What? If this was Marlene's idea of revenge for that comment Bethany had made earlier... But the camera was on her, so she made sure she was the consummate pediatric professional as she gave her expert opinion.

She'd thought she was doing pretty well, but then, from the corner of her eye, she saw Tyler glance at his watch. Just the way he had when she'd bored him with her pitch. No doubt he was counting the seconds until he could get all the attention back on himself and his precious foundation. Until he could forget Ben's existence.

"How did you come to get involved with young Ben?" Marlene asked her.

"I've been fortunate to have my research into childhood kidney disease funded by the generosity of Tyler Warrington and the Warrington Foundation," she said.

She caught Tyler's surprised, pleased look. Good, she had his full attention. "Or should I say, it used to be funded," she amended. "Unfortunately the foundation hasn't renewed its grant, so if I want to make real progress in the battle against childhood kidney disease, I need to look elsewhere." She sensed rather than saw Tyler's shock. *Take that, Mr. Hotshot Philanthropist.*

"If I get more money," Bethany said, "I know my work can make a difference." At first, she talked fast, not wanting to give Marlene any chance to break in. Then she realized the presenter had eased back in her chair and, beyond chipping in with the occasional "uh-huh," was going to let her say her piece. She slowed her pace, made sure she got across several important points about childhood kidney disease and the im-

portance of securing extra research funds. She talked for wha
felt like two whole minutes.

By the time the cameras went off them and the ad break
kicked in, Tyler was ready to explode. Thanks to Bethany's
hijack, he'd barely gotten a word in, and this was his last
chance to impress Washington. She'd hitched a ride on his
wagon, then proceeded to shove him off it!

"Thanks for letting me say so much about my research,"
she was saying now as she shook Marlene's hand while Tyler
stood fuming to one side.

The other woman's mouth twisted in a wry smile. "I didn't
have much choice, after you made it plain you doubted my
professionalism."

"Oh." Bethany blushed—and so she damn well should,
Tyler thought. "Sorry about that."

"I'm just glad you didn't say it on air." A giggle softened
the talk-show host's sophistication and made her look a lot
more attractive, though Bethany was the prettier of the two.
"It would've livened the segment up if you had."

Yeah, and hadn't it needed livening up, with Bethany going
on about kidney disease.

"If you two have finished your girl talk," Tyler said with a
smoothness that didn't entirely hide his fury, "we have a baby
here who needs his lunch."

Bethany's face held a hint of gloating and a whole lot of
"since when do you care about the baby?" And, dammit, she
still looked pretty. She said goodbye to Marlene and headed
for the door, her hips swinging beneath a soft turquoise skirt
he'd never seen before, her high-heeled shoes drawing his attention to her slim ankles. Tyler picked up Ben in his car seat
and followed her.

Ben was tired—overtired—and on the way home he started

to squall. Bethany turned around in her seat and tried to soothe him, but nothing worked. When the din got so loud Tyler couldn't concentrate on driving, he pulled over.

"You'd better get in the back and give him a bottle, or something," he snapped.

She did as he suggested, and it seemed to calm Ben. Tyler pulled out into traffic again, but within a minute Ben was pulling away from the bottle, crying angrily.

"I think he's teething, he's been extra drooly the past few days."

Huh, she managed to speak civilly enough when it was about Ben. In the rearview mirror, Tyler saw her lean over to drop a kiss on the baby's head. Then she began to sing: "Tom, Tom, the piper's son, stole a pig and away did run. The pig was eat and Tom was beat, and Tom ran crying down the street."

Her voice was so soft, Tyler had to strain to hear the words. He grunted sour disapproval. "I can't believe you think a rhyme about juvenile delinquency and child abuse is fit for a baby's ears."

"Shut up," she said with an anger that shocked him.

CHAPTER FIFTEEN

BETHANY DECIDED they shouldn't take Ben with them to see his mother. Having him there could make the meeting too emotional. Tyler was in full agreement.

When she thought about the options available to Ben and his mom, none of them included Bethany having any ongoing responsibility for the little boy. Nor Tyler. Though Tyler hadn't yet told social services about the woman coming forward. Inevitably, she would be investigated, possibly charged by the police. If she loved Ben and could look after him, if her abandonment had been a moment's desperation, prison would be a terrible outcome. Tyler might need to offer his lawyer's assistance to keep mother and baby together.

Bethany wished she could feel happier for Ben as they walked up the path of the shabby but clean white clapboard house in Clayton County.

The woman who answered the doorbell was older than Bethany expected. Tall, skinny—as she'd appeared in the security footage—with a child Bethany judged to be about two years old perched on her hip.

"Alice James?" Tyler said.

She looked eagerly past Bethany and Tyler. "Where's Davey?"

That must be Ben's real name.

Tyler introduced himself and Bethany. He said with that charming smile that could sell sand to a Bedouin, "Before we return your son to you, we want to be sure you have everything you need to look after him." Bethany assumed he hadn't mentioned the inevitable involvement of the authorities in this process because he didn't want to alarm her.

She looked suspicious. "He's my baby, he should be here with me."

"Ms. James, we need to understand why you left Ben, and how your circumstances have changed so that you now feel able to have him back," Bethany said.

Tears welled up in the woman's eyes. "I'll never forgive myself for leaving my baby." She buried her face against the toddler's neck.

Tyler put an arm across her shoulders and shepherded her inside. As they followed her down a hallway that smelled of boiled vegetables, Bethany glanced up at Tyler. He was frowning, his eyes on Ben's mother's back. Alice led them into a small living room, furnished with a worn green couch, a set of nested tables and not much else. In a corner, two more children, identical twins, were playing. Bethany judged them to be around four years old.

They sat on the couch, and Bethany invited the woman to talk about her family. Seemed there was no man around, and Alice, understandably, was too busy looking after the kids to go out to work.

"Tell us about...Davey," Tyler said.

She drew a deep breath. "He was born October fifteenth." That fit with Bethany's conclusions about Ben's age. "I had him here at home, with the midwife. It all went very easily. I'm used to it." She sniffed. "He was a lovely baby, right from the start. Quiet, not a screamer like my other kids." She picked up a piece of paper from the topmost of the nested tables. "Here's his birth certificate."

Bethany scanned the document. Davey Dwayne James, born October fifteenth to Alice Catherine James. Father: Joseph Stanners. Bethany wondered if Mr. Stanners knew he had a child.

"I'm on my own, and it all got too much." Alice's voice wobbled. "The kids had ear infections, they were all so sick, I couldn't cope. I thought, why am I doing this, when I'm such a bad mother? I saw a couple of articles about you in the newspaper—" she nodded to Tyler "—and you seemed so nice, I thought you'd be a good person to have Davey."

That lamentable piece of logic aside, Bethany found herself feeling sorry for the woman.

His eyes fixed on Alice, Tyler said, "Tell us about the day you left him at my office."

She buried her face in her hands. "I asked my neighbor to look after the other kids—she was rude about it, she always is, but she said she'd mind them for a couple of hours. I put Davey in the bag—"

"What color was the bag?" Tyler asked.

Bethany stared at him. Surely he didn't doubt the poor woman's story?

Alice blinked. "Green. It was one I had from high school. It's all faded from the sun."

"What were you wearing that day?"

Alice described her clothing, which matched what they'd seen on the security tape. "I was afraid someone would recognize my scarf, so I threw that and the hat away." She fixed him with an accusing look. "Don't you believe I'm Davey's mother?"

Tyler hesitated. "We were expecting someone younger."

That started her crying again. "I'm only twenty-six, but I look ten years older and that's because of all these kids."

"You don't look a day over twenty-five," Tyler said politely.

Alice managed a watery smile.

Then he said, "You must be proud of your kids, they're all so cute."

That dried Alice's eyes. He continued, "But while I may be biased, I think Davey's the cutest of the lot." He turned to Bethany. "We're really going to miss the little guy, aren't we, hon?" He clamped a hand down on her knee, gave it a shake.

Hon? And what was with the knee groping? His eyes were steely, so she didn't argue. "We sure are."

"I can't wait to have him home," Alice confessed. "I've missed him so much."

"He's adorable," Tyler said. "He's going to have hair like yours."

Alice touched a hand to her wavy blond locks, thin like the rest of her. "I think you're right."

Tyler studied her face. "He has your eyes, too." The other woman flushed.

"He's all-round a great kid," Tyler said. "You can already tell he's got so much personality, that birthmark is never going to bother him." He squeezed Bethany's knee, choking the question she would have blurted.

"N-no," Alice agreed uncertainly. "I guess not."

"I mean, right now it's pretty big," Tyler said. "But hardly anyone gets to see his chest, and we're so used to it already, we barely notice it." He turned to Bethany. "You're pretty sure it's going to fade, right, hon?"

"I—yes." Bethany dredged her memories of medical school. "Most strawberry birthmarks disappear by the time the child is ten years old."

"Did the doctors say much about it to you?" Tyler asked Alice.

The woman had turned white. "I haven't taken him to a doctor yet."

Bethany let slip a cry of shock. Tyler stood, tugged her to her feet. "I don't know what your game is, Ms. James, but I know for sure you're not that baby's mother."

Alice clutched the hem of Tyler's jacket. "I knew he doesn't have a birthmark, you had me confused. Please," she said as she began to cry, "I was a surrogate for another couple. I gave my Davey away. But I can't stop thinking about him. I need him. I need a baby."

BETHANY WEPT on the way home. The tears started as a trickle of moisture and overflowed into a river.

"How did you know?" she sobbed to Tyler after he'd gotten off his cell phone from the police and social services. He'd also acted on what seemed a very natural instinct after what they'd just been through, and called his mom to check that Ben was okay.

He kept his eyes on the road. "It was her shoulders."

Bethany stared at him, confused.

"She had broader shoulders than the woman on the tape," he said.

"You remember that?"

"When it comes to women's figures, I have excellent recall." He was half joking, but Bethany couldn't summon a smile.

"I can't believe someone would try that. I can't believe I believed her."

"If anyone else turns up, we'll insist on DNA tests."

She reached over, put her hand over his on the steering wheel. "Tyler, I can't thank you enough."

He glanced briefly at her. "If we hadn't figured it out, social services would have. I didn't want to lose Ben, so I was looking for obstacles. I lucked out big-time."

Bethany wasn't so sure social services would have seen through the woman. But she focused on his other words. "You didn't want Ben to leave?"

He ignored her. "Bethany, things aren't going well between you and me—" understatement of the decade "—but for Ben's sake, please don't quit before we find his real mom." His hands tightened on the wheel. "I'm sick at the thought of how vulnerable he is. I don't trust anyone else to look after him. Apart from me and you."

He pulled in to his mother's driveway, and Bethany breathed easier knowing Ben was safe just a few yards away.

"What if we don't find his mom anytime soon?" she asked. "I can't stay forever."

He switched off the engine. "I don't know, I can't think that far ahead right now." He ran a hand down his face. "Bethany, please, just…stay."

He only wanted her for Ben.

"I'll stay," she said.

BETHANY AND TYLER fell into an uneasy truce. It was hard for Bethany to remain spitting mad at him after he'd saved Ben from that woman.

Ben thrived in blissful ignorance of his narrow escape; Tyler went to work as normal, though he phoned several times each day to check on Ben. Bethany started applying for jobs.

She should be talking to other research teams, submitting applications to funding organizations, but she was so tired of talking, thinking, living kidney research that she couldn't face it. She told herself she'd find a six-month hospital contract, then revisit the research options. But some of the jobs she applied for were permanent positions.

SOMETHING'S WRONG with Ben. Bethany sat bolt upright in bed. The clock on her nightstand said six forty-five; it was Monday morning. She threw the covers aside, raced out of her room—and bumped right into Tyler.

"Did you get up to see to Ben in the night?" he demanded.

"No, did you?" Without waiting for a reply, she charged down the hall. Tyler was on her heels, and when she came to a stop in the nursery doorway, he bumped into her. He steadied her with his hands on his shoulders.

They both stared at Ben, lying there with his eyes closed, his thumb in his mouth, his cheeks moving rhythmically as he sucked.

"He's asleep." Tyler whispered the obvious.

"He slept through the night," Bethany murmured. "The first time."

By unspoken mutual agreement, they backed out of the doorway.

Now Bethany realized she was wearing only her skimpy MCG T-shirt. Tyler had noticed too, and his eyes darkened as he stared down at her.

"Bethany." He reached out, smoothed her tousled hair.

She stepped back. "Don't," she said. "Not unless you're going to say something I want to hear."

He held her gaze for a long moment. Downstairs, the phone rang. "I'll get that," he said.

Bethany went to put on her robe before she headed downstairs to make coffee. Tyler was in the kitchen, talking on the phone. It seemed to her he was standing at attention.

He listened for the next few minutes, occasionally agreeing

with whoever he was talking to, sometimes asking brief questions such as, "How soon?" and "When will you announce it?" At one stage he said, "Sir, I'm honored." The call ended with thanks on Tyler's part.

He was grinning from ear to ear as he said to Bethany, "That was the secretary of health and human services, calling on his way to catch a flight to London. Looks like I have a new job."

She listened, first in bemusement, then in growing outrage as he told her about a think tank in Washington, D.C., set up to help families. Tyler had been invited to chair it, and it was obvious the invitation wasn't a surprise.

"You knew you were up for the job." She interrupted his monologue.

"I heard a rumor," he corrected. He poured coffee into two mugs, pushed one across the island to her.

Bethany ignored it. "That's why you wanted to keep Ben, why you did all those interviews. Ben gave you a positive association with parents and kids."

Tyler stirred sugar into his coffee, said nothing.

"None of those interviews were to help the foundation," she said. "They were all about you. Only you."

"They did help the foundation," he said coolly.

Her lip curled. "Will you move to Washington?"

"It's a full-time job."

"Who'll run the foundation?"

"The foundation was never going to be the rest of my life," he said. "I have several very competent executives, one of them will step up to the plate."

"But you're the best." She knew that now.

He shrugged.

"You used Ben," Bethany said. "And now you're abandoning him and the foundation."

"I'll admit I did keep Ben at first because of the job," he said. "But I've grown very fond of him. I won't leave before he's settled, either with his mom or a long-term foster placement."

She snorted.

His eyes narrowed. "You can't talk about using Ben. You used him to get to me."

"I cared about him from the start."

"Really?" He launched a hard, accusing look at her. "It suited you to look after Ben. If this job had been an obstacle to your precious research, you never would have done it."

Tyler knew he was right, and it seemed Bethany did too, because her eyes widened, then she clammed up and stormed out of the room. *Good.*

He wandered into the living room, threw himself onto a couch and thought about his new job. He should be thrilled at the prospect.

But he wasn't enjoying the moment as much as he should, and that was Bethany's fault.

TYLER WAS LATE for work, and since Olivia had a policy of not starting work before him, she had time to attend to some personal correspondence. Such as her astronomical credit-card bills. Three major shopping sprees had resulted in four new pairs of shoes and a beaded evening purse in a shade of purple she wouldn't be seen carrying. Then there was the Venetian-glass vase to complement her collection, a new dinner set and an antique brass candlestick.

Silas would hate it all.

Good.

Bad.

She loved the man. She wasn't supposed to fall in love with

im until she knew he would always put her first, and she could no longer be certain of that. But she loved him anyway. It was going to make life complicated. Much more complicated than she liked it to be.

Olivia pulled the telephone directory out of her desk and began searching for the numbers she needed.

With luck, she could make her calls and skip out of the office before Tyler got here.

STILL REELING from Tyler's news, Bethany took Ben on a visit to Susan that she'd arranged earlier in the week. But she was in no mood to be sociable, and it seemed Susan hadn't heard about the D.C. appointment yet, so conversation was difficult. The visit didn't last long.

On the way back, she drove past Emory University and it reminded her it had been a while since she'd visited the pediatric kidney patients. Last time she'd visited, Tyler had gone with her.

The thought soured in her mouth and she tried to recall some of the more pleasant memories of that day. The pervasive cheerfulness among the kids after Tyler talked to them. The fun they'd had with the nurses afterward. That teenage girl who'd asked if Ben would rather be with his mom, making Tyler aware of how much he would miss Ben when he left.

Bethany froze. Ahead of her the red light turned green. The driver behind honked his horn. Still, she didn't move.

That girl, the teenager…she was Ben's mother. Her build—her shoulders—fit with the young woman on the video, and she'd been so upset about Ben's feelings. Not exactly conclusive evidence, Bethany knew, but the hunch she had about this was almost overwhelming.

Bethany pulled ahead, prompted by the mounting dir
behind her. She broke a personal rule by pulling out her cel
phone while she was driving to call Tyler.

"I've found Ben's mother," she said. "I know it's her."

BETHANY AND TYLER arrived at the hospital at one. Bethany
described the girl to the senior receptionist, a woman whom
she knew slightly, and asked if she was a regular visitor to the
hospital. The girl's blond dreadlocks were sufficient for the
receptionist to identify her.

"That'll be Kylie Carter. She visits her mom—Nancy
Carter, stomach cancer—every day."

"Is she here now?" Tyler asked.

The nurse nodded. "She comes while her younger siblings
are in school. Ward ten, room 203."

When they found the right room, they stopped outside
Bethany said, "I'll ask her to come out, in case her mom
doesn't know she had a baby."

"She may not have," Tyler said. "This is a very long shot."
He sounded almost as if he hoped Bethany was wrong.

The girl—Kylie—looked up at Bethany's entrance. Her
face paled, then reddened.

"Excuse me, Mrs. Carter," Bethany said to her mother
thin and pale in the bed. "I'm Dr. Bethany Hart, I'd like a word
with your daughter."

The mother waved weakly. Kylie sprang out of the vinyl
visitor's chair and followed Bethany. When she saw Tyler
in the corridor, her shoulders slumped and she burst into
tears, looking more like a baby herself than someone who'd
given birth.

Bethany wrapped her arms around the girl. "It's okay,
sweetie, we want to help you."

After a minute the storm of tears subsided. Kylie pulled away from Bethany, her shoulders squared in defiance, but her limbs trembling. "Wh-where's my baby?"

"He's with my mother," Tyler said. "Just for a few hours."

"Are you going to report me to the cops? Because my mom is really sick, and if she hears about this she might—"

"We want to help you," Bethany said again. An inquiry at the nurses' station gave them access to an empty room. Kylie sat on the bed, Bethany beside her.

"Tell us about Ben," Tyler said.

"I called him Jordan," Kylie said. "I didn't want to put his name in the note because there were people who would've known he was mine. But Ben's nice too."

"When was he born?" Bethany asked.

"October twelfth. At a clinic in Houston."

"Was anyone with you?"

"One of the nuns I'd been staying with—they have a home for single mothers." Kylie gave a mighty sniff. "My boyfriend, Marcus, left me right before that."

"How did you end up in Houston?" Tyler asked.

"Mom was really mad when I got pregnant. She did the same thing—that's how she ended up with me—and she wanted me to be different. I was sixteen and Marcus was nineteen. Mom complained to the police about statutory rape and got social services involved. I loved Marcus, so we ran away."

Bethany gripped her hand, squeezed it. The girl must have been terrified, giving birth with no one she loved at hand.

"When did you come back to Atlanta?" Tyler said. "And why did you give Ben away?"

Her lip quivered. "I called home, I was so lonely. The kids told me Mom was sick and there was no one to look after them. I wanted to come back, but I knew I couldn't look after

Ben as well as the kids and Mom. I saw your picture in the newspaper, you looked nice and kind."

He made a stifled sound.

"I told Mom I'd had a late miscarriage." She hung her head. "How is Jordan—Ben?"

"He slept through the night for the first time last night," Bethany said. "Maybe he knew we were about to find his mommy."

Tears sprang to Kylie's eyes again. "I miss him so much. But I can't look after him. I can't work, not with Mom to visit and the other kids to look after, and there's no money and no time."

"We can fix that," Tyler said.

SOON THEY WOULD KNOW for sure if Kylie was Ben's mother— she'd taken a DNA test. But Tyler's instinct told him she was the real deal. His lawyer, Malcolm Farthing, came to the office for a meeting two days after they'd found Kylie.

"You know, Tyler, if you want to keep this baby, you could contest the mother."

Keep Ben? Tyler half rose from his chair, then gripped the arms, forced himself to sit down again, to say without excitement, "He's Kylie's child."

"Whom she abandoned," Malcolm said smoothly, "with a request that you adopt the boy. She didn't come forward, you and Dr. Hart tracked her down. It appears she's in no position to raise the child herself, she doesn't have any extended family who can support her…" He shuffled his papers. "Fact is, if we're thinking about what's best for the baby, there's every chance Ben will be better off with you. You can afford the best child care, he'll never want for anything—"

"And I love him," Tyler said sharply.

Malcolm pursed his lips. "That, too."

Tyler pictured a scenario where he kept Ben and they had their own little family. Him and Ben and—not Bethany, but eventually, maybe someday, a woman he wanted to marry. A woman who was selfless, but not too selfless. He had trouble conjuring that, so he pushed the thought aside.

But Kylie…she was Ben's mother. She was desperate. Brave. Was it right to take a child from his mother?

Caring wasn't about money… Bethany and Ben had shown him that. Yet the lawyer was right, Tyler's wealth would ensure Ben had security. And Tyler didn't want to lose Ben.

He thought about it so long without speaking that Malcolm glanced at his watch and cleared his throat.

"You're right," Tyler said. "Money talks."

CHAPTER SIXTEEN

IT TOOK an appallingly short time—almost no time at all—for the arrangements to be made.

By ten o'clock Thursday morning, the removal guys had packaged up most of the nursery's contents and started on the trip across town to Kylie's home.

Tyler, holding Ben, sat down in the armchair that was one of the few furnishings that remained in the room. He was due to deliver Ben to Kylie in an hour. He couldn't imagine how empty the house would feel. Bethany would move out, too, of course. Yesterday she'd attended a job interview at Piedmont Hospital for a full-time resident position.

He shifted in the seat. Maybe it was the transition from upright to half lying down, but Ben started to whimper. Tyler felt like doing the same.

"Hush, baby." He ran a finger down Ben's cheek.

He'd seen Bethany do that with calming effect, but now Ben's whine turned into something nearer a wail. Tyler jiggled the baby on his shoulder, but Ben squalled louder.

It was about now that Bethany would start to sing. Tyler managed a "la-la-la" under his breath. Ben's cries approached a shriek.

Bethany had said he was teething, and his cheeks had two bright red patches, so Tyler assumed the poor kid was in pain.

He didn't want Ben's last memory of his time with Tyler to be full of pain. He knew Ben didn't have that kind of memory, but still… He sighed. How could he ever have thought it would be easy to give Ben back?

Reluctantly, rustily, he began to sing.

"Twinkle, twinkle, little star…"

Ben's eyes unscrunched.

"How I wonder what you are."

Was it his imagination, or was Ben quieting?

"Up above the world so high, like a diamond in the sky…"

At least this rhyme bore some resemblance to reality, Tyler told himself. Not like some of Bethany's ditties about cows jumping over the moon, or farmers' wives cutting off mice's tails.

"Twinkle, twinkle, little star, how I wonder what you are."

Ben's distress had wound down to a quiet sobbing. By the time Tyler sang the song through once again, the baby had stuck his thumb in his mouth and was watching Tyler with big eyes.

Tyler studied the little boy in his arms until he couldn't see for the haze in front of his eyes. "You're my little star, kid." He blinked, but somehow a drop of moisture escaped and landed on Ben's arm. Tyler brushed it away with his thumb.

"Tyler?" Bethany's voice from the doorway made him jump a mile high.

"What do you want?" he said roughly, not looking at her.

"I, uh, thought I heard singing." She came into the room, pretty in that copper-colored dress Sabrina had helped her buy.

He cleared his throat. "I don't think so. Ben sure wasn't singing."

She looked at him, at his possessive hold on Ben, at his face, which was no doubt red and possibly even damp. She put a hand on his shoulder and squeezed sympathetically. "Bonded, huh?"

What was the point of denying, to himself or to her, the overwhelming love he felt for Ben? He looked up at Bethany, met her eyes for what felt like the first moment of honesty between them in a long while. "Superglue."

WITH THE ATMOSPHERE still so strained between her and Tyler in the lead-up to Ben's departure, Bethany had asked Susan for the details of Tyler's arrangements for Kylie and Ben.

Susan had told her that Tyler had paid for Kylie's mom, Nancy, to move into a private room in the hospital, where she could have her family around her. The doctors had started another round of chemotherapy—Nancy wanted to try every last option—but they were predicting she'd need hospice care in another couple of months. Tyler had promised Kylie he'd pay for that, too.

He'd paid off the mortgage on the family's home—Susan assured Bethany it was a laughably small amount for him—and with the help of a guidance counselor worked with Kylie to devise a plan for her to finish high school at a school that catered to single moms by providing on-site child care. Tyler would fund an after-school sitter for the other kids so Kylie and Ben could visit Nancy each day. He'd met with social services to make sure Kylie wasn't in any trouble, and that they would keep an eye on the family. It wouldn't be easy for Kylie, but the girl seemed determined to succeed.

For a guy who didn't like to do more than sign checks, it was an impressive effort.

With Ben gone, there was nothing to keep Bethany at Tyler's house. After he left to take Ben to his new home, she started packing. She hadn't finished by the time he got back.

He showed up in the doorway of her room, took in the sight

of her suitcase, the pile of clothes on the bed. "You're going back to your apartment?"

She nodded. "I need to visit my parents for a couple of days, too. I still haven't told them I didn't get the foundation's money, and I owe them some kind of explanation as to why I haven't bothered to find an alternative source of funds."

"*They* owe you," he said. "They owe you years of love."

Bethany dropped her chin to her chest, didn't want to engage in talk of love with him, when he didn't love her. She rummaged in her pocket. "I found Ben gumming this a couple of days ago."

She held it out to him. His silver pen. His bemused frown as he turned the object over between his fingers suggested he'd forgotten its existence.

"So Ben had it all along, huh?"

"I haven't seen it before… He may have just found it tucked in a fold of his stroller."

Tyler clicked the nib down, then up again. "Was he enjoying it? I could give it back to him—you said he needs hard things to gum while he's teething."

"A twelve-hundred-dollar pen would be overkill." When he looked as if he was about to argue, she added, "The pen isn't child safe, it's sharp and it might have small parts he could choke on."

Tyler shoved it into his pocket as if he never wanted to see it again. Did he remember how horrified he'd been when she'd lost it?

She stacked a pile of clothes in the suitcase. Then took most of them out again, dropped them on the floor.

"Why did you do that?"

"You're right, I do have awful clothes. I'm going to get rid of them. All of them."

"Peaches, I'm a hundred percent in favor of you going without clothes, but I'm not sure Atlanta is ready for it."

The *Peaches* made her eyes sting, but it was so nice to have him talk to her in that light, teasing, Tyler voice that she let herself laugh. "I have the things I bought with Sabrina, and she said she has a couple more to pass on to me. Anything of hers will be so tasteful, even I can't go wrong."

He nodded, but it seemed he wasn't really listening. "What happened about the job at Piedmont?"

"It's mine if I want it."

"That's great."

"I'm not sure I do. I still want to get back into research, and there's always a possibility of—" she concentrated on zipping up her half-empty case "—Toronto."

"You don't mean that," he said dangerously.

"What's it to you if I go to Toronto?" she challenged him. Tyler's eyes shot daggers, but he didn't reply.

She hefted the case off the bed. "Okay, I'm done."

They both knew it was more than her packing that was done. *I'm done living with you. I'm done laughing with you, crying over you. I'm done waiting for you to love me back. We're done.*

He carried her case downstairs. The cab she'd ordered was waiting. Bethany halted beside it, gave him one last chance to ask her to stay.

"Thanks," he said, "for all you did for Ben."

Dammit, that was all he planned to say. How could he be so dense?

"It hurt you horribly to give Ben back," she said. Susan had told her Tyler's lawyer had suggested he keep the baby— Bethany knew how tempted he must have been. She could hardly bear to think of not seeing Ben again herself, was deliberately *not* thinking about it. It would be just as bad for Tyler.

He shook his head impatiently.

"You gave up something infinitely precious because it was he right thing, the unselfish thing, to do," she persisted.

"That wasn't it at all," he growled.

Beneath his words, Bethany saw the truth. Tyler had made a huge sacrifice. But it had hurt too much. He didn't want to risk that hurt again.

She had no answer to that.

As if he saw her concession of defeat, he opened the taxi door, waited for her to get in. Then he shut it firmly, finally.

She was out of Tyler Warrington's life as surely as if she'd never been in it.

TYLER HAD EXPECTED to miss Ben horribly, and he did. What he hadn't expected was that nothing would feel right without Bethany. Not even aspects of his life where she'd barely been involved—work and social events. And lunch with Mom on Sunday had been so flat, the whole family had noticed.

A part of him had wanted to ask Bethany to stay. But for what? She'd been the mother of "his" child the last couple of months—of course he felt some attachment to her. But now Ben was gone, there was nothing between them.

Apart from an all-consuming desire to take her to bed. *I'll get over that.*

Talking to her was a lot of fun, too. He couldn't think of a single conversation that wasn't better for having it with Bethany. And, of course, she was pretty sharp when it came to interpreting his family.

And what about when he went to visit Ben, which Kylie had promised he could do? If Bethany came, they could talk about what Ben was up to, share their memories of his time with them.

Dammit, the new appreciation of life he'd experienced recently came from sharing everything with Bethany. Garnering her disapproval, teasing her, making her laugh against her will. Being driven crazy with desire for her.

He remembered the day they'd disgraced themselves, both too cowardly to tell Sabrina she had cereal in her hair. Those midnight rendezvous in the nursery with Ben. The night he'd nearly made love to her.

She'd been gone five days and his home had gone back to being just a house.

He reminded himself he hadn't liked having her constantly judging him. With his next breath, he admitted it had been strangely comforting to know she saw his faults and…liked him anyway.

He loved that she wasn't Little Miss Perfect, either. Not just her truly awful clothes, which he acknowledged with a twinge of regret might be a thing of the past, but the way she assumed the worst of him, even as she manipulated him to her own ends. She made him laugh, some of the outrageous accusations she leveled at him.

She made him laugh, full stop.

Right now, he didn't feel like laughing at all.

"I DIDN'T GET the funding." Bethany was beyond sugarcoating the news for her parents.

Her mother's face crumpled. "Oh, Bethany." Not sympathy. Accusation.

"I'm still trying other organizations." Okay, maybe she wasn't beyond sugarcoating.

Her father let out a whistling breath between his teeth, his eyes on his wife. He shook his head but didn't say anything.

Bethany saw how worried he was for her mom.

Suddenly, she was sick of bearing the brunt of the responsibility for making something out of Melanie's death.

"It wasn't my fault," she said.

"I'm sure you did your best," her father said heavily. "I suppose that foundation has a lot of people asking for money."

"I mean," Bethany said, "it wasn't my fault Melanie died."

Her mother flinched, and her dad's gaze turned reproachful.

"No one's ever blamed you," he said.

"Not out loud," Bethany admitted. "But you've said it in the way you don't love me, the way you don't love Ryan, because neither of us could save Melanie."

Her mom's fists clenched in her lap. "That's not true, we do love you."

"Then you loved Melanie the best, and I guess someone has to be loved the best, so that's all right." The words poured out of Bethany in a torrent. "But it's not fair to take it out on us. It's not fair to duck out of life because the one you loved most has gone. Give us a chance, Mom, Dad. Get some help to get better, and give me and Ryan a chance to be part of a real family—or say goodbye to us both."

ADMITTING HE WAS WRONG didn't come easily to Tyler. But if he was going to be a better person, that was what he'd have to do. He couldn't afford to screw things up with Bethany, so he decided to practice on his brother.

He found Max with Jake, poring over architectural plans for a new condo development.

Max looked pleased to see him, and Tyler realized he felt the same. "Can we talk?" he asked.

Max waved him to a seat. "Go ahead."

"It's kind of private." Tyler looked at Jake, who got to his feet.

"Sit down," Max told their cousin lazily. "Tyler probably just wants to show off about his new job."

Jake sank down again.

"Mom told you," Tyler said.

Max nodded. After a moment, he said, "Congratulations." He stood, offered Tyler his hand. "Getting this think-tank job—it's a big deal. You've done well, Tyler."

"Not bad for a guy who couldn't hold down a job in his own family's business," Tyler agreed. So much for admitting he was wrong—it was harder than he'd thought. "I didn't mean that," he said. "I'm here to say you did the right thing firing me."

Max protested, but not too hard. Tyler grinned. "I could have done the marketing job well, but I didn't. I was coasting, and you knew it."

Max lifted one shoulder. "I could have given you another chance. I pushed you out as fast as I could."

"I was pretty mad," Tyler said. "And hurt that Mom took your side, like she always does when it comes to the business."

"She takes your side with everything else," Max said gruffly.

Tyler nodded. "That's the other thing I'm here to say. Mom loves you just as much as she loves me."

Jake groaned. "Do I have to listen to this?"

"Whatever it is you're trying to do—" Max shifted in his chair "—you don't have to. I've always known you're Mom's favorite." The words came out in a rush, as if he'd been holding them in for a long time, then his jaw slackened.

"I don't see it," Tyler said frankly. "But Bethany tells me it's true, and I believe her."

Max looked shocked at the acknowledgment, then maddened. Perhaps he'd been hoping Tyler would say Max was wrong about Mom. Oops. Maybe this wasn't such a smart idea. Tyler tried a lighter approach. "I know it annoys you when Mom wants me rather than you to charm the old ladies—"

"It doesn't annoy me," Max said, visibly annoyed. The

temperature in the room seemed to have gone up a couple of notches.

"You guys have got this all wrong." Jake's laconic interruption arrested the tension. Tyler sat back, looked at his cousin. "There's only one favorite in your mom's life, and that's Mitzy."

Tyler laughed first, then Max joined in. Tyler sent his brother a look that requested a truce, and received a not-unfriendly shrug in reply.

"If your visit here is a prelude to any kind of heart-to-heart with Bethany," Max said with uncanny fraternal acuity, "you might want to plan what you're going to say a little better."

Tyler grinned. Okay, so he hadn't made the best job of hashing things out with Max. But surely they could move forward from here.

"What's happening with the cute kidney doctor?" Jake asked. "Is she available?"

"Never to you," Tyler said.

OLIVIA PARKED out front of Silas's house and wished she was a less selfish, nobler woman. One who wanted what was best for Silas, instead of just worrying about how miserable she was without him.

She got out of the car, pulled her sable coat tighter around her.

He must have seen her coming, for he opened the door as she stepped onto the porch. The sight of him filling the door frame set her stomach fluttering.

The hope in his eyes told her she was doing the right thing.

"You're not the only one who has something to confess," she said before she even stepped inside.

He took her hands in his, tugged her over the threshold. "Tell me, my love."

No wariness, no sign that he would allow anything she'd done to change the way he felt about her.

"I want you to know that I'm selfish, shallow and demanding."

He smiled, and he seemed almost boyish. "Those are the things I love most about you."

That couldn't be true. Slightly less confidently, she said, "I was so worried about what my friends would think of you, I didn't tell them about you. I wouldn't have taken you to that ball if you hadn't let me choose your clothes."

He chuckled. "I could have slapped you for that."

She gaped. "You knew?"

He shrugged. "I love you," he said, "no matter what."

"I'm not willing to take second place. Not to Anna, not to those frogs. Not to anything, not ever."

"You'll always come first," he said.

Tears sprang to her eyes, because this was where she still couldn't be certain. "How do I know you mean it?"

He dropped a kiss on her lips, one so sweet that she almost caved right then and there. Then he led her to the living room, pushed her gently onto a sofa and sat down next to her.

"You know that the Warrington Foundation gave me the money for the frogs," he said.

She nodded.

"I've wound up my involvement, organized the trust to run without me." He kissed her hand. "I've made my peace in here—" he touched Olivia's hand to his chest "—with Anna. I loved her. I did something stupid, something terrible. I have to live with the consequences."

"Which brings me to my next confession." She drew a deep breath. "Silas, I visited your children."

His jaw dropped.

"I know it was forward of me, but I had to tell Jemma and Paul what a wonderful man you are. I told them you'd made a mistake and they had to forgive you." She said proudly, "Paul seemed ready to talk to you. Jemma might be a tougher nut to crack, but I told her I'd keep calling, keep visiting, until she agreed."

"Darling." He pulled her into his arms, kissed her tenderly. "You're amazing."

When he looked at her like that, Olivia *felt* amazing.

Silas knuckled his eyes. "I love you, Olivia, but I understand you might not truly believe that until I'm ninety-nine and no longer capable of saying it. But I'll be in the bed next to yours in the nursing home and inside I'll be saying I told you so."

She laughed and then she cried and then she kissed him with all the passion, all the love, she had. "I love you, too. No matter what. And that means I'm going to take the risk. I want to be with you always."

He kissed her so hard she couldn't breathe. "I know it's only a tiny risk," she assured him.

"Infinitesimal." He kissed her again, did incredible things to her mouth with his tongue.

When the kiss ended, she sighed against his chest. "Does this mean we're engaged?"

"Hell, no!"

His vehemence startled her. "But you said—"

He hauled her back into his arms. "I love you too much to get engaged and have you change your mind."

"I won't," she protested. "Silas, I've never felt like this before, not for any of my fiancés."

"Darling, I know I told you to take a risk, but I'm not as brave as you. We're not getting engaged, we're getting married." He kissed the tip of her nose. "Today."

"Silas!"

He looked at his watch. "It's a four-hour drive to Nashville, where there's no waiting period, no blood test. We can have a license by three o'clock and be married by four."

"But I want a proper wedding with a five-thousand-dollar dress and hundreds of guests."

"Too bad." He stood, fished in his pocket for his car keys. "We can do the big event later—after we're married. I'm not going to risk losing you, Olivia." He pulled her to her feet, silenced any further protests with a kiss.

Olivia followed him out the door, happier than she'd known it was possible to be. She might be about to marry a man who was wearing jeans with holes in them and non-matching sneakers, but she would travel to her wedding in a Maserati.

TYLER HAD CALLED Bethany and asked her to come to his house. "It's urgent," he said. Then he hung up.

Heedless of the extravagance, she took a cab. It could be a crisis, something to do with Ben. Even if it wasn't, she was desperate enough to see Tyler again that she wanted to get there as fast as possible.

When the taxi pulled up outside his house, Tyler stood in the doorway, waiting. Tall, gorgeous, the man she loved. And yet, not the same man.

This Tyler looked as if he didn't have a designer suit to his name. He wore baggy sweatpants, a ratty T-shirt that couldn't have belonged to him—he must have wrestled it off some homeless guy—and his feet were bare. His hair was rumpled, not in a sexy way—though she found it sexy anyway. He looked as if he hadn't slept in a couple of nights.

"Bethany." His gaze skimmed her new outfit, a wrap dress,

in green wool, her curves, her hair. "You look fantastic." He sounded hungry. For her?

Bethany's stomach lurched in response, and she put a hand to it. "What's so urgent?"

She followed him into the house and realized it felt more like home than anywhere else in the world.

"I have something for you." He led the way to the dining room. On the antique wooden table sat a familiar, faded green duffel bag, incongruous in the luxury of the room.

"Another baby?" she said stupidly.

He smiled, a grim movement of the lips. "No, but that's not to say I didn't think about using that ploy, before I hit on the rather obvious idea of giving you money."

She lost the end of that sentence in her focus on the first part. "A ploy to what?"

He picked up the bag, tossed it to her.

Bethany caught it. At first glance, she thought it was empty. Then she saw a small rectangle of paper. She pulled it out, dropped the bag on the carpet so she could examine her find.

"It's—Tyler, it's a check for a hundred thousand dollars." Made out to her.

"It's your research money," Tyler said.

"But you said the foundation won't fund two projects in the same field."

"This check isn't from the foundation."

She glanced down at the slip of paper. The account name swam in front of her. "This is your personal check."

He nodded. "I wish your dream wasn't to sacrifice yourself on the altar of your sister's memory, but it is, so I'm damn well going to help you climb up there. Then I'm going to hang around until you're ready to get down again."

"I don't understand," she said.

"I want you to come to Washington with me. There's a team there working in the same field. I spoke to the doctor in charge and he'd welcome another fully funded researcher on board."

She knew the team he meant—they were top-notch. "You said Toronto were the best people to do the work."

"It's your dream," he said again. "I can't say it makes a lot of sense to me, and I sure can't say I'm happy about it. But if we're going to get married I don't want to spend the rest of my life being nagged by you about your kidney research." He pulled her into a loose embrace. "Besides, I've met my in-laws, and you know what they're like about this kidney stuff."

She put a hand to his chest. "Did you say *get married?*"

He sighed. "I can't see any way around it. You're not likely to stay with me if I keep dating other women, are you?"

"I'd kill you if you even *thought* about dating other women," she said. "Tyler, you don't need a babysitter, you don't need female companionship, you don't need a woman to tell you you're wonderful—"

"It would be too damn bad if I did, with you around," he interrupted.

"So why are you even talking about me and marriage in the same breath?"

"Why do you think?" He smiled so tenderly, so *lovingly,* it took her breath away. "I love you, Bethany."

She couldn't speak.

"Here, I'll show you." He let go of her so he could reach into his back pocket. He pulled out his wallet, produced his driver's license. "Look." He pointed to the small print.

It said Tyler was registered as an organ donor.

Laughter welled within Bethany, bubbled over.

"Hey," he protested. "I just signed up to give away some of the best parts of me when I die."

"And this is proof that you love me?" she teased, seeing the way his mind was working and loving him even more.

"These guys have to wait until I'm dead." He stuffed the license back in his wallet, tossed it onto the dining table. "But you—" he took her in his arms again "—you get all of me right now. You want a kidney, it's yours." His eyes darkened. "And you already have my heart."

"Oh." It was hardly expressive of what she felt, but it seemed sufficient for Tyler to claim her mouth in a scorching kiss.

Bethany let her lips, her tongue, say what she needed to. When Tyler pulled away, he was shaking. He held her close, his chin resting on her head.

"I know you're way too good for me," he said. "Too kind, too nice."

"Too smart," she inserted.

"I don't think so," he said smugly. "If you were at all smart, you'd have figured out by now that I'm crazy about you, and you'd have worked out some way to take advantage of my pitiful state."

Bethany had never seen anyone less deserving of pity.

"But even though you're all of those things and I don't deserve you," he said, serious now, "I love you too much to let a better man have you. Be mine, Bethany, for always."

She swallowed an instantaneous *yes.* "Are you sure this isn't because you miss Ben? Because you associate me with him, which makes you emotionally vulnerable to me?"

"That's what I've been telling myself the last week," he said. "I do miss Ben, like crazy. But the way I feel about you is…well, it's all about you." He looked into her eyes. "Bethany, put me out of my misery. Do you love me?"

"For someone who knows a lot about women, you're pretty dumb," she said. "Of course I love you, you idiot."

He shook his head at his own stupidity. "I don't know how I didn't figure that out, given those endearments you lavish on me." He put a finger under her chin, tilted it. "I can't wait to get you into bed."

"Yes, please," she said.

"We'll get married," he said. "We'll have children."

"Yes, please," she said happily.

Tyler's face clouded. "It would be great if we still had Ben, wouldn't it? But we can get started on those kids right away, if you want."

"We might have one sooner than you think," Bethany said. "I told my parents I plan to invite Ryan to live with me. That means with you." She held her breath and watched him process that.

"Uh, great." He thought some more, then said firmly, "You're right, it's a great idea. We'd better start checking out schools. Day schools, no more boarding."

Selfish playboy Tyler Warrington was taking on her brother, just like that? He was putty in her hands—the power almost made Bethany dizzy.

"There's something I have to do," she said, "and I really hate to do it."

"It doesn't involve kidneys, does it?"

"Sort of." She picked up the check she'd dropped on the table. She tore it in half.

"But—"

She put a finger to his lips, smiled when he kissed it. "Tyler, you made the right decision giving that money to Toronto. I hadn't realized I don't even like doing research. I like working with kids—I was getting more satisfaction out of my E.R. work than anything else."

He kissed her. "So that's what you want to do? Be an E.R. doctor?"

She shook her head. "I've seen an awful lot of illness in my life. I want to treat sick kids, but I also want to see healthy kids, help them stay that way. I want to work in a private practice, with lower-income families—you'll have to subsidize me with your fabulous wealth, of course."

"Of course."

"I want to help them make the most of what they're doing right, treat them when they're going wrong."

He nuzzled her neck, sending shivers through her. "That sounds flexible enough for us to fit our own children in somewhere along the line."

Bethany nodded. "Though in some ways I'll always feel as if Ben was our first child."

"Me too." He gazed down into her eyes. "He brought us together."

"I love you, Tyler."

His kiss was thorough, demanding, rapturous. Bethany wanted it to last forever.

From a distance, she heard the doorbell.

Tyler broke off the kiss to say, "Ignore it," then he kissed her again.

But the bell rang again, and again, and again. Finally he released her.

"Dammit," he growled as he strode to the door. "If it's those religious nuts in the white robes, they can go to hell."

"With your reputation, I daresay that's where they think you're going," Bethany pointed out.

He yanked the door open.

"Kylie." All heat was gone from his voice.

Bethany came out into the entryway. Kylie stood on the

doorstep, Ben in his stroller in front of her. He'd grown, even in a week, and he was more adorable than ever.

"Come in." Tyler picked up the front of the stroller and lifted it over the doorstep.

Kylie's smile was tremulous but happy. "I've brought him home. To you."

EPILOGUE

JUST WHEN TYLER thought he couldn't get any happier...he did.

He and Bethany—his sexy, gorgeous, adorable wife—had Ben back in their home, and the adoption would be through any day now.

Kylie was as excited about it as they were—she loved her son, but she was certain she wasn't ready to be a mother.

She needed to focus on her own family, on her mom, whose life had been blessedly extended, but who wouldn't last much longer now. Some time in the future, Kylie wanted to go to college, then get a job working with kids. One day, she'd told them, she wanted to get married, have a family of her own, do it all properly this time.

But for now, she wanted to be an aunt to Ben, and a much-loved member of the extended Warrington family. Just like Ryan, and just like Silas and Olivia, the unlikeliest couple Tyler had ever known—and, next to him and Bethany, the happiest.

With Ben and Kylie in their lives, Tyler and Bethany hadn't been able to move to Washington—he'd had to pass on the think-tank job. But that was okay, Tyler was full of ideas for the Warrington Foundation—he'd talked them through with Max, and the new direction they'd set had him excited about his work.

Best of all, he had Bethany. Just looking at her made him

want to laugh out loud—then kiss her senseless. He couldn't wait to spend the rest of his life with her, with their family.

Who'd have thought caring could be so much fun?

* * * * *

*Mills & Boon® Special Moments™
brings you a sneak preview.*

In The Single Dad's Virgin Wife *sensible Tricia is
determined to keep things between her and gorgeous
new boss Noah strictly business. Yet fighting her
attraction to the eligible dad of four could
prove impossible...*

*Turn the page for a peek at this fantastic new story
from Susan Crosby, available next month in
Mills & Boon® Special Moments™!*

*Don't forget you can still find all your favourite
Superromance and Special Edition stories
every month in Special Moments™!*

The Single Dad's Virgin Wife
by
Susan Crosby

Tricia McBride came to a quick stop a few feet from the interview room of At Your Service, a prestigious Sacramento domestic-and-clerical-help agency. She stared in disbelief at the owner, Denise Watson, who'd been filling her in on the details of a job opening.

"Hold on a second," Tricia said. "Let me get this straight. I'm not being interviewed by the person I would be working for, this Noah Falcon? I would be taking the job, boss unseen?"

"That sums it up," Denise replied. "It happens all the time, Tricia."

"It does?"

"Remember, I screen all my potential employers, just as I do my employees. If you find yourself in an impossible situation, you'll leave, but I don't think that'll be the case. Noah's a successful business owner, a widower with four children. Pillar of the community."

"Yet he's not doing the interviewing." Tricia didn't like how two and two were adding up. "There's something you're not telling me."

Denise hesitated. "Well, to be honest, he doesn't know his current employee is quitting. She told Noah's brother in confidence, and he decided to take matters into his own hands and do the hiring himself."

"Why's that?"

"You can ask him yourself." Denise opened the door, leaving Tricia no choice but to follow her inside.

An attractive man about her own age stood. Denise made the introductions. "Tricia McBride, this is David Falcon."

Greetings were exchanged, then Denise left them alone.

"Your résumé is impressive," David said, taking his seat at the conference table again.

It is? Tricia thought, but she said thank you then sat. "Why me, Mr. Falcon?"

He raised his brows at her directness. "Why not you, Ms. McBride?"

"I'm sure Denise told you I'll be leaving Sacramento in January to move to San Diego to start a new job. I would be in your brother's employ less than three months. That seems unfair to the family."

"And you're absolutely committed to this other job?"

"Yes, absolutely, unequivocally. I've given my word."

"Just checking," he said with a smile. "You know, it's obviously not the ideal situation for us. But the important thing is that we'll have that three-month cushion to find someone perfect, someone who *will* stay. Who knows, it could happen next week, and you'd be on your way. We're not guaranteeing the job for the whole three months, either. But in the past Noah has been forced into making expedient choices. You'll be giving him the luxury of time to find just the right person."

"By that you mean he loses employees frequently?"

David hesitated. "My brother tends to hire people fresh out of college who don't have a clue about life yet, not to mention how to handle four children. You were a kindergarten teacher, which leads me to believe that you like children, certainly a necessity for the job, plus you have actual experience working with them. You're thirty-four, so you have life skills, as well. Denise has done a thorough background check on you, and I feel comfortable that you'll be an asset."

She eyed him directly, not easily fooled. "And what's the real reason you're doing this behind his back?"

He half smiled. "Truth? Noah's children are in need of a woman like you, even if it's only for a few months. Their mother died three years ago. The house is...quiet. They need laughter. And someone who will stand toe-to-toe with Noah."

"Why?"

"He needs help, but he usually resists suggestions. Noah is still grieving. He doesn't know how to deal with his children."

"*Deal* with them?"

"Wrong word, I guess. He loves them. He just doesn't know how to show it."

He sounded to Tricia like a man out of his element and on the edge. "When Denise called me yesterday to talk about the job she made it seem like a nanny position, but after the details she gave me today, I'd say it's beyond that."

"It's more teacher than nanny. The kids are homeschooled, so your teaching background is important."

"Homeschooling four children is a far cry from being a nanny."

"Which is why the salary is so high. But the kids are bright and eager to learn."

"How old are they?"

"The boys are nine and the girls are twelve."

"Twins? As in two sets?"

He gave her a dry, apologetic smile. "Which is the other reason the salary is high. Yes, two sets of twins, who aren't nearly as intimidating as you might imagine. Just the idea of them tends to scare off the prospective help, which is why I asked Denise not to mention it."

"I'm really not sure about this…."

"I understand your reservations, but if you'll just give it a chance…" He leaned forward. "Denise is good at what she does, finding the right person for the job. In fact, she's downright uncanny at it. Why don't I just take you to Noah's house now, while he's at the office? You can meet the children and see the environment."

The children. Tricia pictured them, sad, and lonely for a father who didn't know how to show he loved them. She blew out a breath, trying to dispatch the heart-tugging image. "Where does he live?"

"About an hour's drive north of Sacramento, a little town called Chance City, although not within the town itself."

"You mean it's in the *country?*" Tricia couldn't contain her horror at the idea. She'd spent her entire life in the city. She liked concrete and grocery stores and fast-food restaurants.

"Depends on what you mean by country. It's in the Sierra foothills," David said. "His home is large and comfortable, on ten acres of property."

"As in no neighbors for ten acres?" This was getting worse and worse.

"Or thereabouts."

"So, I'd have to live in? What about my house? I'm getting it ready to put on the market."

"You could get Saturdays and Sundays off. He can hire weekend help locally, if he wants to," David said.

Silence blanketed the room. Living in, with weekends off. Not exactly what she'd signed up for. Or expected. Then

gain, it was only for three months, and her mantra of the
ast year kept repeating in her head: *Life is short. Make it
n adventure.* She just needed to keep her usual safety net
n place, too.

"Okay," she said at last. "Let's go check it out."

SPECIAL MOMENTS™ 2-in-1

Coming next month

THE MAN BEHIND THE COP by Janice Kay Johnson

Detective Bruce Walker never risks emotional entanglements. Then he starts to fall for Karin Jorgenson. He needs to trust himself enough to show her the real man inside.

THE SINGLE DAD'S VIRGIN WIFE by Susan Crosby

When Tricia McBride agreed to care for single dad Noah Falcon's two sets of twins, she didn't expect what began as strictly business would become pure pleasure…

BABY MAKES THREE by Molly O'Keefe

When Gabe Mitchell turns to his ex-wife for help, he can't ignore the sparks that are still between them. Can they forget the heartbreak of the past to find a future?

HEALING THE COWBOY'S HEART by Judy Duarte

Laid up after a car crash, rodeo cowboy Matt Clayton was understandably surly. But Tori McKenzie took every opportunity to get him back in the saddle…and falling for her

HER MIRACLE MAN by Karen Sandler

Fate brought her to the mountain retreat of millionaire Jack Traynor during a storm. She had no idea who she was – but Jack's protective ways had her wondering if it mattered.

NO PLACE LIKE HOME by Margaret Wilson

All Bree McInnes has to do is make it through the summer without anyone discovering her secrets. That's complicated when her sexy boss begins to pay her a *lot* of attention.

On sale 18th September 2009

Available at WHSmith, Tesco, ASDA, Eason and all good bookshops.
For full Mills & Boon range including eBooks visit
www.millsandboon.co.uk

SPECIAL MOMENTS™

Single titles coming next month

THE PRINCE'S COWGIRL BRIDE
by Brenda Harlen

Undercover as a commoner, playboy Prince Marcus Santiago found himself working as a ranch hand for Jewel Callahan – the cowgirl who was capturing his heart.

THE BOSS'S CHRISTMAS PROPOSAL
by Allison Leigh

Greg Sherman's new staff member is Kimi Taka, hotel heiress. She's young, a party girl, and – he assumes – just working for kicks. But could Kimi offer him so much more?

THE BRIDE WITH NO NAME
by Marie Ferrarella

After Trevor Marlowe's heroic rescue of a drowning woman, he took the amnesia victim in – and fell in love. Then her fiancé showed up on Trevor's doorstep...

THE DAD NEXT DOOR
by CJ Carmichael

When Gavin Gray and his young daughter move in next door, Allison is drawn into their lives...until Gavin's ex-wife returns seeking a second chance.

On sale 18th September 2009

Available at WHSmith, Tesco, ASDA, Eason and all good bookshops.
For full Mills & Boon range including eBooks visit
www.millsandboon.co.uk

2 FREE BOOKS
AND A SURPRISE GIFT

We would like to take this opportunity to thank you for reading this Mills & Boon® book by offering you the chance to take TWO more specially selected books from the Special Moments™ series absolutely FREE! We're also making this offer to introduce you to the benefits of the Mills & Boon® Book Club™—

- **FREE home delivery**
- **FREE gifts and competitions**
- **FREE monthly Newsletter**
- **Exclusive Mills & Boon Book Club offers**
- **Books available before they're in the shops**

Accepting these FREE books and gift places you under no obligation to buy, you may cancel at any time, even after receiving your free books. Simply complete your details below and return the entire page to the address below. You don't even need a stamp!

YES Please send me 2 free Special Moments books and a surprise gift. I understand that unless you hear from me, I will receive 5 superb new stories every month, including a 2-in-1 book priced at £4.99 and three single books priced at £3.19 each, postage and packing free. I am under no obligation to purchase any books and may cancel my subscription at any time. The free books and gift will be mine to keep in any case.

Ms/Mrs/Miss/Mr _____ Initials _____

Surname _____
Address _____

_____ Postcode _____

Send this whole page to: Mills & Boon Book Club, Free Book Offer, FREEPOST NAT 10298, Richmond, TW9 1BR